A Sea of Golden Chains

BACKWARD FAIRY TALES
BOOK TWO

CALLIE THOMAS

Author Callie Thomas

Also by Callie Thomas

Backward Fairy Tales Series

A Forest of Stolen Memories (Book 1)

A Sea of Golden Chains (Book 2)

Autumn Fairy Tales Series

Jacklyn and the Twisted Beanstalk: A Jack and the Beanstalk Retelling

Sacrificed Hearts Series

Mask of Deception and Sacrifice

Anthologies

The Sun Still Rises—A charity collection of YA fantasy stories in honor of Lani Forbes

**A Forest of
Stolen Memories***

Callie Thomas

**A Sea of
Golden Chains**

Callie Thomas

The Kindle Vella Version

A Sea of Golden Chains was originally published on Kindle Vella, bundled at the end of *A Forest of Stolen Memories*. It was written in a serial format with a weekly episode released from August 2022 to July 2023. Each episode contains author notes that reveal some behind-the-scenes information on the story and the characters. All bonus episodes earned thanks to reader interaction (likes and voting on content) are included in this version.

What is different in this version?

- New character artwork! A sweet picture of Ryken and Marigold in a swoony underwater moment.
- A beautiful map of Hanalla.
- Refreshed content! Extra details were added with another round of editing to enhance the reading experience.
- Ryken's two bonus chapters are now at the end of the book for easy access.

For the perfectionist, it's okay to make mistakes. There is beauty in all things, including your flaws.

❤

For my older sisters, who were my inspiration for Roselyn and Marigold's relationship. Families always have their rocky moments, but in the end, we'd do anything for each other.

❤

For every reader whose heart belongs to the sea—you really are mermaids in disguise.

Contents

"A mermaid does not fear the depths, for she is no stranger of the darkness and the cold. It was the darkness that made her scales shine so brightly, and it was the cold that made her heart so warm. She does not fear the deep for she has been to the bottom and knows that she can rise."

— MERMAID PHANTOM

ARUKAH ISLANDS

Taika

SEA OF THIEVES

N

Glenton

Windcrest

Mistbrooke

Cadell

Bressal

HANALLA

Overboard

Forget happily ever after—she just wanted to live.

"You kill her. I'm no murderer."

My eyes shot open at the threat, the brown burlap blocking my vision. The scratchy sack reeked of rotten potatoes and scraped against my cheeks. Proof these last few days weren't a nightmare.

Days ago, en route to Roselyn's wedding, two men had attacked our royal carriage and held me at knifepoint. Bound and gagged, I watched as all my possessions went up in flames. On the side of the carriage, Cadell's royal insignia, the five-pointed crown, blackened as it curled in on itself in the fire. The windows shook, smoke billowing from the seals. The poor footman pounded against the glass—locked inside alive.

I cringed. Squeezing my eyes closed, I wished the memory away, but it was useless. It repeated like another form of punishment. His tortured screams reminding me I couldn't save him.

What kind of madness was this? Who killed innocent people and abducted a young woman just because she was easy prey?

If only I hadn't traveled alone. Thinking the footman would be enough protection, I had refused the extra guards my sister requested. My pride had cost me . . . and now I was alone.

Was help on the way?

Or did my family not know I was missing? They had to be expecting me. Except . . . my last words with my sister were far from kind. I was ashamed to admit they were hateful even. A moment where I had let my jealousy get the better of me. After years of growing up in her shadow, I had finally snapped.

Perhaps my family assumed I wasn't coming. No matter the argument, I would never be so callous as to miss her special day with her beloved prince.

But in the end, I did miss it. One week bled into two, maybe even three. It was difficult to keep track when mornings and nights were identical under the burlap sack. Disoriented, I couldn't guess where I was. They didn't stop every day. Nor did they feed me every day.

Not that I had much of an appetite. My stomach was sick with fear, wondering which day would be my last.

Until yesterday, it felt like we were going in circles. This morning I knew. The salty breeze and the cry of seagulls told me we were on the coast, somewhere close to Windcrest . . . and far from my home.

The thought alone had me weeping silently in the darkness. I needed to be quiet and obedient so my captors wouldn't scream at me again. How was it my fault I wasn't someone else?

I wasn't even myself anymore. That Marigold disappeared the day they stole me from the carriage. Now my clothes were stiff, caked with dirt and sweat. Limp strands hung at my shoulders, my blonde hair in greasy clumps instead of soft curls. Riding on the floor in the back of the wagon had done me no favors. Fish nets tangled around my entire body, weighed down by heavy buoys that pinned me to the wooden floor. There wasn't a place on my body that didn't ache or wasn't covered in bruises.

"This is what we agreed on. I took care of the footman, and now you're supposed to deal with her." The gruff words jolted me back to the present.

"This is your plan, Des. You do it."

Hands tied, I remained motionless as I listened. Even though it ached, I kept my head at the same awkward angle it had landed from when my captors tossed me on the floor like garbage. They argued a lot, so this wasn't anything out of the ordinary. Yet, the topic at hand was new and not one I'd overheard before.

You kill her. I swallowed the lump in my throat.

"Me? You're the one that botched it, Fitz. You done snatched the wrong girl, and now we're stuck with this nobody," Desmond growled. A sentiment I'd heard repeatedly since I'd been taken.

I forced my breathing to remain steady with the same soft puffs of air that I used when my sister would sneak out our bedroom window while I pretended not to notice. The sister who these idiots thought they took. But no. Instead, they got me. What had the man said?

A nobody.

A few days ago, I would have cried at the insult, but my mind had leapt to survival. How could I get out of these binds? They only removed the sack to let me eat and drink. After years of following the rules and priding myself on my obedience, figuring out how to break them was harder than I realized. What if I made a mistake? Then they would kill me outright for being rebellious. My thoughts of escape disappeared as quickly as they had come.

What would Rose do?

She would have run before they threw her on their fishing boat. The ground rocked beneath me, a slight swaying that had made me ill at first but now was a calming sensation.

"I can't. She has kind eyes," Fitz complained.

"You can't even see her eyes with the sack over her head. Go on, do it quick before she wakes. I don't want to listen to her blubbering all day again."

"Des——"

"Don't you say it."

"—she looks like an angel. I just can't. You do it and I'll wash your clothes for a week."

"You already wash my clothes. Here, hold the knife like this and aim for her heart. It will be painless for her."

"You promise? It won't hurt her?" Bootsteps thudded on wood, the beams beneath me vibrating.

"Stop!" I croaked, my throat raw from sobbing. Only a few pinpricks of light made it through the material, so I couldn't see how close he was.

"She's awake," Fitz cried out.

"I'm not deaf. I heard her." The sack was snatched off my head, the bright light burning my eyes. "Hello, sunshine. Thought you could be sneaky and eavesdrop on us, did you?"

I blinked, trying to focus on the weaker man of the two. Fitz was gentler than the other when he threw me in the wagon and when he tied my restraints. Almost as if he cared, he would even ask me if I needed something, like a sip of water. Perhaps he still had a tiny conscience inside his large frame because he quickly tucked the knife behind his back, perspiration beading on his wide forehead.

"Please, don't kill me. I promise not to tell anyone who you are or what happened," I begged.

"Stand up," Desmond said. Tall and skinny like a malnourished tree, he scowled down at me, his teeth rotten and black. "Now."

A whimper escaped my lips, my face crumbling at his icy command. I knew what was coming. The fact we were out in the middle of the sea wasn't lost on me. The turquoise water sparkled, the liquid so clear I could easily spot the brightly colored fish swimming below.

Who knew what else was down there?

Far from my home in Cadell, the people on the coast here in Windcrest were different. Superstitious. Fishermen refused to dip one toe in these crystal waters. They were too fearful of the strange creatures, half fish and half man, that lurked below the surface. Merfolk, they called them. Scavengers who were always searching for their next treasure. And according to legend, humans were said to be a favorite collectible.

It was hogwash, yet they still spread the lies from generation to generation, as my grandfather passed them down to Rosey and me. My mother was torn between the two kingdoms, the farm life of Cadell and the clothing shop in Windcrest. She encouraged us not to believe everything we heard.

Though one thing they said was true: once you lived by the sea, you could never leave it.

It seemed I wouldn't be leaving it either.

"Quit your stalling and get on your feet." Fingers clamped around my arm, jerking me upright.

My mind raced. "I know Prince Alexander. He is my friend and will give you whatever you want if you let me go."

"The prince only cares about one thing—and it ain't you." He pointed the end of the knife at me.

"He's to marry Rose, my sister——"

"Stop talking!"

"—and she could get him to give you anything——"

His dirty hand struck so quickly I didn't even see it. My head whipped to the left, my cheek burning as I stumbled backward into the boat's railing. Shock left me tongue-tied. I had never been struck before. My fingers trembled as I pressed them to my heated skin.

"I said to *shut up*."

I nodded, always one to follow instructions. What had come over me to be so disobedient? *Rules, rules, I must follow the rules.*

"Careful, Des. You almost sent her overboard."

Waves lapped hungrily at the side of the boat, rocking us back and forth. I nearly stumbled again, gripping the worn railing with my tied hands.

A cruel glint reflected in Desmond's eyes. He tilted his greasy head, regarding me with a huff. Then he took a step toward me. His worn boots thudded against the frail wood, the force swaying the boat.

My fingernails dug into the rail as I leaned away.

"It's time to get rid of the dead weight."

Before I could argue, plead, or cry, he pushed me over the edge. The world spun. A flash of sky, the bright sun, and then the clear blue waters rapidly approaching until—*splash!*

Surprisingly warm, like tepid bathwater, the ocean gobbled me up faster than I anticipated. My gown bubbled, a buoy of sorts, and it bought me a few seconds before panic settled in.

I can't swim with my arms and legs bound!

I kicked out, but the rope held my legs together, each thrash of movement rubbing my skin raw. My hands were also useless, painfully tied at my wrists. No matter how much I twisted to keep afloat, gravity pulled me down until the water level reached my chin.

"Save her!" Fitz shouted. His torso balanced on the rail as he reached a hand for me.

I was desperate enough to reach out to anyone, including him, for help, but the ocean's hold was too tight. There was barely enough time for a quick breath of air before I submerged completely.

Noises muffled, accentuating the soft lull of the current, so tranquil and relaxing as it pulled me to my death. Salt stung my eyes as I searched for the seabed, trying to see how much farther until I hit the bottom. It was too deep, the distance hidden in the murky darkness. The endless drop nailed another spike of fear into my chest.

There is nowhere to go but down.

The last of the air escaped from under my skirt, and the light of the sun dimmed as I drifted lower. The more I struggled, the quicker I sank, and the more my lungs began to ache.

Bubbles burst from my lips as I expelled a breath, instinct demanding I inhale. The edges of my vision darkened, and my limbs grew heavy, no longer fighting against the bonds that held me.

Regret filled me. This was the end, and what had I done with my life? *Nothing.* A poor farmer's daughter whose greatest achievement was being related to someone who was marrying a prince.

But what about me?

What happened to the girl who always followed the rules? Who kept her head down and picked up the slack others left behind? Who always put others' needs before her own?

Life was unfair. What was the point of doing everything right when it made everything go all wrong?

A mixture of fury and resentment churned in my chest, and I clenched my hands together as a scream tore from me. Frustration over a future that would never be. Jealousy over my sister's perfect life, followed by the crushing guilt of even thinking it. The insanity that I would find myself at the bottom of the . . .

The garble of bubbles strung into notes, long and haunting. A song, echoing across the coral reefs such that a school of fish swimming past stopped to stare as if they understood me. Like they could hear the misery in my soul. Notes grew louder, a lullaby of the sea, rising and falling on their own.

How was I doing this?

The answer doesn't matter—I ran out of time.

The last of my air ran out and halted the music. The melancholy tune drifted away in the current, softening in the distance until the ocean was silent again.

My lungs cramped, screaming for air. Then the terror took over and controlled me like I was a puppet on a string. Terror like I'd never felt before. Even worse than when Desmond held a knife to my throat. I flailed against my binds like a wild woman, the pressure of the depths popping my ears as I continued downward.

I had to breathe. *Now.*

Movement flashed in the corner of my eye, a flick of a fin. A large fish had darted by, probably hungry for a snack. *Great.* Drowning or being eaten by a shark? Which would be worse?

My eyes drifted shut, calmness filling me. Nothing mattered. I didn't matter. My limbs grew heavy, tired from fighting. I relaxed and let whichever fate wanted me come to claim me.

Funny, I had always wanted to swim in the sea. I guess I got one thing I wanted in life.

Water crashed against the front of my body like a wave pushing me back, but I didn't move, my dress taut around my waist as if it had caught on something.

I shouldn't look.

I mustn't.

But I had to know. My curiosity always got the better of me, and I cracked my eyes open a sliver.

It wasn't a shark—but a man. And he was close. Too close. His handsome face seemed too perfect to be real. Of course he wasn't real. My mind must have imagined him so I wasn't alone when the end came. Except there was something not quite right about him. Was he . . . smelling me? My vision was fading, and just like my limbs, my eyelids were no longer under my control.

Something cold wrapped around my neck, sending jolts down my nerves and heating my flesh until I was sure I was burning from the inside out.

My jaw relaxed, and the saltwater rushed through my mouth and nose. The water stung as it poured down my throat. Dizzy, my body unclenched, confusing the water for air. But I didn't care because the darkness had finally come.

My lungs gave up. My heart must have, too, since the soft thumps were quiet.

Then I died.

A Second Chance

D arkness wrapped me in its tight embrace. But I wasn't alone.

"Who are you?" A voice rang out of the void, the tone neutral.

A nobody, I thought, not quite here or there.

"Hmm . . . that is not what I see, my child. There is a light inside you that refuses to be snuffed out. Though you are lost, you are not alone." The words echoed in the emptiness of my mind.

Lost? Ha! I'm already gone. Leave me in peace.

"If that is what you wish, I will. But the path home is not far."

Home? To my family?

"Yes. There are many who are searching for you."

As if summoned, voices roared in my head, all in mid-conversation, the words overlapping each other in a chaos of noise.

"Marigold," one cried out.

"Have you seen my daughter?" my mother asked, distraught, her voice cracking.

"—taken her——" said a familiar female voice.

"We've looked everywhere."

"—disappeared like magic——"

"Don't give up," urged a male voice in a whisper. It was different from the rest. Softer, like a caress in the darkness.

More voices thundered over him.

"—that poor girl."

"Send out more men. We will find her."

"She is alive. I can't explain it, but I know she's out there—and I will never stop looking for her," Rose promised with an authority I had never heard before. I tried to hold on to my sister's words, the lilt to her voice, and the emotion behind it. *Rosey.* She cared about me even after everything I had said.

A bucket of sound doused my thoughts, my senses overloaded. So many voices, they shouted in the void until I couldn't take it any longer.

Stop!

The immediate quiet was jarring.

"You are not forgotten," the calm voice reminded.

Who are you?

"I am many things—the grains of sand on the shore, the hum of the rippling tides, the sunlight glinting off the horizon, the creatures that swim below and fly high into the clouds. The world spins at my command, and my breath gives it life. The real question is—who are you?"

I am Marigold Alysa Bellmond.

"What do you seek, Marigold of Cadell?"

Life. I want to experience life.

"What would you do for a second chance?"

Wait—can you really do that?

"I can." The voice chuckled.

Could I trust this mysterious voice? Luck hadn't been kind to me. But at this point, what did I have to lose?

I yearned for another chance. There had to be more to life than tears and disappointment. Was it greedy to ask for more? To ask for happiness and excitement . . . and love? To see my family one last time and make amends—or just to say goodbye?

Resolve built in my chest, giving me strength. I refused to accept defeat.

Please! Help me. I would do anything for you.

"Then open your eyes—and live."

My eyes flew wide as my heart started again, zealous pumps to make up for lost time. I gasped, inhaling a gulp of salty water into my mouth.

Muscles in my neck tickled, a new sensation that startled me. Water whooshed through the two slits behind each of my ears before I could choke on it.

What just happened? Who was that voice, and how was I still under-water—alive?

Everything's all right. I'm all right. I soothed myself before panic overrode my good judgment. I only needed to swim to the surface. Easy. Don't think about anything else . . . like the slits behind my ears. A shiver raced down my spine, making me cringe. Or that I was alone in the ocean without a soul around. Or the fact I'd been submerged for who knew how long.

I was probably going to die again.

My hands trembled, and the urge to scream itched in the back of my throat.

Don't think about it. Stick to the facts and what I can control.

Where was I? From there, I could gauge the distance upward.

My golden hair drifted around me like tentacles in my vision. I lifted my hand to push it away, but the other one followed. I was still bound.

I swallowed on instinct, and I cried out, bubbles escaping my nose and mouth. Something solid wrapped around my neck, its jagged teeth burrowed into my flesh. My throat throbbed all the way up to my ears, and even the gentlest wave bit like the stab of a knife.

I traced a finger along the piece of metal clamped around my throat, tortuous jewelry, the surface smooth and cool under my fingertips. Wincing, I searched for a clasp until I couldn't take the pain anymore.

Who knew where it had come from, but I was stuck with it for now until I could find help removing it.

I'm all right, I encouraged myself. *It's just a piece of . . . jewelry, that's all.*

Careful to avoid the metal choker, I wrestled my thick hair back enough that I could see, but my vision was still blurry. A thickness coated the tops of my eyeballs, causing me to blink at the strange feeling. But the saltwater no longer stung, and with each blink, the formations around me sharpened into focus.

Seaweed swayed from the ocean's bed, its long green fingers a bright contrast to the darkness of the cave I found myself in. Porous rocks formed tunnels and tiny windows around the open area. Yellow beams shone through the holes in the rocks at the ceiling, with one larger opening above me that I might be able to squeeze through.

In the distance, the unsettling darkness morphed into gray, visible enough despite the minimal rays of light. Small fish darted in one of the holes, but otherwise, I seemed to be alone.

How did I get here?

Soft white light illuminated the dark space like underwater candles. Glowing spiral shells were scattered throughout the cavern, stuck to random surfaces of the rocks. One of the closest nautilus shells on a nearby rock detached, floating for a moment before landing on my arm. I brought it closer for inspection. The light of the shell was bright, highlighting my pale skin. It shook as two little antennae slid from the base and pointed in my direction.

Uh, a strange little thing.

Twisting my arms against the rope at my wrist, I peeled the shell from my skin, my arm still glowing from where it had rested. The antennae bent backward, keeping an unsettling watch over me as I placed it back on the rock.

Slimy seaweed brushed over the soles of my feet and I jolted, inhaling another mouthful of water. I closed my eyes, the pain from the necklace combining with the tickling sensation when the water exited out behind my ears. But the rush of water also brought relief, like a breath of air, that I took a few more short gulps on my own without my neck hurting.

Breathing . . . underwater? Maybe it was part of the gift of this second chance.

Fabric tangled around my legs and I kicked out, my feet bare. I sighed in frustration. Rope restricted my movement, the knots tight below my knees. But even if my hands and feet were free, I wasn't a strong swimmer. We had a shallow pond beside our apple orchard back home. Perfect for hot summer days. Father allowed us to swim after our chores were completed, but I never played or swam around. Instead, I would sink to the rocky bottom. The muffled noise in the water was peaceful. Sound would mute and the world would pause, if only for a second before I had to kick up for air.

There was nothing peaceful about sinking to the bottom of the ocean.

I'm all right, I reminded myself as my body shook.

The gray shadows of the tunnels were full of twists and turns. A maze? What other sea creatures would be waiting for me there? I glanced up at the larger hole in the ceiling again. Perhaps the direct route would be the safest.

A flash of silver caught my attention. The water rippled, my hair loose and dancing with the waves. Clawing the strands away, I froze as the man from before glided in the water on his stomach toward me. His skin was opal gray, glossy and smooth, his muscular arms at his side. Cautious, he approached, his eyes scanning my face.

Ha! I hadn't imagined him. Was he the voice from before? Had he saved me?

The water shifted as his body straightened into a vertical position. My eyes went wide. *Oh, my goodness . . . where is his shirt?* His nostrils flared and he tilted his head, his sandy hair almost as long as my own floating around him, the ends tipped in navy ink. A click and hum variation sounded, bringing my eyes to his lips. It repeated, slower this time. *Click, clickety-click, hummm, click.*

Wary, I tensed as he inched closer. My heartbeat thudded like a drum in my ears. I leaned back. He was here to save me, right?

After a few moments, he shrugged, opening an oyster—no, a clam —with his sharp nails. He dug his fingers in it before pulling out an amethyst-colored pearl glowing against his fingers. Unable to control myself, I leaned in, admiring the pulsing light.

Over the last few months, I had lived above my grandparents' dress shop. I had sewn thousands of pearls on dresses, gowns, hats, shawls, and gloves and knew they came in many sizes and colors. Except this color. I had never seen a purple one before.

His tail brushed against my leg. Long and dark, it appeared bluish in the shadows. The slanted beams of light reflected off his scales, the edges glittering flecks of silver. How odd—unlike the vertical fish tails my grandfather caught in his nets, his was horizontal. It flicked a few times, keeping him upright while he watched me study him. The tip of his tail fanned out in flowy tendrils, swishing in the current with the fabric of my dress. More elegant than—

Um . . . did I just say tail?

I screeched, shooting back into a barnacle-covered rock.

I'm not all right, my mind chanted.

"Beware of the sea, my sweet girl." My grandfather's warning rang in my head. "It deceives with its beauty, luring even a seasoned sailor to his doom. The ocean remembers your promises and will always come to collect what is due. It summons the Merfolk, the warriors of water, to claim any treasure the sea demands—including you."

Impossible! There were no such things as Merfolk. My grandfather's old stories couldn't be true.

And yet, a real and absolutely not fake merman hovered a few inches from me. Was the lack of air causing me to hallucinate?

They aren't real. He's not real. I repeated this over and over. What would be next? Did magic exist too? Now I sounded as crazy as my grandfather.

What kind of a second chance was this? Nothing made sense.

I relied on order. Things needed to be organized and put in their place. How could I put things in their place if I had no idea what was going on? What was happening with my body? My vision was sharper and clearer than before, even in the darker waters. I could breathe underwater, and a strange necklace had fused itself to my skin. Oh, and I could sing underwater.

Could this be a dream? Did I hit my head on the boat and Desmond was waiting for me to wake up?

No . . . because I could feel everything—including the touch of this merman. His long fingers scooped the curtain of hair blocking my face. Too close, he crowded into my space, his aqua-blue eyes curious and staring into my own as if he was trying to tell me something.

He offered the pearl, lifting it to my mouth.

He wants me to eat the glowing purple thing? Gross.

Pinching my lips together, I turned away and pressed into the rock, scanning for the quickest escape route.

Scowling at my refusal, he tried again, more forcefully this time. Turning my head left and right, I evaded his attempts. He persisted until I knocked his hand away.

"No," I said, or at least I tried. The word was garbled in bubbles, unintelligible to even me.

Then he growled. Animalistic and unnatural, his growl was a mix between a wolf and whale that I didn't think was possible. It had been a mistake to think this creature was human. Fear had me kicking off the rock, desperate for escape. I glided higher to the hole above me, straining my bound hands for the small ray of light. Before my fingers could touch the moss around the opening, the weight around my neck jerked me to a stop. The force of it spun me sideways, my feet scraping into the ceiling of the underwater cave.

A scream ripped out of me as a sharp pain radiated from my neck outward. My maroon frock swirled around my legs, disappearing in and out of focus as my vision flickered.

My scream morphed into notes, a mournful song, and my heart squeezed in despair as I sang it. The notes echoed off the rocky walls and down the cavern, surrounding me in sadness.

Metal rattled behind me, a long chain with an attached anchor that was wedged into the rock formation. The length of it was taut and connected to . . . *me*.

Grasping the golden chain, I frantically yanked at the end in the rock. The chain attached to the choker around my neck. I wasn't wearing jewelry—it was a leash.

And the merman was using it to reel me back to him.

Chained

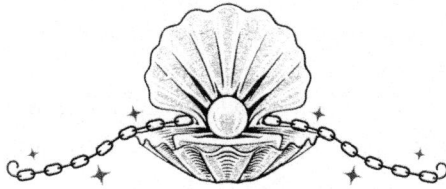

Link by link, he dragged me back to him. The merman's muscles bulged as he wrapped the chain around his forearm. I resisted, refusing to make it easy for him—thrashing and kicking until the chain wrenched my head back.

Another sharp stab pierced my neck, drilling deep into my nerves such that I closed my eyes as the wooziness overtook me. My arms fell limp at my side. I gasped for breath, greedily gulping the water for relief as I had before. But the next time I opened my mouth, a round object was forced past my lips. A large hand pressed against my mouth to keep me from spitting it out.

Weak from the pain, my eyes fluttered open.

It reminded me of when I first saw the merman. He could easily be mistaken for a human. He had an oval face and a strong jawline, but it didn't look like he smiled often. *Do Merfolk even smile?* His mouth was wider than normal and paired with full lips in a dark coral color, giving him a more sensual appearance. With an average nose, his nostrils flared as he breathed. While he didn't have facial hair, he had light brown wisps of lashes under thick dark brows that added to the human illusion.

If I hadn't seen his tail, I wouldn't have known.

His eyes drifted across my face, mimicking my perusal. Up close, his eyes were a startling aqua. Hypnotic. The way the ocean brought me peace, I sensed his eyes were cut from the same blue cloth.

We floated in this stalemate for some time, staring at each other but communicating nothing.

Why? I wanted to ask him. *Why me?*

Frustration rippled off of him as he continued to hold my stare. His other hand flexed, holding the coiled chain.

He hummed, a high to low swoop that sounded like a barked command.

Stiffening my back, I narrowed my gaze at him as an unhealthy amount of stubbornness filled me. He could hold me forever—I wouldn't swallow it.

Click, clickety-click, hummm, click. His strange call was long and drawn out . . . a warning.

Why was it so important to him that I swallowed it? If he wanted me dead, wouldn't he have just let me drown? Why save me? I still didn't understand.

Just thinking of the pearl, my tongue itched to inspect it. It slid across the strange object clamped between my teeth. Circular and smooth, it was warm to the touch. Then, unexpectedly, it popped open. A sticky liquid oozed out, clinging to my tongue like a thick paste.

I gagged.

The sour taste was a disgusting combination of curdled milk and fermented cheese. It dissolved in my mouth, leaving the horrible taste behind. Tingles traveled through my body, zipping through my veins from my head to my toes in a burst of energy.

In an instant, the ache in my neck lessened.

The merman nodded and released my mouth. He pointed to my collar.

I ignored him, spitting and raking my fingers down my tongue. Now what? Was something going to happen? I dipped my head low, bracing for the side effects.

With a soft hum, he reached for me.

I swatted his hand away. Since I had been taken from my family and home, I had been shoved, dragged, and thrown across the countryside. I had been roughly handled to the point my arms were covered in bruises. I didn't need anyone else touching me without my permission.

I curled into myself and turned away as much as the chain allowed. Hopefully, he'd take the hint.

My hair floated around me, a halo of gold, and I brushed it from my face, but it came back again. What I had once prided myself over had become nothing more than a nuisance in the water. As I swiped at it again, the merman caught my bound wrists in his hand. Staring at the rope, he poked at the knot.

He hummed. A pitiful sound, short and quick. His eyes creased as he scratched at the binding.

Maybe . . . just maybe . . . could he be helping me?

The thought evaporated with a snap as he opened his mouth, revealing a row of sharp teeth and paralyzing me in place. So many teeth. I couldn't stop staring at the hideous sight of them.

My grandfather was right. These creatures had an ethereal beauty on the outside only to mask the monster on the inside. Was that part of the lure? Perhaps I had fallen for it too. For a moment, I had let my guard down.

I strained against my leash, my chain rattling as I trembled. My hands cupped over my mouth, preventing my cries from calling him any closer.

The merman ran a hand across his face, inspecting his fingers, confused.

What else had my grandfather said? Why hadn't I paid more attention? Did Merfolk eat people? I guessed I was about to find out.

He brought the rope to his mouth and shredded it into pieces. When he was done, he didn't let go, tracing his thumbs over the backs of my freed hands.

Too afraid to blink, I watched the rope particles drifting in the water. *That could have been me.*

His brows slanted up, his touch gentle. Pulling my fingers closer, he inspected them one at a time. When he sniffed them, he caught my gaze over our locked hands. Then, instead of releasing me, he placed my palm over his chest where his heart would be—at least if he were human.

Scandalous!

Heat tingled my cheeks as I stared at my splayed fingers on his bare chest. Since I had noticed his indecent attire, I had kept my eyes from straying to this part of his body. What was I to do when it was directly in front of me? Skin smooth and glossy, it was cool to the touch. Compared to his muscular physique, I felt scrawny and malnourished. Even our skin color differed, his void of color and pale next to mine.

His heart thumped in steady beats. Evenly paced and calm, it sounded more like a human heartbeat. The rhythm was oddly comforting.

He hummed, content.

The rumble shook my fingers, and I snapped out of my musings.

What am I doing? Even in the sea, rules of propriety existed. I didn't know this merman, nor did I know if he followed the rules of proper etiquette. Rules that had been ingrained in me since I learned to walk. Though I was lowborn, my mother raised my sister and me to be ladies. Mother would faint if she had any idea what I was doing right now.

Especially if she knew I liked it.

What is wrong with me?

I jerked away, but he followed, tilting his head at my reaction. It was as if he heard something I didn't.

His eyes met mine, aqua orbs that made my heart race differently than before. Could he hear it beating out of my chest?

"What do you want from me?" I asked, bubbles rising from my lips. Shaking my head, I knew he couldn't understand. Speaking underwater was pointless.

How else could we communicate?

A wailing sob echoed through the tunnels. So faint, I was surprised I heard it.

The merman tensed, whipping around to the tunnel opening. His tail beat against the current, angry flicks that propelled him upward. On his lower back, a small dorsal fin protruded in the same pearl gray as his skin, blending into the dark scales of his tail.

Another mark on his right arm drew my curiosity. A strip of his skin was indented, wrapping around his bicep. It seemed as if something ornamental had circled tightly there for a long time, and now it was missing.

He glanced over his shoulder at me, frowned, then shot off toward the tunnel and disappeared.

Sighing, I leaned back against the rock.

A merman. I survived my first encounter with one of those mythological creatures. Would I be so lucky next time?

I didn't want to find out. I wanted to be long gone before he returned with whatever made that wailing sob. More Merfolk? No, thanks. One was enough for me.

Surrounded by sand, rocks, and tiny patches of seaweed growing on the floor and through the cavern walls, there wasn't much I could use to aid my escape. The chain had to be broken for me to fit through the hole above, or I had to carry the chain with the attached anchor through the tunnel. I dug through the loose rocks hidden in the seabed. A large fossil-covered stone required two hands to pull out. It seemed sturdy enough for the task.

Unfortunately, it was only more time wasted. No matter how long I beat the stone against the rock crevice, it wouldn't pull free.

My chain only allowed me to go so far. I couldn't touch the top of the ceiling or make it halfway to the tunnel the merman had exited.

I was trapped.

Alone for hours, boredom set in. I counted the glowing shells on the rocks—seventy-two—and messily braided my hair, tying it with a piece of seaweed. Keeping my mind busy gave me purpose. It also distracted me from the memory of his sharp teeth.

I held out my freed hands. Those same sharp teeth that had chewed through my binds.

If he wanted to help me, then why did he leave me chained up?

I understood mermen as well as I did men—not at all.

Secretly, I had always thought I'd end up an old maid. I didn't fit in anywhere. I was quiet and meek, and if it weren't for my voice, I'd probably blend into the background.

Was that what had happened with my family? Now that I was out of sight, was I out of mind?

I'd been given this opportunity—a second chance. What would I do with it?

Immediately, my sister's face came to mind. The guilt from my words ached in my chest as much as the choker around my neck. I had to make things right between us.

The path home is not far . . .

Would I even have a home to go back to? I estimated the royal

19

wedding was a week or so ago. A princess by now, Rose and my parents would have moved into the castle after the ceremony. They were probably laughing over glasses of wine and expensive chocolates, enjoying the fineries of royal life.

My stomach rumbled in protest. How many days since I had last eaten? Yesterday, Fitz had given me stale bread and a questionable chunk of cheese, but the way my stomach gurgled, I'd have guessed it had been months.

Eventually, my body grew weary. Was it the pearl? Or a day of exhaustion? Whatever the case, I used the chain like a blanket to hold me closer to the ground. I rested my cheek on my arm and traced my finger in the sand, the motion soothing. I fell asleep staring at my name scrawled on the ocean floor.

I dreamed of sunshine. The warmth of the summer rays heating my skin as Rosey and I picked wildflowers in the meadow by Mistbrooke Forest. We hadn't been there since we were children. A cool breeze whipped from the trees. Flowers stirred, their sweet aroma reminding me of my youth. Rose laughed, chaining the flowers together as she always did. I held one blossom under my nose, plucking a petal off to watch it spin through the air.

My sister seemed older, like she had lost her spark of innocence from when I saw her last. A crown of flowers rested on her hair, a childish accessory, but on her, it looked as regal as if it were made for a queen. She hummed as she worked, a new song I had never heard before.

"Why are you making another crown?"

"This one's for you," Rose said, looking up. "I wish you'd come back."

"Me too," I agreed.

"So much has happened since you've been gone. I don't know if I'm as brave and strong as you are. You always do the right thing no matter the consequence."

The emotion behind her words sent a chill down my spine. A raw honesty that felt so real . . . too real.

"You've never said that to me before."

She tensed, her red ringlets swaying. Her eyes narrowed as they studied my face.

"What?" I asked.

"Is this a dream?"

"What else could it be?" I said with a shrug, releasing my daisy into the breeze. "Magic doesn't exist."

She leaned forward, her green eyes bright—the same green color as my own.

"It does exist."

"Now you sound like Grandfather." I blinked, suddenly remembering the merman. Could my grandfather be right about magic as well?

"Goldie . . . I swear I've had this same dream a thousand times. You have never responded this way. Is this really you?"

"This is my dream. Of course it's me."

She squealed, crawling over flowers to get to me. Shadows flickered. The space between us lengthened like a long tunnel.

"What's happening?" I cried out, grabbing the blades of grass to gain my balance.

"Where are you? Tell me quick!"

Before I could answer, the winds picked up, howling like a beast. A crack of lightning struck the ground between us. Fire whooshed up, a barrier that crackled and hissed.

Was this real? Had I somehow connected to her in a dream?

"The sea," I shouted. "I'm in the sea."

The roar of the wind was too loud. I prayed she had heard me.

The ground cracked and the field shook. Thick blades of grass peeled back and sucked me into the dark hole, the bottom full of water. I called out, scratching at the walls until the hole above me closed.

I woke up with a start. Bubbles floated from my lips as I panted.

The cave was the same as when I had fallen asleep curled up in the sand. Glowing shells twinkled in the darkness, flickering to the tune of the calming waves.

A silly dream and nothing more.

But if it was a dream . . . then why did the smell of smoke linger?

I didn't have time to dwell on it. The merman had returned with something flesh-colored wiggling in his hands.

Let Me Go

I scrambled from under the heavy chain. Darting up, I held on to the end of it to keep from floating upward.

The merman swam across the cave, his scales catching the fragments of light from the glowing shells. I couldn't tell what wiggled in his grip. Whatever it was, it fought so violently he needed two hands to hold it.

Click, clickety-click, hummm, click, he called out, his greeting echoing off the walls as he approached.

I shrank away, my fingers clinging to the rough surface of the rocks behind me for support. Tingles of panic surged through my stomach. What should I do? Every time I fought back, it resulted in me getting hurt. Desmond had slapped me. The choker strangled my neck.

I was tired of fighting. I was tired of pain. I was tired of the unknown. Chained, I was at his mercy. I couldn't even say I had lost control because I'd never had it in the first place.

I should just give up and accept my fate.

Preparing for the worst, I turned my cheek.

Horrible scenarios circled in my mind, most of them involving his sharp teeth. Were the rumors true? Had he considered me a treasure to keep chained in his lair . . . forever? Didn't he realize I was thrown overboard because I was worthless? A nobody? What would happen when he came to the same conclusion?

I trembled. It wouldn't be good.

Softer this time, the merman called to me.

I peeked over my shoulder at the melancholy sound. His head was tilted, his brown hair swirling around him like a cloud. He sniffed the water near me while his aqua eyes held mine, never blinking.

Though I couldn't communicate with him, his eyes conveyed more than I expected. An inquisitive glint, like I was a puzzle he didn't know how to solve. It seemed as if he was cataloging my every move—including how my dress swayed with the flow of water.

The thin material refused to stay down. I brushed it back in place, but the movement stirred the other side, a never-ending battle I was losing. It was impossible to keep my feet and ankles covered. Another etiquette rule broken. *I apologize, Mother.*

His tail brushed against my leg like a caress. I jolted out of my thoughts of rules. His jaw ticked, amused. Had he done that on purpose?

The merman's lips parted, then snapped closed as he settled on a strained smile. Ducking his head, he lifted his hands to present the wriggling object still fighting for its freedom.

I know what that feels like.

It had large glassy eyes—wait—not an object, but a fish. Upon closer inspection, it was a sunrise perch. A common, medium-sized fish found close to the shores of Windcrest. A fisherman's staple, it loved the warmer waters of the coast. At least I hadn't traveled far from where Desmond and Fitz had so kindly left me to die.

The merman shook the fish as if I had missed his gift.

What was I supposed to do with that? I held up my palms and declined.

He growled, impatient. Then he shoved it at me, the fish's tail smacking my chest. Slimy, the fish's squishy body made me cringe. My grandfather had caught a netful of fish every day during my stay with him. He had insisted that I know how to clean and cook them. A required family skill. But lucky Rose had missed that ritual. Not one day passed that I didn't hold a fish—sometimes still alive—in my hands. It was disgusting. And when I left for Rose's wedding, I vowed never to hold one again.

Yet here I was.

He held it against me with one hand forcefully enough to pin me to the rock. Using his other hand, he pointed to his open mouth.

Teeth. So many sharp teeth. Could there be more than last time?

I pushed against his forearms. His muscles corded up his biceps. I could sense the strength in them and the fact he restrained himself. He wasn't even trying. Who knew what he could do if he were really angry?

I shivered at the thought.

His mouth curled down at the corners. He relaxed, pulling the fish away. I quickly wiped off my dress, the slimy residue stuck to the fabric.

With a sigh, he let the perch go. The fish darted off and out the exit of the cave without a second thought, leaving a trail of bubbles behind him. I smiled and wondered if there was hope for me yet.

But the merman's hands were still full. Another clam rested in his palm—like from before. He pried it open and retrieved the purple pearl inside.

Oh, no. Not again.

As I kicked off the rock, he snatched my dress in his fist and brought me back to him, my arms flailing in resistance. It seemed the fish and I had switched places.

Another call, high to low, as he watched me squirm.

Minutes passed, and my stamina drained. I gulped liquid until I eventually gave up, too exhausted to fight anymore. Panting, I noticed his bored expression. Exasperated, like I was the one being difficult.

Again, he reminded me more of a human than a creature.

It was odd. Even without me fighting, he still didn't move. His eyes trailed along my face and over my hair, stopping on the long twist of my braid.

He placed two gentle fingers on it, tensing as if he would snatch them back at the first sudden move. When I didn't, he grew bolder. He ran his hand down the length of my braid until he got to the end, his thumb twisting the seaweed that held it together.

With a flick, he tore the seaweed tie in half and released my hair from the bind.

Fear held me in place as he untwisted my hair so that it floated around me. He used both hands to carefully scoop it back from my face. My cheeks heated, the gesture more intimate than it should be. Weeks without a kind touch had scrambled my emotions. Had I almost leaned into his hand?

Wait. Both hands. He no longer held me as he was distracted by the texture of my hair.

Not wanting to waste the opportunity, I reared back, tucking my knees to my chest, and kicked him with everything I had. Off guard, he flew backward for a split second before using his momentum to somersault in reverse and flip up closer to me than before, his teeth bared.

Clicking and humming, his strange noises echoed in the small space. Curt and sharp, though I couldn't understand what he was saying, only that I had displeased him. *Good.* Now we could both be unhappy.

For the first time, I didn't cower. I held my ground, leaning forward with a growl of my own. I didn't want that nasty pearl again. I had no plans of making it easy for him.

His eyes widened, dilating. Anger glittered there, giving them a frosty appearance.

He held up the purple pearl. In the darkness, it emitted a purple glow. Streaks of color altered the hue of the surrounding water and his skin. I closed my mouth, sucking my lips in. With another growl, he moved forward and tapped it to my mouth as if I didn't understand.

Oh, I understand what he wants just fine.

I spun away. I didn't make it far before both of his arms encircled my waist and pulled my back flat to his chest. He growled low, a menacing echo that made the hairs on my arms rise.

The chain caught between us, the end rattling with each jerk of movement as I fought him. Unable to untangle myself from his steel grip, I connected my heel to some part of his tail. Roaring, he retaliated by knocking my feet forward with a swift thrash of his fin. I still didn't surrender. Instead, I jammed my elbow into his side.

His grip tightened, and his teeth pierced the flesh of my shoulder. The pain froze me in place. I closed my eyes and screamed.

The merman tensed at the sound and immediately released my shoulder. My hair whipped around as he spun me in his arms. Red ribbons floated above my skin. I applied pressure to the cut, wincing as the sea salt stung the open wound.

He . . . *bit* me.

His blue eyes pinched at the corners, his tail curling around my calves. He made soothing noises, humming low by my ear as he pulled me into an embrace.

The water smelled acidic—of blood. It signaled like a compass, a bright arrow in the current to the wound on my shoulder. Even with my eyes closed, I could sense the direction the blood was coming from and that the wound was fresh.

My scream morphed into notes but was cut short as he shoved the pearl in my open mouth. It broke open as soon as it touched my tongue. Just as sticky as before, I had to peel my tongue from the roof of my mouth. I gagged, choking on the sour texture.

Heat sizzled under my tongue. Then it shot off as before, racing through my veins. My shoulder itched, a scratchy tickle, and goosebumps sprinkled my skin in response. The merman grabbed my wrist before I could claw at the offending flesh.

"Let me go, you monster," I shouted, but the words were muffled by the whoosh of waves. My expression conveyed what my words could not.

Had the pearl made my wound worse? No, it was quite the opposite. My skin stretched, knitting itself closed with invisible needles. In an instant, the pain stopped. My skin appeared as it had before—completely healed. Even the traces of blood faded from the current.

Was that . . . *magic*?

He ran a finger over my shoulder, grimacing. His finger brushed against my choker and a voice penetrated my thoughts as clearly as my own.

Sorry.

I stiffened. That was not my voice. It was also not the voice that saved me. Was it him? The merman's voice in my head? Or was that my imagination? But the voice continued.

Your human skin is weak. I forgot.

Had the impossible become possible?

Out of everything that had happened, nothing should surprise me now. I was breathing underwater, and I thought nothing could top that. But hearing him speak inside my mind? I had no words for that. Grandfather absolutely did not mention this little tidbit.

The merman had apologized too. Surprisingly, he had a conscience and emotions beyond animalistic ones. This meant I could possibly convince him that holding me hostage was wrong.

If he could talk to me . . . could I talk to him?

I responded in my thoughts without hesitation. *Don't ever bite me again.*

The merman shot six feet away, his eyes wide and arms outstretched. His reaction displayed a new emotion I hadn't seen on him—fear.

You Are Mine

Was he scared of . . . me? Or was this some Merfolk thing?

It could have been the sound of a different voice in his head. If I hadn't heard the other voice earlier, I would have been scared too. Whatever it was, I had to figure out how to recreate the exact moment again. If there was a chance he could understand me, then there was a chance I could persuade him to remove my chain.

My fingers pressed into the metal around my throat. *Interesting.* The pain from my choker and the weight of the chain were barely noticeable. The bruised spots on my arms ached less too.

It was almost as if my body had adjusted. The water was less resistant and more natural to the point it felt like nothing. The longer I was submerged, the more my body changed. Not in a good way. I didn't want to conform to my surroundings—I wanted to return to normal.

If only he would let me explain the misunderstanding. It was a mix-up from the beginning. I belonged in the sea as much as he belonged on dry land. He had to understand.

Hello? I thought, wondering if our connection still held. He didn't react. Hyper-focused, his eyes tracked me in a predatory way. I strained to listen, hoping for the echo of his voice again—anything. But it was just the soft swish of the current. A sick feeling settled in my stomach at the thought that I might have to be touching him for us to communicate.

How did one tell a merman that we got off on the wrong foot—uh, fin?—without using words? Body language?

I lifted a few fingers and waved. Immediately, his gaze snapped to my hand. I grabbed the cool metal of the chain and shook it, the noise clanging and scaring a small school of fish upward and out of the hole in the rocky ceiling.

When he didn't move, I pointed up. He mimicked my gesture. *Yes.* I nodded my head enthusiastically, my hair whipping about my shoulders. With two hands, I pointed to the hole the fish swam out of. A quick glance up and he returned his attention back to me, a scowl darkening his features. He sliced his hand diagonally through the water. A clear sign of disapproval.

I scrubbed a hand down my face and held in a frustrating scream. Gestures weren't enough. I would have to convince him with words.

Pushing off the rock, I glided toward him, ignoring the memory of how this beastly creature had just sunk his teeth into me seconds ago. I had to get close enough to touch him so I could speak to him.

The merman flicked his tail up and then slammed it down, knocking me back with a blast of water. As strong as physical hands, the water carried me to my original position. My hair wrapped around my face in such a tangle that I didn't see the rock until I collided with it. My gown floated up around my knees. *Oh, goodness!* I yanked the fabric down, covering my rope-bound legs.

He called out, a low-pitched hum.

What could I do? It wasn't like I knew how to speak his language. Except . . . what had I heard him say?

Click, clickety-click, hummm, click. I called to him, remembering the phrase he used. But poorly mimicked, my tongue couldn't click to the roof of my mouth like it could on dry land. It was the best I could do underwater.

His mouth parted, and the tension eased out of his shoulders. He leaned forward, barking three grunts.

Did I say the right thing? I hoped so. I smiled, one of my sweetest smiles that I had spent hours practicing in a mirror. "One day, you will charm some lucky boy," Rosey had joked. Who knew I'd have to use it on a merman.

He blinked at me, still unsure.

Click, clickety-click, hummm, click, I repeated and held up an outstretched hand for him.

Water rippled as he shot through the space between us, grabbing my hand in his. He rested it on his bare chest like before, making my heart skip a beat. Before I could jerk it away, he pressed it into the hard ridges of his muscle, holding it in place.

I ordered my body to relax so I could test this theory.

Can you hear me . . . ? If he could, he didn't respond.

His thumb slowly glided up mine, leaving a trail of tingles in its wake. A soft smile hung on his lips. Handsome. He was so distractingly handsome. His hair swayed in the current off of his left shoulder. Was it as soft as it looked?

It was hard to gather my thoughts with him so near. His shoulders were wide, taking up most of my personal space as he constantly seemed to do. The skin of his torso had an iridescent glow, highlighting each muscle as he flexed with each swish of his tail. His dark tail went well past my feet, just as powerful as his upper half. With all the swimming, it was no wonder he was so enormous. *Stop staring at him!* Embarrassed, I forced my eyes up and off the chiseled chest inches from my face. Suddenly, I was lost in his eyes and thick lashes. A tenderness showed beneath the surface.

How did he seem so human sometimes? And other times . . . not?

Or was I trying to make him into something he wasn't?

The steady beats under my fingertips were soothing. My trained smile melted into something more genuine.

He scooped my hair from my cheek and tucked it behind me while his eyes trailed over my face. Leaning in, he breathed in my scent and left a heated aroma of his own. Odd that I didn't notice his smell before when it seemed so intense now.

Not a usual scent I could describe, like flowers or food, but it was more of an instinct. Like who he was. *Male.* I sniffed again, trying to understand it. No, not just a male—my eyes went wide—but a male who was interested . . . in me.

I swallowed, the metal around my throat constricting the movement. What could he tell from my scent?

The merman leaned in closer. The tip of his finger skimmed over the healed spot on my shoulder. The fresh patch of skin zinged with nerves, sensitive to the lightest touch. My thoughts completely dissolved, and I focused only on the trail of tingles that spread when his fingers glided up to my neck.

Don't be mad, he said in my mind. Soft like velvet, even his voice was seductive. I curled my own hand over his, pressing it into my collar. His chest rumbled. It reminded me of our barn cat purring in the morning sun.

The collar. I could hear him because he was touching my collar.

I'm not, I responded, keeping my eyes on his.

His hand on my neck tensed. I tightened my grip as he tried to pull away.

Don't be scared, I thought.

He froze. *Scared?*

Of me.

His mouth broke into a wide, sharp-toothed smile. I cringed, averting my eyes. *I would never be scared of you. We are one.*

I snapped back to face him, frowning. *We absolutely are not. Don't say that.*

He winked. *I said nothing. You intrude into my mind. What are you?*

"Me?" I said, shock making me forget we were speaking through thoughts.

You smell . . . He leaned in the rest of the way, his nose pressing into my shoulder. Water tickled as he took another breath. *You smell new.*

Heat flooded my cheeks. *Oh, Mother. I'm doing a terrible job with these rules.*

Mother? Is that your name?

What? No! I forgot you could hear me.

I am Ryken. Tell me what to call you.

Marigold, I replied after a long moment.

He breathed deeply, his lips accidentally bumping my skin, and I shivered. *Marigold, I sense you now.*

Things were spiraling out of my control. I was practically in his embrace, his head in my neck. How had things escalated? I needed a breath that didn't have his scent coated in it. Each touch from him distracted and teased me in a way that left me confused. My mind wiped of everything but him.

I need a minute. Or perhaps longer. Can you ... not be so close?

I won't bite you.

I appreciate that. But I still need for you to move—I gave his chest a shove—*back.*

Ryken groaned. *You delay the inevitable. You are mine.*

I jerked my hand away, surprising him so that his head snapped back. This time I sliced my hand in the water to gesture my response: *no.* I belonged to no one. I was not a trinket he could collect.

He snatched my hand back and pressed it against his chest while his other hand touched my choker. The fear of hearing me in his mind gone.

Listen, he demanded.

To what? The thumping sounded louder in the quiet when I wasn't focused on his thoughts. A steady rhythm, strong enough that my hand shook with each beat.

Listen. Then he pressed my free hand against my own heart. I arched away, objecting to his hands moving lower on my body.

You are too bold, I scolded.

He tilted his head, his face scrunching in confusion.

Then I heard it. Our hearts thumped in unison.

We beat as one.

I don't understand. No. I refused to understand.

I already told you. You are mine.

I wiggled against his hold. *I'm not.*

He growled. Not realizing his own strength, he held me tighter, flush against him. *I don't know what to make of you. You should not be awake, and you are. You should be starving, but you're not. You speak in my mind and I in yours—it's unheard of. More puzzling is that you haven't completed the transformation.*

The fight left my body, and I floated in place.

The ... what?

You are still human. You should be asleep until you are not. He shrugged as if it wasn't out of the ordinary that I should be anything other than human.

Of course I am. What else would I be? I felt numb.

You smelled human before, but now you smell different . . . a mix?

You're wrong. He had to be.

He hummed, thoughtful. *I will take you to Orion. He will know.*

Take me? Does that mean I'm leaving the cave?

I'm not sure you should. You have no tail, and your skin is weak.

Is that a bad thing?

He grumbled, his tail swishing angrily. *Yes.*

I was willing to take the chance. Whoever this Orion was, he wasn't here. Here I was trapped. But there? There led to new possibilities.

Where is he?

He's preparing for tonight's ceremony at Coral Courtyard.

What kind of ceremony? Like an offering? A human offering? My eyes widened. Was I swimming into a trap?

Not to worry. It's for anointing the new Collectors. I'll stay close.

And if we go . . . you'll unchain me?

His eyebrows pinched together. *I know I shouldn't, but it's distracting knowing you have awakened and I'm not here to watch you. It will be hard to focus during the ceremony without you by my side.*

So . . . yes? We're going? I clasped my hands together, focusing on the part I cared about. Freedom.

Yes, under one condition. You don't try to escape.

I promise, I lied. As soon as I could, I was heading to the surface.

Don't promise me. He crossed his fingers and held them to his forehead.

I bit my lip, knowing exactly what he wanted. Not just any promise, but a sacred promise. It proved the merit of an oath taker, increasing the value of their word or action. For if they were dishonest, the sea would know.

What happens if a vow is broken? I asked.

He was silent for a moment. The corner of his mouth pinched. *I won't let you break it.*

He avoided my eyes like he avoided the question.

My grandfather had warned me of broken vows since I was young, but it was based on rumors. People disappeared at night and were never

33

seen again, with only puddles of water left in their empty homes. Nobody had any evidence to prove them as lies. So, the rumors spread. They whispered of horrors that sent shivers down my spine: for every broken vow, there was a broken corpse floating in the depths of the sea. Lost forever, they remained condemned—even in death.

Rumors were only that—lies spread by fear. But still, I had never dared to utter those words before. While most of Windcrest's superstitions were laughable, this one had a deadly ending on which I wasn't willing to risk my life.

My eyes flicked up and landed on Ryken. I had to convince him to release me. But challenging the sea? What if I was wrong? I flexed my hand, thinking.

"Beware of the sea, my sweet girl." My grandfather's warning repeated, his words urgent.

I sighed. What choice did I have?

I won't leave you. Let the seas take me if I do, I vowed. I ignored the dip in water temperature and tapped my crossed fingers to my forehead. *Now, unchain me.*

One of Many

Do you understand what you have promised? Ryken frowned. His aqua eyes hardened as he scanned my face. *There's no going back.*

I do. I had carefully chosen my wording by promising to stay with him versus escaping. I chewed on my lip, thinking. Could he grant me permission to leave and visit my family? Technically, I wouldn't be breaking my promise. It would be like a vacation . . . which meant if I left, I had to come back. Was there a time limit on how long I could be gone? Months? Years?

Rose would tell me to do it and ask questions later. But if I was wrong and broke the vow, my life would be on the line.

One challenge at a time. First, he needed to fulfill his side of the promise.

His hand slowly slid up my back. The fabric of my dress was a flimsy barrier. I felt him trace each bump of my spine.

You are . . . small. His grip softened into a gentle cradle.

I raised a brow. *Or maybe you're just big.*

He hesitated, then shook his head. *No. You're small. Breakable.*

You're stalling on your end of the bargain. I grabbed the chain and shook it to remind him.

A low growl rumbled in his chest. *I'm warning you if you'd just listen. Once you leave the protection of the cave, you can't return. Only those that haven't awakened may rest here. Out there, you're vulnerable.*

His hand cradling my neck twisted a latch. The high-pitched grinding of metal on metal warbled in the waves just before the heavy weight dropped from around my neck. The golden tint from the chain reflected against the rock wall as it sank, landing in a heap on the sand.

One more, I reminded him. I tapped the metal around my neck—the collar.

He shook his head. *No, that one must stay.*

I ground my teeth. *But you said—*

If you take it off, you will die. His blunt tone stopped my tirade. My lips parted as I took that in. He rubbed a knuckle under my chin. *Don't keep your mouth open unless you want a school of fish living in there.*

I cringed and closed my mouth so quickly that my teeth cracked together. Using two hands, I pushed off his chest, overwhelmed by his proximity. I needed to teach him about personal space. Could a merman be trained? Ryken required a lesson in proper etiquette of how one behaved in the presence of a woman—or even a human in general.

He released me, eyeing me carefully as he swam backward.

Without the weight of the chain, I drifted up, not quite high enough to reach the ceiling, but high enough that I didn't have the ground or rock wall to propel off. My arms waved about, trying to lower myself back down, my legs still tied and useless.

Ryken swam up, his arms crossed, while he watched me struggle. Somehow, I had flipped upside down. I tried to kick to right myself, only to knock my skirt down. *Oh, goodness.* He didn't offer help but mirrored my position, his hair hanging down.

His lips quivered as he placed a hand on my collar. *What are you doing?*

Swimming. I glared at him. *It's the rope. Can you cut it off too?*

But I had lost his attention. He caught sight of my foot, and his eyes went wide. *What is this called?*

My feet?

Feet, he repeated in awe. Releasing me, he swam closer to my toes. I scrambled to right myself, but I only shifted sideways. He grabbed my ankle, pulling closer to sniff my sole.

The bubbles from his nose tickled the arch of my foot, and I couldn't stop the laugh that erupted from me. His eyes shot to mine, curious. He leaned forward and blew another string of bubbles along my heel.

I squeezed my eyes closed, and another wave of laughter burst out, twisting into a melody. It was lighter and laced with joy, the higher notes ricocheting off the walls.

Ryken grabbed my hands, pulling me upright. His mouth set in a firm line as he touched my collar. *As much as I love your ballad, you shouldn't sing once we leave here. The others will think you are calling to them.*

Calling who? More Merfolk? That was the last thing I wanted. *I can't control it.*

Then consider it another reason to keep your mouth closed. It's time to go.

Can you cut the rope? I pointed to my knees.

Rope?

The one on my legs—Ryken! I cried out when he practically lifted my skirt over my head. He flicked it back down just as fast before the blush could spread across my face. Shock rendered me speechless. Was there no privacy in the sea?

Never have I been treated with such disrespect, I huffed. *You don't—*I couldn't believe I had to express this—*lift a woman's skirt.* Desmond and Fitz never behaved in an ungentlemanly fashion toward me. Well, they did try to kill me—but at least my virtue was intact. Ryken appeared clueless about his actions, a bland expression on his face. That didn't excuse his behavior. I tried to slap him, but he snatched my wrist before the blow landed.

You're a very violent human. Once you can swim, you'll be a skilled hunter. Not as good as me, but decent.

I groaned. He was dense. Couldn't he tell I was furious? Just as I thought of kicking him again, he opened his mouth to reveal the pointy tips of his teeth. A reminder of the last time I fought him.

I jutted out my chin and turned away.

Are you done? We have to go, he barked.

You are the most vexing creature. Wait—go? You didn't cut the rope.

You don't need it cut.

I sputtered. *But I need my legs to swim.*

37

Yes and no. You'll have to learn to swim without two legs. Consider it practice. He placed my hand on his dorsal fin at the base of his spine. *Hold on.*

He didn't give me even a second to prepare before he took off. I grabbed on to him with white-knuckled fingers. Water whipped across my face as we weaved through the dim tunnels. Objects passed by in a blur of scenery, too fast to recognize. A female whimper vibrated from the right, startling me so that I lost my grip when Ryken shot off around the corner and sent me tumbling into another small cave.

A cave that was occupied.

Motionless, a lone mermaid floated in the middle of the open area, her eyes closed. Her tail glittered like jewels, a soft lavender with specks of silver that melted into a burnt orange at her hips and upward. The scales crisscrossed above her navel and covered her modestly over her chest. Her arms stretched above her head, her wrists limp. Silky black hair swayed to the ocean's current, her ends dark blue like Ryken's.

I gasped, my eyes locking on the golden band around her throat. I touched my collar in wonder. Due to its location, I hadn't seen the one I was wearing. If mine was anything like hers, it was the most exquisite thing I'd ever worn. Her choker sparkled like pure gold, an inch thick, which explained the weight. A long chain attached to the back and connected to an anchor on the seabed.

She was just like me. Which caused me to wonder—if she existed, were there more of us?

I paused at a thought. Had Ryken brought her here? If so, how many others had he collected before me? I frowned, strangely disappointed.

Was I one of many?

She didn't deserve to be down here any more than I did. Why keep any of us? To transform us? Her skin had the same glossy tint as Ryken's. Hopefully, it wasn't too late to save her. There had to be something human left in her.

I had to free her. Kicking and digging through the water, I managed to tread in place before a pair of hands wrapped around me from behind, one landing on my choker.

You let go.

Who is she? I demanded, flipping around to gauge his response.

38

He stared at the unconscious figure, only now noticing her over my shoulder. *I don't know.*

I pointed at her, my temper flaring again. *Why did you chain her up?*

He tilted his head. *I didn't.*

Oh. I blew out a breath, my anger deflating. *Did you chain me?*

Yes. Your song called to me.

My song? But not hers?

She is Trexton's. He'll be furious if he finds us here. We don't like to share.

I unconsciously touched my healed shoulder. *And he would attack me?*

Ryken smiled, cold and deadly. *He would regret it if he tried.*

For once, I appreciated that razor-sharp smile.

I glanced back at her. *Can we free her?*

Not yet. When she awakens, Trexton will let her go. Until then, the chain keeps her from scraping against the rocks.

I wanted to keep pressing him. It felt wrong to leave her, but how would I carry her out? I couldn't swim as it was.

Ryken's hand gripped mine. *Come.*

No. I tugged at my hand. *I have so many questions.*

He pressed his lips together, his eyes darting around. *Now is not the time.*

My questions spewed forth anyway. *What is this place? A prison? Why must we transform? And what does that even mean? Why us? How many more of us do you have chained down here?*

Me? How many do I have? He halted at that, his eyebrows high.

Had I offended him?

You, only you.

He paused as if he had something more he wanted to say but then decided against it, glancing down. His aroma changed, the surrounding liquid swirling with disappointment. With a sigh, he squeezed my hand and guided us out of the mermaid's cavern.

Slower this time, he led us down the main tunnel. Every few feet, we passed by another cave entrance with another sleeping mermaid chained inside. All were similar in appearance except for the variety of tail colors. Ryken sped up, his hand tight around mine. I lost track of how many mermaids we passed.

How long did they stay that way? How long had I been there before I woke up? My list of questions kept growing.

We barreled out into the open waters. Shadows danced in my vision, too dark for me to focus on. Hopefully, it was seaweed and not a fish swimming around me. I closed my mouth—just to be safe.

Either it was nighttime or we were so deep that the light from above couldn't reach us.

Ryken dropped my hand, leaving me alone in the darkness. I surprised myself by immediately reaching out to find him again. Another swing of an arm and I hit his chest with a whack. He hummed, a soothing noise that would have brought me more comfort if I could see him clearly.

Marigold, he said through our connection. At the sound of my name, the spike of anxiety ebbed away.

You let go, I accused.

I had to block the cavern's entrance. I'm here now. He placed my hand on his heart, the steady thuds calling out to my own. My heartbeat slowed to match his. *I'd never leave without you.* His voice was velvet again, his words humming in my mind.

I didn't want it to be comforting . . . but it was.

Another sign I had been down here too long. As soon as I learned about my transformation from this Orion person, I'd talk to Ryken about the possibility of returning home.

Are we going to the ceremony? I asked.

Shaking his head, he responded, *There's something I want to show you first.*

He let go of my collar and flicked his tail to shoot us in motion. Up we went, climbing out of the darker depths. The farther we swam, the bluer the water became, so clear I could see out for miles. From every angle, it was nothing but endless water. We sped up, zooming over the coral reefs, the fish scattering in panic as we passed. Then we skimmed over fields of seaweed, the tips grazing down the front of my gown and tickling my toes. It smelled of earth, of nature, reminding me of wandering through the apple orchard back home. In the distance, a huge sea turtle turned its head at our approach. Its shell was as wide as our kitchen table, and I marveled at its size as we swam beneath it. Soon, tiny fish flanked us on both sides and joined us for a few minutes. Their bodies were a rainbow of vibrant colors, weaving between Ryken and me as they kept pace with us.

How did I not know there was an entire world beneath these crystal depths?

After a bit, I caught myself smiling, the ride smoother than riding on horseback. Exhilaration fluttered my stomach as we dove over a trench. I stretched out my hand, enjoying the whip of the current between my fingertips.

Faster, I wanted to tell him. Faster until I was like a shooting star. A streak of bubbles across the sea—free to soar wherever I wished.

Down below, buried in the rubble, was a sunken tradership, its masts snapped in half and lying on its side. The sails, riddled with holes, billowed against the current like it was still sailing to port. Algae covered the wooden planks and camouflaged the vessel in the surrounding seagrass.

Ryken gestured to it with his hand, slowing down as he brought us closer to the ship. We entered through a jagged hole in the side, the frayed beams suspiciously scratched and gnawed away as if on purpose.

Gloomy without the sunlight, the inside was a mess of broken furniture and who knew what else. I glanced back to the opening, wanting to be in the colorful world of sea life again.

This is where we live.

I touched a barnacle-encrusted beam, the wood flaking under my fingers. *Who is* we? *Is there someone else here?* Had I missed them in the darkness? I turned to scan the wreckage of the ship.

He scooped the hair from my face, a tangled mess from our swim.

I mean us. You and me.

My heart skipped in fear. Us? Live together? The weight of his words pressed as heavily as the shackles he had removed. I shrank away from his intense stare, his eyes heated with possession.

What did he want from me?

Time to Go

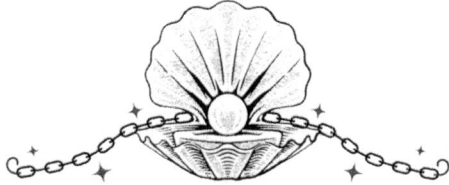

R yken's hungry eyes raked over me like I was his favorite dish he couldn't wait to devour. Since I'd met him, he had been under the impression there was a romantic commitment between us. *Me...with a merman? Ridiculous,* I scoffed.

I had agreed to nothing of the sort. There was no "us"—nor would there ever be. Leading him on, even for my own benefit, would be a dangerous game I didn't want to play. It was best if he knew upfront there wasn't a future for us.

Not that I had any experience in declining suitors. Nobody was knocking down the door for my hand in marriage. Mother had focused on getting Rose married before setting her matchmaking schemes on me. Rose had constantly reminded me of my good fortune. Why Mother even bothered with Rose when Prince Alexander had his sights set on my sister made no sense.

Just like it made no sense that Ryken thought I belonged to him.

My vision adjusted to the gloom. The ship's lower deck was long, crammed with crates and oversized barrels. It must have been a stocked ship when it sunk, as random junk and debris littered the floor.

The tight quarters heightened my awareness of his presence. Ryken circled me twice, inching closer with each lap. When he stopped, his tail still wrapped around my feet, lost in the fabric of my skirt.

One thing about him, he was persistent.

I held out a hand as a barrier to keep him from leaning in farther. My hair drifted above my shoulders from the movement. He brushed his fingers through it, running his hand all the way to the tips. It was long enough for him to bring to his face, sniffing the ends.

Enough was enough. I snatched my hair back, twisting it at the nape of my neck and tucking it under.

Click, clickety-click, hummm, click, he called to me.

I shook my head, causing the corners of his mouth to crease into a deep frown. Ryken pointed to my collar.

I agreed, dropping my arm so he could touch it. But he was sneaky. His whole hand pressed against my throat. His thumb traced along my sensitive flesh and followed the line of the choker.

What's wrong? he asked calmly.

Ryken, you know I can't stay here with you.

You are not ready. I understand.

No, you don't. I clamped my hand over his, halting his distracting thumb. *I will never be ready.*

His jaw clenched. *You called to me. I heard your ballad, and I accepted.*

I told you I can't control it. My eyes widened at an idea. *Is there another mermaid in that cave that can sing to you? Then you could let me go?*

He growled. *We can never be parted—our hearts are synchronized. Your song sings in my veins, fills my soul, and beats in my heart. We have only one mate for our entire lives. You are mine.*

Forever? My jaw fell open, and he nudged it closed with the pad of his finger.

Until we die.

But . . . I don't even know you, and I didn't agree to this eternal commitment. Don't I have some say in the matter?

Destinies were set before our creation. Your mind will catch up to your heart soon. I can wait.

Was it my destiny for you to chain me here against my will?

You aren't chained. He tilted his head.

Then let me go.

I'm protecting you. Your body is changing, so it's not safe for you to be on land.

I touched the small flap behind my ears—my gills to breathe underwater. Ryken was right about that, at least; I was changing, which was why I needed to get out while I still could. The porthole to my right beckoned my escape.

Only death will meet you on the sandy shore. Don't think about it, Marigold.

Everything will kill me eventually. In fact, I think I died already.

His tail drooped. *You . . . did?*

Yes, a voice spoke to me. Did you hear it?

He paled. *No. What did it say?*

That my home was closer than I thought. And then it asked me what I would do for a second chance.

What did you agree to? he demanded.

Anything. Then I woke up—alive.

Anything? He whipped away, swimming back and forth around the cluttered room before returning to me to touch my throat again.

Do you know who that was? I asked.

I can guess, but it seems impossible. Why would Ruah wake you early? Before your transformation was complete?

Ruah—who? An invisible force stirred the current.

The sea. You made a promise directly to the sea . . . an open promise too.

I gulped a mouthful of water. Now I had two promises? One was bad enough . . .

How do I talk to it?

You don't. Ruah only speaks to a select few.

Like you?

Ryken glanced down and then away. *Yes. But that's different. I'm a Collector, which is an honor chosen at birth. Once my ceremony is complete, Ruah will tell me the times and places to gather.*

Collector? Of what? All these random things?

It was as if someone had opened all the cabinets and drawers and dumped all their contents on the floor. Decorative statues, mirrors, clothes, furniture, dishes, pictures—plus even more buried beneath it. It rivaled the pit on the outskirts of Cadell where we disposed of our garbage.

My fingers itched to tidy and organize.

Things? They aren't just things. His eyes lit up as he picked up a black button off the floor. *It's treasure.*

I gave him a side-eye. *It's a button.*

Button, he whispered. *What does it do?*

It goes on clothes or items to keep them in a certain position.

Show me. He offered it to me.

Oh, uh, it needs to be attached to something. I pushed his trinket away. *Are we not in a rush for the ceremony?*

The ceremony! Ryken's eyes went wide and he shot off, bubbly foam following him.

Panicked, he searched around the ship, digging through the scattered objects across the floor. Rejected items were quickly chucked over his shoulder, creating an even bigger mess. Candlesticks, silverware, jewelry—was that a *real* diamond necklace?—boots, daggers, books, plates, baskets, teacups, coins—too many human items to name.

Where had he found all this?

He screeched by a weathered barrel, diving to pick up a small box buried behind it. I stretched to see him unlatch the lid and open it. With a sigh, he closed his eyes and took a moment before pulling out a pair of golden wrist cuffs. They were a smaller version of what I wore around my neck, but they glittered just as brightly. After placing them on his wrists, he swam over to me, visibly more composed.

I'm ready now. Do you need assistance out of . . . what is this called? He plucked at the capped sleeve of my gown.

It was a newer style that was popular in Windcrest. Due to the constant hot weather, they preferred cotton clothes in lighter shades that flowed on the ocean's breeze. Cadell had a more traditional style with high necks and darker, thicker fabrics for the colder months. We were not wealthy enough to afford the cost of a double wardrobe for both cities, so we repurposed outfits to fit both locations. This maroon gown was dark, matching the colors of Cadell, but in a soft cotton which had kept me cool these last few months. Grandmother had sewn me a special wrap, the collar lined with fox fur, for the snow season.

Unfortunately, Desmond had burned it up with the rest of my belongings.

I blinked, recalling Ryken's last question. Did he say *out* of? As in the *removal* of my clothes? And here I was, shocked when he flipped up my skirt. Frowning, I pressed his hand into my collar.

Absolutely not! My gown covers my body and protects me from prying eyes.

Ryken squinted. *Protects you from what?*

From people—or mermen—looking at me while I'm indisposed.

Why hide? You are who you are.

I crossed my arms. *I'm not hiding.*

He raised a brow in challenge.

But I'm also not taking it off. Think of this as a human thing. I need it. Nonnegotiable.

If you must . . . but the others will think you're strange.

I don't care. I am who I am, I repeated, smiling sweetly at him.

Your choice. Ryken shrugged. *Time to go.*

My courage wavered. The thought of being surrounded by Merfolk had my stomach fluttering with nerves.

You're safe with me. I won't let anything happen to you. He held out his hand, expecting me to take it. This time, he didn't snatch or grab but was patient even though I knew he was in a rush.

Did I believe him? This creature I had met less than a day ago and had chained me up in a cave? A wise person would say no. But maybe there was some truth in what he had said about our connection. Because with every beat of my heart, I knew he was trustworthy. That he wasn't just saying it to get me to comply with his wishes.

How did I know these things? It was like trusting the sun would rise each morning. But it didn't mean I had to like it.

Sighing, I placed my palm over his.

Before we leave, there are a few things you should know. First, don't stare into their eyes or get into their faces. It's aggressive, and they could take it as a threatening gesture. Second, don't touch them. Touch is another way we communicate. You don't want to send the wrong message.

You touch me all the time.

It's hard to resist instinct. He smirked. *Third, don't sing.*

You already said that one.

Because it's important. Merfolk don't sing. Or at least there hasn't been a siren in years. Your gift is . . . one that others might try to hoard for themselves.

Like when you took me and chained me up?

He sucked in a breath, my words derailing him. *I saved you. My heart beat for you so that you could live.*

And the other mermaid? She was once someone's daughter or sister. You stole her from her family. Only a heartless monster would want—

We're dying, he blurted, startling me out of my tirade. *All the mermaids are gone. The only ones left are the ones we've transformed. But they only birth males. It's an endless cycle. Our race is struggling to survive. But I promise, we never steal them—we save them from death and give them life in a new form. Even you were dying when I found you.*

Yes, but—

Ruah normally instructs us who to save. Except you. You called to me with your song, begging for help. You were so weak . . . I was afraid I was going to lose you. I gave you medicine to help you recover faster . . . or tried to. You're quite violent. He shot me a pointed look.

Medicine? Please tell me you don't mean that disgusting pearl.

It heals and provides stamina. What was I to do? I couldn't let you waste away.

Had he been helping me the whole time? I tried to think back, to see it through his eyes. I escaped death, but at what cost? Was I now his betrothed?

He whispered, *I can't undo our bond. I'm sorry.*

I placed a hand over my racing heart.

His aqua eyes held mine. *I meant what I said—I will wait until you're ready. You may feel differently after your transformation.*

If he thought that, then the chance of me returning to the surface was slipping like sand through my fingers. He'd never let me go.

Ryken tugged on my hand, signaling our departure.

We swam out the way we came, our hands linked as he pulled me through the kelp forest. Tall stalks of kelp swayed in the water, so thick I could stay hidden at the bottom unseen. They grazed my face and arms as we zigzagged through them. A swarm of jellyfish floated above us, pinkish to the point of being translucent, their tentacles outstretched like a deadly net.

Since I had never been in the ocean before, I had never been stung. Grandfather, on the other hand, carried a white scar, like a hot iron brand had wrapped around his forearm. Back when he was a young man still learning his knots, he had stuck his whole arm in his net while pulling his haul onto the deck. A jellyfish had been trapped inside. A mistake he never forgot. Even in his old age, the groove was still visible.

My eyes rested on the mark on Ryken's bicep, and I wondered if the same thing had happened to him. Did it bother him during the hot months too? Not that I cared, of course. It was more from curiosity.

As if he sensed my thoughts on him, he glanced over his shoulder at me. Unable to stop it, a blush covered my cheeks and marked me with guilt. He smiled, pleased, then threaded our fingers together.

I should say something . . . but I could only focus on his large hand engulfing mine. Even with his strength, he applied only gentle pressure as if I were a delicate flower.

He was built for battle: strength, speed, and a mouth full of sharp teeth. Yet with me, he was the opposite.

The kelp forest ended abruptly, and the arch of a cave appeared before us. Flat pieces of coral sprawled out like a rug to the entrance. Their scarlet tops opened and closed, a living rock. A school of fish ducked beneath them, startled at our arrival.

More coral was embedded into the cave's entrance like broken tree branches blocking the path. It didn't deter Ryken. He tucked me close, his grip moving around my waist. We entered the narrow opening and continued down the hollow tunnel. Swimming above me, he held me to his chest. His back arched up and down, like the crest of a wave, the movement rippling down his body to the end of his tail, propelling us forward in the water.

Don't be so stiff, he suggested. *Feel my movement and practice.*

I don't want to feel anything, I said, sulking. I wanted to walk, not swim.

He held me a little tighter. *That's fine with me. I can carry you everywhere if you don't want to learn to swim.*

My retort dissolved on my tongue as the tunnel emptied us into a wide, oval-shaped cavern. The high walls were covered in seagrass and yellow flowers—or were those yellow anemones? They were difficult to identify in the crowded space.

Merfolk lined the walls, leaving the center empty. They stiffened as we entered the open space. I tasted their presence in the water, a delayed warning of a nearby predator.

My surprised yelp released a stream of bubbles. If I didn't have their attention before, I did now.

Hundreds of wary eyes locked on me. A few bared their teeth and growled.

Ryken...

He gave me a comforting squeeze, his arm still around my waist. *I'm here. I won't leave you.*

All at once, the cavern filled with irate chatter. It was so loud that I covered my ears to block out the hums and angry grunts of the Merfolk as they voiced their disapproval. An animalistic roar drowned out the others, a wild sound that sent a chill down my spine. It vibrated off the walls with such ferocity. Frightened, I turned to burrow into Ryken's chest.

This was a terrible idea.

Defective

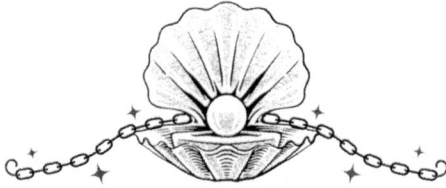

The roar silenced the cavern. My hand rested on Ryken's chest, his heart racing under my fingers. His unsteady beats frightened me most of all. Did he know something I didn't?

A wave pushed into my back as something swam up behind me. Tingles pricked my neck in apprehension. Whatever it was, I closed my eyes and rested my forehead against Ryken's chest. I was putting all my trust in him at this point.

The low hum of Merfolk sounded behind me in whatever language they spoke. Ryken responded, his hand gripping my waist as he hummed a range of octaves sprinkled with some sporadic clicks.

After a moment, Ryken touched my collar. *Turn around. Orion wants to see you.*

I nodded, taking a breath of courage before I peeked over my shoulder.

An older merman hovered behind me, his arms crossed. A satchel bulging with items hung over his shoulder. He wasn't as frightening as I had originally thought.

Similar in stature to Ryken, though his back was slightly hunched as if the weight of his bulky frame had worn him down over time. His high cheekbones were smooth and his aqua eyes sharp. Compared to Ryken, he could have been the same age with his wrinkle-free skin. But his short, wispy hairs gave him away. They fanned around his head like a white crown.

He huffed at me, pinching his lips. Confidence that spoke of authority oozed from him.

Stop staring, Ryken ordered. *Look down.*

I obeyed. It was easy to fall into my old habits and follow orders again.

Orion hummed in a harsh tone. I flinched at the sound, keeping my eyes fixed on his silver tail. It didn't have the sparkle or allure like Ryken's. Silver wasn't a common color for scales here. The majority of the Merfolk had green, blue, or purple tails.

Ryken's grip tightened, and he hugged me to him. His response was clipped, practically a growl.

What did he say? This was worse than people whispering behind my back. I felt invisible as they talked like I didn't exist. It was my fate, and I deserved to have a say in it. *Translate, Ryken.*

He said you're defective. You didn't transform properly, and the kindest thing we could do—he inhaled with a growl—*is kill you.*

"Kill me . . . ?" I mumbled. Even with my second chance, everything was going wrong. Betrayal swept through me, followed by a numbing shock. What was I thinking, trusting Ryken to bring me here? I had expected answers, not to be fighting for my life.

I told him I'll kill anyone who touches you—including him. He pressed his hand over my heart. *You are mine.* The honesty in his words sang like a promise.

Orion hummed a long note, arguing without words.

Ryken responded, equally agitated. He gestured to his bicep to make a point.

The longer they bickered, the louder the urge to flee screamed in the back of my mind. I scanned the cavern for the closest exit. But the Merfolk flanked us from every angle. I would have to leave from the main entrance we'd entered through. I would be lucky to swim halfway there without being caught, especially with my legs still bound.

At least the Merfolk were distracted. They leaned in and listened, enthralled with Ryken and Orion's disagreement. Their tails thrashed in excitement.

He said he won't kill you. Ryken's voice startled me.

51

I sighed in relief.

You are still part mermaid, even if the process hasn't been completed yet. We must be patient and ask Ruah for guidance before we make any rash decisions.

Ruah, again. Whoever it was had saved me a second time.

Now, come. We must get in our place so the ceremony can start.

He tugged me into the circle of Merfolk. A few of the mermaids stared unabashedly. Sections of their dark hair were braided with shells and fishing wire and lay against their pale gray skin. Their tails were stunning—vibrant scales of two colors mixing in perfect harmony. I scanned their faces, looking for fear or pleas for help. But they were calm, whispering to one another. Did they remember their old lives? Or were their memories removed like their legs?

And if they did forget . . . would that mean I would forget too? My family? My home? Myself?

I touched my collar without thinking. One of them mimicked me, tilting her head to the side. Her eyes flicked to the merman between us. His tail was a brown earthy color. It was the same shade as an old frock I had worn on the farm. It was an ugly color on the fabric as well as on scales.

He grunted. My eyes snapped up to meet his. They were the same blue as Ryken's, but his glinted in irritation. The current carried the ends of my dress toward him, grazing his tail. Scowling, he slapped it away like an annoying insect.

I flinched back and collided into the wall that was Ryken. He swept my hair over my shoulder, his fingers grazing my neck. *What's wrong?*

Besides everyone trying to kill me?

They agreed to let you live.

Let me live . . . I rolled my eyes and glanced away. The merman next to me had shifted closer without me noticing, his long brown hair tickling my arm. I shrunk back when he leaned over to sniff me.

In a blur of movement, Ryken struck out and gripped the merman around the neck. Snarling, he gave him a vicious shake before shoving him a few feet away. The surrounding mermen hissed in response. Another swam over, his teeth showing. Whipping his tail, Ryken shot a blast of water and knocked him backward, spinning him in place.

Ryken curled his tail around my legs and wrapped his arms around my middle. He growled, low and menacing over my shoulder, warning any merman who thought to approach. They gave us a wide berth, moving away until we had almost a whole corner to ourselves. For once, I felt safe being so close to him.

I placed his hand on my collar. Guilt at my thoughts from earlier turned in my stomach. How easily I had assumed the worst of him.

Thank you, I thought.

He narrowed his eyes. *For what?*

For protecting me.

He shook his head, his long hair swaying. *If they attack you, they are attacking me. I earned my title for a reason. They should know better than to challenge me.*

Your title?

As a Collector.

How would you being a treasure hunter . . . ? My question trailed off at the long trumpet call. I wasn't the only one. Everyone's attention fell on the lone merman in the middle of the circle. Orion held a conch to his lips, sounding the beginning of the ceremony.

Ryken's tail twitched, either with nerves or enthusiasm—I couldn't tell which.

When Orion let out a reverent hum, everyone stood straight. He held a purple crystal in a shell. The glow from the light drew me in, and I drifted closer. It reminded me of the pearl, and I wondered if this was something they had to digest. I gagged again at the memory. Maybe it tasted better to the Merfolk.

Three mermen separated from the rest, their tails also silver. They joined Orion in the middle of the cave and formed a line with their backs to me. The rest of the Merfolk turned to stare at us.

Ryken faced me and placed his hands on my shoulders. *Wait here. Nobody will bother you.*

You're leaving me alone after they said they wanted to kill me? I reached out to grab his hand, suddenly frantic at the thought of being parted from him. *Don't leave me.*

He stiffened; even his tail stopped. *I wouldn't. I will only be a few strokes away.* Then he reluctantly untangled our fingers. *I have to do this. Wait for me?*

Staring into his eyes, the need to argue dissolved. He seemed to be as uncomfortable about this as I was.

I nodded and watched him join the other three mermen at the end of the line. He glanced over his shoulder at me as soon as he stopped, looking like he was about to bolt back to me. What was this connection between us? Hadn't I been trying to escape from him yesterday?

I forced a smile, hoping to alleviate his worry. Instead, his brows furrowed, suspicious of my agreeable mood. He rubbed the back of his neck and turned to Orion.

Without Ryken close, I felt like something was missing. It was unnerving. Biting my lip, I strained to see over the four mermen's backs.

Not having a translator, I observed the events of the ceremony in utter confusion. Everyone else participated, chanting in clicks and hums after Orion spoke. He offered up the scallop shell like a platter. One by one, the four silver-tailed merman placed their palms over the crystal. He released the shell, and it hovered in place by an unseen force.

The temperature of the water dipped. The water circled around each of the mermen into a whirlpool that picked up speed.

Next, Orion pulled out a solid gold dagger from his satchel, holding it up for the crowd to see. At the sight of it, the Merfolk erupted in whooping calls, bouncing in place and unable to contain their excitement. Orion pointed the tip of the weapon at the chest of the merman in front of him. The Merfolk's voices joined into a chant, repeating with a slow and steady beat. With each call, Orion rotated the tip of the dagger between the four mermen. My heart matched the beat, convulsing each time the dagger landed on Ryken. The chant picked up the tempo, building the tension in the cave. I followed the golden tip until it was too fast to see. Then the chanting abruptly stopped and so did the dagger, the blade pointing at Ryken's heart.

My fears overtook me, and my only thoughts were of his safety. I shrieked, paddling toward him in hopes of protecting him. He turned wide-eyed, already attuned to my noises. He caught my dress just before the undertow of the whirlpool sucked me in and yanked me to his side, keeping me from being pulled under.

Having him close felt right. I threw my arms around his neck. Safe. He was safe.

Are you hurt? Did someone touch you? He peeled me off of him. His hands trailed over my arms and neck, lifting my chin to search my face.

I blushed at my overreaction. The need to protect had been overwhelming. But now that I was next to him, it dwindled away, leaving me with only embarrassment. Had I just screamed and flung myself on him in a cave full of Merfolk?

Marigold? he pressed, his thumb rubbing up my jaw. *Speak to me.*

Yes, yes. I'm all right.

Are you sure?

Yes. I swallowed my pride. *I was worried when I saw the knife. Just a little bit.*

His lips twitched. *You were worried . . . for me?*

I couldn't find my voice to admit it again, so I nodded.

Instantly, his aroma was overpowering. I breathed it in, letting his familiar scent comfort me.

Ryken turned, clicking and making noises to the group. All eyes snapped back to me, their chuckles leaving me confused.

What did you say? I demanded. My cheeks heated even more.

I said you were my protector—coming to rescue me.

Groaning, I covered my face with my hands.

Orion spoke to Ryken, his eyes on me. Hopefully, he wouldn't change his mind about killing me because I ruined his ceremony.

Ryken smiled, showcasing his many teeth. *Ruah has spoken. You may stay by my side for the rest of the ceremony.*

Ruah was here? Just now? How did I miss it?

Ruah is everywhere.

Where? I swiveled in place, looking for someone that stood out. After the ceremony, I'd have to have Ryken introduce me.

Orion dashed around the other mermen to hover behind us. The four mermen floated face forward, their long hair whipping around from the whirlpool.

They all wore matching wrist cuffs. But more surprising was that each of the other three had a gold band wrapped around one bicep. Scanning the room, I noted they weren't the only ones. Many of the mermen around the cave wore them on their arms.

But Ryken's was missing.

Orion drew out his dagger from his satchel again, holding it up

55

above him. Frowning, he glanced at me before swimming behind the merman next to us. He gathered their hair, wrapping it around his wrist so it was taut. Then he hacked away at the strands, inches from his scalp. The merman's face was scrunched, his head bowed.

Don't panic, Ryken whispered even though nobody could hear him but me. *It doesn't hurt. It's a great sacrifice that we give up to honor Ruah. We are meant to be humble.*

But . . . it will grow back?

No. His voice was quiet. *It wouldn't be much of a sacrifice if it did.* He sighed. *Besides, it's just hair.*

Something about his tone made me think it was more than that.

Orion cut the other mermen's hair, finally stopping behind us. Ryken's head jerked back from Orion's tight hold, and his eyes squeezed shut. I didn't think as I grabbed his hand in mine.

He blinked his eyes open. The corner of his mouth lifted in a sad smile. Sections were removed one at a time, and I never let go.

When Orion was done, he returned to the center of the circle where the crystal grew in brightness. Turning toward the whirlpools, he threw the hair clippings in the current, immediately disappearing into the foamy rapids.

The whirlpools churned, building momentum and growing wider around each merman as they waited with arms outstretched. Ripples from the wave crashed into me, the undertow clawing at my skirt. Orion's hand gripped my upper arm to pull me to safety.

I screamed as the top of Ryken's head disappeared from view into the swirl of foam and bubbles. The scream morphed into a low, haunting melody. I didn't care. Instead, I sang louder, ignoring the strange looks from Orion. Ryken would come back. He had to. He would hear my song and return. He was the only one who had helped me since this whole ordeal started.

I just . . . I just needed him back.

The whirlpool matched my song. The foam inched closer. Bubbles formed a curtain of privacy. Each change in my notes sent another batch of bubbles upward. Once I saw his face, the song died in my throat.

The bubbles drifted away, the four mermen still in the same position. But they were different. Their bodies were covered in translucent armor, solid but made completely from water. A circlet in the shape of a scallop shell rested on each of their foreheads. On each chest hung a clear breastplate of water that swirled and foamed as if angry at being contained. They each extended their hands, and a wavy longsword materialized in their grips from nothing but liquid.

While the hilts of the swords glittered in refined silver, the water blades were translucent aqua. The color matched their eyes and shone with an inner glow.

The light of the blades pulsed, drawing my attention, before they let loose a thundering boom of light, blinding me in white.

A sudden dizziness overtook me. All my energy drained like liquid through a funnel, and I was lifeless. As I thought to call for Ryken, his face appeared in the glowing white light of my vision—stoic, handsome, and invincible.

With one look at his face, I collapsed.

I Like It

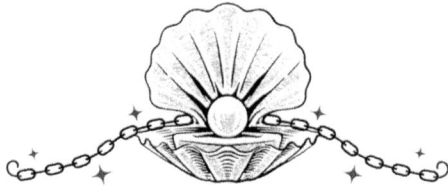

The undertow clawed at my hair and the fabric of my gown, invisible fingers hungry for more. Darkness crept across my vision until there was nothing. Limp, I dangled in the current, being tossed about and too exhausted to care. A voice called my name off in the distance.

Ryken. My anchor. I strained to hear him over the whoosh of the waves.

My stomach flipped like when I tumbled from a tree in the orchard. But this time, the falling sensation didn't stop. I faded in and out of consciousness, tucked in the safety of Ryken's arms during the swim back to the sunken ship.

What was happening to me? I wanted to demand answers, but my eyelids were weighted down, refusing to open.

His words echoed like a whisper in my mind. *Stop fighting, Marigold.*

So I did, and the darkness overtook me completely.

It was a dreamless sleep, like staggering through a never-ending dark tunnel. When I woke, I snapped to a sitting position. A stool tumbled off my chest, a weight to keep me from floating away.

My mouth was sour, tasting suspiciously like that purple pearl again. *Ugh!* I wiped a hand across my lips. It would take hours for that taste to go away.

Where was that merman? I had a few things to say to him about feeding me when I was asleep.

The ship was quiet. It rocked in the gentle current, the wooden planks creaking as it swayed. Alone, my gaze trailed over the piles of junk surrounding me while I pieced together what I remembered before I fainted.

Orion's scowling face as he told Ryken that he would let me live. The golden knife that he used to cut off the hair of the four mermen. The armor made of water. Ryken's face in the white light appearing otherworldly and unlike himself.

Warriors of water. My grandfather's words came back to me. An underwater army? Why? Did Orion plan on attacking the surrounding kingdoms?

I worried my lip, thinking of my sister in her new role as princess. Would she be safe? Cadell bordered the water the same as Windcrest. Whereas Windcrest had sandy shores leading straight to the Sea of Thieves, Cadell had cliffs overlooking the same turquoise waters from high above. Would the soldiers be desperate enough to scale the cliffs?

If the Merfolk were interested in gaining power, it was easy to guess which kingdom they would target. Cadell reigned over the five territories: Cadell, Windcrest, Glenton, Mistbrooke, and Bressal. Though the last two kingdoms were obliterated centuries ago in the Battle of the Bones. Since then, none of the kingdoms thought to usurp Cadell for fear of the same outcome.

It was a lot of speculation, but I couldn't stop worrying over my sister, who would be collateral damage because she married Prince Alexander.

Rubbing a hand over my eyes, I wondered if I was letting my imagination get the better of me. With a sigh, I leaned back to stare at the rotting board of the ceiling. The wooden grains were dark, covered in green-haired algae that floated in the water like tiny waving fingers. It was more than I could see before. I blinked at my improved vision and noticed other details around me. Little details, the particles in the water crystal clear, even in the gloomy shadows.

Oh, no. Was I changing? I flipped up my skirt in a panic, then relaxed into a barrel at the sight of my pale legs. Thankfully, I was still human.

I scrubbed a hand down my face, hoping to erase the cobwebs of sleep that wouldn't let me go. It felt like I hadn't slept in a long time.

A high-pitched cry echoed from outside the ship, screeching like a panicked animal. The noise grew louder as Ryken flew through the jagged opening, his eyes wildly searching the ship. At first glance, it was odd to see him without his usual long locks. Orion did a terrible job. The ends were uneven and butchered—I had seen sheered sheep with better haircuts.

I raised my hand and waved. His alert eyes locked onto me, and he swam quickly to my side.

Before I could move around the oversized rolled-up rug, Ryken let out a mewling noise and gathered me into his arms. Squeezing me tight, a spew of bubbles flew from my lips in discomfort. He rested his forehead on mine, taking steady gulps of water.

His fingers threaded through my hair. The gesture more for his comfort than mine. He slid them through the strands and stopped at my collar.

Marigold. It was a sigh and a plea at the same time. It was one hushed word, but I felt everything behind it—fear, loneliness, longing, relief, and thankfulness.

What had I missed? *What is it?*

I had this feeling that you needed me. You're still too weak . . . I shouldn't have left you.

I'm better now, just tired.

Eat, he growled. *You can't transform if you don't eat and sleep. Your body isn't strong enough. My heart had to beat for yours again. You were lucky I was there.*

Did I die? My voice trembled in my thoughts.

Some of his anger seeped out. *No, but you were unconscious for a while. It scared me. You have to stop fighting the process.*

I don't want to transform.

He made a noise somewhere between a growl and groan. *You don't have a choice. Your body can't handle the in-between.*

I looked down, refusing to argue about something that would never happen. My eyes stopped on his bare chest, and my thoughts scattered.

Where is your armor?

Shaking his head, he struggled to follow the conversation. *My armor? I only wear it when I am called.*

Who calls you? Orion? Is he your king?

We don't need a king when we have Ruah.

Oh, I wasn't introduced at the ceremony.

I told you it doesn't work that way.

He ran a hand through his hair, startling at the short length, then his body sagged in memory. He pulled at the ends like his strength alone could make it longer.

I twisted my hands together, unsure how to comfort him. He turned his head away. I picked up his hand and pressed it to my collar.

You know, short hair is in style in Windcrest.

It doesn't bother me.

But I could smell his lie.

Slowly, I reached out to touch the ends. *It's a little uneven. I could fix that for you. I've trimmed my father's before. There should be a pair of scissors somewhere in this mess.*

I buried both hands in his hair, raking my fingers close to his scalp and pulling outward to measure the length on both sides of his head. Orion hadn't cared about style or precision when he hacked it off. Some chunks were nearly an inch off. I leaned over his shoulder to check the back. It was even worse there, almost three inches off.

My next gulp of water was doused in his scent. So intense I could taste it on my tongue. Overwhelmed, my eyes snapped to him. His eyes were closed, and his body completely relaxed. I hadn't realized I was smushed against him.

On the other hand, he was paying very close attention.

Oh, sorry.

His hand gripped my waist as I jerked away, holding me in place.

Never apologize for touching me. I . . . I like it.

Blushing, I turned away. *Ryken, don't say things like that.*

I didn't say it. I thought it.

I kept my eyes on the porthole in the distance, embarrassed to my core.

Now this is me saying I liked it.

Click, hum, oooh. The last note was soft, repeating in my thoughts even when his voice had stopped. His bubbles tickled my neck and I flinched, trying to keep up my stern face. His half-smile gave him a look of pure innocence, but I knew better. He blew more bubbles into my neck and I squealed, laughing.

Why do you do that? he asked.

Do what? I caught myself smiling and immediately stopped.

You laugh at the bubbles. Are they funny?

Another laugh spurted out at his question. *It tickles.*

Hmm. It must be your weak human skin.

Oh, Ryken. I lifted my eyes to the ceiling and begged for patience. *Do you want me to fix your hair or not?*

He shrugged, swimming away to an overflowing pile of boots. He picked at one of the laces, watching me under his lashes. His dark tail extended behind him, the silver scales more prominent than before. The sparkle was fascinating, alluring in a way that almost called me to him.

My eyes went wide at the direction my thoughts were turning. I'd be concerned about my declining mental state, but it wasn't the strangest thing that had happened to me today.

Scissors, I reminded myself and spun away. *I swear I saw them somewhere.* Gripping the toppled furniture, I pulled myself through the wreckage, searching the items scattered across the floor. There was enough rusted armor to equip ten guards and enough place settings to fill a banquet table. I picked up two more teacups. Perhaps it could fill a servant's table too.

I froze at the dagger, then snuck a glance at Ryken to see if he noticed the weapon. Immersed with his own findings, he distractedly swung the door of a birdcage open and close. Not wanting to miss my opportunity, I snatched the weapon up. It had a plain brown leather handle with a rusted blade. To not arouse suspicion, I floated slowly behind a barrel and ducked out of sight. Could I cut the binding around my legs before he found out?

A bark of alarm made me jump, and I quickly tucked the weapon under a moldy blanket just as he came speeding around the barrel. He swam up to me and shot out his hand to my collar.

Why are you hiding? His eyes narrowed.

I'm looking for—as luck would have it, a pair of scissors were tangled up with some jewelry a few feet from me—*these!* I picked them up and slid my fingers in them, showing him how they opened and closed. With the rust, it took a little extra force to get the metal to move. His agitation evaporated at the delight of the object.

What is it?

They are scissors. You can cut things with them.

Show me.

I snipped a tiny bow off my gown and held it up.

Oooh, like teeth. He nodded in understanding. *A weapon.*

I stared at the pointy tip, frowning at the dark direction of my thoughts. Could I use the scissors or the dagger to fight my way to the surface? Immediately, I was sick with guilt for even thinking of it. Hurt Ryken? Never.

I panicked when Orion held a knife at his chest. The thought of anyone hurting him caused my heart to flutter.

What do I do? he asked, his aqua eyes wide and trusting.

Hold still. Which he did quite well despite his curious nature. I trimmed little sections, trying not to think about how strange an underwater haircut was. It was just another thing to add to my list for today.

His hair was soft, the texture reminding me of rose petals. I shook my head as I snipped. It was the fine balance of the Merfolk, equally beautiful and powerful. My eyes strayed to the hard lines of muscle on his back. Distracted, I nearly trimmed off my finger.

Focus, Marigold, I reminded myself.

I swam back around, admiring my handiwork. The sides were shorter than the current fashion, but it made his face leaner and accented his strong jawline. I left the top a little longer, his brown hair floating across his forehead.

Goodness, had I made him more handsome?

Ryken touched my collar. *Why are you upset? Is it bad?*

No, it looks good on you, I thought quietly.

If you like it, then—he grabbed my hand and placed it on his chest. Instead of thoughts, he spoke in his language—*Click, hum, oooh.*

Now, how do I say I don't like something?

He frowned. *Hummm, click, huff, huff.*

What about the one you said before? Click, clickety-click, hummm, click. What does this mean?

A knowing smile spread across his face. *It's my heart's . . . ugh, what's the word? Reflection! My mate.*

Oh. I thought back, blushing. Had I called him that?

My stomach used the lull in the conversation to noisily remind us it had been days since my last meal. What I wouldn't give for a piping hot bowl of stew with crusty fresh bread. My stomach growled again, agreeing.

You must eat, Ryken reminded me. *Fish?*

I shook my head and wrinkled my nose.

His jaw dropped. *But fish are delicious.*

I eat them cooked.

Cooked? He tilted his head.

As in heated over a fire.

He crossed his arms. *No fire.*

Obviously, I said with a laugh. *So, no fish for me, thank you.*

Seaweed? he suggested.

I made a face.

Urchin?

I don't even know what that is, but it sounds disgusting.

I'll find you some, and you will try it. He leaned back and rubbed his hands together as if the matter was settled.

No, I won't. But he didn't hear my retort since he no longer touched my collar. I reached for him, but he smirked and swam out of reach. He stopped at the hole in the wall and held his hand out, gesturing for me to wait. Flicking his tail, he dove out the opening.

I counted to ten, waiting to see if Ryken would return. When it was safe, I flipped the blanket back and yanked the dagger out. The blade was dull, but it would have to suffice.

The last of these ropes had to go.

I managed to saw through one of the coils of rope around my legs when a light flashed from a nearby barrel. An ivory hand mirror cast a column of light upward to the top deck like a signal beacon. Curious, I paddled closer to inspect it. Was it catching sunlight from somewhere? As I picked it up, it hummed and let out a whiny pitch.

It required both hands to hold. The handle vibrated and shook my arms all the way up to my shoulders. It rippled across the surface like melted metal until Rose's face appeared in the reflection. Her red hair was matted in clumps around her sweaty face. Sallower than I had ever seen her. She turned her face into her pillow and moaned.

My stomach flipped at the sound. Something was wrong . . . was she hurt? Sick? Was she alone?

"Rose," I cried, her name garbled in the water.

Like the clanging of a warning bell, my instincts screamed she needed me—*now*.

Last Words

Rose's reflection moaned again, and she threw an arm over her face. I stiffened, the warning bell chiming again. My father always joked how the Bellmond blood must have been blessed since neither my sister nor I were ever ill. No coughs, sniffles, or rashes. Ever.

Then she had to be injured.

"Rose," I called out over and over. Could she hear my voice as I heard hers? The water distorted my words, but maybe just the noise alone would bring her attention to me.

When I placed a fingertip on her reflection, she vanished, and the mirror returned to normal.

I let out a frustrated scream, the end of it harmonizing into my song.

First the dream and now this. Was someone toying with me and using my sister as bait? Why else would they keep dangling her in front of me only to snatch her away?

Or maybe it was to warn me. My fingers tightened on the mirror's handle. What if I was the only one who could help her? I lifted the mirror, my own reflection staring back.

Whether traveling in the back of Desmond's wagon or trapped under the sea, the lack of sun had left my skin pale. Not a grayish tint like Ryken's, but like I hadn't seen a ray of sunshine in months. Blue veins wound under my skin like rivers on a map.

But it still didn't compare to Rose's sickly green appearance. I blew out a breath of bubbles, my stomach knotting.

What would she do if I needed help? *Anything.* Well, at least that was before our last argument. Now I wasn't so sure.

Would she even want me there to help her? My heated words lingered at the edge of my mind. I didn't want to remember them.

But they came all the same, filling me with regret and shame.

Our cottage replaced the sunken ship, my memory of the last time I had seen her returning. Our home, small that it was, still sent a bolt of homesickness through me. The fire flickering in the hearth, Mother's current sewing project draped across the rocking chair, Father's hats hanging by the front door, and the four of us squished together around our tiny table for a family meal.

It was home.

Mother and Father were discussing the preparations for Rose's departure while she pushed her vegetables around on her plate. Her red hair was down in loose curls, the ends covering her dirt-stained apron. She had been quieter than normal since she sat down, though it wasn't unusual for her head to be lost in the clouds. But that day she seemed worried.

Over what? I had no idea. Her life was perfect.

She was living the dream of every peasant here in Cadell. She had won the heart of the crown prince. More than that. Prince Alexander was besotted, sneaking over to our cottage more times than I could count—almost daily. Of course, Rose never allowed me to spend time with him and whisked him away to keep him for herself.

Whispers of the two of them spread, and Father worried about the time they spent together as an unwed couple. With summer approaching, he planned to send Roselyn to our grandparents' dress shop in Windcrest to help during the busy summer months.

"Distance would do you both some good," he suggested.

She sighed. "You don't understand. He gets into these moods, Pa. If I'm not there to calm him down . . . I don't know what will happen."

I rolled my eyes at her dramatics. The prince was always in a cheerful mood when he visited. Sometimes he brought me sweets or books from the castle. If he was so terrible, then why did she spend all her time with him?

"If you don't want to go, then just say it." I turned to my father and sent him my sunniest smile. "Send me, Father. My thread lines are always straight."

Mother patted my hand. "I know they are, but this isn't about you. When your time comes, you will be an excellent assistant for your grandmother. But this time, it's about Rosey."

I crossed my arms with a pout. *It is always about Rose.* There was something about her that drew people to her—even the animals came to her when she sang. I loved my sister, but sometimes . . . she just didn't appreciate what she had.

This was an opportunity for her—why wasn't she more excited? A break from mucking the stalls and harvesting apples. I had been to Windcrest once when I was little and Grandfather fell ill. Everything was whitewashed and clean. Flowers lined the streets, and the shops were full of exotic goods from sea traders. Their castle was beautiful—as if constructed by the sea itself. The outside walls were made of crushed shells and adorned with sea glass and seashells like something from a storybook.

I wished I could go back. Sometimes it felt like the salty breezes beckoned me to return. Even here in Cadell, miles away from the cliffs overlooking the sea, I caught a whiff of it in the air. It was a shame we didn't live closer . . . instead we were stuck next to a haunted forest.

Two loud knocks pounded at our entry, immediately ending the discussion around me.

"Open the door by royal behest," a voice demanded from outside.

We turned to Rose in expectation, but she only shrugged, just as clueless as the rest of us.

When the door rattled again, my father jogged across the room and opened it.

"Your Royal Highness?" Father jerked back at the number of royal guards escorting the prince. Usually he came alone.

"May I please come in?"

Father opened the door wide. Rose stood, rattling the dishes on the table.

"Prince Alexander?" she squeaked.

"Oh, my darling." He rushed into our cottage, his presence filling the confined space. The prince's red cape flapped behind him. His royal attire gleamed in the firelight, out of place in our drab farmhouse.

When he threw his arms around her, Rose's green eyes went wide. He pulled her close, desperately clinging to her. A familiar embrace that was inappropriate for too many reasons to count. My mother clicked her tongue in disapproval but was wise enough to keep silent since our front door was littered with royal guards.

"Don't," Rose whispered. "I'm filthy from the garden."

"I don't care," he whispered back, his words muffled in her hair. "I thought you had left already."

"I leave in a week."

The prince leaned back, a hard look in his eyes. "I forbid it."

A wistful sigh escaped me. Rose was the luckiest. I hoped one day I'd find true love like she did.

Mother had taken a protective stance behind my chair, her hands gripping my shoulders. Though the prince dropped by often, this formal visit seemed different.

"To what do we owe the honor of your presence, Your Highness?" my father asked.

"I want to ask you for your daughter's hand in marriage."

Rose sucked in a breath. She stepped back, but the prince refused to release her hand. "Xander . . ."

My mother clicked her tongue again at the informal nickname.

A large smile spread across the prince's handsome face. "I've been thinking nonstop about what you said. The only thing holding us back are your concerns for your family. I have a solution that will ease your worries."

"Worries? About us?" Father asked, red splotches covering his face. "There is nothing to worry about. You provide well for all your subjects, Your Highness."

"I will take care of everything," Prince Alexander promised her, his words smooth and deep, like even they were dipped in gold.

"Everything?" Rose repeated.

"In exchange for your hand in marriage, I will pay off your family's debt on this cottage. It will be theirs in full."

Mother's grip pinched my shoulders.

"That is too much——" my father started, but the prince silenced him with a raised hand.

"And a dowry for Marigold. Five hundred crowns would be more than enough to bring any man, though I doubt she will need my assistance."

I tensed in my chair, my fingers gripping the edge of the table. A dowry? For me? Overcome with giddiness, I marveled at the idea. A door of opportunities would be unlocked. I could marry for love or at least have some choice in who I settled with.

It was more than I could have imagined. A priceless gift.

"I'll give you anything to prove my love, Rosey. Marry me. Then they'll never separate us again."

Rose glanced at me then away, her eyes misting. Her lips trembled as she said, "Can I think about it?"

I gasped. Unease settled in the pit of my stomach as I watched the prince's jaw tighten. Had anyone said no to him before?

"Think about it?" he asked, his voice eerily low.

How could she refuse *the prince*? While he'd always been nice to our family, rumors circulated of his erratic behavior. Fits of anger and jealousy as quickly as the changing wind. If that was true, he'd never marry Rose now that she had offended him.

The merriment over my dowry disintegrated before I could take my next breath. With one question, Rose changed the course of our future —and not for the better.

But why? Didn't she love him?

"What is there to think about? I offered you everything you request-ed." He dropped her hand in disgust. "I don't understand why every-thing needs to be difficult with you, Roselyn."

"It's not me, Alex. It's you," my sister bit back.

Another round of gasps circled the room—mine included.

"Roselyn Vera. You forget your place," my father warned, sweat beading his brow.

"She knows her place. It's at my side," the prince growled. "I'm not in the mood for one of your games."

"It's not a *game*. It's my life," she said, building in volume until the last word ended with a pent-up scream. When she finally stopped, the room hung on the silence, a tension right before the crack of thunder.

Eyes wide, I stared at her, unable to comprehend what I had witnessed.

"Then you can be alone forever," the prince whispered. The two of them glared at one another, far from the romantic proposal it had started as. When she didn't respond, he stormed out, knocking our door into the wall in his haste.

"Protect us, Sea of Providence. My child's stubbornness may kill us all," my mother groaned.

Bowing her head, Rose burst into tears.

She turned him down.

Enraged, I shot to my feet, brushing my mother away. How could Rose be so selfish? Everything would have been provided for us, and we'd finally not have the chains of poverty tight around our necks.

All she had to do was say yes.

"Call him back," I seethed.

"Goldie, you don't understand."

I stomped around the table. Torn between wanting to comfort her and shake some sense into her. Instead I balled up my hands, refusing to do either.

"Oh, I understand. You're spoiled and selfish. Because of your outburst, we have to scrape together for another winter. You took my future and threw it away. Why? I thought you loved me."

Rose wiped her wet cheeks. "Of course I love you. It's always been the two of us."

"Us? I rarely see you. It's about you, Rose. It always has been. My life, Mother's and Father's, even the prince's—everyone dances to your tune. I'm sick of it. I've covered for you more times than I can count and pulled your load plus my own when you and the prince run off to who knows where. I've asked nothing from you—*ever*. And the one time something good comes my way, a chance for me to find my own happiness, you can't say yes?"

"Sweetheart, calm down. You're upsetting your sister." My father placed a comforting hand on Rose's shoulder.

"I'm upsetting her? *Me?*" I pointed at her. "She refused the prince's proposal."

Mother cleared her throat as she eyed my sister. "Perhaps it's for the best."

71

I sputtered. Was I the only sane person in the room?

"Please, don't be mad at me," Rose begged.

"Marigold's just in shock, like the rest of us," my father stated.

"Shock? I'm well beyond that. You would've been a princess, Rose, *a princess*. What's there to say no to? People to pamper you day and night. A wardrobe bursting with silks and jewels. Never-ending trays of meats and cheeses—you'd never be hungry again. We would never be hungry again." I stopped mid-ramble, taking a deep gulp of air. My throat swelled as I put the pieces of my thoughts together. "I feel . . . betrayed."

She was by my side in an instant, her hands cradling my cheeks. Whispering like when we shared secrets under my covers. "I would never."

"Is it the Sorcerer's curse on the royal family? Are you afraid?"

"No, I don't believe in that magical nonsense."

"Then why? Don't you love him?"

"I—I—I don't know." She bit her lip. "Maybe?"

"Couldn't you pretend? For us? For me?" I begged.

She looked at her worn boots.

"How can you be so selfish?" Anger had me bucking from her grip. "At least think of Mother and Father. Not having the debt of the farm would be such a burden off their shoulders."

"Marigold, that's enough," Father thundered.

"I have thought about it—every time he's asked me," Rose blurted, then slapped a palm over her mouth.

Mother groaned, pressing the heels of her palms into her eyes.

I blinked at Rose. How many times had she refused the prince? How many opportunities had she declined that could have helped us improve our financial situation?

"Where is my sister who promised to take care of me and save me from the dragons of this world?" My heart felt empty. Like every word she had ever spoken was meaningless.

Her eyes misted over. "Goldie, I am keeping my promise. Not everything is what it seems."

"Like you?"

"Quiet! Both of you. This has gone on long enough." Mother intervened, moving between us.

The part of me that obeyed rose up inside me at her tone. But my anger refused to subside, boiling inside of me from years of staying quiet. I couldn't stop myself from getting one final jab in.

"Sometimes I wonder if I'd be better off with no sister at all." Hot tears spilled down my cheeks. "I don't need anything from you—not now, not ever. Just leave me alone."

Heated last words I regretted with my entire being. Jealousy had blinded me, and I didn't realize we wouldn't speak again. Rose accepted the prince's proposal the next day and was whisked off to the castle.

She took my response to heart. I wasn't allowed to enter the castle to visit her. Nor did she return home again.

I pressed the mirror to my chest, my tears mixing with the saltwater. Was it too late to apologize? To tell her that she was worth more than all the crowns in Cadell?

Wasn't that what second chances were for? To fix mistakes?

I snatched the dagger from the rubble and returned to sawing my bindings with a feverish intensity.

I was going home.

Be Warned

y fingers cramped, and the skin of my palm chaffed from the grooves of the dagger's handle. But I didn't stop sawing. The memory of Rose's pale face fueled me through the pain.

The reality I had been avoiding hit me.

Whether I acknowledged it or not, I was changing. Granted, it was a slow process, but one still happening. How much time did I have before I grew a tail? Chain or no chain—I was trapped in the sea. I'd never get to walk through the wildflowers, ride horses around the countryside, or dance at my wedding. Would I even have a wedding?

Time was floating away without me. Numbers and days scattered in every direction like bubbles circulating in the water. I'd never be able to catch them all and get those moments back. I couldn't focus on everything all at once, so what was the most important?

My family and Rose.

This might be my last opportunity to see them—to say goodbye. My heart ached at the possibility of never reconciling with Rose.

Last time, it had been Rose who had made the peace offering. Now, it was up to me to take the first step and make things right. But with her illness, who knew how much time I had to make amends? Was Mother with her? Father? Prince Alexander?

I thought back to Rose's declaration, to the agony in those three words—*it's my life.*

Had she truly not wanted to marry the prince? My selfish actions could have forced her hand and bound her into a loveless marriage.

Bile churned in my stomach. What had I done?

Fueled by my guilt, I sawed feverishly through the ropes, almost halfway through before I realized Ryken had returned. His scent drifted on the current, stopping me mid-saw.

Normally, his smell reminded me of laundered clothes drying in the sunshine kissed with a salty breeze. But now it was a sharp odor, a warning. I stiffened, my body on full alert. All my senses overloaded me at once as my heart rate sped up, my neck pulsing with frantic beats.

I turned slowly to the barrel behind me and peeked over the top. There was no one. The hairs on the back of my neck insisted otherwise.

Click.

My head snapped back at the noise, my eyes colliding with Ryken's above me. He hovered at the ceiling, his aqua eyes freezing the water between us. His nostrils flared with each breath. His tail rippled behind him with each angry whip, the end flowing like shimmering silk. He held himself back, his arms extended behind him, his nails deep into the rotted wooden planks.

He sprang forward, diving straight down at me.

I shrieked in surprise. Ducking, I threw an arm over my head, the forgotten dagger slipping from my fingers. Muscles in my shoulder and back tensed, waiting for him to plow into me.

But he didn't.

Under the cover of my arm, I could sense him next to me. My skin tingled at his close proximity, vibrating with his awareness. The bubbles from his breath caressed my shoulder, crowding into my personal space. I tensed as his arm wrapped around my back, pulling me upright with a sudden jerk.

Unable to hide, I took in his cool stare. He bared his teeth, and I cowered on instinct, but his grip was like steel, reeling me closer. Wild emotions flickered across his face. Before, I might have been frightened by his anger. But now it was the scathing glare of disappointment that did me in.

It wounded just as much as his bite.

You promised, he roared into my mind.

One of his hands glided up into my hair. It curled around the strands, yanking my head sideways, allowing him full access to my throat. The water lapped at my skin from his long intake of breath. His hand on my back uncurled until his heated palm pressed into my spine.

I flailed against him, not appreciating being hauled about. His grip tightened, holding me still before touching my collar.

Let me go, I ordered.

You said you wouldn't escape. You lied.

I need my legs to swim, I argued.

Let go of your human ideas. You don't need your legs to swim, just as you don't need air to breathe. I see the desperation in your eyes for a life you can never have. It's gone. You have to learn to live without your legs.

I don't want to, I shouted, stubbornly holding his glare.

He growled. *Your choices will be the death of us. What am I to do with you?* He took another gulp, breathing in my scent. *I know you should be punished.* His words tapered off as he studied me. The tension in his body drained, the hard ridges of him molding into me. *But I can't do it.*

His grip on my hair gentled until he cradled my head, allowing me to relax. After a moment, he shot forward, his mouth aimed for my throat. It was too fast for me to react. But there was no pinch of teeth or sting of pain. Instead, my skin sizzled. Molten hot, it burned from the press of his lips between my collar and flesh. I didn't want to feel anything, but my body refused to listen to my demands.

Is it me?

I barely heard his whispered question as I was lost in the sensation of his lips resting on my throat.

Do you wish you were claimed by another?

No, I responded, surprising myself at my outburst. It was the truth, though. Was it because of our connection? Or were my emotions getting involved? For the first time, someone made me feel special.

Then . . . why? Why remove it if you weren't trying to escape?

Ryken's voice cracked, but he still didn't lift his head to look at me. It triggered something within me, and I placed a protective arm around him. I knew what it felt like to be inadequate. I didn't want to be the one that caused him to feel that way.

Your mirror showed me my sister. She is sick, Ryken. I wanted to say more, but the fear of losing her rose up and clogged my throat. My lips trembled as I swallowed it back down. *I have to get back to her.*

Mirror? I don't understand.

Something is wrong with her. Please let me go to help her. There must be something I can do.

You can't.

I panicked at the finality of his tone and grabbed his shoulders in desperation, his head popping up. *If I go, I promise to come back.*

Don't make me more promises. You have enough debts on your life already. You belong to the sea—just like I do.

Ryken, I begged, *please. Don't you have family? Someone you care about?*

A dejected smile pulled up one corner of his lips. *You. You are my family. Collectors don't have family. We are created with a singular purpose for Ruah's choosing. Not that a mate is forbidden, but my responsibility will leave little time for a family.*

What responsibility? What will you collect? I asked, tilting my head.

Broken promises.

I stared, wondering if I had misheard him.

Or, I should say—I will collect the people that break their promises, so they may endure their judgment. He gave me a pointed look.

Wh-wh-what do you do with them?

The sea takes them and decides if their lives are worth saving.

Are they?

He shrugged. *Sometimes.*

Wait! Does that mean you can travel on land?

I will when I am called.

I reeled back. *How? What? But you have no legs!*

Ruah will provide what I need when the time comes. I haven't been called yet to know firsthand, but Orion said it will be similar to the ceremony. Four elite warriors are sent at Ruah's command, one to aid each Collector during his duty. They offer their strength, agility, and speed . . . among other things.

I still didn't understand. Ryken on land? How was it possible? Was that what the armor was that he had to wear? And who even was Ruah? There were too many questions to focus on just one.

How will you know when you have to collect . . . people?

The sea tells me. You have the promise mark on your forehead. It is unseeable to your human eyes, but to my people, we see it and know.

Know what?

That you made a promise to the sea. Your life is not your own.

And if I break my promise? Guiltily, I glanced down and remembered the vow I had made in exchange for my second chance. Perhaps promising *anything* wasn't the wisest decision.

Click, clickety-click, hummm, click. I won't let anything happen to you. You are mine to protect.

I don't want to break my promise, but I also can't leave my sister knowing that she needs me.

What does she need?

She needs—my eyes opened wide, and I sucked in a gulp of water—*your pearl! The medicine you gave me. Where do you get it?*

An underwater cavern where you woke up. It's full of them.

Could we get another one so I can give it to her?

We could, but——

Grinning, I nodded. *Yes! We can go together.*

Together? Collecting himself, he shook his head. *No, no, no. You cannot go to the surface.*

I blew out a frustrated breath of bubbles. *Fine. I'll stay in the water. Let me pass a message and the pearl to someone on the shoreline.*

We do not speak to humans. It's our first and most important rule. They bring war and chaos.

And you already broke it—I'm human.

You aren't human. You're . . . I don't know what you are.

I'll transform. I'll stop fighting and finish the process if you help me do this. I crossed my arms and hoped he couldn't tell I had no idea how to fulfill my side of the bargain.

His nostrils flared. *You have to transform anyway.*

He was calling my bluff. I had to up the stakes. I placed my hand on his heart, and he froze. *Imagine if it was me that was unwell. Wouldn't you do everything in your power to save me?*

Seconds stretched into minutes. His impassive face left me doubtful if I had a bargaining chip at all.

One message?

I blew out a slew of bubbles as I threw my arms around his neck, hugging him tight. *Oh, thank you, Ryken, thank you.*

You must stay in the water the entire time.

I will, I will.

Laughing, I leaned back to beam a smile at him, and his words turned into gibberish. His mouth hung slack.

But the contentment was too hard to contain. The wedge between Rose and me had rested heavily on my heart. More than I realized. Perhaps I wouldn't get to leave the ocean, but at least I could make peace in one aspect of my life. Thinking of my healed shoulder, I had faith the pearl would cure Rose of her ailment.

When can we leave? Now?

You're too weak to go anywhere without eating. I brought you the urchin. He swam over to the entrance and gathered a handful of balls with brightly colored spikes poking out of the top. He broke it in half, revealing an orange goop in the middle. *Here. Eat.*

I thought of arguing, but I didn't want him to change his mind about helping me.

And you're sure it's safe? I had never eaten raw meat before, yet my stomach gurgled in excitement.

It is, he replied with a sly smile.

I took the squishy piece he offered and quickly popped it into my mouth before I could talk myself out of it. Creamy and sweet, it practically melted on my tongue with flavors of buttery sea salt. Not as terrible as I feared it would be.

Now can we go?

That wasn't enough. More.

He broke more apart, offering them to me one after another. After a dozen urchins and a stem of green bubbles he called sea grapes, my stomach stretched to capacity. Not that it needed much since it was used to being empty.

I tried again. *Now?*

He shook his head, watching me with a twinkle of laughter in his eyes. *Yes, impatient one. We can go. But be warned, Marigold. This is a onetime visit, and then we'll never speak of it again. You must forget your past life and accept your new future. No more negotiations. No more pleas. You have been given the gift of life in exchange for your allegiance to*

Ruah's kingdom. By not completely transforming, you put your life—and mine—at risk.

What will happen? My stomach dropped at his serious expression.

The sea will come to collect what is owed . . . and there won't be anything I can do to save you from its wrath.

Stormy Seas

The cost for life was a life indebted. I knew a payment would be required—I had promised anything. But my entire life pledged to a stranger?

I stared down at the empty urchin shell. Ryken's warning made my full belly twist again. Was I just another human trinket to be collected like all this junk scattered at my feet? It was still my life, and I was in control, even if a stranger was dictating the rules. Rules that could cost me my life if I broke them.

Who even was this Ruah? Neither here nor there, they were powerful enough to command me through my thoughts and save me from the black void of death. Who was I to deserve Ruah's attention? I was a farmer's daughter. A seamstress of no worth. Why save me when there were more worthy people with higher rank and influence? What did I have that others did not? Was it my voice?

Ryken had to know more.

Who is Ruah? And where is their kingdom?

Ruah is the creator and ruler of all things. Human kingdoms exchange crowns on a whim, but only Ruah can grant true sovereignty. The Chosen has claimed his throne with his queen at his side. Through his reign, peace will be restored across the lands. Not only here but beyond

Hanalla to all the continents. Ruah's magic flows outward to form invisible veins that connect us no matter our location. From the music of the crashing waves to the wind whistling through the leaves in the forest to the pulsing drum in the boglands and the vibrations in the cracks of the rocks at Mt. Cynale. It's a reminder that we are not alone.

I blinked, remembering the voice—Ruah—had said the same thing.

Where do I fall in a world of magic I don't understand? Why me?

Only Ruah knows. You probably serve a greater purpose than you think. Ryken shrugged as if it made sense to him. Then he grabbed both of my hands, lifting me upward and wrapping an arm around me. He scooped my hair away before it became trapped between us.

What? He stared down at me.

You always surprise me with your gentleness.

I'm not gentle. I'm a fierce warrior. He flicked his tail and sent a shockwave of water into a lone barrel beside us. The wood exploded on contact, the fragments and long splinters shooting in all directions. His top lip lifted in a satisfied snarl before his eyes went wide at the incoming debris. He tucked me to his side and batted the pieces away with his free hand.

When the water was clear, his tail flicked again in excitement. *See? Fierce.*

A soft smile quivered on my lips. *Of course.*

His eyebrows shot down. *You don't believe me.*

Oh, I believe you. He had a way of being both. Just as he had a way of being both animalistic and human. *Please don't break anything else to prove a point.*

He huffed. *Your human body will require sleep soon, so we must hurry.*

Holding his palm out, I placed mine in his, the smooth texture of his skin bringing me a sense of security. He led me from the ship, swimming with ease for the both of us. I held out a hand to catch the flow of the current between my fingers and caught him sneaking glances at me when he thought I wasn't looking. Retracing our route from yesterday, I admired the scenery through new eyes, the sights more beautiful the second time around. My vision was clearer than before. Microscopic fish were visible from over a mile away. Even the colors were more vibrant.

The ruby red of the coral bled into many shades, brighter at the ends and darkening into the color of blood in the middle. A fuzzy film coated the blades of seagrass, tickling my skin as we swam through the field. Distracted by the details and sharp colors, I nearly missed our arrival at the stone front entrance.

Wait here. You're not allowed in.

I floated to a flattop boulder covered in holes in the middle of a patch of seagrass. I sat on top, my legs dangling over the edge, and clasped my hands together on my lap. *I'll wait.*

He stared at me for a moment before he turned to slip behind the stone, leaving me alone.

I kicked down the ends of my dress that had ballooned around my knees. Fabric in the water was nothing but frustration. But what was the alternative? Wearing nothing? My cheeks pinked, and I shifted uncomfortably on the hard rock. Would I be confident enough after I transformed?

Marigold of Cadell.

My back stiffened at the voice.

Do not be afraid.

Not just any voice—no, it was *the* voice I had been waiting for. All my thoughts evaporated but one—had I failed my second chance?

I can explain, Ruah.

Explain? I see your heart. Your actions are not selfish. Your sister's heart appeared the same.

Roselyn? I rolled onto my knees and scanned the empty waters. *Do you know her? Is she safe?*

I know every heart that beats, and hers is as strong as ever. Her path is set before her, as is yours, if only you choose to walk it.

Walk? Or swim?

It depends on you. You always have free will, and I will never force your decisions.

But I'll die again if I don't transform.

Will you? Haven't you wondered why I woke you early? As much as you deny it, you do have a purpose, my child.

What? What do you want from me? My fists balled at my sides.

Patience. You will know soon enough.

I spun around at the light tap on my shoulder. Ryken tilted his head, his nostrils flaring. *What is wrong? Why are you scared?*

Ruah is here.

Ruah is everywhere.

But I mean here-here, as in talking to me.

A sharp-toothed smile stretched across his face. *And now you will transform?*

Actually, no. I met his smug smile with my own. *I'm told to be patient until my purpose is revealed.*

His smile fell, and the water reeked of panic. *Are you leaving me?*

The word "no" was on the tip of my tongue so quickly it left me paralyzed. I refused to fall for his beauty and charms. *Ruah said I awoke early for a reason.*

He nodded, his face pinched. *Whatever your purpose, it will be a great honor for you.*

It doesn't mean I'm leaving you.

Yet. Lowering his lashes, he lifted the strands of my hair, rubbing his thumb over the ends. *I don't know if I can let you go. This will be a test for me as well.* He sighed. *Now let's deliver your message.*

Ryken was quiet on the swim upward. Not that I had much to say, as Ruah's conversation repeated in my head.

The sea thrashed the closer we got to the surface. He stopped us every so often, pointing to my ears. I had grown accustomed to the pressure of the deep water, and my ears popped as they adjusted on the swim back up.

Dark, angry storm clouds tumbled across the skies. Thick with streaks of white as lightning shot out in a jagged line. Just before we reached the surface, a crack of thunder vibrated through the current, rumbling through me.

What if there was no one nearby because of the storm? Would Ryken give me another chance on a sunny day?

I raised a hand past the water line. My lips parted with a shaky breath at the thought of seeing land sooner than I expected. I marveled at the sensations, savoring them. The wind swirled between my fingers as I turned my hand back and forth. This could be the last time raindrops would splatter against my skin.

I kicked with my legs, wanting to break through the roll of the waves. Ryken reached out and gripped my bicep to pull me back under the water. Where my eyes had been skyward, his were locked on me.

Maybe this is a bad idea.

No, Ryken. We are already here. How far are we from shore?

He didn't answer, his eyes scanning my face.

Ryken. I said his name again and jarred him out of his internal debate.

You stay down here and let me check. He glided upward until his head was out of the water. His tail swished about until the end of it slapped against my shoulder and slid slowly down my arm. It curled around my back, holding me in a hug. The tips of his tail drifted in the current at my waist, silky across my forearm. I turned my palm over, letting the glittering silver graze over my hand in a seductive dance.

The length of his tail was almost pressed to the side of my face. Up close, each scale was iridescent. Sparkling with silver, the darkness shimmered at the edges and highlighted the fan-shaped scales. Each scale pulsed with energy and lured me with its beauty. Would Ryken be mad if I touched one? Would the texture be rough or smooth like his fin? My fingers hovered over his scales as I battled against the rules of propriety ingrained in me.

I shouldn't. But my fingers itched anyway and dared me to close the last inch between us. He was distracted—he wouldn't even notice one little touch.

There wasn't time to make a choice; his tail tightened and flung me up into his waiting arms and the rush of roaring winds.

The air combed over my head, the sensation familiar but strange at the same time. It reminded me of a time before and of a life that had grown dim these last few weeks. It was the gust of freedom. Memories of our farmhouse returned, the same breeze flapping our clothes hanging on the line. Then another memory of me standing at the window of my cramped bedroom above the clothing shop, the salty breeze a song of its own. It hummed along my skin in hypnotic notes to beckon me to the sandy shore.

This was only a small taste but addictive enough that I wanted more. I wanted to be back on the shore with the tide between my toes and the breeze in my hair.

Ryken's face dropped to eye level with mine. His aqua eyes glinted brightly in the storm's gloom. The corners slanted down, saddened by my expression. His thumb traced across my mouth, wiping away my smile. He clicked and hummed phrases. Though I didn't understand, I sensed the melancholy embedded in each syllable.

My heart squeezed. An intense need to comfort overtook me, and I placed my hand on his chest. Immediately, he placed his over mine. Whereas I thought to reassure him, it had the same effect on me.

Click, clickety-click, hummm, click.

I tried to say his name, but my mouth was still submerged and formed only bubbles.

We bobbed in the current, up and down with the crest of each new wave. Everything faded away but Ryken. Would things have been different had he been human? Would I have met him in the shop? On market day in Cadell? Traveling on the roads around Mistbrooke Forest?

Would he have noticed me? Or was it only my song that interested him?

A wave splashed into his back, separating us with the force of it. He called me, but the current had other plans, dragging me under, then tossing me back up to the surface.

A whistle sounded, and I strained to discern the notes over the roaring waves. A fisherman's whistle. It signaled a command to its crew. In an instant, my thoughts righted themselves.

A message. I'm here to deliver a message to my sister.

Movement caught my eye, men aboard a fishing vessel anchored on the sandy beach. They scrambled to gather their things and escape the storm.

People!

I cried out, trying to get their attention, but it was as if my lungs had forgotten how to function. I couldn't gather enough air to speak. Instead, it was a low, gurgling croak.

Ryken wrapped an arm around my waist from behind, dragging me away from the shore. I fought his grip, refusing to let this opportunity pass.

Marigold, he cried in alarm, *what are you doing? Your body needs to stay in the water.*

I had to get the fishermen's attention. Ignoring the merman's growls in my ear, I waved my arms, leaping from the choppy waves as much as he would let me.

I'm sorry, Ryken, but I have to do this.

Desperate, I kicked at him, elbowing him in the stomach. Then I knocked my head into his nose with a solid whack. It was enough to free myself, and I rode the current in, stumbling when my feet caught the shells on the bottom. The waves rushed out to land, only to return to the sea, the foamy fingers almost pulling me with them.

Now only one man was left on the beach. The rest had raced over the dune, ducking for cover. Frantically, I hopped a few feet, the blasted rope hindering my movements, before landing on my knees in the wet sand, trying to scream to grab the last man's attention. My new vision had made him seem closer than he was. His back was to me while he folded his fishing nets, his movements jerky. He snatched his wicker basket full of fish and smashed his white cap to his head to keep it from blowing away.

I stared at my own hands for a moment. The pearl . . . I didn't have it. Ryken had been the one carrying it.

Torn, I glanced back at the ocean to see Ryken swimming as close as he could without leaving the water. He called me to him, a high-pitched wail that reminded me of a seagull's cry. Palms out, I hoped he understood the signal to wait. Not that I was too worried about him coming out on land with his tail. I was more worried that the fisherman would leave without noticing me.

I crawled on all fours, struggling against the rope that bound my legs. Sand clumped to my skin and clothes, a gritty texture. The fabric of my tattered gown dragged through the sand behind me, making each shuffled inch toward the man more difficult than the last.

My chest grew heavy, my muscles weak from the lack of exercise. Even as my strength waned, I fought through the aching spasms. Hopefully Ryken would understand when I returned and would forgive me for lashing out. I had a lifetime to make it up to him. But Rose? I only had this *one* chance. A little discomfort was worth making sure she got my message. The sentiment fueled me a bit farther inland, my lungs burning with adrenaline.

A tingle erupted from my chest, and fear had my eyes going wide. I wrapped my hands around my throat. I tensed as I swallowed air that whipped uselessly through my gills.

My lungs weren't working.

The burning wasn't adrenaline—it was my body demanding oxygen. Pounding on my chest, my insides sloshed with liquid. My lungs were still full of seawater from the day I had almost died.

And now I was drowning again . . . but this time on land.

Not My Bed

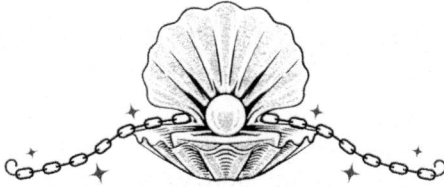

lick, clickety-click, hummm, click. The desperate plea carried on the wind.

I looked over my shoulder through the misting rain. Ryken fought against the choppy waters. Even as each wave slammed into him, he refused to break eye contact. Lightning streaked across the sky just before the crack of thunder.

Lightheaded, I sat back on my heels and swayed, almost tipping over. My vision spotted, and I couldn't tell which direction was the shore and which was the ocean. I tried screaming, coughing, and pounding on my useless chest.

Help! Someone? Anyone?

A white light exploded into my vision, and I rocked back on the sand. Rain splattered my face. I opened my mouth, hoping to catch enough droplets to gulp through my gills.

Was this my punishment for leaving the sea?

"Marigold," a familiar male voice called out. It was faint, drowning in the chaos of the storm. "Don't give up." The phrase and tone were similar, giving me a sense of déjà vu.

I stared at the bright light as the memory resurfaced. I *had* heard it before—after I had died. Not only that, but the voice had been the same one that spoke in my mind every time Ryken touched my choker.

Could that be him? Because . . . I had *heard* it. It wasn't in my mind.

Something slammed into my ribs with enough force that I was sure they were broken. I didn't have time to recover as it repeated, my teeth clattering from the impact. Before I could beg them to stop, the third strike hit me, and warm salt water gushed from my lungs and erupted out of my mouth.

Coughing, I inhaled my first sweet breath of air.

"Ryken . . ." I said, my voice cracking from disuse. His silhouette came into focus above me. Darkness shadowed his face, the light blinding behind him.

"Breathe." His steady hand rested on my heart. The warmth of his fingers scorched me through my damp dress. My heart flipped and then picked up pace from its deathly slow beats. I placed my hand over his, wishing I could see his face.

He hadn't left me.

"Hello?" A distant call from somewhere behind me. The patter of rain and crash of the waves made it sound like a hushed whisper.

Tingles trailed over my skin, leaving me weak. What little energy I had left evaporated at an astounding rate. The dark void called me, and I fought to stay conscious. I held on to Ryken, refusing to be separated.

This sensation was the same as the end of the ceremony. I was standing at the edge of the unknown, and Ryken was my anchor, keeping me safe.

"Sir? Can you hear me?" Closer this time, the voice was a male baritone. One I didn't recognize. He panted his questions. "Do you require assistance?"

The hand on my heart tensed, but Ryken still didn't respond. Was the man talking to us?

"Don't move. Relax," Ryken said softly. Something warm brushed across my forehead, dragging my scraggly loose hair from my face.

"Sir? What are——? *You cad*—get off of her."

Thunder rumbled, echoing in my ears like a clattering of pots in the kitchen. I flinched at the unexpected explosion. Ryken kept me steady, pinning me to the sand with his hand.

Then he turned away with a menacing growl.

What was happening? This was not the time to be useless. I blinked, trying to see.

Crack. A loud, hollow sound, and Ryken's silhouette disappeared, along with the comfort of his hand. Without him, the light grew to a blinding intensity. Squeezing my eyes closed was all the energy I could muster.

Tired. I was so tired. My body went limp, my head lolling to the side and into the gritty sand.

"Miss?" The voice sounded underwater again, garbled and far away, until even my thoughts were lost, swallowing me up in nothingness.

Just like before, I tumbled through the pitch black of my dreams. I screamed into the endless void, frustrated at being dragged from one horrible event to the next.

I focused my thoughts inward, accusing the voice that had told me lies. *You said I wasn't alone. I trusted you.*

Ruah's voice blared in the quiet. "I never left you."

Where's Ryken?

Thoughts for his safety fueled me with an unknown strength. He had saved me . . . again. Perhaps now it was my turn to save him.

"You must do this on your own. Not every path you walk will be easy. Each bump, fall, and disappointment strengthens you for your purpose."

What purpose?

"You will be my voice."

Me? Oh, no, no, no—you have the wrong person. A gust of water or air—I couldn't tell—pierced my chest, stealing my breath away.

"Have faith, not only in me but in yourself. Rise up, my warrior, and *sing*."

How could I? I wasn't in the water. Notes floated in my head like jumbled pages of sheet music. I scoured my memories for the tune I had sung when I called Ryken. If I sang it again, would he hear me and return?

The notes played softly in my head, and then they grew louder until each note surged through me. Energy coursed through my veins, beating like the drum of my heart. Music of my soul. It crescendoed against my skull until I could only find relief by complying with Ruah's request.

Sing.

My eyes sprang open before I hit the first low note. The deep breath I held sputtered out in surprise. Light from a strange room sharpened into focus. Squinting, I noticed the dust motes in the air and a tiny cobweb in the far corner of the wooden ceiling. Birds chattered noisily outside my window, the sun's rays streaking across the quilt over my legs. I pressed a hand on my racing heart. It thudded like I had run across a meadow at full speed versus lying here in . . . someone's bed. *Not my bed.*

Sitting up, a scratchy sheet slid down my front and revealed an ivory cotton nightgown that I definitely hadn't been wearing earlier. *Not my clothes.* I didn't even want to think about how I had gotten into them or who had helped me while I was asleep.

I pinched my forehead where a headache pulsed to the beats of my rapid heart. There had to be a way to release the pressure that had built up. Massaging my temple, I glanced around the tight quarters. Similar in size to the room I had shared with Rose back at the farm, only this one had a child-sized bed against the wall. A misshapen burlap bear flopped to one side on the bed, his one button eye missing. *Not my room.*

Where was I?

Could I have dreamed my time under the sea? Only stories of fabled creatures who lived in my imagination? My heart clenched at the thought of not seeing Ryken again.

I touched my choker and smiled. He was real.

Whispers echoed in the distance. I straightened, narrowing in on the conversation.

"What do we do with her?" It was a woman's voice. The *r* rolled off her tongue, an accent of the Windcrest region. Either my hearing had improved while I slept, or I was more attuned to sound after being submerged for days.

"We have to notify the king." This one was a man with a deeper octave.

"Yes . . . and him? He can't stay here," she insisted.

A roar vibrated through the walls. It shook the candlestick on the nightstand next to me. I placed a hand on my chest so my heart didn't flutter away. The sound wasn't angry; it was forlorn. The beast was frustrated to the point of agony.

Not just any beast—my beast. *Ryken.*

A red-hot fury took me as I leapt from the bed and padded barefoot to the door, swinging it open. A lit candle burned on a table in a dark hallway, shadows dancing on the walls. Stairs disappeared downward in front of me with another wooden door to my left and two more doors in the other direction.

I turned right, following my instinct. I had no idea where I was heading, but my heart somehow already knew the way. The pull in my chest guided me like a compass forward. The floorboard creaked as I moved, and the murmured conversation started again.

"What was that?" the male asked.

"Did he escape? Jacek, don't let him near us."

Boots thudded up the stairs, and I picked up my pace, going straight to the leftmost door where my inner compass pointed.

"My lady, don't go in there," a bearded man pleaded when he reached the top of the landing.

My lady?

I froze with my hand on the doorknob. *Follow the rules. Be obedient,* I reminded myself.

As I went to step back, another roar sounded on the other side. More pitiful than the last one. His voice cracked at the end, raw from overuse.

The heartbreak in his cries was enough that I wanted to claw through the door with my bare hands. Luckily, I didn't have to. The door was unlocked, and I rushed through.

Ryken reclined on a bed in the center of the room. A thick rope tied each of his arms to the wooden headboard, stretching them high above his head. Multiple nails were hammered into the rope and to the wooden bed frame. The frayed ends were tied tight in a Palomar knot, one of the strongest knots fishermen used.

I sank to my knees at his bedside. He tilted his head, angling his good eye at me as it worriedly traveled over my face. His other eye was swollen and black, his cheek a canvas of purple and green, almost distracting me from his blood-crusted lip.

"What have they done to you?" My voice quivered. What had my decision cost him? "I'm so sorry."

Ryken strained against the binding to touch me.

"Release him. Now." I could barely get the words out for the lump of fury in my throat.

"Stay back, my lady. He's gone mad."

"The only one mad here is you. How *dare* you treat him like this," I seethed.

"It was the only way I could rescue you, my lady. He had attacked you and wouldn't let anyone near you. Though I'm happy you're awake, you should be recovering. Let's get you back to the safety of your bed."

The bearded man grabbed my elbow from behind. I shook my arm, trying to dislodge his fingers.

"I belong here—with him. Unhand me this instant."

Pop, pop, pop. Nails shot out of the bed frame as Ryken yanked one arm free and, in one swift movement, whipped the man to him by the throat. His aqua eyes frosted over as his grip tightened until the man's veins bulged on his face.

"Ryken."

He ignored me, his lip curled up in a silent snarl.

"Please don't do this."

He finally turned to me, his eyebrows shooting up.

"We aren't like them. We don't need to resort to violence."

Immediately, the man was flung back to the floor, wheezing for air. He crab-walked backward and tripped over himself as he ran out the door.

With a sigh, Ryken plunged his hand into my hair and cupped the back of my head. He drew me close until our foreheads pressed together. Sand coated his skin, the grains dusting off him and onto me.

"You're safe," he murmured under his breath.

"You . . . speak." More than just his voice had changed. His coloring, though still darker than my pale complexion, took on a human quality. Lightly tan and flushed. Still distractingly attractive.

Our breaths mingled together, the heat of his fanning my face. If I thought I was in trouble before, I was a lost cause now. I had used his merman features to hold my attraction at bay. Now, I had nothing. Even bruised, he was stunning and made me want to melt into his arms. His next breath shuddered out and sent a fresh wave of tingles down my spine. Desire begged me to move forward and press my lips on his, surprising me at the urgency behind it. It took everything I had to glance away and collect myself.

I leaned back, his fingers gliding down my neck to stop at my collar. *I like it better like this. More intimate—just you and me.*

The last thing we needed right now was intimacy. Instead, I needed to figure out where we were and the identities of the people in the other room. Not that I was worried. Ryken wouldn't let anything happen to me. I brushed his hand away and hoped he would focus on the situation at hand.

"I see you're still the same on the inside even if your outside appears different," I said with an eye roll. "We need to get you out of these ropes."

But I knew nothing about knots, and no matter how much I tugged and pulled, I couldn't release him. I'd have to find help.

He rested back on a pillow and smiled, his teeth square and flat, just happy to have me close again. The expression made him wince, and he dabbed his blood-crusted lip. He barely fit on the bed, his feet poking out at the end.

Human feet. Ginormous human feet. How tall was he?

"Ryken, look at you! You have legs."

His cheeks pinked, and he lifted the blanket, his eyebrows shooting up. "Uhh, I think I have more than legs."

I spun away, pressing my hands into my heated cheeks.

"*Goodness.* We don't speak of those things."

"But it's . . . normal?"

I cleared my throat, the topic making it go dry. "Yes. Quite. Now let's talk about something—anything else. Are you injured anywhere else?"

The sheet rustled. "No, only my face. Is this how humans feel all the time? Heavy?" He lifted his arm and watched it drop onto the sheet. "I don't like it. We need to return to the sea."

I placed a gentle hand on his bicep, and his attention snapped back to me. "About that . . ."

"No."

"I didn't finish what I was saying."

"You didn't need to."

"Let me see her one last time. Let me say goodbye to my family. Please, Ryken."

"We were supposed to deliver a message. See how that turned out?" He shook his head, his jaw clamped closed.

95

"We are already on land. The hardest part is over. And look at you——"

"I *did* look. I want my fins back. I want——" His face darkened to a light gray, and the color spread down his naked torso. With a groan, his hips flexed off the bed, rippling across the sheet to the end of the bed where the sheet flung up in the air, and his tail uncoiled to hang over the edge and flop on the floor.

He was back to his merman form, though his facial injuries had transformed with him.

My mouth hung open. "You can change back and forth?"

Ryken spoke in his language with hums, grunts, and clicks.

"I can't understand you."

With a flick of his tail, the rope that had bound his legs dropped in pieces on the floor. He shredded the last rope with his sharp teeth, spitting the rope fragments on the bed.

I wrinkled my nose at his manners. Meanwhile, he appeared satisfied with himself. Now free, he wrapped his arms around my back and pulled me closer. I resisted, pressing my palms against his chest.

He grunted at me.

"No matter how stubborn you are, you can't stay in this form. What are you going to do? Crawl back to the ocean?"

His eyes narrowed, and he brushed his fingers against my choker. *I don't like being human.*

"I didn't like being underwater——" he let out a low growl "——at first either. I had to experience your world through your eyes to see its wonders. It helped me understand you better. I think if you experienced a few days in my world, maybe you would understand me better too."

He was silent, scanning my face.

"We can deliver the pearl to Rose in person. You can meet my family."

He narrowed his eyes.

I sighed, rubbing a hand down my face. What could I say to convince him? His skin twitched beneath my fingers, heating before it softened under my touch. Air hissed between his teeth, followed by a muffled whine.

"I don't have the shell," he said, his voice strained. "I dropped it after they knocked me unconscious. You'd only be able to deliver the message."

Startled, I glanced up at his voice. His coloring had returned to a peachy hue, a light coating of sweat dotting his brow. How did he shift so fast?

Wait a minute—did he say I could deliver the message? I bit my bottom lip, holding in my excitement.

His mouth pulled into a firm no-nonsense line. "Then we return to the sea. I mean it. Even if I have to drag you back with me."

Half-Truths

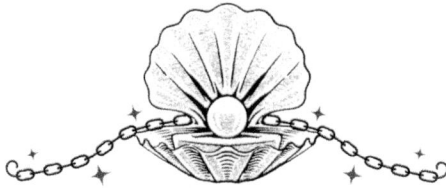

"Thank you, thank you." I threw my arms around his neck and rested my head on his shoulder. His human shoulder—my mind couldn't even fathom him in this new form.

His hand ran down the length of my hair, stopping at my back. "How do you stand this?"

My head dipped back, meeting his eyes. "What? My hair?"

It had been some time since it had a good scrub. Even though my clothes had mysteriously been changed, sand still lodged in the creases of my body and dried salt crusted on my skin.

"All these . . . feelings. It's hard to focus."

I blinked, unsure of what he meant. "Try focusing on one at a time. Which one is the worst?"

"Exhaustion. Normally I'd feel this tired if I swam from one island to another. But today I've done nothing. Why would my body be exhausted?"

"Maybe from shifting between forms?" I suggested.

He yawned and glanced to the side. "I didn't think of that."

"Haven't you done this before?"

His eyes fluttered closed as he collapsed back into the pillow. "No, I had never considered or even desired to shift into a human before . . .

until I saw you on the beach. Now I know . . ." He licked his dry lips, flinching at the wound. "Shifting hurts . . . a lot."

The more he talked, the more hushed his words became. Tilting my ear toward him, I struggled to translate his muffled sentences.

"Can you stand? Walk? We have to get out of here."

His yawn was his only response.

"Ryken——" I stammered when he shifted his weight.

His arms went slack on my back, throwing me off balance. I tipped forward and landed on the sheet on top of his chest. As if he planned it, he tightened his arms, snuggling me closer.

"This is extremely inappropriate."

Mother would faint if she knew I occupied the same room as an indisposed man. But lying on top of him . . . in my nightgown? *Goodness.* I'd get more than an earful. It was one thing when I was trapped under the sea, but now I was back in civilization. What if the man from downstairs returned and caught us like this?

No matter how many times I shoved at his chest, his eyes remained shut.

"Why are my eyes so heavy?" he asked.

"It's the way your body tells you it's time to sleep."

"My kind doesn't need to sleep."

"You will as a human."

He frowned at that. "Why? All you do is make moaning noises like you're in pain."

"Humans need sleep to—*what?*—have you been watching me while I sleep?" Shocked, I tried to pull back, but his heavy limbs held me in place.

". . . protect you . . ." he mumbled, his voice drifting off. ". . . stay with me."

"I can't." But my heart tensed, reluctant to leave. It didn't help that my resistance melted the longer I stared at him. How was he so adorably handsome just lying there? Probably because he wasn't into mischief for once. His hair had dried with a subtle wave, like the ocean had styled it and left a hint of the sea breeze in the strands. Long lashes rested on his cheeks, his bruised eye bold in contrast to the off-white pillowcase. My fingers hovered over his cheekbone where the black color ended, and I wished I could somehow make it disappear.

"Ryken?" I whispered. He didn't respond, his steady breaths tickling my wrist.

I swallowed at a sickening thought. What if I had caused these bruises during my escape? Instinct wanted me to blame the bearded man from earlier. But it could easily have been me.

I rested my fingertips on his bruise and let out a sigh of relief that it was cool to the touch. No infection. My thumb brushed gently over the spot, a wave of guilt crashing into me with each swipe.

"I'm sorry," I said and didn't think twice when I bent forward to press a soft kiss over the mark, my eyes closing for a brief moment. He twitched, sucking in a breath, but quickly settled back into steady, rhythmic breathing.

As I pulled away, the dead weight of his arms flopped on the bed. I dragged the sheet over the muscles of his chest—*don't stare*—and tucked him in as I would a small child. There was no way I could lug him unconscious out of the room. For now, we were stuck here. Arms crossed, I stood next to the bed, unable to walk away even as he slept.

Look at me. I'm not any better, watching him while he's sleeping. I sighed.

What was I to do with him? The corner of my mouth pinched. A strange need to protect him coursed through me. Was it the collar? Or was it something more? No longer trapped in the water, I could easily walk out the door, yet I was still standing there.

What was I doing, anyway? Had I really promised to transform after I said goodbye to my family? And what would that mean for us afterward? Would he become my husband? *Do Merfolk even get married?*

"You . . . you soothed him to sleep?"

Gasping, I spun at the voice. I had been so absorbed with Ryken I didn't hear the man sneak in.

"Who are you?" I held up a hand when he took a step farther into the room, my eyes locked on the fishing spear clutched in his grip. *"Stay back."*

"I'm Jacek." Nodding, he placed the spear at his feet and raised both arms up from his crouched position. "I'm not going to hurt you, my lady. This was for your protection."

My lady . . . again?

"You are confused. I'm a farmer's daughter and nothing more."

"Yes, of course, my—uh—miss. Come downstairs where it is safe."

I stepped back until my legs bumped into the bed frame. After Desmond and Fritz, I wouldn't be blindly walking away with anyone. Especially if that meant leaving Ryken here alone and vulnerable.

"I am safe. He wouldn't hurt me. Or you."

He grumbled like he didn't believe me. "My wife, Caitlyn, and son, Mattis, are downstairs. Begging your pardon, but I have to lock this door to keep them safe from whoever that is." His eyes flicked behind me to Ryken's sleeping form.

"His name is Ryken," I snapped. "And I don't appreciate you tying and locking him up."

Jacek stiffened. "Did you release him?"

I couldn't exactly say he chewed the ropes off. "The restraints were unnecessary."

He paled two shades and shuffled backward toward the door. "Protect us, Sea of Providence. This woman has set the monster free."

"He's no monster," I shouted, my words sparking with fury. "He saved me from drowning. If not for him, I'd be dead. When the storm came through——"

"The storm? Is he a fisherman?"

I shook my head at the swift change of subject. "Um, no." I glanced at him over my shoulder. "He's a collector of things . . . like a trader."

Jacek scrubbed a hand down his shabby beard. "A trader?"

"Yes, he collects many items in his ship. Almost too many."

"Where are you docked?"

I coughed, struggling with my half-truths. "Unfortunately, it sank to the bottom of the sea."

He stood, his brown eyes twinkling with what I hoped was pity. "I'm so sorry. To lose your own ship would drive any sailor to the brink of madness. And then almost losing you too? I don't blame him for lashing out." Stooping back down, he grabbed his spear before strolling back to the door. "I'll talk to Caitlyn. See if I can't explain the situation. She doesn't want Mattis in any danger."

My anger fizzled out, and I wondered if had been too quick to judge him. I didn't approve of how Jacek treated Ryken, but I could understand the need to protect their family. They only needed to have a conversation with him and then they'd know how sweet he actually was.

"He won't be. I promise." I crossed my fingers, tapping them on my forehead in a binding vow. What was one more?

Jacek's eyebrows shot up. "You can't make a promise for someone else. Each promise binds to that soul. But I appreciate your gesture." He nodded again and left.

I turned back to Ryken. Kneeling beside his bed, I rested my cheek on my folded arms. "You better behave, Ryken," I whispered to him.

"Hello?"

A boy, eight or nine at the most, peeked around the doorframe. His mop of brown hair hung over his eyes, and he swiped it away with the back of his hand.

"Hello. Who are you?" I asked, wondering if this was Jacek's son.

"Mattis. Who are you?"

"I'm Marigold."

"Are you the one that's going to make us rich?"

I let out a laugh. "Unfortunately, no. I think that's Lady Luck. And she has stayed far away from me lately."

"Oh," he said sadly. "Are you staying?"

A woman screamed from downstairs, a blood-curdling sound.

Jacek's frantic call for his son had Mattis's face flushing.

"I—uh—need to go."

Curious, I spied through the open door just in time to see the boy race down the stairs.

"Momma, Momma! I'm right here."

"You stay away from those strangers. Do you hear me?" A woman's voice, the same one I'd heard earlier.

"Yes, ma'am."

"Now scoot. You might have to stay at Rogan's house tonight."

"Again?" Mattis whined. "Can I at least get Bungo?"

"Not right now. Our guest is still sleeping."

"Marigold is awake. I've talked to her, and she wasn't scary at all."

I snuck down the hall at my name and pressed onto the wall beside the staircase.

"Marigold?" Caitlyn whispered. "Are you sure that's her name?"

"Yes. She told me so herself."

"Jacek," she cried out, running into another room.

"I know you're there," the boy called up to me after a minute.

I leaned farther away.

"I can see your shadow." He thumped up the stairs as he climbed.

There wasn't any point in hiding, so I waited for him at the landing.

"Found you." He smiled, his front tooth missing. "Can I get Bungo from my room? It's hard to sleep without him."

"Bungo? I don't know——"

He walked away before I could finish, entering the room I had been sleeping in. A minute later, he returned with his burlap bear under one arm.

"Is the man feeling better? He was crying a lot. Does he have nightmares too?"

I forced a smile. Ryken had been crying? "Something like that."

The boy looked at his bear, turning it back and forth. "Here." He pushed his toy into my hands. "He can sleep with Bungo. I'm old enough to go another night without him. Just one night, though. I will need him back tomorrow."

I cradled the misshapen animal—handmade by the looks of it. Several seams were coming undone, and fluff poked out of one of his paws. I hugged him to my chest, my heart overflowing at Mattis's kindness. If only all humans could be this generous. "Thank you for sharing him. Are you sure that it's all right?"

The boy stared at the bear, his eyes the same dirty-brown color as his father's. "Yes. But one night only. Deal?"

I nodded. "Deal."

"Mattis," Caitlyn called out, her voice high-pitched.

We both turned, meeting her eyes at the foot of the stairs.

"Oh, no. I'm so sorry. Did he bother you when he grabbed his toy, my lady?" She sent Mattis a stern look. "I had told him to wait."

I placed a hand on his shoulder. "Quite the opposite, actually. He displayed such kindness by offering my—uh, er—friend his stuffed Bungo to sleep with."

Mattis's chest puffed out. "See, Momma?" He looked up at me with an adoring glance, so sweet it melted my defenses.

His mother rushed up the steps, curtsying at the top. "I'm Caitlyn, my lady. It is a pleasure to meet you, but if you don't mind me suggesting, perhaps we may dress you for the day before you go wandering about."

A burning trail of embarrassment raced up my neck and across my cheeks. Had I been standing in the hallway in a sheer ivory nightgown? *Oh, goodness.* And I had talked to Jacek wearing this too. I brought Bungo up to cover my face.

"Yes, please," I squeaked.

"I thought you looked nice," Mattis added as his mother ushered me back into my room. His mother clicked the door closed in his face before he could follow us in. She hissed at him through the crack of the door. "Scoot, Mattis. Go play."

She spun around, smiling again. High on her head, her reddish-brown hair twisted into a neat bun, the color reminding me of my sister.

"My lady?" Caitlyn repeated, and I blinked away from her hair to her concerned expression.

"I'm not a lady," I said. I touched my collar around my neck, wondering if she mistook my status because of the golden choker.

Her face scrunched up in confusion. "Miss?"

"Marigold would be better."

Dark blue eyes widened as she inched closer. "Where are you from?"

The sea. The phrase popped into my mind before I could take my next breath, shocking me speechless.

"You don't have to answer. I know you and your husband had a traumatic incident when your ship sank." She raised a knowing brow and walked to the wardrobe while I gaped at her like a fish. She pulled out a sky blue frock, two shades faded from washings.

"We are about the same size. Would this be okay?"

My throat worked as I struggled to collect all my thoughts. "Uh, yes, please. Thank you."

She pulled the gown over my head just as I went to comment about the husband reference.

"You don't have to say anything more about it. He called for his mate. For you. It was easy to put together."

Next, she shoved my arms through the sleeve holes and buttoned the back of my dress. "I don't think you should be shy about it. He's quite handsome, my lady, even if he is mentally unwell."

"I'm not a lady," I repeated again. Did everyone think Ryken was my husband? "And there's nothing wrong with him. He was trying to protect me."

"Of course. As you said. But he is your husband?" She leaned in closer, making me fidget under her scrutiny.

"No. He is not. More of a friend—a close one. I heard in some places they refer to friends as mates. You misheard." It could be true. I hadn't traveled everywhere to count this as a falsehood.

"Yes, miss." She nodded again, sliding my feet into a pair of black slippers, then stood. "Blue looks beautiful on you."

Why did it feel like she didn't believe me? My father always told me I was a terrible liar. This was why following the rules made things less complicated—and back then, there was nothing to lie about. Then I met a merman, and all of that went out the window.

I sighed.

"Are you hungry?"

"I am, which is odd since I just ate."

"You've been asleep for three days."

I stumbled back into the wardrobe. Three days? My sense of time was completely off. Then another thought hit me, and I narrowed my eyes.

"Has Ryken been tied up in that room for——" I took a calming breath "——three days? With no food or water?" My voice broke on the last word. My poor merman. No wonder he was so distraught.

She bobbed her head. "Yes, my lady. It's just the three of us here, and we had to protect our family."

The air around me shifted, and a confidence filled me that had me slowly crossing the wooden floor. I stared her down until her eyes finally dropped to her work boots. "He is not to be bound or starved like a prisoner. You treat him as you would treat me—with respect."

"Yes, my lady."

I ground my teeth at the phrase.

"Please go fetch me a clean pair of your husband's clothes, your sewing basket, and a glass of water. When he wakes up, we will be leaving."

New Rules

yken slept through the rest of the day. Sitting in a chair by his bed, I listened to his heavy breathing. It had a steady rhythm that reminded me of the hum of waves crashing onto the shore. Oddly enough, it comforted me while I let out the seams in the clothes Caitlyn had given me.

Numerous times she appeared at the door, clearing her throat to grab my attention. Her eyes sparkled with curiosity as she wondered at the circumstances that had left Ryken unclothed. Never brave enough to ask, she fidgeted as she waited, the room filled with her unspoken questions.

She cleared her throat.

Ryken's leg twitched under the sheets. On his stomach, one arm escaped the tangle of cotton as he stretched out his hand to rest on my knee while I worked. It didn't matter if I moved my knee. In minutes, it would return, startling me so that I jabbed myself with the needle one too many times.

Eventually, I gave up and let him rest it there, the heat of his palm boiling through the layers of my dress.

"Yes, Caitlyn?" I asked, not bothering to look up from my stitching.

She opened her mouth to say something and then quickly snapped it shut again, squirming nervously. After a moment of silence, she spoke.

"You are most welcome to stay as long as you please. Though I have some concerns about your friend staying. He damaged our wagon on your journey here. As it is, Jacek has to travel to Windcrest to purchase a new axel wheel."

I swiveled toward her, Ryken's hand dropping to the floor. "Oh, do you think that we might travel with him?" If I could get to Windcrest, I could meet my grandparents at their shop.

"I'm afraid not. He has to travel by horseback since our wagon requires repair. But perhaps we might send word home for you?" She tilted her head, stepping into the room.

"Could you?" My voice spiked in excitement.

"Of course. They must be worried sick about you. My penmanship is shaky, but I can write the note for you should you need help."

"It's not necessary, thank you. Prince Alexander taught my sister and me how to write."

Caitlyn's eyes widened, and she pressed her hand on her chest. "Save my soul, I had hoped, but now I think my suspicions might be correct. Are you the lost sister? The one everyone is looking for?"

Everyone was looking for me?

"I, uh, don't know. I'm just . . . me?"

"Are you Marigold Bellmond?"

My heart thudded nervously at hearing my full name on her lips. Immediately, Ryken's hand plopped back on my knee. "I am."

In a whoosh of fabric, Caitlyn raced across the room to grip the back of my chair, laughing with pure joy. "Is it you? Truly? To think you've been sleeping under our roof for days."

Her enthusiasm had me shifting away.

"We must notify the king of your safety," she informed me, nodding as she thought.

"The king? Why?" Why would King Baxton need to be involved? Though the poor man had been on his sickbed for the last month, the king of Cadell still sent goosebumps down my arms. Cold and calculating, he ruled with an iron fist over the other territories. I doubted he worried over the return of an unacquainted peasant. "Could we send word to my sister or the prince instead?"

She squinted at me. "Prince Vox or Prince Vian?"

"Not the princes of Windcrest. I mean Prince Alexander of Cadell.

He is to marry my sister, Roselyn. I'm not sure if you have heard about their ceremony. That's where I was heading before I was abducted in transit."

She bit her lip, hesitating before she answered. "But Prince Alexander is . . . uh . . . yes, I know who you speak of, but I still have to follow the decree. We must inform the king first if you are found. Jacek will ride out tonight and can deliver any letters you wish to send."

"I'd prefer to go myself——"

"*No,*" she half-shouted, then slapped a hand on her mouth when Ryken let out a startled snore. "What I mean to say is that we would love to escort you to the castle ourselves, but the wagon is unavailable. Besides that, your friend is unwell. He needs time to recover. By then, Jacek will have returned to fix the wagon."

"I thought you were unsure of Ryken staying here."

"As a mother, I can't help but worry about the safety of my son. I'd be lying if I didn't say his inhuman strength wasn't alarming. He crushed the wagon with his bare hands."

I took in Ryken's slack face, boyish-looking, with his mouth slightly open. Deceptively innocent. I wondered what other trouble he had caused while I was sleeping.

"He was frightened," I whispered, knowing full well it was a terrible excuse.

"I'll send Mattis to a friend's house while Jacek is gone."

"No, Momma," the little boy shouted from the hallway and scurried into view. His large eyes welled with unshed tears as Caitlyn rushed to his side, a protective barrier between him and Ryken. "Don't send me away."

"Mattis, you know it's rude to eavesdrop. We've talked about this. I don't want you anywhere near this man. It's not safe."

"How come she can be next to him then?" Mattis glared up at his mom.

"I'm not her mother, but I am yours. So you better mind my words, or you'll be chopping firewood for a week."

The boy grumbled as his mother led him from the room.

Alone again with Ryken, I picked up the forgotten pants from my lap, but my mind refused to focus on the mundane task. Why would

King Baxton want to know when I had been found? Had my sister asked her father-in-law to search for me? Was she worried about me?

Did she miss me?

Suddenly, I was in motion. Ryken pulled my chair closer to the bed, his ocean-colored eyes focused on me. The chair scraped across the wood, a rumbling noise that rattled the seat. I clutched the clothes to my chest, wincing as I stabbed myself with the needle. The shaking stopped when the side of the chair tapped the mattress.

Ryken blinked at me, his pupils dilating. He clicked and hummed, then shook his head. "My head is full of water."

"We call that groggy. Are you better now that you have rested?"

"My eyes don't hurt, but I still ache all over."

"It will fade as you wake up."

"I thought I was awake."

"You'll wake up more. Here, I have a cup of water for you to drink."

Sitting up, he eyed the metal cup I placed in his hand. "Drink it?" He stared at the clear liquid inside. "There isn't much in here. I can't cover my whole body with it." He raised the cup over his head, and I stopped him just before he poured the contents over himself.

"Drink, Ryken. Like this," I lifted it to my lips, the cool temperature soothing as I sipped. Almost the same temperature as the sea. And for a moment, the thought of dumping the liquid over my body like Ryken had almost done didn't seem like such a ridiculous idea.

"Why?" He took a massive gulp, choked, and sprayed a fountain of water across the bed.

Oh, goodness.

"Humans need water to survive." I patted his back while his shoulders shook with each cough. "Swallow it like food. Don't inhale it."

Doubled over, he hacked until his face turned red. "I don't like this feeling."

I bit my lips to keep from laughing when he held up the offending cup as if it had attacked him on purpose. The merman had never had to worry about water in his lungs before.

Ryken tried again, a smaller, more cautious sip. His lip curled up. "It doesn't taste right."

Now I couldn't contain it, laughing at his disgusted face. "Well, it's not ocean water. This is fresh water from the nearby river."

"I don't like it."

"It's just something new, and you're not used to it. Transitioning is hard at first. Be patient, and you'll get the hang of it."

He scoffed. Shifting in the sheet, he moved to whip back the bedding.

"Wait," I screeched, throwing my hands on top of his. "We need to set some rules."

"Rules?"

"Yes. Things are different between us now that you have changed forms. You have to stay clothed, at least while you are in human form. I don't think there is a pair of clothes that can fit you when you have your tail. This also means no shifting in front of anyone else."

"Only you." The corner of his mouth ticked up.

I narrowed my eyes at him. "This also means no shifting to your human form so that you are naked in my presence. The clothing rule applies *especially* to me. It's a way of showing me respect."

He stuck out his lip in a pout.

"I mean it, Ryken. Keep your clothes on. Or maybe it would be safer for you to wait in the sea until I return?"

"Not an option," he growled.

"Then you have to blend in. Life is different up here, and we are a modest community. When we see things that are strange or unexplainable, we become defensive. As you saw with Jacek and Caitlyn, we fear the unknown. It's why they tied you up."

"Oh? I thought it was because I bit him."

"*What?*"

Ryken lifted one shoulder in an innocent shrug.

I blew out a slow breath. "New rule. No biting people."

"I don't——"

I held up a hand to cut off his complaint. "I hear you. You don't like it. This isn't forever, and as soon as we see my family, we can go home."

He straightened. "Home?"

Had I said home? It was a slip, of course. "The sea, I mean."

Nodding, he glanced down at my hand resting on his. He flipped his over so our palms touched. "I promise to try my best."

Our heads bowed as we stared at our joined hands. It was different from the grayish skin I remembered. His skin was soft now and smooth, warm to my touch. More of what I was used to seeing in a male but less of what made Ryken himself. I frowned, not sure if I wanted to change him into something he wasn't.

But wasn't that what was happening to me?

"Will this make you happy?" he whispered. "Happy enough to stay with me?"

"I hope so," I replied. It had to. I was returning to the sea afterward whether I was happy or not. But life with Ryken wouldn't be so terrible. He was humorous at times and compassionate. And the fact that he cared about my happiness at all made him even more endearing. The exact opposite of the scary creatures from the stories I had been told growing up.

Perhaps I enjoyed spending time with him more than I realized.

"I feel . . ." he started, his face pinched. His index finger trailed down mine. "I don't know how to describe it."

"Better?" I suggested.

"It's more. I feel more of everything—even you."

I didn't know what to make of that.

"Before, it was instinct. I used my senses and made my decisions from there. But now my insides are twisted in thoughts and feelings."

"New emotions?"

"When I touch you, it's . . . I don't know how to describe it."

Embarrassed, I leaned away. His fingers clamped over mine to stop my withdrawal. "No. It feels good. There is so much more—*agh*, feeling?—as a human. It's overwhelming but in an addictive way. Like I want more of you. Not just your touch but your thoughts and words. Everything that is you." He sighed and scooted away. "I'm not explaining this well."

His confession left me speechless. I knew the electric attraction from the moment we met. But there was more? Ryken had feelings for me? Warmth spread in my chest, and I pressed my free hand on my heart, the thudding shaking my fingers.

"Does it feel the same for you?" he asked, his voice like gravel.

My throat constricted. The thoughts I had kept locked away in the deepest corners of my mind slammed against the steel cage of decorum I had erected. Feelings, emotions, attraction . . . one didn't talk about these things with a potential suitor.

But one thought had already slipped through the bars, and my eyes dipped to his lips.

Kiss him.

I shouldn't.

"Marigold?" he asked, moving an inch closer to breathe in my scent.

No, I shouldn't. It was not done. It was scandalous enough to even think of kissing someone I wasn't married to, plus a lady would never make the first move.

But I'm not a lady, I reminded myself.

"I feel . . ." Ryken's voice shook, his face confused.

A throat cleared in the doorway. It sent me shooting so far away from him I nearly flipped the chair over. *Oh, gracious. What had I been thinking—or doing?!*

"Yes, Caitlyn?" I asked, my voice sounding like a stranger's.

She stared at Ryken, worrying the lace at her sleeve. "I made luncheon downstairs if you want to join me. I didn't know *he* was up."

"Ryken. His name is Ryken." I refused to meet his glance. As it was, my neck flushed at his intense scrutiny.

"I apologize, miss. I'll slice up some more cheese and bread should Ryken want to join us." She spun on her heel, leaving us as silently as she had arrived.

I rubbed a hand down my face. That was a close call. The more time I spent with him, the more addled my thoughts became. I shouldn't even be alone in a room with him without a chaperone. If Caitlyn or Jacek told anyone, my reputation would go up in flames. No wonder she was asking me if he was my husband. I bit my lip and turned to face him.

Ryken, my husband?

He tilted his head, confused by my expression. I mean—we could marry. Wasn't that where this was all headed? That I was his mate? But I didn't want to be chosen because of my song or to be some mermaid breeder. I wanted what my parents had and what Rose had—*love.*

Fleeting feelings were not enough for me.

I stood, strangely disappointed. "I'm going downstairs. See if I can figure out where we are."

"I'm coming too."

"You aren't dressed. And no, the sheet doesn't count. Here, these clothes are as big as I could make them." I went to hand them to him and stopped, shaking my head when I realized he had no idea what I was talking about. "You put them on like this."

Throwing the shirt over my head, I pushed my arms through the sleeves, the ends dangling well past my hands. The cotton shirt engulfed me. Even the hem of the shirt hung to my thigh. Oddly enough, wearing a man's clothes, his clothes, felt more intimate than I realized it would.

I cleared my throat, continuing. "Pants have one hole for each leg. This button goes in the front and should be waist level." I held them out in front of him.

"A button? Like from the ship?"

"Yes. It will help keep your pants from falling down." I removed the shirt and folded both pieces to offer back to him.

Ryken pinched his brows at the list of instructions, standing to grab the clothing bundle. For a brief second, he towered over me before he crumbled in place.

I threw my arms around him to keep him upright. "Lock your knees."

He did, finally standing on wobbly legs. A smile lit up his face over the small accomplishment. It was infectious, and I couldn't help but return it.

Before the sheet could slip from his body, I wrapped it around his torso and wide shoulders. With each loop around his body, his frown deepened.

"I still don't understand clothes," he grumbled. "They're restricting like the rope."

"What is confusing? Those areas of your body are meant to be kept private. You'd frighten the townsfolk with your boldness. Nobody wants to see you walking around stark naked."

"Nobody?" he pressed. "Not even you?"

My stomach fluttered at his low tone. I fumbled with the sheet, gaining my composure.

"No. Not even me." I met his eyes and cinched the sheet tight with extra force to make a point.

A wolfish smile spread across his face, and my stomach fluttered again. He leaned forward, inhaling my scent.

"Liar."

"You can't possibly tell——"

113

"It's your scent. I can always tell."

"Stop that," I demanded. "Those are my personal thoughts and feelings."

"You've been thinking about it?" he practically purred at me.

Mortified, I spun on my heel to the door, nervous about having him too close when I no longer trusted myself.

"Wait, Marigold." He stumbled a few steps before he crashed to the floor in a puddle of sheets.

I turned around, concerned despite his earlier teasing. "Are you hurt?"

"You made moving look easy. It wasn't."

I returned to his side. "You're strong. All you need is some practice." I offered both my hands in assistance.

The air twinged like mischief, and just before he grabbed my hands, I snatched them back, sending him a stern look.

"If you think to pull me to the floor, I'm not going to help you."

He lifted a brow, smirking. "Now who is reading thoughts?"

Soothing the Beast

I shook my head at his mischievous grin and placed my hands on my hips. "New rule—no smelling to read my thoughts or emotions."

"I can't agree to that. It just . . . happens. You would need to stop emitting the scent."

"I'm not emitting anything," I growled at him.

"Like now, I can smell your displeasure." He took a long inhale. "Hmm, and something more."

"*Ryken,* do you want me to help you? Or do you want me to leave you here on the floor?"

He peered up at me through his lashes. "Help me."

"Then stop smelling me and give me your hands. You're one exasperating merman," I grumbled, struggling to get him back on his shaky legs.

"Me? You have it backward. The whole reason we are on land is because of you."

I glanced away at the truth.

"These legs are broken. Why won't they hold still?" He beat on the side of his thigh with his fist.

"Don't forget you have human skin, *weak* as you like to call it. So go easy on yourself. I'm heading downstairs. Try to practice your balance and change while I'm gone."

"Balance?" His eyes went wide as much as his swollen eye would let him. "I'll go down with you."

"You sure about that?" I pressed my finger to the middle of his chest, lifting a brow. Deadweight, he toppled backward onto the bed. I laughed as he scowled up at me.

"Marigold . . ."

"Clothes," I reminded him, picking them off the floor and tossing them next to him on the bed. It was nice to be the one bossing him around for a change. "Do you want food?"

"Marigold, don't you leave me here."

"I'm not leaving the house."

"What's a house?" He made a grab for me, and I easily stepped out of reach. "Show me how you move so quickly."

I rubbed a hand across my face. "I'm not showing you my legs. We can practice walking later. First, get dressed. It's the most important."

He was still complaining as I strolled out of the room. Footsteps rushed down the stairs. When I checked the stairwell, it was empty. Had Mattis been eavesdropping again?

I continued down into the heart of the house. All at once, I missed our cottage.

Their place was small but homey. A decorative quilt hung on a long wall, patterned with yellow fish and blue ocean swirls. It was almost as beautiful as the tapestries of bluebells over their fireplace mantle. The detailed work on the stitching was exceptional. I walked around the oval table in the middle of the room to get a close-up view.

Green flecks shimmered in the fabric, not quite cloth, but not something I had seen done before. When I reached out to investigate, a voice jerked me back.

"It's seaweed," Caitlyn said from the door to the kitchen. "I only add little pieces for detail." She joined me to admire her handiwork.

"I'm not familiar with that technique. It's creative."

She sent me a shy smile. "Thank you. That means a lot, knowing the quality of clothes you sew in Windcrest."

I turned back to the tapestry, a chill going down my spine. It was odd to talk to a stranger who knew things about me when I knew absolutely nothing about her.

I cleared my throat, hoping to get the topic off of me. "How far are we from Windcrest?"

"A few hours. This is Amille. We are a small fishing village. There are many scattered down the coastline. It's easier to be closer to the sea for Jacek's work than to commute from Windcrest."

I had never heard of Amille. But I had also never left home before my trip to work at my grandparents' shop.

"How far to the shore?"

"By wagon or horse? Not far. By foot? An hour walk or so."

Good. I let out a relieved sigh. If we were too close to the water, Ryken would be tempted to whisk me back to the sea.

A loud boom rattled the ceiling. Caitlyn and I tilted our heads up in unison as two more bangs sounded.

Ryken.

"Should you go check on him?"

It was probably what he wanted me to do, that sneak.

I found him crawling down the hallway, his legs dragging behind him. Thankfully, he was dressed. He stared up at me pitifully with his one black eye.

"Oh, Ryken. You couldn't be patient, could you?"

Droplets beaded on his brow, and he wiped it away, his top lip lifted. "What is that?"

"When you're overheated, you sweat."

"I don——"

"I know. You don't like it," I finished for him. "It's summertime, so be prepared to sweat a lot."

He shuddered.

"Here. Take my hand so we can get you back on your feet."

With a grunt, I pulled him upright again, his arm bumping into the wall. He overcorrected and slammed into the other wall with a thud.

"Easy."

Ryken straightened as he gained his balance. When he swayed, he reached desperately to cling to my shoulder. The weight of it nearly brought us both tumbling down the stairs.

"Not so hard, or we are both going to fall."

"It's this human body," Ryken growled, and another fresh batch of sweat dotted his forehead.

I tried to rotate him around to go back to his room, but he gripped the corner of the wall.

I blew a lock of hair from my face. "I don't know if I can help you down the stairs."

"Please," he begged.

My resistance melted the longer I stared at his bruised face, his eyes pleading. He didn't want to be cooped up in that tiny space. Honestly, I didn't blame him. Having the freedom of the ocean and then being trapped in a room big enough for one bed could make anyone desperate. Agreeing, I changed my stance and directed us to the stairs.

Each step made him sway, even with his grip tight on the railing. His arm around my shoulders had ridden up and was wrapped around my neck, bending it toward him. I hissed in pain.

Be gentle, Ryken. You're making it hard for me to breathe.

He loosened his hold and gave me a sheepish expression. *Sorry.*

"Miss? Do you require assistance?"

He stiffened. *Tell her no.*

You tell her. You have a voice.

He ground his teeth. *I don't talk to humans.*

She already heard you speak.

Yes, but not to her.

Should I remind you that I'm human? Or that you look more like a human than a merman?

He whipped his head away, refusing to respond to that statement.

"Thank you, Caitlyn. Your assistance would be most appreciated."

His aqua eyes snapped to me in outrage.

Next time, you say something. Your weight is more than I can handle, and I'd prefer it if we didn't tumble down the stairs.

Caitlyn forced a smile, regretting her offer with each step she took toward the scowling man in disheveled clothes.

Don't bite her, I reminded him. *She's helping.*

He let go of my neck, obviously done with listening to me. I still gave him a quick look to behave before she reached us.

With mild grumbling, Ryken let Caitlyn grab his other arm.

118

Together, the two of us got him into the chair at the table. We were both heaving for air, and I thanked her for helping.

Meanwhile, Ryken remained silent. Not because of his stubbornness, but because he was too distracted. His mouth parted as he stared around the room, inspecting each item on the wall and furniture around us.

Pulling out the chair next to him, I joined him at the table so he wasn't alone. Not that he was aware of my presence at all. His head swiveled back and forth, up and down, cataloging all the items to probably ask me about later.

I rested my chin on my palm, watching his excitement grow. Everything was new to him.

"I've never seen so many things before." He spoke without realizing it. "I don't know which one to ask about first."

The door opened, and the laughter floating in from outside cut off abruptly. Jacek stumbled to a stop, narrowing in on Ryken sitting casually at his table.

"Uh, hello," Jacek said, his voice wavering.

Ryken let out a low snarl. He draped a hand across my lap, leaning over me to bare his teeth at the other man. So close, his scent reeked of his fury.

I jabbed him in the ribs, silencing him.

"Father? Why did you—? Oh! Hello, Marigold." Mattis ducked under Jacek's arm, his cheeks flushed and his brown eyes twinkling.

Ryken tensed at the boy's appearance.

"Mattis, I told you I would get your book for you."

The child ignored him, darting past him to skip up to the table.

"Is this your friend? Did you give him Bungo?"

Ryken blinked in shock, mouthing the word Bungo.

"Mattis! Get back," Jacek barked, sprinting over to his son.

Caitlyn rushed from the kitchen, a tea towel over one shoulder. When she spotted her son, she let out a high-pitched shriek and dropped the cloth.

Jacek jerked the boy back by the shoulders, his arms crisscrossing protectively over Mattis's chest.

"Caitlyn, it's under control."

Racing to Mattis, she dropped to her knees, her hands searching for cuts and bruises on his body. "Are you okay? Did he hurt you?"

"Momma, I'm fine." Mattis batted away his mother's searching fingers.

She threw her arms around Mattis despite his muffled complaints. "You said you were taking him," she accused over his shoulder.

"I did, but you know Mattis. If he can't have his bear, he wants his book."

"Please don't be upset. I was only saying hello," the boy complained, his lip jutting out from the arguing.

She pulled back. "You should have listened to your father."

"I was talking to Marigold," Mattis said, pointing at me.

"We set rules for a reason," Jacek argued. He wrenched the boy from Caitlyn's desperate hold and spun him toward the open door. "We have talked about this. Do we need to have another discussion on obedience and respect?"

Ryken glanced between the three of them, overwhelmed by all the shouting.

Even I flinched at the loud noises, and I wondered if the peaceful-ness of the rushing water had spoiled me these last few days. Since being back on land, noises were louder than usual. I caught myself flinching often.

"Please don't make me leave," Mattis whined.

Caitlyn and Jacek's voices overlapped with each other as they argued, their words harsh.

"Wait," Ryken shouted above the noise. Eyebrows high, his large eyes locked on me in surprise.

"Yes, they heard you. You may as well keep talking," I whispered.

"He can stay," Ryken added quickly. He flushed, the rosy color highlighting his cheekbones attractively. "I have no quarrel with him."

Jacek pulled up the sleeve of his shirt, revealing a bandaged arm. "Excuse me if it's hard for me to trust you while I'm still carrying your mark on my arm."

"You touched my mate."

"I saved her," Jacek snapped back.

"You took her from me."

Jacek sputtered and gestured to me. "She's right there."

Ryken turned to me, frustration pouring from him. I placed his hand on the back of my neck so it touched my choker.

Breathe. They are just trying to understand you, I said calmly.

I don't like anyone touching you but me.

Warmth filled my stomach. *Nobody is touching me right now but you. But sometimes, it's all right to let others help us. We are relying on their generosity. This is their home, like our ship, yes? They took us in and are allowing us to stay here until they can fix the wagon you destroyed. You didn't mention that, by the way.*

He swallowed.

You can't just attack people for touching me.

I can.

I narrowed my gaze. *But you shouldn't. He wasn't hurting me, so there's no reason to harm anyone over such a minor matter.*

It didn't feel minor. He touched his chest. *Something broke inside me when I saw him carry you inside . . . I thought I wouldn't see you again.*

"What's happening?" Caitlyn asked Jacek.

"I think she is soothing him again."

Look at me. Nobody has taken me.

I'm always looking at you.

I grinned at him despite myself. *Ryken . . .*

A secret smile stretched across his face, and my breath caught in my throat. Tingles spread where his thumb caressed the skin at my collar. *It's true.*

I turned away, unable to handle his intensity, especially with onlookers watching from the other side of the room. *I think you should be nice to them. Maybe start with an apology.*

He grumbled, wiggling in his seat.

You can do it.

"I'm sorry for the . . . wagon." It took him a moment to remember the word.

And . . . I added.

"And for biting you," Ryken mumbled.

I squeezed his hand in reassurance.

Caitlyn and Jacek looked at each other, confused. Her face pinched for a moment, and he gave her an angry shake of his head. Jacek stepped around Mattis and said, "We are sorry too. About your eye, tying you up, and . . . well, everything. We didn't want you attacking anyone else."

Ryken nodded, his eyes darting to me. *Happy?*

I looked down at our tangled fingers, his index looped through three of mine. *Yes. Try not to snarl anymore. Humans don't do that.*

But—I'm not human?

Blending in, remember? You don't want to be tied up again.

He frowned, glancing away.

"Can I stay now?" Mattis piped up in the silence.

"*No,*" both Caitlyn and Jacek said at the same time.

"I can keep an eye on Ryken," I said, drawing their attention. "If that will make you feel better. It's only until you fix the wagon, right? A day or two at the most?"

"I gave you my word I wouldn't hurt him," Ryken reminded them, shooting to his feet. He lasted a second before he toppled to the floor, taking his chair with him.

"Ryken," I cried out and knelt down next to him.

Rubbing his head, he sat up, and color flooded his cheeks again.

"Is he paralyzed?" Jacek whispered to Caitlyn.

"I don't know, but I had to help her carry him down the stairs."

"Hmm, maybe it would be okay for Mattis to stay."

Caitlyn gasped. "You can't be serious."

"It's two days, darling. Two. Just make them comfortable for a little while longer." He gave her a look I couldn't comprehend.

She nodded, twisting her hands. "If you insist."

Jacek slapped his hands together, causing Ryken and me to flinch, then rubbed them together in excitement. "Did you hear that, son? You can stay. But don't overcrowd them. Or pester them with questions."

"I won't, Father. Can I go get my book now?"

"Yes," Caitlyn responded. She worried her lip as she watched the boy jog up the stairs.

"Don't worry so much, darling. It will all be fine." He placed an arm around his wife and led her back to the kitchen where her worried whispers were a rumble of noises I couldn't understand.

I placed a hand on Ryken's cheek, twisting him to face me. "Are you all right? It's just us."

"I am. It's confusing, and I feel . . . weak. I can't even stand on my own." He blew out a pent-up breath. "I don't like it."

"You aren't weak. I believe you destroyed a wagon with only your hands."

He grinned. "I did."

"You're strong enough to do this. You just need practice until it becomes second nature. Until then, you can lean on me."

Ryken grabbed my offered hands so I could help him to his feet. When he started to lean, I put a supportive arm around his middle.

"Hey, you did it," Mattis cheered on the stairwell. With a large book tucked under his arm, he thumped down the stairs. Skipping the last two steps, he jumped to the main level, rattling the floorboards beneath us.

"Mattis," Caitlyn scolded from the other room.

"Oops. I'm not supposed to do that," he mumbled guiltily.

"Oops?" Ryken asked, tilting his head for an explanation.

"It's something you say when you make a mistake," I said.

"Oops," Ryken repeated, nodding.

Mattis laughed, a youthful sound of innocence. "You're funny."

The corner of Ryken's mouth twitched.

I helped him into his seat and surprised myself when I caught my hand running over his hair. But Ryken was too focused on the boy who took the seat across from him.

He dropped the book on the table. "You like books?"

Ryken shrugged.

"I do," Mattis continued. "They're full of magical places, battles, quests, and strange creatures. It's more exciting than catching fish."

"I like reading," I said, joining them.

"Real books? Or the girly stuff with kisses?" Mattis stuck his tongue out.

Ryken perked up and waited for my response.

"Fairy tales are classic. They have everything you just mentioned plus a love story woven in."

"Yuck. I skip those parts."

"Why?" I smiled at his reaction. "It's part of the story."

"It's gross. Why would I want to read about wooing someone when

I can read about sword fights instead? I made my own wooden one." He held an imaginary sword in his hand and waved it in a mock parlay.

"Wooing?" Ryken asked.

Mattis wrinkled his nose. "You know, where the prince does nice things for the princess? Flowers, candy, poems—ugh, it's disgusting."

I barked out a laugh and covered my mouth.

"Why? Why does he woo her?" Ryken pressed.

"Because he likes her? I don't know. But it has to be done if he wants to marry her."

"Marry?" Ryken leaned forward. "I don't know this word. Explain."

"I think that is enough questions for today," I jumped in.

Mattis ignored me. "If you want to be with one person forever, then you have to marry them. That lets everyone know you belong together. My parents are married. They had a ceremony and everything. Then I came along after that." He rolled his eyes. "Now, back to my sword. Do you want to see it?"

Ryken blinked at the boy, looking more confused than ever. "Yes."

Mattis took off with a hoot of excitement, running out the door so fast that he didn't bother to shut it behind him.

I grabbed the book, ignoring Ryken's hard stare. "Oh, this is *The Return to the Emerald Isle.* I read it when I was about his age. Well, actually, Rose read it to me. Can you read? If so, you might like it. It's about a voyage across the sea to find the missing king. I think it mentions Merfolk in it—*what?* Why do you keep staring at me?"

Ryken smirked, my nerves jittering.

"I know what I've been doing wrong."

"Besides biting people?" I lifted a brow.

"I've been treating you like a mermaid when I should be treating you like a human." He leaned in, his scent intoxicating. Picking up a loose strand of my hair, he rubbed it between two fingers. "I'm going to woo you, Marigold. Whatever I have to do so it's not just a sacred promise binding us together." He placed his fingertips on my collar, and my eyes fluttered closed at his touch. *Until you understand that our souls are one.* The heat of his breath tickled my cheek. *Then you will claim me.*

I shivered in anticipation.

Blending In

The echo of his words turned my insides to jelly. Eyes still closed, I leaned into his touch. His thumb traced up my neck and followed the shape of my jaw. The quiet moment hung between us, heightening my sense of longing.

I focused on the sound of his breathing, the erratic breaths he was having a difficult time controlling. An ocean breeze clung to him, mixing with his masculine scent, his desire and interest tainting the air.

"I feel . . . " he said and trailed off. His chair creaked, fabric rustling from his movement.

I tilted my face, sending up a silent offer. My trembling lips parted as I waited for him to close the distance.

It was just one kiss, I reasoned. A harmless kiss. Perhaps once I knew what it felt like, I'd stop thinking about it so much. No more thoughts about consequences or rules—I only wanted to feel his lips on mine.

When another minute stretched by, I shifted closer in case he missed my subtle gesture.

What are you doing? His voice whispered into my thoughts.

I'm waiting.

For what?

For you.

His hand tensed on my skin. *For me? Am I supposed to be doing something?*

Opening my eyes, I took in his confused expression.

He wasn't going to kiss me. That knowledge smacked with disappointment. What had he meant earlier about wooing? Was I too forward? Or was there something wrong with me that he found distasteful? The more questions that flew through my mind, the more my heart sank. My cheeks reddened as I scooted back in my chair and untangled his fingers from my neck.

I didn't understand him at all.

"Marigold?" he asked, his voice thicker than usual. "What happened?"

"Nothing," I said. Turning back to the table, I traced the letters of Mattis's storybook.

"You're . . . " He took a deep breath, and his eyes went wide. "You're upset."

I shot him a look. How did he think I would feel after being rejected?

"Stop smelling me."

"I don't understand. I didn't do anything."

"That's the point—you didn't do anything," I complained, then rose to my feet. Evading his reaching hands, I moved around to the other side of the table. I leaned against the chair to stare at him. "I don't want to talk about it."

"Talk about what?" Caitlyn asked from the doorway. She carried a wooden tray with four empty mugs into the room. One glance at my face and she stopped in place. "Is everything all right?"

"Yes, I'm just homesick is all."

Ryken narrowed his eyes at that.

She clucked her tongue and continued forward the last two steps to place the tray on the table. She moved Mattis's book to a nearby bookshelf. "You poor thing. I can imagine you would be after being away so long."

I sat in the chair across from Ryken. "Yes, it's been a long few weeks."

Caitlyn's hand clumsily knocked into the mugs. She placed a hand over one before it tipped over. "Weeks?"

"It could be a month. It was hard to keep track of time at the beginning . . . when they . . . " I swallowed. The first days after being kidnapped rushed back to me. Days and nights overlapped with each other. The only thing that remained was my constant state of fear.

"They? You mean those thieves? Don't you worry about them. They'll be rotting behind bars until they are old and gray."

"They were caught?" My stomach clenched. "Where are they being held?"

"Oh, miss. You're getting all worked up. That's not good for the complexion."

"Caitlyn. Where? Are they here in Windcrest?" My knees quaked under the table, rattling the glasses. Why was I worried? They were imprisoned and wouldn't be coming back to finish the job.

"They are in Cadell. Like I said, don't you worry."

I stiffened when the tip of Ryken's toes touched mine. He watched me, cataloging my reactions and not looking pleased with his findings.

"What men?" Ryken asked, his voice low.

"The ones who threw me into the sea." Desmond's angry face floated in front of my vision.

Ryken tilted his head. "I thought you fell."

"Desmond pushed me."

Blinking, he looked to the left and then back at me. "But you were bound."

"I was."

"How could you swim if . . . ?" His lips slammed together as he collected himself. His nails curled on the table as he growled, "Tell me everything."

"I don't like to think about it," I whispered.

The silence had a pressure that weighed down on me. I wrapped my arms around my middle, hoping Caitlyn and Ryken would talk of something else. Where was Mattis when I needed him?

"Nobody will touch you again," Ryken promised with such ferocity that I jumped in my seat. "You are mine."

Caitlyn coughed, backing away slowly. "I'll just, uh, go get the pitcher."

We barely noticed she had left, staring at each other across the table.

"When we see your sister, I want to see them too."

I paused. "Why?"

"To thank them for their stupidity. They led me to you after all . . . and maybe to punch them in the face. I can do both."

I smiled despite myself. "I don't want to see them."

"You should. Confront your fear and look them in the eyes. Show them you are stronger than they will ever be. You cannot be broken."

My throat tightened with emotion, my eyes misting. "Thank you."

"But mostly it's for me to punch them." He leaned forward with a charming smile, and a swarm of butterflies took flight in my stomach. "There was no rule for that."

I laughed. "No, not yet."

"I like your laugh," he said.

"I like your smile." I had no idea what came over me to say that. But it was worth it to see his smile stretch across his face, radiating happiness.

He opened his mouth to say more, but Caitlyn hurried back into the room, spoiling the moment.

"Here, take this," Caitlyn said, handing Ryken a mug of water.

He took it with two hands, the water sloshing over the edge as he adjusted his strength.

"I'll bring out your luncheon in a moment. Jacek is leaving, and I had hoped to say goodbye."

"Please, let me help." I tried to get up, but her hands pressed me back into my seat.

"It's an honor to be of service, miss. Please, just give me a moment."

At my nod, she scurried from the room.

The splattering of liquid hitting the floor had me whipping back to Ryken, his back stiff as his lips parted. "Oops."

But his cup remained upright. Then I noticed water dripping from his earlobe by his gills. Did he . . . breathe in the water?

"What was that?" Caitlyn called, her footsteps echoing as she approached the doorway.

My mind raced with what to do, and I scanned the table, my eyes landing on my still full cup.

"I'm sorry," I said to Ryken and lifted the glass.

"Sorry? For whaaa——?"

I tossed the contents of my drink in his face.

He sat motionless across from me, rivulets of water trailing down the planes of his irritated face. My mouth hung ajar, surprised by my own actions.

"My word," Caitlyn said as she turned the corner to the messy aftermath. Her eyes darted nervously between us. "I'll get the mop."

"No, please. Let me clean it——" The last word ended on a screech. Cool water splashed across my face like a liquid slap. I sprang out of my chair, wiping the droplets from my eyes.

Blinking, I turned back to Ryken as he placed his now empty cup with a thud on the table.

"Mop, yes. Let me, uh, go get that," she rambled as she ran from the room.

"Ryken," I scolded, shaking my dripping hands.

"You did it first."

"Yes, but I was trying to cover up your mistake."

"Was this not a human custom?" He smirked knowingly, fully aware there was no such thing.

"Remember, you need me to walk. I'd be a little nicer if I were you."

"You won't let me be nicer."

Groaning, I turned away. He was an incorrigible flirt sometimes, but I caught myself smiling anyway. Then I touched my lips, confused as I remembered his rejection. Why did he say things like that? Was he only teasing?

As I cleaned up the mess, Mattis barged back into the house, his brown eyes sparkling as he brought his makeshift sword over. Instead of coming to me, he stopped at Ryken's side. The merman startled at this, surprised at the boy's attention.

"Look! Here it is. I crafted it myself from a branch. When I get older, I'm going to get a real one," Mattis said. He held up his weapon to show Ryken.

Ryken's eyes slid to mine for a second, and as I was about to intervene, he turned to the boy and said calmly, "Mattis, is it? I'm Ryken."

"I know, silly."

Ryken blinked at the boy, not sure what to do.

"Do you like it?" Mattis asked, turning it back and forth.

"It's fine craftsmanship. Well done. Now, may I ask what you plan to do with your sword?"

His smile flickered for a second as he thought. "I will fight thieves and monsters just like in my stories."

Ryken nodded. "A valiant answer. Do you promise to use your skills for goodness and truth? To instill peace and not destruction? Where I'm from, to wield a weapon is an honor, one the holder must earn."

Mattis hung on his every word. "Yes, yes. I promise."

"May I?" Ryken reached out and adjusted the boy's grip on the handle. "Not so high, or you'll slice a hand, yes? Balance allows for smoother swings and more control."

"Will you teach me?" Mattis asked, his voice in awe as he swung his sword in the new position.

"I've never taught a youngling before."

"I'm a quick learner."

"I believe you. You seem strong and quick on your feet."

Mattis's toothless grin lit up his face. "I am. And you? Were you injured in battle? Is that why you can't walk?"

"Uh . . ." Ryken looked to me for help.

"He's recovering from a big change. It will take him a bit to be steady on his feet again."

Ryken forced a smile.

"I'll help you," Mattis insisted. "I'm good at walking, but I'm especially good at running."

"You would help me?" Ryken asked slowly, mulling over the words.

"Think of it as a trade. The sooner you can walk, the sooner you can teach me how to use my sword. Maybe by the end of the week, I'll be as good as you. How long have you been practicing?"

"Since I was your age."

"Really?"

"Yes, every day. Though some days, training wasn't holding a sword but gaining knowledge. Weapons come in all shapes."

"I'll practice every day," Mattis said, nodding along.

"Can you teach me too?" I asked suddenly. The thought of being able to protect myself brought me peace of mind. I didn't want to live in fear for the rest of my life.

Ryken's aqua-blue eyes flashed, pleased by my request. "I'd be honored."

Mattis clapped his hands. Delighted by the idea, he ran outside to find a suitable branch I could use for a sword.

Ryken was still staring at the open door, sucking on his bottom lip as he thought. "He may be the first human I've liked. Maybe the younglings are not so bad."

"What about me?"

His eyes slid to me. "You can breathe underwater, which doesn't sound human to me."

Glass shattered in the kitchen, spiking my pulse. Both Ryken and I rose to our feet at the noise. Had Caitlyn overheard?

"Sorry for the ruckus. Clumsy fingers," Caitlyn called out, laughing nervously.

I turned to ask Ryken's opinion when I noticed he was standing, a little wobbly, but still he was upright on his own.

"Marigold, do you see?"

"I'm looking right at you." I laughed, melting at the wonder in his eyes. "At this rate, you'll be walking in no time."

"I hope so. I need to be able to keep up with you."

Standing, even for a short period, tapped Ryken's strength. We stumbled up the stairs where, after an embarrassing discussion of what a chamber pot was, I left him to rest. Exhausted myself, I fell into my own bed and slept until the late hours when I woke with a start as if something had shaken me awake.

But it was just me.

Unable to go back to sleep, I tossed and turned, incapable of finding a comfortable position in the lumpy bed. I reflected on Ryken's words. About how he wanted to woo me so that I claimed him. It conflicted with his response when I offered my lips for a kiss. What exactly did he want from me? All he did was leave me more confused.

The floorboard creaked in the hallway. I sat up, worried about Ryken. I twisted a strand of my hair while I debated if one little noise was worth investigating. But my curiosity won out, and I opened my bedroom door to check on him. I didn't need to venture far, as I saw a glimpse of him when he stepped down the stairs.

"Ryken?" I whisper-screamed. How was he walking so easily?

I sprinted to the stairwell. He was already turning at the floor landing and heading to the door. His body was illuminated, his water armor from the ceremony shimmering in the darkness. With stiff movements, he moved with purpose, focused on his task.

My hand clasped the banister as I finally understood. Ryken had said Ruah would provide what he needed when the time came. It explained why he practically jogged down the stairs with expert footing when he could barely stand earlier in the day. That, and he was wearing his water armor again, the unnatural glow of it slanting across the walls.

He was Collecting.

With silent footsteps, he walked outside and into the night, leaving the door open behind him.

My heart clenched at his disappearance, and a frantic need to be close to him clouded my reasoning. I didn't hesitate as I rushed down the stairs and sprinted out into the darkness after him.

He was going nowhere without me.

Where You Belong

My eyes adjusted to the night as soon as I stepped outside. I scanned the surrounding field, a few tall pines scattered across the acres of untamed grass. A small path led from the house, curving down and around until it disappeared from view in the distance.

Ryken's glow made him easy to spot, but he was already yards ahead of me, moving at an unnatural speed. Instinct pushed me forward, my feet crunching against the pebble path. Moonlight cloaked the field in beige, dewdrops sparkling in the grass.

In a full sprint, I pushed myself to the limit, pumping my arms as I closed some of the distance between us. Gasping for breath, I entered a small patch of evergreens that led me off the normal walking trail.

The air was muggy and thick, and an uncomfortable layer of sweat clung to my skin. It dripped into my eyes, stinging on contact. I squinted, swiping it away. Vision blurring, I struggled to focus on Ryken's form ahead of me.

"Ryken," I called out. The glow from his torso was barely visible through the gap between the trees. Then it winked out like a candle flame.

Which tree did he go behind? This tree? Or that one?

Panting, I stumbled to a stop and spun in place. Dread crawled up my spine. Everything looked the same. A pale moonbeam brightened the pathway I entered from, but I knew if I continued any farther, there was a chance I'd lose my way.

I glanced over my shoulder, my self-preservation reminding me how dangerous this was. Alone in the night, barefoot, and only in my night-gown? I was asking for trouble. My inner voice, the one I always listened to, demanded I return to my bed. What if someone happened upon me?

But then my heart contracted in fear. *Ryken*. He could be in trouble.

Debating, I stared down at my hands, knowing I was wasting precious seconds as Ryken put more distance between us. Even if he was in trouble, what could I do to help him? I had no magic armor or weapon.

I balled my hands into fists. They were tiny, human hands, smaller than most. But I wasn't completely human, was I? Nor was I as small as others had me believe.

My eyes snapped up as a wave of determination surged through me. I could do this. Small didn't always equate to weak.

I took a deep breath, my thoughts on Ryken, and jerked in surprise at his scent in the air. The more I focused on it, the more his scent morphed into invisible arrows, pointing a zigzag path up and to the left. It was strong and fresh, only minutes old.

I chased after them, following the path and ignoring the voice of reason, and dashed deeper into the woods. It wasn't a straight path as it weaved across the untraveled ground, the foliage so thick in places that my arms were sliced on the branches. When I turned the next corner, I found myself in front of a stream, the scent trail ending at the water's edge.

Water no deeper than my ankles trickled by over the moss-covered rocks and rushed off to twist around the trees. Had I made a wrong turn?

I turned back the way I came, breathing the air and hoping for the same instinct to take over. It was as if the scent ended here, but he was nowhere to be seen.

A hand clasped my shoulder, whirling me around. I lifted my hands, prepared to strike out if necessary, but I dropped them on a sigh at Ryken's illuminated face. Emotionless, he stared down at me, showing no signs of recognition in his vacant eyes—dimmer than his normal shade. His circlet pulsed, blinding me with the light.

"You do not belong here," he said stiffly. "Go back."

Abruptly, he shoved me away before I could reply. I stumbled into a tree.

"Leave." The word was cold and empty.

"No." My heart thudded as I pressed closer, crossing my arms defiantly. What had gotten into him?

"Leave, or I will make you."

"You would never——"

Light radiated off his circlet, a whining pitch that built as the beam grew in intensity. I held up a hand, shielding my eyes. They drooped before I crashed to my knees.

"Ryken . . ." My voice cracked.

The light flickered.

"Sleep."

And I did, crumbling onto the forest floor.

I woke up sometime later, my body jostling in the air. Somehow I found myself upside down, blinking at the stretch of blurry sand as we moved. Ryken's hand gripped my thigh, holding me in place as he carried me over his shoulder. But we weren't alone. A man rested on his other shoulder, his loose hair and arms bobbing with each step.

I heard it then, the crash of waves on the shore. It whispered a seductive hum, begging me to return home. With each wave, the memory of cool, salty waters tingled across my skin, emphasizing how dry and sticky it was now. The desire to dive back into the refreshing liquid consumed my thoughts. To wash off this world and return to the peacefulness of the sea again.

Suddenly, Ryken stopped moving. As I turned to peer over my shoulder, he dropped me at his feet. The cool splash of liquid greeted me like an old friend, the crest of the wave breaking into my lap. The tide rushed back, gripping my gown like hands, gently beckoning me to the deeper waters.

The strange man landed next to me, splattering wet sand onto my face and chest. Arms tangled about him, he lay motionless with his face turned away.

"What have you done?" I said, pressing the back of my hand to my mouth. Was he dead?

"There is a price to pay for a broken promise," Ryken said, sounding like a stranger. The wave hit us at the same time. Whereas mine felt like a bubbly caress, the water slammed into the man so hard that his arms flailed out just before the tide flowed out, rolling the man on his side over and over until he disappeared beneath the foamy crests.

I gasped, my stomach coiling into knots.

"You remain," Ryken said, staring down at me.

"What about the man? Where did he go?" I scrambled to my feet, searching the dark waters.

"You are of the ocean . . . yet you did not return. The ocean grants you freedom—why?"

"Ryken. Did you hear me? Where did the man go?"

"Where he belongs—where you belong." The glow of his skin startled me back a step.

"You can't force me back to the sea." The water lapped at my feet. "I didn't break my vows."

He tilted his head and reached out a hand for me, and I dodged it. "Do not be afraid."

"You aren't Ryken. Don't touch me."

"He is me and I am him. I won't let any harm come to his mate."

"I'm not his . . . *fine.*" Whatever they needed to believe so I stayed safe.

In a blur of light, he was in front of me, his hands like iron on my shoulders. "I see now. I know who you are."

"You should. We've spent a few days together," I grumbled.

Not-Ryken smiled. "I've been waiting for you."

I tensed. "Waiting for me? Why?"

"You are the song in the darkness. The beginning to the end. Your voice will start it all."

"I don't understand." I placed my palms on his chest, and he flinched.

"Don't do that." He wiped my hands from him. "Don't call to him. You are a distraction."

"I didn't call anyone," I stuttered as he loomed over me. *Ryken,* I remembered. *It's still Ryken in there.*

He sighed and held out his palm. "Touch me."

"No." I twisted away, but he followed me, too close.

"Your mate insists."

"No, thank you." I walked backward in the surf, the tide tugging the hem of my nightgown.

"He is concerned for you. Touch me." The light of his circlet pulsed, and I watched my hand move on its own to rest on Ryken's cheek. His eyes fluttered closed at my touch. He swayed forward, wrapping an arm around my back. When his eyes opened, they were a clear aqua, twinkling in recognition. *Click, clickety-click, hummm, click.*

"Ryken," I breathed, throwing myself into his embrace.

His other arm wrapped around me, drawing me to him. His nose pressed into my hair, breathing me in. "You followed me?"

"I was worried," I said into his armor.

He chuckled, giving me a squeeze. "Protecting me again?"

I nodded, my cheek rubbing on the hard surface of his armor, a power I didn't understand flowing through him. He didn't need my protection at all. But he had it nonetheless.

His hand glided down my hair. "I can't stay. I have to finish. There are more."

"Why are you not yourself? Who was I speaking to?"

"He is one of the four elite warriors, the ones who have always aided the Collectors throughout time. During my ceremony, Tzedek and I were tethered, united in Ruah's mission. He shall return to lead me when it's time to collect broken vows. With Tzedek, I am faster, stronger, and more efficient. He helps me remain neutral and focus on my task. But he wasn't prepared for you. You easily distracted me." As I pulled back, he cupped my face, tilting it up. My cheeks heated at the thought that he might kiss me right here in the moonlight. But after staring at me for a moment, he only touched our foreheads together. "I'm sorry."

"Sorry?" I closed my eyes at his protective scent.

"I'm sorry you had to see it. Your heart is too soft for what I do." The breath from his lips brushed across my own.

I trembled.

"Is that what will happen . . . to me? If I break my promises?"

He winced. "No, no. I won't let it."

"But it would. This would be my fate."

He said it himself—he couldn't save me if the sea decided to take me.

"Consequences are required for the greater good. It keeps peace in the chaos."

His curt tone had me jumping back so quickly I landed on my bottom in the surf again. It wasn't Ryken.

"Your free will is a power you must wield wisely. Your choices will affect us all."

"Stay back," I demanded, hoping I sounded more threatening than I felt.

"It's time for you to leave. There is more work to be done."

"I'm not going anywhere without Ryken," I countered, my eyes narrowing.

"He is pleased . . . I am not. This ends now."

The light from the circlet shone brighter than the sun, blasting me flat into the water and knocking me unconscious again.

My next breath had my eyes shooting open, daylight reflecting on the ceiling above. The weight of the comforter was heavy and warm, the sun's rays pouring in from the window. How long had I been sleeping? I scrubbed a hand down my face, dusting off bits of sand. Events from the night before replayed again in my head as I rubbed the sandy grains between my fingers.

What had happened? How did I end up in bed? And where was Ryken?

A soft snore sounded from my side, startling me sideways into the wall. *Is there someone in bed with me?*

My Favorite Thing

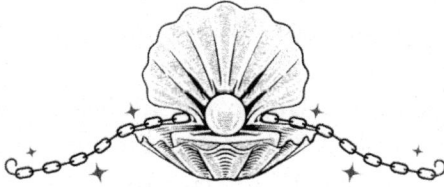

The weight of the comforter shifted and then settled back into place. While I was under the bedding, something—or someone—was on top. I pulled back the extra pillow to reveal Ryken's slack mouth, his breathing deep and heavy. His armor was gone, leaving him in the same clothing I had sewn yesterday, covered in sand.

Stunned, I blinked at him as I wondered if my imagination was playing tricks on me. My chest rose and fell, picking up speed as my anxiety spiked. This was more than breaking the rules. The heat of embarrassment set my body on fire.

Don't lose control, I reminded myself, taking a shaky breath. *Nobody knows he is in here but me. Fix the problem and worry about the consequences later.*

"Ryken," I whispered. I had to figure out a way to lug him out of my room before Caitlyn noticed. "You need to get up."

When he didn't move, I shook him.

He still didn't respond, continuing to snore into the bedding.

Why was he even in here? I tried to be furious with him, but my frown pulled up at the corner the longer I stared at his relaxed face. He seemed so peaceful lying there, the light highlighting his features in a way that made the butterflies take flight in my stomach. His eye had healed some, more green smudges than black. Did he get more hand-some each day? I brushed back a loose strand of hair from his forehead. Or was I just falling for him despite myself?

My eyes widened at that. I had to get out of this bed and into some fresh air that didn't smell like him. I crawled out of the cocoon of sheets, escaping the weight of his heavy arm, and tiptoed out the door. As I clicked it closed, a voice piped up behind me.

"Good morning, Marigold," Mattis said. "Have you seen Ryken? He's not in his bed."

My face flushed scarlet. "Uh, no. I'm sure he's around."

"Around? He can't walk." He squinted at me. "You all right?"

"Wonderful. How about breakfast?" I pressed a hand onto his shoulder to steer him to the stairs.

"It's closer to afternoon tea. Momma said you were sleeping the day away."

I coughed, looking for a distraction. "Bungo! Did you grab him from Ryken's room?"

"I did. He ate breakfast with me, then sat with me while I worked on your sword." His chestnut eyes lit at that. "Do you want to see it? It's almost ready."

Nodding, I agreed as we walked down the stairs. The boy took off to the kitchen as soon as we arrived at the main level.

"Momma, Marigold is awake. You told me to tell you."

"Honey, not so loud. I'm right here." She came around the corner, giving me a curious look. "Good morning to you. Did you sleep well?"

I glanced away. "Surprisingly, yes."

"Good, good." She wiped her hands on the cotton apron tied around her waist. "By chance, did you have a moonlight swim last night?"

"Uh . . ."

"I only ask since the front door was left ajar and there were tracks of sand leading up to your chambers."

"Sorry about the mess. I needed a walk to clear my head."

"And I see some of the beach is still clinging to your nightgown."

Brown splotches stained my hem, the fringe lace stiff. I was so focused on sneaking out of the room that I had forgotten to change into clothes. What was the matter with me? Walking around in nothing but

140

a nightgown *again*? It was as if the urgency to cover up was lessening each day.

I am still human, I reminded myself and forced my arms around my chest, my cheeks heating in concern.

"No need to fret. It's easily washed. First, let me help you change into another gown, miss."

"No," I said a little louder than I meant to. "I can do it myself. But I would love a cup of tea."

Caitlyn smiled, nodding. "Yes, of course. I'll boil up some water."

A thud sounded from upstairs. We both glanced at the ceiling.

"Odd. I thought he was gone." She shrugged and returned to the kitchen.

I raced back up the stairs as soon as I was alone again, rushing back into my room. Ryken sat on the floor, knees bent, rubbing the back of his head. He scowled at his legs.

"I fell."

I shut the door behind me. "I heard."

"Can you help me?"

"Yes, of course." I wrapped an arm around his waist, helping him stay centered as he rose to his feet. "*Easy.* Focus on staying balanced."

"What do you think I've been doing?" he grumbled.

"Don't get gruff with me. I'm only trying to help."

Ryken blew out a breath. "Sorry. I'm just . . . frustrated."

"I know. You'll get it soon enough. Let's walk you to your chamber."

"Why do we not share the same . . . chamber?"

"Rules."

"I don't like rules."

I tried not to laugh and failed. "Nobody does."

"But you do."

"They are comforting, I guess. I like having structure and things I can rely on."

"You are my comfort."

"Oh, Ryken." I shook my head as I smiled. I led him into the hall-way. "You shouldn't say things like that."

"Why not? Why should I have to lie about how I feel about you to please other people? Or follow rules I don't understand? Out of everything on land, you are my favorite thing."

His words stole the breath from my lungs. His favorite? Had anyone called me their favorite before?

He stopped me with a jerk of his arm, forcing me to look at him. "Did you hear me?"

"I did. I've just never had anyone say things like that to me before. Sometimes . . . I don't know how to respond." I tried to glance down, but his hand held my chin and prevented me from breaking his stare.

"Just be honest. What was the first thing you wanted to say?"

I squeezed my eyes shut, my nose scrunching. His fingers brushed along my jaw to my collar.

You can tell me this way. Then it's only you and me.

My heart hammered in my chest. I knew even if he couldn't hear the erratic beats, he could smell my nerves. He was patient—so patient—waiting for my response. I opened my eyes to see him studying my features.

I took a long breath and let it out on a sigh. *You are my favorite thing too.*

Am I? His thumb traced the skin of my neck.

"Ryken, you're back," Mattis called out as he jogged over to us.

Ryken's gaze didn't waver from me. "Of course, I would never leave her," he said. "I'd always come back."

"Really?" The thought of him always being close did something to my insides.

You are mine.

The phrase was like a slap of reality. He still considered me a treasure to be collected. I didn't want to be owned—I wanted to be loved. Frowning, I stepped back.

"You're upset," he said.

"I'm all right."

He stepped toward me. "No, you're not."

I blinked at him. He was standing on his own, and he didn't even realize it. I shuffled back another step. "Ryken?"

"I don't like this game where you pull away and then lie about it." His jaw ticked as he closed the distance between us.

142

Again and again, he matched my stride, too caught up in the conversation to notice he moved on his own.

"Tell me the truth. What is happening?" Ryken demanded.

I stepped away, and he followed.

"You're walking, Ryken. That's what is happening," Mattis said, appearing at Ryken's side with a goofy grin on his face.

Ryken glanced at his legs, confused. "Walking?"

"Yes, look at how far we are. We are at your doorway."

He focused back on me, taking a few steps until he could reach me. "We aren't finished with our conversation."

"What conversation?" Mattis asked, kicking up the loose granules of sand on the floor. "And why are you so sandy? Momma has been cleaning it up all morning. You're going to be in trouble if she catches you."

"Ryken, why don't you sit for a moment while I go change," I suggested while Mattis started talking about a strange yellow bird he found in a tree.

Ryken's hand linked with mine. "Stay with me."

The pleading look in his eyes almost made me agree. But my ingrained propriety had me shaking my head and returning to my chamber to change into another clean frock after I washed in the basin.

When I returned to help Ryken, I paused in the doorway, listening to him and Mattis talk.

"See? That's a faster way to do a button."

"Thank you," Ryken mumbled, fiddling with one of his shirt buttons.

"Momma told me to just practice. Same with walking, I bet. Then you'll be running and jumping and climbing———"

"Running? Jumping?"

"Watch me," Mattis said, sprinting in a circle. "I could go faster if I had more room. This is a jump." He jumped in place, knees high, then landed on the floor with a thud.

"You didn't fall," Ryken said, leaning forward to watch Mattis's legs move.

"Not unless I want to." Mattis laughed.

"You are very wise for a youngling."

"You must have sailed from a faraway place. Normally, they call me a child."

"Child," Ryken repeated.

"What's it like where you're from?" the boy asked.

Ryken blinked as he thought. "We have different rules we follow. They are strict since there aren't many of us left. We like our freedom but function better as a group. Though we are powerful, we will always choose peace instead. Our world is bright, full of colors, but the sound is quiet. It's never too hot or too cold. It's always the perfect temperature."

"How far is it from here? Could I visit?"

"It's . . . far enough. I don't get to meet new people often."

Mattis pouted. "Oh. Do you think it's like my book?"

Ryken lifted a shoulder. "I don't know. You mean your wooing book?"

"*Adventure* book."

"Could you read it to me? Then I could tell you if it is similar or not."

"I could read it," I chimed in, leaning on the doorframe.

Mattis spun at my entrance. "Oh, would you? It's always better when someone else reads."

"I'd love to. It's been a long time since I read it with my sister."

"Is she far away too?"

"Yes, in a way. She lives in Cadell. She is a princess by now."

Mattis scratched his head. "Princess? There's no princess in Cadell."

The smile dropped from my face. "You're mistaken. She is there with her prince."

The boy tapped his lip. "No prince, either."

I took off, rushing down the stairs, ignoring Ryken's calls.

"Caitlyn," I called out, banging out the back door.

She turned, the wet laundry flapping on the line behind her.

I didn't give her a second, bombarding her with questions. "Where is the princess of Cadell? Is she all right?"

"Princess?" She swallowed. "There's no princess. Only the king and queen rule the kingdom."

"The king married?" When did King Baxton have time to search for a bride when he was confined to his sickbed?

"Yes. Wait—no. This is confusing. You're thinking of the old king. He went mad searching for his missing bride. Then when he found her, she killed him——" she lowered her voice and leaned in, glancing around us as if we were being watched "——with *magic*."

I gasped. People were publicly wielding magic? But it was outlawed and punishable by death. Anyone who performed magic stated they were in league with the Sorcerer. Though the old man had never been seen, his stories were infamous and passed on from generation to generation. He lurked in the shadows of Mistbrooke Forest, plotting his revenge against the royal kingdom.

Truth or fable, I didn't get anywhere near the haunted forest to find out.

"And now this murderer is ruling Cadell?" Where was my sister in all of this? Back at the cottage? Was she safe?

"They call her the Queen of Hearts because she uses her magic to enchant the hearts of others. The poor king was so lovesick that he tried to burn down the entire forest to get to her. Her people may be entranced under her spell, but our king has warned us to keep our distance. It's best you stay away from Cadell too."

"Our king?"

"King Galon of Windcrest. He's the only one that cares about his people and their safety. She has been forcing all the territories to accept all forms of magic, encouraging it so much that she decreed a new law."

Magic was taking over Cadell? Prince Alexander always said magic was a vile thing, stealing what mattered most. And he would know. As a child, he had lost his mother to the Sorcerer's curse that plagued his royal family. Sometimes I would catch his envious eye at our family gatherings.

Were he and Rose able to escape to safety before the evil queen attacked?

It sounded similar to a fantasy story I had read in a book. Curses, enchanted forests, and an evil queen? How could this be real?

A week ago, I wouldn't have believed Caitlyn's rambling at all. But Ryken and his underwater world had opened my eyes to magic. He wasn't in league with the Sorcerer and was unaware of the magic in Mistbrooke Forest. Were there two types of magic? Good versus evil? Light versus dark?

Caitlyn shook her head at my silence. "Don't believe me? I wouldn't believe myself either if I were you. Do you know who she ended up marrying? The king of Mistbrooke."

I made a face. "There is no one in those woods but the Sorcerer."

"But it's true. The Sorcerer kept him hidden away. The king stole her from Cadell, and together they claimed Cadell's throne. The Keeper of Flames and the Queen of Hearts, they're a deadly combination."

"Flames?" I recalled Ryken's water armor. Was that why it was made of water? "How did I miss all of this?"

"A lot happened while you were . . . sailing, was it?" she asked, piercing me with her gaze.

I took a step back. The guilt of my lies hung like a tangible weight around my neck. "Yes, sea traders of sorts. I have to talk to Ryken. Excuse me, please."

I raced back to the house, Caitlyn's eyes boring into my spine as I went. This changed everything. We needed to leave immediately.

Where are you, Rosey?

Torn

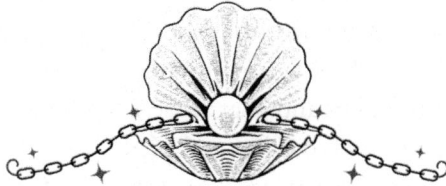

Barging through the door, I was so lost in thought that I nearly knocked Mattis over. His two wooden swords tumbled to the ground. Bending down, he swiped them up and tucked them under his arm.

"Sorry about that. I'm in a rush," I said, patting his shoulder.

When I moved to step around him, he planted himself in my path. He blinked up at me, frowning. "Where are you going?"

"Something has come up, and it's time for us to leave."

The boy's lips parted in a silent gasp. "But—you just arrived. You can't leave yet. We haven't learned how to fight."

"I know. . . and I am sorry." I weaved around him, searching for Ryken on the empty stairwell. "It's just that my sister is unwell."

"Oh?"

"And I need to go find her and make sure she isn't hurt." Rose's image from the mirror flashed in my mind, her face twisted in discomfort. Could her ailment be magic related? Did something happen when she escaped the castle?

"Who would want to hurt your sister?" Mattis's question jolted me out of my anxious thoughts.

"I think the Queen of Hearts might."

He gasped and wrapped his small arms around my waist, stopping me from climbing the stairs. "Please don't go. I've overheard Father talk of war. You'll have no protection at the castle."

"I'll be her protection," Ryken said from the upper landing. He leaned heavily against the wall, his eyes locked on mine.

"No offense, but you can barely walk," the boy scoffed.

Ryken growled at that.

I sent him a sharp look before turning to Mattis. "We aren't storming the castle or charging into battle. I'm visiting my grandparents' shop first to see if they have heard anything. There's a possibility that Alex whisked her to safety and that Rose is hiding there. If that's the case, I might not even need to travel to Cadell."

"Travel to Cadell? When are you leaving?" Caitlyn said as she rounded the corner from the kitchen, her empty wicker basket resting on her hip.

"Today, if possible," I said.

"So soon? Jacek hasn't even returned."

"I'm afraid I've stayed longer than I initially planned. It's just that——" I glanced up at Ryken, who had plopped down on the stairs to sit "——there were a few complications."

Changing tactics, Mattis ran to his mother's side. "But we haven't played swords or read the book yet. Please make them stay."

Caitlyn nibbled her lip, walking into the room and resting her basket on the table. "We can't make them do anything. But I will point out that your friend doesn't seem well enough to travel."

"Where she goes, I go too," Ryken said, his eyebrows lowering.

"I'm not leaving you, Ryken. I just need to figure it out." I turned to Caitlyn. "Do you have an extra horse by chance?" It was a risk. Riding double with Ryken would tarnish my reputation, but I could dismount on the outskirts of Windcrest before anyone spotted us.

"Horse?" Ryken asked.

Shaking her head, Caitlyn replied, "No, Jacek took our only one. He will return tomorrow. Can't you wait one more night?"

One more night? Didn't she realize that every second mattered? I was torn between wanting to race to find Rose and staying with Ryken until he figured out his footing. I couldn't leave him. I scrubbed a hand down my face, spinning to the stairs and then back to her again. "What about your neighbors? Could we borrow one from them?"

"You could. It's just that we're a poor village. Borrowing a horse is equivalent to losing a day's worth of wages. They're unable to cart their daily haul home."

Sighing, I knew what it was like to live day to day. A disease devoured half of our apple orchard two springtimes ago, leading to a desperate winter. Luckily, Prince Alexander had gifted my family—well, Rose—with extra provisions so that we could survive the season.

I took a deep breath and counted to three before releasing it. There was no other way—I had to wait for the wagon. Either that or I'd have to leave Ryken behind . . . and I couldn't do it. My heart twisted at the mere thought.

I closed my eyes as an idle feeling gnawed at me, like precious time slipping by while I stood here useless. If only it were as easy to take Ryken with me as it was when he carried me around the ocean.

A hand pressed on top of mine on the banister. Ryken had scooted down the steps, his head tilted as he watched me.

"Don't be sad. I will walk with you," he said, his eyes shining with determination.

"Ryken, no." I shook my head, more at myself than at him. My impatience was forcing him when he wasn't ready. "You still need more practice."

He lifted himself to stand anyway, and I pressed my hands into his chest to stop him from swaying forward.

"Lead the way." He draped an arm around my shoulders.

"Wait, wait." Caitlyn rushed forward, her hands outstretched. "There are thieves on the roads. I can't possibly let you go in good conscience."

Desmond and Fitz. I shuddered and curled into Ryken's side. Though they were behind bars, there were plenty more like them out there. The last time I traveled, I had a false sense of security because of the royal insignia on the carriage. But even that wasn't enough to deter the criminals. How much more would I attract criminals if I went on foot? I couldn't outrun anyone, and neither could Ryken.

"You're right."

She nodded quickly. "Yes, walking on foot is dangerous lately. You don't know who is human and who is an Enchanter."

"Enchanter?" Ryken and I asked at the same time.

"It's what the people of Mistbrooke are calling themselves. The Sorcerer is teaching them how to use their magic. The King of Flames's army is growing larger by the minute. Dark times are coming, miss. It's best you stay off the roads until all the Enchanters are captured and destroyed."

"Not all magic is bad," Ryken said, tilting his head. When Caitlyn whipped her head toward him, he quickly added, "Or so I have heard."

"It's evil is what it is. Unnatural. It changes the laws of nature and forces people to act against their will. Nobody deserves that type of power."

Only Ruah, I thought. But I must have mumbled it, as Caitlyn leaned forward, her eyebrows high.

"Ruah?" she repeated. "That name hasn't been uttered in centuries. A childhood story from so long ago that I'm surprised you heard of it in Cadell."

"My grandparents are from Windcrest," I reminded her.

"Oh, that's right. Won't it be wonderful that you will see them tomorrow?" Caitlyn beamed a smile at me. "Why don't you go outside and enjoy the rest of the day? You've been sleeping most of it away. I'll get started on supper after I finish a few more chores." She hummed as she snatched the basket off the table, ruffled Mattis's hair as she passed him, and then returned to the kitchen.

"Are we going?" Ryken asked, looking down at me.

"Yes, tomorrow, it seems," I grumbled.

"I'm sorry. I know I'm the one slowing us down."

"No, I'm actually amazed at how far you've come in so little time. You were taking steps on your own earlier."

"Yeah, could we sword fight now?" Mattis asked.

We both jerked in surprise, having forgotten the boy. His large brown eyes pleaded with Ryken, apparently sensing he was the weaker one between us.

Ryken's mouth fell open and then closed in a fishlike gesture. "Uh."

"Maybe you could help guide him around outside first?" I suggested. Ryken needed to learn how to balance soon if war was on the horizon. The faster we could get to Windcrest so I knew my sister and family were safe, the sooner I could say my final farewells and return to the sea. Hopefully, we would be deep in the peaceful waters before all the chaos on land occurred.

Tightening my hold on his arm, I navigated us out the main door.

Ryken halted in the doorframe, his breath rushing from him. His eyes were wide, flicking quickly from one thing to another as he noted each new detail. The pebble path, the sparse row of pine trees that dotted a trail, the lush green grass that Mattis took off in—already in an imaginary battle. His eyebrow twitched at the sight of a scarlet-colored butterfly flittering between buttercups sprinkled through the thick grass.

"What do you think?" I asked.

He didn't respond, overwhelmed with his surroundings like I had been with the clutter on our ship. "Can I touch them?"

"It depends. Which thing?"

"That yellow thing."

"Oh, that's a flower. Yes, you can touch it."

For the next few hours, we inspected every flower, insect, animal, and rock. Ryken wanted to know its name, if you could eat it, and what its purpose was. It was actually quite sweet.

Mattis lost interest in swordplay, loving the new game where he taught Ryken how to see the shapes in the clouds as they lay back amidst the wildflowers. Watching the two of them together did something in my chest. I was small compared to Ryken, but Mattis? Ryken dwarfed him. I waited for the merman to grow weary of the boy's interruptions, but he seemed just as fascinated with the boy as the boy was with him.

It reminded me of the many times Rose and I had done the same thing. Times we had laughed and created stories while staring at the sky, wondering what our futures had in store for us. She never imagined she would catch the eye of a prince.

Ryken laughed a deep chuckle and turned to meet my eyes over the distance. My heart caught on the sound, my hand resting on my chest. I supposed I wasn't that different from Rose . . . I hadn't expected to be charmed by a merman.

He tilted his head, watching me for a moment before I glanced away, busying myself by dusting the dirt off my lap where I sat in the field. Why was it so hard for me to be as direct and honest as Ryken? How freeing that must be for him to say whatever was on his mind or do whatever he wished.

A buttercup appeared in front of my nose, my eyes crossing at its nearness.

"For you," Ryken said.

"For me?" I picked the small flower from his grip. Nobody had given me a flower before. My voice shook as I spoke. "Thank you."

"The color reminds me of your hair. It was one of the first things I noticed about you."

Surprised, I turned to him. He sat next to me, his fingers playing with the end of one of my long curls.

"My hair? I thought it was my song?"

"I saw your beauty first, then I heard you."

"But . . . I didn't see you."

"That doesn't mean I wasn't there watching you."

My cheeks heated, and I returned my attention back to the flower. *What do I say to that?*

"Marigold," he whispered, leaning in so close that goosebumps spread across my neck. "Don't hide from me."

I turned back, our noses almost touching. "I'm not."

The corner of his mouth came up. "Liar."

His aqua eyes sparkled in the sunlight, unashamedly trailing my features. The way he looked at me made me weak—hooded eyes that stared into my soul and saw something I had yet to find in myself. I couldn't breathe. I couldn't think. How was it that I had captured his attention? My fingers fidgeted in my lap as an urge came to trace his cheekbones, the slope of his nose, the fullness of his lips, to curl my hands in his hair and kiss his bruises away.

My eyes widened at the scandalous direction my thoughts had turned, and I dropped my gaze.

Click, clickety-click, hummm, click. "I will wait until you're ready."

The breeze picked up, ruffling my hair over my shoulder and across my face to dance in the air. The smell of him drifted over me as comforting as a hug. It almost made me forget why we had left the ocean in the first place. But a lone daisy in the field popped the hazy bubble around me.

My sister's favorite flower. *Rosey.*

Ryken's shoulder pressed against mine, a subtle pressure of reassurance that I leaned into.

"Don't be sad," he said.

I lifted a shoulder. "It's hard not to be."

"Your sister?"

I nodded.

"We will find her, and then you will be happy again."

If only it were that simple. "What if she can't be cured? What if I don't make it to her in time?" My throat constricted.

"I'm sorry I don't have the answers. What I do know is that whatever happens, you won't be alone. The good, the bad, and everything in between, I am here by your side."

My eyes misted, and I blinked the moisture away. But unwanted tears escaped, and I brushed them away with a flick of my finger.

"What are those?" Ryken asked, turning my face to him. He sniffed at my cheeks. "Seawater?"

A laugh bubbled up from me at his innocent stare. "These are tears, Ry. Sometimes when you're sad enough, it happens."

His face crumbled. "Oh." He touched a finger to one. "How do I make them stop?"

"You don't. But knowing you care helps, and so does the flower." I held up the buttercup.

"I can get you more if you want. Mattis said giving flowers means you like someone."

"Did he now?" I chuckled and wiped away the last of my tears.

"One might not be enough. How many do you think you need? Hundreds? Thousands?"

"*Thousands?*" I smiled at the outrageous number. He grinned back. "No, one is perfect." I slid the bloom behind my ear.

He cupped my chin, my heartbeat picking up its tempo. His thumbs rushed over my cheeks still damp from tears. He leaned forward and rested his forehead on mine, his eyes closed. A calm filled me, and I sighed.

"I feel . . ." Ryken started, pinching his lips in frustration at his lack of words.

Just then, Mattis called for us, excited to show us a frog he had caught in a mud puddle.

Holding each other's stare, we both eased back, fighting the magnetic pull that held us together. I placed my hand over his just as he drew away. "I feel it too."

He hummed, content.

I eventually left them chattering about frogs and their long, sticky tongues and offered my help to Caitlyn as she prepared our evening meal. Moving around the kitchen brought a sense of comfort, like I was home. I sliced carrots, the motion relaxing; it kept my mind focused on the task rather than straying to my worries of war, my sister's health, and the ominous Queen of Hearts.

I'd forgotten about my troubles completely when I crawled into bed, still chuckling at Ryken's reaction to using silverware when he ate. It was almost as hilarious as watching Caitlyn's aghast expression when he gave up on the "human torture device" known as a spoon and just slurped from the bowl.

He complained again when I dropped him off at his chamber, reluctant to sleep in separate beds. As handsome as his pout was, I didn't fall for it. I gave him Bungo to snuggle with instead, which he was still holding to his chest when I left him.

When sleep came, I dozed off with his face at the forefront of my thoughts, smiling into my pillow as I dreamed of him.

In the hushed silence of the night, a faint rap sounded at the front door. Even as quiet as it was, it echoed in my ears and jarred me awake. I shot upright in bed, my eyes adjusting quickly to the darkness. Footsteps shuffled by my door, and a slow glow illuminated the cracks in the door-frame as they passed, then faded out as they continued onward. Curious, I eased from my bed and tiptoed closer to my door, listening to the creaking of the stairs as the wanderer scurried downstairs.

Was it Ryken? Collecting so soon?

I knew I shouldn't follow him again, but I crept out of my chamber anyway. Candlelight from downstairs cast long gray shadows on the wall and ceiling. I pressed close to the wall, peeking around the corner to the main level.

Another knock. The bolt turned with a clank. Whispers drifted up, crystal clear.

"Jacek? You're back early," Caitlyn said, her voice high.

"We had to rush. The Queen of Hearts must have scouts nearby. She knows Marigold is somewhere in Windcrest."

Unable to stop myself, I gasped and slapped a hand over my mouth. Why would the queen be searching for me? What could I have that was of any value? Did she think to use me to get back at my sister or the prince?

"What was that?" Jacek asked, rushing into view before I could jerk out of sight. He wore a mud-colored cloak with the hood pushed back. Candlelight highlighted half of his face, the other half hidden in shadows. "My lady? What are you doing up at this hour? The rooster has yet to crow."

"I heard a knock at the door."

"It was just me." Jacek placed one hand on the banister and beckoned me with his other. "Will you please come down? I don't want to wake Mattis with our voices."

I glanced at the boy's closed door and nodded. As I reached the bottom of the landing, Caitlyn fingered the tie of her dressing gown, refusing to meet my eyes. Pausing, I realized I had once again ventured downstairs in just my nightgown.

"Goodness, I'm so sorry." I crossed an arm over my chest. "I forgot to put something decent on. Let me——"

"I'll get it for you, miss," she interrupted and dodged past me up the stairs.

"Caitlyn," I whispered, but she was already out of sight.

I turned back to Jacek and forced a smile, shifting awkwardly. "Sorry. Uh. Your trip went well?"

"Very well, actually. It exceeded my expectations." His abnormally wide smile filled me with a sense of unease.

"All right," I said. "If all is well, then I shall return to bed."

His hand whipped out, gripping my forearm and preventing my escape. "Please, stay and chat for a moment, will you? I'd love to hear what I missed while I was gone."

"Oh, nothing really." The pinpricks of foreboding nicked my shoulder blades, spreading down my spine. I let out a small sigh of relief at the sound of footsteps on the landing.

Caitlyn rushed back down the stairs, carrying a neat stack of linen.

My black slippers rested on top of the pile. Wordlessly, she placed them in my arms, glancing anywhere but at me.

"I thought you'd bring a dressing gown or a wrap."

She didn't respond, refusing to look my way.

"Caitlyn?"

Her head jerked up, surprised. "Yes, miss?"

"Is everything all right?" If I had been human, I would have missed the smell of fear oozing from her skin.

"Of course. Why wouldn't it be?" She barked a laugh, a forced sound.

An odor permeated around me. The wrongness of it made me flinch —it smelled of dishonesty. Why would they lie? A flash of warning shot through me, my prey instinct activating, and my need to flee had my eyes darting around the room for the nearest exit. *Run.*

"My lady, do not panic. Remember, we are helping you," Jacek said gruffly when I took a step away.

I looked down at his hand bruising my arm. "This doesn't feel like helping."

Jacek shushed me with a shake. "Lower your voice. Don't wake Mattis."

I mulled that over, my chest rising and falling. *Is it really Mattis he is worried about waking?* My narrowed eyes snapped directly to his in a challenge. *Or is it Ryken?*

Just as I opened my mouth to scream, Jacek pulled a silver dagger from the folds of his cloak. An expensive piece, the dagger glittered with sapphires and diamonds. It was out of place among the possessions of his home. But Jacek seemed at ease handling it and held the blade near my neck.

"Don't make a sound."

My heart thudded at his betrayal . . . at Caitlyn's betrayal. Only hours ago, we had been swapping stories at the dinner table.

"Jacek," Caitlyn hissed and placed a hand on his arm. "Is this necessary? She's a good girl—obedient—she wouldn't cause trouble. Right, miss?"

"Of course. There is no need to threaten." I swallowed the lump stuck in my throat. How did I keep finding myself at the end of a weapon?

156

"I'm not taking any chances in case she tries to run."

A fist pounded at the door, cutting off his sentence. The three of us swiveled toward the sound as tension filled the air. Whatever was outside had both Jacek's and Caitlyn's hearts racing so loudly, I could hear them as clearly as my own.

"Open up by royal behest," called a deep voice from the other side.

The Lost Sister

J acek slapped a hand over my mouth. A fishy smell wafted up from his skin, making me gag.

"Not one peep from you. Do you hear me?" His grip tightened on my cheekbones, squeezing my skin. "And don't get any ideas. I know you and your sister are runners."

Rose had run? Where? I opened my mouth to ask, but he squeezed my jaw until I cried out, my eyes watering from the pain.

"What did I say?" he growled in my ear.

"Jacek, stop. You're going to bruise her."

His hold loosened, my skin still throbbing. "Open it, Caitlyn. Make sure it's not a trap."

Flustered, she dipped her head in a quick nod and opened the door a crack. "Yes? Can I help you?"

"Is this the home of Jacek Cotter?"

"It is."

"We are here on behalf of King Galon in reference to Mr. Cotter's request. I will need to verify her identity, and if her claims are true, then deliver her to His Majesty post haste. Is the young woman here presently?"

Caitlyn peeked over her shoulder at me, her lips pinched. She shuffled from foot to foot.

I tried to shake my head, willing her not to betray me further, but Jacek's grip held me in place.

"Madame?" the voice on the other side of the door asked.

"Caitlyn," Jacek whisper-screamed.

A gloved hand snaked through the opening to grip the edge of the door. "If you do not comply, I will be forced to search the premises. If I catch you hiding her, you'll have broken the king's decree and thereby forfeited your finder's fee."

"She's here," Caitlyn blurted, opening the door wider.

A tall man stood outside, a navy blue cloak draped over his shoulders, his face hidden in the shadows of the hood. Large pearls dotted the edges of the fabric, set in gold.

"Good choice," the man said, entering the house. He flicked back his hood when he saw me, stopping mid-step. "Is this her? Then release her immediately. She is a guest of the royal family and will not be mistreated."

Jacek let go so quickly that I stumbled forward, squeezing my pile of clothes to my chest as I fought for my balance.

"What is happening?" I asked, my eyes darting between the three of them. Caitlyn looked away, her ears pink. I turned to the stranger. "Who are you?"

"It doesn't matter who I am. What matters is if you are who you say you are. What is your name?"

I took a step back. Why should I tell this stranger anything? And why was he so concerned about my identity?

"If you run, it will prove your guilt, and I will have to resort to less chivalrous behavior. We do not take kindly to scammers. Please, just answer the question." He rested his hand on the hilt of his sword.

"I'm Marigold," I said with a shaky breath.

"They all say that. What is your family name?"

Why did I need to prove who I was? I rubbed my fingers over the gown's coarse fabric. "Bellmond."

He nodded. "Where are you from?"

I blinked, and then my nerves made me stutter. "Th-the kingdom of Cadell."

"Why are you not there?"

"I was abducted by thieves en route to my sister's wedding. They

159

burned the carriage . . . and the poor footman that was sent to collect me."

The stranger shifted toward me, his eyes narrowing. "Go on."

"Desmond said they made a mistake. They were supposed to grab my sister, Rose, who was going to marry Prince Alexander. When they found out I was not of any worth, they threw me into the Sea of Thieves."

"And you lived? Where have you been all this time?"

I pressed a finger to my choker. "Ryken saved me and has been protecting me ever since."

"Who might that be, my lady? A fisherman from Windcrest?"

Words failed me. The truth was more dangerous than lies.

"He's upstairs," Jacek informed him, arms crossed. "There's something not right about him. He's a wild man. I'd appreciate it if you took him with you too."

"It will have to be approved by King Galon. My orders are to escort the girl to safety."

Some of the tension released from my shoulders. *Finally, someone providing aid.*

"Are you going to help me get home to my family?" I asked.

"I'm only authorized to bring you to Windcrest. If King Galon decides it is best for you to return to Cadell, he will order me to do so."

"And if he doesn't?"

"Then he's doing it to keep you alive, my lady. The place you call home is not the same as when you last left it."

It was hard to believe magic had overtaken the kingdom. Was the Sorcerer fulfilling his prophecy? I shivered. "Honestly, I don't care about going back to Cadell. I'm just searching for my family to make sure they are all right after the new queen and king took over the castle."

He made a noise in the back of his throat and covered his mouth, thinking. He sent Jacek a look I didn't understand. He carefully chose his words. "I'll inform His Majesty of your request."

"Really?" Perhaps King Galon was a more kind-hearted, attentive monarch than King Baxton was. The latter wouldn't have given a care to any peasant's worries. "He would help me?"

"He is concerned for your safety. That's why I am here—to bring you under his protection. The problem is that many have impersonated you."

I frowned. "Pretend to be me? What is the point of that?"

"Everyone has a reason, but you are more valuable than you realize."

"Is it because the Queen of Hearts is looking for me?"

He cleared his throat. "It's one of the reasons. Glenton is searching for you too."

The kingdom hidden in the mountains? I had never stepped foot anywhere near Glenton's borders. How did they know of me—a farmer's daughter?

"What will they do with me?"

"I can't speak for the other kingdoms, but Windcrest is offering a safe haven. As long as you stay with us and wear our colors, we will provide for you."

"I'm not a prisoner?"

He smiled. "No, my lady."

"Then why was I being held at knifepoint?" I sent a scathing look to Jacek.

"Because of the bounty on your head. It makes some act with less-than-civil manners," the man spat, also sending Jacek a glare.

"*What?* People are paying to find me?"

"Everyone wants to find the lost sister. But I still have not verified that you are, in fact, her."

"And you would know me? I've never met you before in my life."

He laughed at that. "That is a point in your favor. It is true. We have never met before. But I have seen numerous drawings and sketches of you. Come closer so that I may see you better."

I shuffled forward obediently.

"May I?" he asked but didn't wait for my approval. With gentle fingers, he lifted my chin and turned my face left and right. "She has marks on her skin. That will be deducted from your fee. She was to be delivered unharmed." He touched my collar. "What is this?"

"Jewelry," I lied.

"Interesting that the thieves didn't take this when they threw you into the sea."

"Ryken gave it to me afterward."

The man stepped back and rubbed his chin. "Is this man from

another kingdom? Windcrest needs to be prepared if another territory is involved."

"He's a trader of sorts."

The stranger leaned down until we were eye to eye. "Why does that sound like a lie?"

I lifted my chin. "Why would I lie?"

"If either of you stole it, the king will send payment to the original owner. We want no discord or war over a trinket. Consider it a gift from the royal family."

"It already *was* a gift," I snapped back. My hands curled into fists. Now he thought me a thief?

He raised a brow at me and leaned back. Did I cross a line with my outburst? Would he still offer aid? He turned to Jacek and said, "I think she is lying, but she is the mirror image of the sketches I have of her. I will escort her in hopes that she will be more honest in the presence of the king."

Snapping his fingers, the stranger summoned another guard. He unloaded the items from my arms and exited the cottage.

"I'm not going anywhere without Ryken." I dug in my heels as the man pressed a hand on my back to guide me through the door.

"We can discuss it in the carriage." He gestured to a guard outside as if the matter was settled. "Come, we must make haste. The enemy approaches."

"I'm not moving until——"

The man snatched me up in one fluid movement, tossing me over his shoulder and marching out of the house. The world was upside down and a blur as he crunched down the pebble path. I kicked and wiggled, pounding my fist on his back. More men in chain mail with blue tunics lined the yard, waiting for us to approach.

When I realized my attempts to escape were futile, I screamed. *Please, let Ryken hear me and wake up,* I prayed.

"Door," he commanded over my wailing.

He climbed into the carriage and placed me carefully on the seat next to my clothes. I swung out at him as soon as I got my bearings, but he ducked just in time. "You'll thank me for saving you from that family. Money-hungry peasants. Who knows who they would have sold you to for a sack of crowns? Be happy it was King Galon. Mrs. Pretta, you have a task ahead of you."

I swung my fist again, but he was already climbing out the door.

A cough had me freezing in place, and I finally noticed there was another person in the carriage with me. A middle-aged woman scowled at me in distaste. Her silver hair was braided like a crown so tightly that it pulled her eyebrows up in a surprised expression. She wore a peach-colored gown, soft and sewn in a light cotton material. The neckline was high, showing her elite status, and covered in tiny sapphires.

She tsk-tsked. "Uncivilized, disheveled, unclean, and dreadfully poor manners—you have a lot to learn."

The door shut, jarring me from my seat in a panic, then the carriage jerked into motion, sending me off my feet and into the angry woman. Her top lip curled as she shoved me off her lap and onto the floor.

"Wait! Stop the carriage," I screamed. *Ryken . . .* we left without him. A frenzy overtook me. *"Stop!"*

"My word, what a ruckus you are making. Compose yourself, girl."

"There's been some mistake. Ryken is back there, I can't—I won't leave him behind. We need to turn the carriage around this instant."

The carriage jostled, sending me on my rear.

"I'm adding ungraceful and stubborn to the list. I'm not sure you're worth the journey."

"Then why fetch me in the first place?" I growled.

"I'm afraid it's not my call, but I'll give my findings to His Majesty."

Mrs. Pretta could blather on to whomever she liked—I wasn't planning on sticking around. I had to get back to Ryken. I leapt up to grab the handle of the door.

She clapped her hands together, a deafening sound.

"You ungrateful child. Sit on that bench. *Now.*"

My mouth dropped at the scolding, and I stumbled back into the seat despite myself. The old Marigold hadn't disappeared after all.

"Listen to me before you make a life-altering decision based on emotion. You are being offered a chance to rise above your station. You might not get another opportunity. And shut your mouth. You look like a fish."

My mouth clicked closed, my teeth rattling.

163

"Good girl. Obedient, I'll add that to your list." Apparently, my only good quality.

"What list? And why are you making one?"

"I'm here to groom you. You are to be surrounded by royalty, and you must look the part."

"I'm not royalty."

She looked down her nose at me with a haughty sniff. "I can tell. You will need a brand-new wardrobe and—*where are your shoes?* Oh, Sea of Providence, give me strength."

"You're not listening to me. My . . . friend is back at that house. I'm not going anywhere without him."

"You have a nice, commanding tone, but I dare say it's wasted on me. I have taught more royals than years you have been alive."

"I don't care what you think." I stood again on shaky feet, the carriage rocking beneath me. "I'm not staying."

Her dark eyes glittered with boredom. "Then leave and see what happens."

"You'll let me go?"

She pulled a cream-colored fan from the pocket of her gown. Flicking her wrist, she opened it in a dramatic snap. "I'm adding slow-witted to your list."

My face scrunched up, and I opened the carriage door, the landscape rolling by. I leaned out, staring at the caravan of soldiers leading and trailing the carriage. Way more soldiers than I expected. Why were there so many?

"Are they all for me?"

"Yes, and you're going to fall if you lean out any farther. Do you want to be trampled by horses?"

I shut the door, blinking in thought.

"Why does King Galon want me this much that he sent an army to fetch me?"

Mrs. Pretta stopped fanning herself, a thin smile on her dark-colored lips. "It's not you, so to speak. It's what you can do for him."

That made absolutely zero sense. What could I do? Sing? Sew?

"What does he want?"

"What all men want—money and power."

"Not all men want that . . ." I touched my collar.

164

Her back straightened. "From where did you steal that?"

My eyes snapped to hers. "I did not steal it. It was a gift from someone special."

Mrs. Pretta closed her fan against her open palm. "First lesson, leave the past behind you—especially men."

My heart twisted at her cold words.

"Never," I said, meaning it with everything inside of me. Forget Ryken? *Impossible.* It would be like forgetting how to breathe.

This woman wouldn't understand—I barely understood our connection. All I knew was that I had to find him, and nothing would be right until we were reunited again.

Then I opened the carriage door again and jumped.

A Ruse Gone Wrong

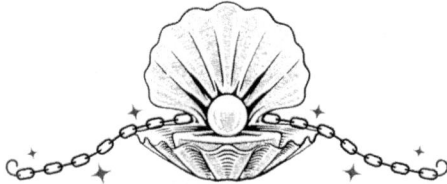

I hadn't thought this through at all.

One moment I was flying in the air, then the next my shoulder slammed into the ground, followed by a hollow-sounding thump when my head collided with a boulder. But I didn't stop there. Bouncing head over heels, I tumbled over and down a grassy hill, picking up momentum with each roll. Every rock, branch, and prickly bush jabbed into my flesh until I eventually crash-landed into the base of a tree.

My head spun, the clouds in the sky a whirlpool of swirling soft blues and amber from the rising sun. I couldn't focus on anything, and the constant spinning turned my stomach.

That might have been the stupidest thing I had ever done . . . I was lucky I hadn't been trampled by a horse like Mrs. Pretta had warned might happen.

A man approached, his chain mail jingling with each rushed step. "Did you just leap out of a moving carriage?"

I groaned. It was the man from before. *So much for a quick escape.*

"We were sent to protect you from attackers, but who is going to protect you from yourself? Is this a common thing for you?"

"It was a first for me . . . and probably a last." I sat up and hissed out a breath. To say everything hurt was an understatement. I tried to focus on what hurt the least and failed. A warm drop of liquid splattered on my arm, which instantly distracted me. Ruby in color, I squinted at it in confusion.

"You're bleeding," he said in shock.

"I am." Another droplet plopped on top of the first.

He sighed. "I'm going to pick you up now. Please don't scream again."

"But I don't want to go to Windcrest," I complained as he gently scooped me out of the weeds.

"I will pass your request to His Majesty when we get there."

With each step he took, my rebuttal rattled in my skull like pebbles in a boot. Squinting, I forgot what I had been talking about. Why was I being so difficult? That wasn't like me.

"All right," I agreed, feeling woozy. Another drop of blood dripped onto my ivory nightgown, the scarlet color seeping into the fabric in an almost floral shape, like a blooming red rose.

My thoughts turned to my sister and her red hair.

"My sister has beautiful red hair. I wish mine was red too."

"Uh. You don't look so well." He picked up his pace and jogged back up the hill, my arms flopping uselessly in the air. "I think you might have hit your head a little too——"

Tingles shot down my spine as bile burned its way up my throat, and I leaned away from him to vomit on the ground by his feet.

"I don't feel well," I said. The words slurred on my tongue and sounded like gibberish even to me.

"Mrs. Pretta," he cried out, alarmed.

A blurry guard opened the carriage door. He appeared to be sideways, standing on the carriage's side. *No, that's not right.* My head had lolled to the side and skewed my view. The guard stretched, forming an identical twin. They both stared at me in horror.

"Sir, that's . . . a lot of blood."

"Quiet, Sai. Mrs. Pretta!" the man holding me screamed again as he leapt through the doorway.

"I'm not deaf. There is no cause for you——" She inhaled sharply. "Oh my. Is she alive?"

At some point, my eyes had closed, but sounds and smells filled my mind as if I could see them. Their frantic heartbeats overlapped with each other, echoing off the walls of the small space and mapping the dimensions of the carriage in my mind. Their fear polluted the air, sending a prickle of warning down my spine.

"For all our sakes, she better be. Take her."

"No, she'll ruin my new gown——" She ended on a high-pitched squeal when he tossed me in her lap. "Wren, you wretched man."

I wished Ryken were here instead of these strange people tossing me back and forth. "Ryken will come for me," I warned them. "I hope he is wearing his water armor when he does, then you'll be sorry."

"Water armor?" Mrs. Pretta asked.

"She has been talking nonsense. Ignore her and hold on to this."

Riiip.

Something soft pressed against my hairline. Pain shot through my skull and my eyelids fluttered at the pressure.

Tired. I was so exhausted. Even my heartbeat had slowed to prepare for sleep.

"Keep consistent pressure on the wound."

"I am not a healer. Where are you going? Don't you dare leave me with her."

The carriage jostled, its one step creaking as Wren exited.

"Whatever you do, don't let her die," he said with a sense of finality. The door slammed so loudly that I whimpered.

"Oh, my lady. I don't . . . don't know what to do." Her hand trembled against my forehead.

I fought to stay conscious by listening to Mrs. Pretta's frantic breathing. Truth be told, I was terrified. Strange things happened to me whenever I fainted. My body transformed little by little, and I didn't want to be in the middle of Windcrest when my transformation completed.

I wanted Ryken to be there. Would he be excited? Would I be? Just thinking his name made my heart sputter. How far away was I now? At the daunting speed we were going, we had to be close to the castle.

My awareness gradually returned. My head still throbbed, but the fear of fainting had dissipated, and my stomach had stopped churning.

When the soft clopping of the horses' hooves on the road changed to clacking against stone, my suspicions were confirmed. We were already in town. But which quarter of Windcrest?

Memories of the beautiful kingdom appeared as if I summoned them. The white castle was more a work of art than a fortress. Its varying blue sea glass shimmered in the sunlight and was a beacon of welcome to ships returning from sea. It was the centerpiece of the kingdom, raised higher than the rest of the buildings, even higher than the tallest tower in Cadell. Though their towers weren't actual dwelling spaces but rather lookouts for the safety of the kingdom. Surrounding the castle was a freshwater moat full of silver trout and sharp-toothed zebra piranhas. Swimming wasn't recommended. The water from the moat poured in from a long river that traveled straight from the mountains of Glenton and flowed out to the Sea of Thieves. An arched bridge with fish carved into its mahogany beams provided the only path across the moat to the castle.

Outside the moat, the city was divided into quarters. The Breezeway quarter was home to the upper nobility if they didn't have lodging in the castle. Pit was the shadier quarter and was littered with gambling halls, black markets, beggars, and seedy residents with a different set of rules than the rest of Windcrest. King Galon kept that quarter heavily guarded.

The Halberts quarter was full of elegant shops and markets where most of the citizens did their shopping. My grandparents' clothing shop was in Halberts, the quarter between Pit and Breezeway, though they could only afford a location closer to the Pit side of the line. Rent doubled and tripled the closer you were to Breezeway.

The last quarter was the Mull quarter. It was where the average resident lived if they had escaped Pit but couldn't afford Breezeway.

Voices chattered from outside, the bustling of the town filtering through the carriage walls. Based on the noise and excitement, it sounded like we were in Halberts. Vendors shouted their deals of the day as we bumped down the cobblestone road. My grandparents were so close. Perhaps now would have been a better time to leap from the carriage.

I peeked through my eyelashes to see Mrs. Pretta worrying her lower lip, her eyes glazed in thought. She held me in place with one hand, and with the other, she pressed a red cloth to my forehead. The navy curtains were closed, darkening the interior of the carriage.

Why was Windcrest so desperate to bring me here?

Nobody ever gave straight answers when I asked. Sometimes silence was the best tactic. I quickly shut my eyes and held my body still so she wouldn't notice I was awake.

Spying was easy. I had plenty of practice when traveling with Des and Fitz.

The carriage stopped abruptly, but Mrs. Pretta's steel grip held me in place so I didn't jostle.

"My lady?" she asked, her voice high. "I beg of you, please, do not depart this world on my lap."

Some part of me almost wished I could just to torment her.

The door opened, and a pair of strong hands lifted me up, cradling me to his chain mail. His musky scent was the same as before. What had Mrs. Pretta called him? Wren? Maybe these new instincts were more useful than I thought.

Wren shifted me higher, and I let my head droop to the side for the full effect.

"Be more careful, Wren. She's a delicate thing."

I bit my tongue to keep my opinion to myself.

"Delicate?" He grunted. "She jumped out of a moving carriage and survived. She just needs to hold still long enough for her wound to heal shut."

"I think it has, but I kept pressure on it anyway. I wiped away some of the mess, but there is nothing to do about the stain on my gown." She sighed.

"Just buy a new one."

After covering my body with fabric—a blanket?—we were on the move again, faster now. He held me snug to his chest so my loose limbs didn't flop.

"Why are we at the servants' entrance?" Mrs. Pretta asked.

"Nobody can see her like this."

"Yes, I didn't consider that. They'll assume we have harmed her on purpose."

"Exactly. Remind me how this happened. You told her she could leave?"

"Well . . . I didn't think the ninny would actually jump."

I gritted my teeth under the fabric.

"Careful how you speak, madame. If word about this travels back to the royal family, you could be on the streets in Pit."

She grumbled something unintelligible as we climbed a flight of stairs.

"Do you think she does magic?"

"I don't know. I hope not."

"Wouldn't that be a good thing? She could protect us."

"But for how long? When she finds out the truth——"

"What are you two doing whispering in the halls?" An authoritative voice joined the conversation, startling me. His Windcrest accent was thick, the r's rolling longer than necessary.

"Your Highness," they both exclaimed. Wren's arms turned ridged, almost crushing me to him.

Oh, goodness. A royal?

"What do you have there, Wren?" Footsteps tapped closer. "Or should I ask, *whom* do you have there?"

"A lady King Galon requested me—I mean us—to escort to the castle. I'm to put her in the Peacock Room, Your Highness."

Wren shifted to move, but a hand pressed against my side, halting him.

"Just one moment. Please remove the cloak. I have a right to know who she is just as much as my father does."

"As you wish, Your Highness." Wren sighed just before cool air brushed across my face.

My heartbeat thudded in my ears as I held as still as possible. Even one flinch would be a giveaway that I was awake and alert.

"It's her," the prince whispered with a mix of surprise and despair.

"We believe so. Her likeness is uncanny, but her story doesn't add up. She might not have felt comfortable speaking with servants, Your Highness."

"She is smaller than I anticipated," the prince said, distracted. "What's your impression of her, Wren?"

Mrs. Pretta cleared her throat. "I've spent the most time with her, so I would be the best person to answer that question. I have already started a composition of her traits, including problem areas that will need to be smoothed out. I could say the same of your social manners, Prince Vian. I know I taught you better. Perhaps you should sit in on her lessons."

Someone chuckled.

"Mrs. Pretta, it's been ages since I was in your schoolroom, and with just one scolding, I feel ten years younger again. I have missed our verbal spars. But you are absolutely correct about my ill manners. My sincerest apologies that I didn't greet you sooner. Might I add that you look lovely as ever? Is that a new gown?"

"Your charms do not work on me, Prince Vian."

"Admit it, you always liked me best. My brother is a bore, and my sister made you want to leap into the sea."

"I will admit no such thing. I have no favorites."

"*Ha!* Your secret is safe with me. Now tell me, what do you think of your new pupil?"

"She'll be a challenge. One of the most stubborn I've ever seen. But she won't bore you, though I do have some concerns about her memory."

His teasing tone dropped, suddenly turning serious. "Was she cursed as well?"

Cursed?! Who was cursed?

"No, she knows who she is, but——"

"Your Highness, might I suggest we discuss this in a more private location than in the castle corridors?" Wren cut in.

"Oh. Yes, yes. That is wise. We wouldn't want rumors to spread. Where is she staying? The Peacock Room? That's next to Vella's chamber," the prince said.

"The king had hopes that a new friend would be just what Princess Vella needed."

"My sister has been through enough. I wish he'd just leave her be. She's coping the only way she knows how," the prince snapped.

"Of course, Your Highness. I didn't mean to upset you."

"Agh, sorry, Wren. I shouldn't have taken my frustration out on you. You know Vella is special to me. Father can do what he wishes to my life, but Vella needs consistency."

"You don't have to apologize to me," Wren humbly replied.

"Don't you go undoing all my hard work. Prince or not, we should always pride ourselves on not letting emotion get the best of us. Well done, Prince Vian."

"Thank you, Mrs. Pretta. I told you I was your favorite," the prince joked.

Mrs. Pretta giggled. *Giggled.* My eyelashes may have fluttered in my attempt not to roll them.

We continued down the hall as they talked of less interesting topics. The friendly manner between prince and servant was . . . unexpected. Prince Alexander would order his guards or servants about whenever I saw him on market day. And nobody would *dare* scold him as Mrs. Pretta had just done to Prince Vian.

My neck ached as much as my head at this point. It had been in this awkward angle for hours. But the pain was worth it. People were keeping secrets from me? Curses, memory loss, and who knew what else. I wished Wren hadn't interrupted Mrs. Pretta about my memory. What could I be forgetting? There were no gaps. Unless, perhaps when I was abducted? Maybe it was a week more? Or a week less? Then I fell into the sea and met Ryken.

Oh, Ryken. How would I get back to him? I'd have to formulate a plan as soon as I "woke" from this ruse.

I sighed.

"Did you hear that?" Prince Vian asked, sounding unnecessarily close. "Was that her?"

"I heard nothing, Your Highness," Wren said.

"She makes little noises here and there. It reassures me that she's still alive. She had me worried a few times," Mrs. Pretta said.

"Hmm. How long ago did you say she fainted?"

"Hours, I believe," Mrs. Pretta added thoughtfully.

"She seems well besides the nasty knot on her head. Her cheeks are pink, and her complexion appears normal."

"She looks a little grayish to me," Mrs. Pretta said with a click of her tongue. "Very odd indeed."

Gray?! I was most definitely not gray.

"She's from Cadell. All their people are pale," Wren pointed out. He shrugged, my body jiggling from his gesture.

When something touched my cheek, I stopped breathing. Everything inside of me screamed to pull away from the stranger's touch.

"She feels fine," the prince said, sounding as if he were puzzling over a great mystery. His fingers brushed across my cheekbone one more time before he pulled them away. "Wren, if there is something wrong with her, I demand to be informed about it. Don't leave me in the dark again."

"As you command, Your Highness. There was a little . . . accident on our journey here."

"I presumed something had happened for her to be covered in scratches with blood splattered on her collar. I hope in my father's zeal to find her, you remembered she was to be retrieved unharmed."

"We took great care, Your Highness. It was an eventful journey back from Amille."

We turned right and entered a room full of floral sweetness carried on a fresh sea breeze. While Wren explained why I had blood on my nightgown and why I was wearing a nightgown in the first place, I tried to use my new instincts to "see" the room, but the sound of pouring water scrambled my senses.

Carefully, Wren laid me down on the softest bed ever created. I sank into a cloud of feathers. I forced my hands to remain motionless, even as they itched to caress the silky texture of the sheets. The weight of his cloak remained, covering me neck to toes.

"Should you wash her face? And change her into a clean gown? She's still crusted in blood," the prince suggested, clearly revolted.

I stiffened. *They better not.*

"I can summon a maid, Your Highness. This is a trivial matter you shouldn't concern yourself with. I will wait with her," Mrs. Pretta said.

"Oh, my deepest apologies again, Mrs. Pretta, but I forgot to tell you that my mother requested you return to her side as soon as you stepped foot through the castle doors. She could barely stand one day without her favorite companion."

She sputtered. "Oh, dear, I can't keep Her Majesty waiting. Spit-spat. Both of you, get out now. No male visitors without my watchful eye."

Footsteps echoed away from me.

"Wren?" the prince asked.

"Yes, Your Highness?"

"Schedule a meeting with my family so we can discuss your findings about our newest . . . guest."

"Including the princess?"

"Did I not say family? Yes, Vella too. We all need to be aware of what kind of person is living down the hall from us. Do we even know where her loyalties lie?" He whispered the last question, but I could still hear it despite the gushing water.

"She said all she wants is to find her family."

"Her sister too?"

I clung to the sheet to keep from snapping upward.

"She is confused, even before she banged her head. Did you want me to discuss it now or at the meeting?"

I'm confused? Me? I pinched my lips at the insult.

The prince made a noise in the back of his throat. "I can be patient. Let's wait until we are all together. Wren, I believe Vella is in the library, but I need to grab something from my chambers first. Then I'll meet you at the Lagoon. Mrs. Pretta, would you inform Mother of our special guest's arrival?"

"I shall, Your Highness. She will love to hear how a young woman jumped from a moving carriage."

I might have let a groan slip.

"*What?* I thought she fell out. She jumped? Is she mad?" The prince's voice rose, cracking with fear.

"Worse. She's stubborn, and stubborn people make poor decisions to prove their point." Mrs. Pretta clucked her tongue. "Now, I mean it. Out with you both. I've made the queen wait long enough."

Fabric rustled as they talked, the voices quieting as they moved farther away.

I waited, straining to hear their trailing footsteps over the gushing water nearby. The desire to know what was causing that noise was eating me up inside. Was it a waterfall? Inside the bedroom?

And why was this called the Peacock Room? I was going to scream if there were live birds in here. I didn't like birds. Not one bit. Loud, squawky things.

But I remained strong, in control of myself. To err on the side of caution, I counted to fifty before I opened my eyes. There wasn't even time for me to sit up before a voice thundered.

"*Ah-ha!* I knew you were faking," the prince accused, storming across the room to me.

Secrets Are the Currency

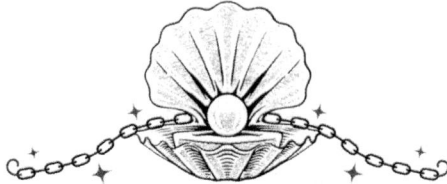

Prince Vian's presence alone exuded enough authority that I froze as he approached.

He was just as I remembered him. Not that we had officially met face-to-face. The royal family was known for venturing out into the shops of the Halberts quarter. I had often noticed him walk past our clothing shop, usually with a female noble hanging off his arm. His skin was dark and glossy, the light from the stained glass windows highlighting it in sapphire. His attire was far from princely, at least compared to the tassels and frills of Prince Alexander's garments. Prince Vian wore a cotton tunic, the high collar trimmed in gold. It was tucked into a pair of brown leather pants, stopping at his ankles, the quality of the material worth more than three months of food for my family. His sandals slapped the back of his feet and mimicked the rapid beats of my heart.

Why was I staring? *Move!*

"Stay back," I demanded as I tried to scramble off the bed. My limbs caught in the soft clutches of the mattress, so I rolled off the bed to get to my feet. "Don't come any closer."

The prince ignored me. His dark eyes narrowed as he quickened his pace. "Who are *you* to give me orders?"

He had a point. What was I thinking expecting a prince to obey my command?

Overcome with dizziness, I stumbled. My vision distorted as I gained my footing. The bump on my head throbbed, but I ran despite the pain.

"Imposter," he said, the word sounding like a curse. "Why are you here?"

Water poured behind a curtain on the wall, the distracting gushing noise I had heard earlier. The clear water landed in a small pool surrounded by rocks and a large bronze peacock statue.

Thank goodness it's not a real bird.

As if it called to me, I raced to the pool. Closer now, the sheer curtain covered an open window that overlooked the moat and beyond, all the way to the bridge leading out of the kingdom. I jumped in with a splash, thankful that the water stopped at chest level. Even half submerged, my skin was singing with joy at the familiar contact.

"You're going to make me chase you into the water?" he asked incredulously.

Ignoring him, I kept my eye on the opening, paddling in desperation.

"Stop, Marigold—if that's even your real name."

Water poured in from outside, over the ledge and down the green tiles to the pool I floated in. I grabbed the ledge just as water splashed behind me, followed by grumbling. The weight of my water-logged dress had me sliding against the tile, too slippery to gain my footing before the prince snatched me back into his arms.

I fought against his hold, frantically reaching for the opening as I tried to dislodge his hands from around me. He spun me to face him, but his fury melted into pity the longer he looked at me. Yet he still kept both my wrists in his iron grip.

"Whoa, hey," he said, some of the anger sizzling out.

A wildness surged through me as I refused to be held captive again. A cry escaped my lips, and I realized that the water streaming down my face wasn't from the pool but was my tears as another sob shook my shoulders. I would not give up.

"I'm not going to hurt you. Be still before you start bleeding again."

My eyes snapped to his. "I will never stop fighting you. Your servant threw me in your carriage and took me from . . . someone special. I need to get back to him."

He froze. His dark eyes slowly traveled across my face, trying to understand. "Took you?"

"You think I like traveling in my nightgown? Of course someone took me." My eyes flicked up to his circlet. His short, frosty-colored hair curled around the golden circlet that wrapped around his head. It was plain in style, like a beaded rope dipped in gold. A reminder of his authority and position. I quickly added, "Your Highness."

"That's a nightgown? I thought it was a frumpy frock." He shifted me away from, still keeping his hands at my wrists. "You promise not to attack me if I release you? I won't hurt you."

"If you release me, I promise not to scream."

He chuckled, a deep rattle in his chest. "My lady, I wouldn't scream unless you have plans of becoming a princess. What do you think people will see when they come bursting into your room?"

"Their prince holding me against my will," I spat.

He rolled his eyes. "No. They will see two people embracing in the bath. So unless you plan to be my wife, I suggest keeping your voice down."

Annoyed, I wanted to smack the smirk right off his face. "I do not want to marry you, Your Highness."

"Am I that terrible to look at? I've been told on numerous occasions——"

"Prince Vian, you forget I lived in Windcrest for months. You may not know me, but I know you. You don't want a wife or anything that would tie you down. Your charming ways are whispered about all the way to Cadell."

"Really? All the way to Cadell? That's impressive." He nodded with a grin. "What else do they say?"

"That isn't something to be proud of," I said flatly. This wasn't where I expected the conversation to be heading.

"Are you curious about the Prince of Windcrest? You only had to ask. There is no reason for you to sneak into the castle to steal a moment with me. I have had many adoring ladies send me notes, flowers, and um, personal items, but breaking into the castle is a new feat. I should congratulate you on your cunning and skill. What would you like as a prize?" His eyebrows wiggled.

My mouth hung open. "I'd like you to release me."

"Not a kiss?"

"Absolutely not a kiss. In fact, I'd like you to remove your hands from me, Your Highness."

He tilted his head, eyeing me like a strange creature. "I was restraining you from hurting yourself."

"I only wish to leave."

"And you may—at any time. But not through the moat. You should know about the fish that reside there. There used to be silver trout, but they were gobbled up by all the zebra piranhas. Insatiable beasts. They'd tear into you, too, if we didn't have a net up around the castle."

I turned to glance out the opening. The tranquil waters appeared inviting, perfect for cooling off on this hot summer day.

"Deceiving, isn't it? Just like you."

I stiffened. "I have not lied, Your Highness."

"Ah, but you should know, secrets are a currency in the castle. I sense you are not being as honest as you say. And you were pretending to sleep—why?"

"Because I wanted to leave, but whenever I ask, nobody would let me go."

Abruptly, he did just that, wading backward in the water. "Then go."

The door to the room clicked open a crack, and the prince shot an arm out to tuck me behind him.

"Vian? I thought I heard your voice. Why are you in here . . . and in the bath?" A soft lilt of a female voice echoed in the chamber. "Where is the girl?"

"Well, this is unfortunate," he mumbled to himself. "She is here, Mother."

Heat flooded my cheeks, and I wondered if escaping through the moat would be less painful than the tingles of mortification racing through me.

"Where? Her bed is empty," the queen said.

"Before you get upset—can I explain first?" he asked, fidgeting.

"What could you possibly need to explain?"

The prince took a sudden step to the side, revealing my presence.

The queen placed a hand to her chest. "*Vian.* She only arrived moments ago. Even for you, this is extreme."

"She was trying to climb out the bath window."

"You expect me to believe that nonsense?" Her spine stiffened as she transformed into her regal stance, her hands clasped at her waist. Her skin was a shade darker than the prince's and contrasted with her neatly braided white hair that wrapped around her golden tiara. The navy blue gown accentuated her curves and flared out at her calves. The hem barely covered her ankles, displaying her golden sandals dotted with pearls.

I bowed my head, feeling inadequate in my wet rags. "It's true, Your Majesty."

Prince Vian pointed to me, nodding dramatically. "See. I'm completely innocent here. Perhaps even heroic."

I turned to him, aghast. "Most definitely not heroic."

He tapped his bottom lip. "It depends on your viewpoint. I think——"

"Mother? Are you in here with Vian?" A younger version of the queen snuck through the crack of the door and shut it behind her. "I thought we were meeting in the Lagoon. Did I mishear?"

Prince Vian groaned, covering his face.

"Vian," the young woman squealed with delight. "You're in the bath . . . with . . . " Her face split into a smile, and she doubled over laughing. "You work fast, brother."

Heat crept up my neck, and I ducked my head.

"You have eyes, my dear Vella. You can obviously see we are clothed."

I swam away from him and cleared my throat. "Excuse me, Your Majesty. May I please say something?"

"Please do. I'd love to get to the bottom of this."

"When I awoke, Prince Vian was already inside this room, and he——"

The queen raised her hand, demanding silence. Even standing in the middle of the bedroom, her demeanor was fit for the throne room. "Vian, were you watching her sleep?"

Bouncing in place, the prince squirmed under his mother's glare, the water rippling around him. He sent me a traitorous look before he replied. "She was already awake when she arrived at the castle. She entered on false pretenses so she could eavesdrop for Cadell."

I sputtered at his implication. "A *spy*? Why would I help the kingdom that turned on their own princess—my own sister? I want nothing to do with your war or with Cadell. Can you blame me for wanting to be as cautious as possible?"

It was as if someone sucked the air from the room. All eyes landed on me, and I questioned if a third eye had suddenly grown on my forehead.

"Interesting . . . " Princess Vella took a teal peacock feather from a glass vase on the table and fanned herself with it. "How will we be able to tell she is who she says she is?"

"My grandparents," I shouted, then flinched at how loud my voice was, even to myself. I continued at a lower octave. "My grandparents could easily identify me. Could we go visit their shop?"

"I think that's an excellent idea," the queen said, tilting her head with practiced grace so that her golden crown twinkled. "Vian, can you escort our guest to Halberts?"

"Right now, Mother? She may not be honest about her identity, but the lump on her head is real."

A small smile pulled at the queen's lips. "Yes, how thoughtful of you. What do you suggest?"

"Tomorrow? After she has rested?"

"That's a splendid idea. I'll inform the guards of the outing."

"May I go too, Mother?" the princess asked, her eyes desperate.

"Not this time, my dear."

"Afraid I'll make a scene again?" The princess whipped the peacock feather through the air. "I have books to read in the library anyway. Tell Wren not to disturb me for the rest of the evening."

"What about dinner? Cook is making your favorite—quail stew."

"I'm not hungry, nor do I care for the company." She spun on her heel and marched to the door to swing it wide. She sent me a sharp look over her shoulder. "I believe you are who you say you are. Sometimes my family has a way of believing the worst of someone without giving them an opportunity to prove differently."

I couldn't get a word in before she dashed out of the room, leaving the rest of us in silence.

"Do you have to be so strict on her, Mother?" the prince complained, stomping out of the bath. Water dripped off his clothes and pooled at his feet. "Nobody is hurting more than her."

"We are all hurting, my young prince. But some of us refuse to let the cracks of our armor show," the queen responded, her words like ice. She opened the door and lifted a white brow. "There are plenty of rumors spreading about our family, and we don't need to add another to the list."

The prince turned to me, frowning. "Like I said before, nobody is holding you against your will. Leave. I was only trying to help." His sandals squished with each stomp toward the door.

As he passed the queen to leave, she issued one final command. "I expect to see you in the Lagoon shortly in a more appropriate wardrobe. Do I make myself clear?"

"Always, Mother."

"If you will excuse us, my lady. I'm sure you are weary and need time to recover from your travels. Welcome to Windcrest." She dipped her head a fraction and followed her son out the door.

Alone, I peeked through the curtain to the city streets on the other side of the moat. If I could swim, perhaps I could make it across. But even unbound I couldn't do more than tread water to keep my head afloat.

Frustrated, I was ready to put this place behind me, but maybe the prince had a point. If the Queen of Hearts was after me, maybe I needed something to protect myself.

I sank beneath the cool water, the feel of it comforting. I wanted to be a child again at the bottom of the pond and let the peaceful noises of the water calm me. But this ache in my chest would never ease until I knew Ryken was safe.

Where was he? I needed him more than ever.

The wet fabric twisted around my body, constraining as much as the rope had. I pulled at the neckline, wishing I could tear the weight of it away.

The stress of everything bubbled up inside of me, and I opened my mouth, a scream tearing through me that sent bubbles scurrying about.

The long note morphed, dropping from its high-pitched wail into the usual pattern of my song. My thoughts turned to Ryken, and I wondered if he could hear me even miles away. Though I was doubtful, a small light of hope had me singing a few moments longer. *Hear my song and return to me,* I begged.

Eventually my screams turned into sobs. I sank to the bottom of the bath and curled into a ball, wishing that something would go right for me. It seemed like I made mistake after mistake after mistake. Was I supposed to leave? Was I supposed to stay? The fear of making a poor choice had me at a standstill.

Are you lost again, my child?

My eyes flew open, and a trail of bubbles poured from my mouth to float to the surface.

Ruah? How did you find me? I perked up, rolling to my knees.

Find you? I never left. You never asked for me.

I blinked. *I didn't know I could. I don't know what to do. Guide me, please.*

There was a long pause. The water swished around me as I spun in a circle, hoping for a clue as to Ruah's true identity.

Go find the princess.

Princess Vella? Why?

I waited for an answer, but none came. I guessed that was the only clue I was going to get.

Breaking through the surface, I scanned the room, but I was still alone. Or was I? Just because Ruah didn't speak didn't mean they weren't there. I didn't need to see a person to know they existed.

Didn't Caitlyn say Ruah was an old childhood story? Could it have been recorded in a book . . . ? *Books!* Princess Vella was in the library.

But I couldn't walk down the halls looking like a drowned rat.

I searched the room, hoping for spare clothes from previous guests. The statue wasn't the only peacock thing I noticed. Feathers lined the headboard, teals and grays, fanning out like the tail feathers of the majestic bird.

Next to the bed were two doors with a double wardrobe built into the wall. A strange contraption like a door that led to a tiny room just for clothes. The first door I opened contained a variety of male garments, sewn of materials we would carry at our shop but none that I'd ever been so lucky enough to wear.

I closed the door and tried the next.

Brightly colored dresses hung in a line. I settled on a cheerful yellow with starfish stitched down the sleeves. I found the undergarments in the drawers of the dresser beside the bed, more blues and trimmed in lace. After dressing, I slipped on a pair of sandals that were a size too big and rushed out the door, nearly slamming into a female guard.

Her brown hair was pulled up high into a ponytail, the ends braided into multiple strands that swayed back and forth when she jerked away from me. Still stunned at the thought of a female guard, I mentally applauded Windcrest for their modern approach. It would be unheard of in Cadell.

"My lady?"

"Marigold, please."

We stared at each other as if she expected something more from me.

"Who are you?" I finally asked.

"Trista, my lady. Prince Vian requested I assist you should you need it. Do you need it?"

"I suppose I do. Do you know where the library is?"

"Yes. Would you like me to escort you? You can't stay long. Dinner is exactly at six."

"I'll be quick."

She nodded, her braids swinging as she pivoted right. I followed behind her, moving down the wide hallway. Similar to the outside of the castle, the walls were made of tabby, a mixture of crushed shells. I found myself tracing bigger shells that protruded from the wall.

Cold air brushed against my legs, the openness of the dress a style I wasn't accustomed to. I may have made outfits from similar materials, but it was always in the floor-length style of Cadell. This dress floated about my ankles, drifting upward with the most subtle of movements. If I hadn't spent days in the water with Ryken trying to keep my dress from going above my head, then I probably would have been more self-conscious than I was.

We took a set of tiled stairs downward, the bright and colorful light from the stained glass windows now replaced with sconces similar to the ones that lined the outside of the castle.

184

Trista stopped and gestured at the door. "Through here, my lady. I'll wait for you outside."

"Oh, you don't have to wait."

"I don't have a choice. It's a direct order, my lady."

"Do you have any other orders? About me?"

"To make sure you arrive to dinner on time."

An odd request. "I will."

My attention turned back to the double doors and I pushed them open, entering the darkened library. A musty smell of books and ink filled the room, the smell of animal hide from the leathers strong enough that I could guess which animal each was made from. I grimaced. I wished I could turn off these new abilities until I needed them.

"Hello?" I called out, noticing a candle on the table at the end of the room. At the sound of my voice, the princess's head popped up from behind a stack of books, her eyes wide.

"Oh. It's you. Come in," Princess Vella murmured as she flipped a page.

Dark shelves lined the walls with row upon row of tomes so heavy that each shelf sagged. Not just along the walls, the bookshelves crowded the middle of the room too. Rows of them that twisted and turned. It reminded me of a hedge maze but with bookshelves. *Could someone get lost in here?*

"Did my brother send you?"

"No, I came on my own. I hope that's all right, Your Highness."

She shrugged. "They know better than to bother me here. Are you looking for a book?"

"Yes, I had hoped you had something about Ruah?"

She squinted. "Ruah?" Her accent held the *r* a little too long as she thought. "Do you have more information?"

"Centuries-old childhood story?"

"Folktales are down this aisle and then two lefts. I'm busy right now," she said with formal finality, ending the conversation.

I wandered for a bit, not finding the right section nor the book I was looking for. But I did find something else of interest in the folktales section—a book about mermen.

I brought it back to the table and sat next to her.

185

She peeked over the books at me. "Can you read it?"

"I can. Prince Alexander taught me."

"I met him once, and once was enough. If I were your sister, I would have run too."

"Run? From the queen?" I rubbed my temple. Why did everything sound like a riddle?

"What are you talking about? And people say I'm the crazy one." The princess rolled her eyes and ducked back behind the books.

"Wait! Please, can you explain what's going on? I feel like everyone is keeping secrets from me."

"You know what they say: secrets are the currency. If you want to know something, you have to pay the price." She lifted a brow, her almond-shaped eyes piercing me with a knowing look.

"I don't have anything. Even the clothes I'm wearing are borrowed."

"We don't care about clothes. Take whatever you want in the guest suites." She shrugged as if thousands of crowns' worth of garments meant nothing. "What I'm more interested in is that."

She pointed to my neck. No, not my neck. My collar.

"Give me that and then we'll talk."

I couldn't give it to her even if I wanted to, but she didn't need to know that. We could both play this bartering game. "How do I even know you have information to give?"

She smirked. "A lot has happened since you went missing a year ago."

The blood drained from my face. "Did you just say a *year*?"

Troublemaker

I missed a whole *year*? How was that possible?

The princess barked a laugh at my confusion, relishing in my discomfort.

"You are jesting," I said. She had to be.

"My brother and I enjoy a good laugh. Not Vox, he's too stuffy for games. And Verona . . ." She swallowed the rest of her sentence.

How could I focus on her ramblings when my world had twisted upside down? My fingers clutched at the leather-bound book, the letters on the cover blurring together.

Lie, it had to be a lie.

I shot to my feet, the chair scraping noisily against the tile. "I don't believe you. What was I thinking? That someone would actually be honest when I ask them a question?"

Spinning to the exit, I clutched the book to my chest while my mind still reeled from the princess's words. What if she was right? What had I missed? Rose's sickly face drifted into my vision.

"Marigold, wait."

Was Ruah wrong? What was the point of coming here and talking to her? It was a complete waste of time. I didn't need to be escorted to my grandparents' shop. I knew where it was, and my skull barely ached anymore. Prince Vian said I could leave anytime, and right now seemed perfect enough.

"Where are you going?" Princess Vella asked, jogging to catch up to me before I reached the door. Her lilac gown swished around her hips as if it were a size too big.

"I'm going to my grandparents'. I have no idea why I'm even here in the first place."

Her dark eyes flicked across my face. "You're serious, aren't you?"

"I'm exhausted from trying to convince people of who I am and the choices I make. I'm not from Windcrest, and you aren't my princess."

"I thought you weren't loyal to Cadell. It sounds like you are."

"I don't belong to Cadell either." A sudden gust blew between us, startling us apart. We glanced around for the source of the wind. But I knew as soon as I caught the briny whiff, the sea smell strong enough to overpower the dank odor of the library, who was sending me a message: Ruah.

I belong to the sea.

"That was . . . odd. I've never noticed a draft down here before," the princess said, still glancing around. "Did you feel that? It was like standing by the surf."

"Why should I answer any of your questions when you don't answer mine?" I turned away, my eyes widening at my curt response. First, I snapped at Prince Vian, and now Princess Vella? Before my abduction, I would never have spoken unkindly to anyone. And of all people, to a princess. She had the power to throw me in the dungeon if she thought it.

With each breath, my blood burned through my veins, spreading through me at lightning speed. It tingled with unfamiliarity, a boldness I didn't understand. As my muscles tensed, a calming sense of strength poured into me. I didn't feel obedient . . . nor did I want to be.

My lashes fluttered with recognition of an emotion I had always envied in my sister—*courage.*

I met the princess's stare over my shoulder.

"All I'm asking for is the truth, Your Highness."

"Sometimes the truth is right in front of you. It's just so obvious that you miss it."

I rolled my eyes at her meaningless response. "Put yourself in my

188

place. I only wish to find my sister, and the only things people tell me are lies and riddles. Why won't you help me?"

"I can't." She held out her palms like they were a scale. "My father is afraid you'll make the wrong choice and upset the balance of the upcoming war. Everything is teetering in place, and your choice will sway the victory." She dropped her right palm dramatically.

"But I'm a peasant who sews ballgowns and picks apples. My decision affects nobody but myself."

"I know you don't consider yourself royalty, but your sister's royal status has elevated yours. You are a lady. Fight it as much as you want, it doesn't change the facts."

"How could one lady tip the scales?"

She glanced around the library before continuing in a whisper. "Only you can control the Queen of Hearts. Now, let us speak of something else before my father finds out I've said anything."

Control her? How could I control a stranger? Blinking, I digested this new bit of information. Was it my connection to Ruah? Or my transformation into a mermaid?

I swallowed. Had Princess Vella learned of my song? Did she think I could control people with it?

"How is he going to stop her?"

She shrugged. "I'm the last person my father would share his plans with. I only hear the reports. The Queen of Hearts is as desperate to find you as you are to find your sister."

"But why is she looking for me?"

"I'm not answering any more questions," she stated, crossing her arms.

"Can you at least tell me who she is? What territory did she come from? There were no Enchanters in Cadell before I left—well, besides the Sorcerer hiding in Mistbrooke Forest. If the kingdom of Mistbrooke has resurrected, what's to say she isn't from Bressal? They are known for their magical illusions and disguises."

The princess squeezed her eyes closed. "I can't imagine a more terrible possibility. We'd all be doomed." She shivered. "Let us speak of something else. Do you play chess? Vox beats me constantly, and I don't think I can handle him flaunting another victory in my face. I miss having someone friendly to play with."

But I couldn't let the subject go. Not when I was so close to the truth. She had to know more.

"Before, you said my sister ran. Who was she running from? The Queen of Hearts?"

Her jaw dropped. "That was a real question? How hard did you bang your head? Wren told me you jumped from a moving carriage."

"Of course it was a real question," I grumbled.

"Then you aren't as smart as I thought you were."

I gaped at her.

"Back to my question about chess. Do you play? My father purchased a special set made with onyx and pearl from one of the sea traders. It's a stunning piece."

"I'm sorry, but do you really think I would stay and play chess with you after you insulted me?"

"I answered your questions. What more do you want from me?"

"Compassion? A friend?"

After a minute of her blank stare, I shook my head and turned toward the door.

"Don't leave. I didn't mean to upset you. I don't . . . have a lot of interaction with people. I know I can come off as rude. Please, let me try again." She glanced down, her eyes on the book clutched in my hand. "What are you reading?"

"Just a book I thought was interesting." My arms tightened around it, squashing it against my chest.

"I've read most of these books. I've probably spent more time here than with the rest of my family." A shy smile pulled at her mouth, the first genuine expression I had seen her make. "I had hoped you'd stay longer."

"I think it's best if I left. I don't belong here."

Princess Vella sighed. "Sometimes I feel the same. Things haven't been the same since——" Her voice cracked, and she pinched her trembling lips closed.

Everyone had their ghosts. "You don't have to talk about it."

She sniffed and stepped back from me. "Sorry . . . I don't know what came over me. I have a special gift of ruining conversations."

"You——" I started, but Trista stuck her head through the opening.

"It's time to leave, my lady. Will you be joining us, Your Highness?"

Trista asked. She pushed the door open with one hand so I could exit.

The princess glanced at me, fidgeting. "I think I am a bit hungry, and I do love quail stew," she admitted.

"I am honored to escort you both, Your Highness."

"Give us one moment," Princess Vella said, angling her head gracefully. She lacked any adornment of a crown or circlet, nothing that would have told me she was royal besides her family's similarity. "Leave the book in the library. The cool air down here keeps the pages from curling. The woes of living in such a hot and humid environment."

She held out her hand, and I resisted, just for a heartbeat, giving back the book. I stared down at the worn cover as if I were giving up Ryken himself.

I can't.

"We can come back after dinner. I feel the same way about books. It's hard to put them down."

A book. That's all this was—an object with no heartbeat. It didn't have turquoise eyes that made my heart flutter, or a smile that I dreamed about at night. I could give this to her.

Gently, she tugged it from my grasp, my fingers still reluctant to let go.

"There is no rush for you to leave the castle. You can come back after dinner and read about——" she glanced at the cover "——mermen. *Mermen?*" Her eyes jumped to mine.

"Yes, I find the Merfolk fascinating." My voice took on a dreamlike tone, and I tried to cover it up with a cough.

The princess placed the book on the table and returned to my side, observing me. "Me too. I'd love to hear your thoughts on these mystical creatures. Do you think they are real like everyone says?"

We walked from the library, and I used our climb up the stairs to stall for extra time. "Yes, but doesn't everyone in Windcrest?"

"I guess we do. There are a few more books like this one in the library. After dinner, I can show them to you. By the time you finish reading them, you'll feel like you've visited Alara yourself."

"I don't think I should stay for dinner. Wait—who's Alara?"

She looped her arm through mine. "It's not a who, but a where— the kingdom of the Merfolk. It's true what they say. Alara is full of treasures they've collected. A kingdom of pure gold."

I opened my mouth to say that Ryken had never mentioned it, but I quickly shut it before I revealed too much. "How much more do you know?"

"Curious? I don't blame you. It's truly a magical place. I'm so excited to have someone to talk to about all of this. Stay just one night. You have to eat, so why not with us?"

Alara floated in my mind. What other information rested in those books? "I mean, I guess I could." It wasn't like I had any crowns on me to pay for food.

"Really, I'm sorry about my behavior earlier. I didn't mean to hurt your feelings. I didn't think you meant it. My mother brings a lot of potential friends around, hoping I'll be like I was before."

"Before when?" I asked as we rounded the corner.

"Before my little sister was taken."

"Oh, I'm so sorry."

The weight of her arm shifted, clutching desperately to mine. "So, I understand the pain of losing a sister. I'll make sure you're reunited with yours."

I wondered if a similar haunted look reflected in my eyes every time I talked to someone too.

"We are alike, you and I," the princess said before she scrunched her nose. "Though I would never get in the bath with my brother. You will have to fill me in on that story later."

Groaning, I lifted my eyes to the ceiling. "Couldn't we pretend it didn't happen?"

"Where is the fun in that?"

We walked down the long hallway, a part of the castle I hadn't been in yet. The rest of the royal family waited by an oversized double door, whispering amongst themselves. Everyone was there but the king.

"Would you be willing to sell your necklace?" The princess studied my collar again.

"No, I could never part with this." I pressed my fingers into the cool surface of my choker. The comfort was instant.

"May I ask how you came by it?"

I sent her a look. This again? "I didn't steal it if that's what you're asking."

"No, I didn't think that. Did someone give it to you?"

"Yes," I said. I had barely responded before she lobbed another question at me.

"How do you take it off? There is no latch," she said, studying my collar.

Perhaps if I shocked her, she'd drop the subject. "It doesn't come off. It's a part of me now and fused into my flesh."

For a moment, it worked. She was speechless. "That sounds horrific."

"It was at first. Now, it———" My vision blurred with the onset of tears. My goodness, where did this onslaught of emotions come from? Blinking, I turned away to collect myself with a couple of shaky breaths. My stomach fluttered just thinking about it. Or to be more precise, thinking of Ryken. "It saved me."

"How?"

"Vella, is she a criminal? What is with the inquisition? Give her some space," Prince Vian said, placing a hand on her shoulder to draw her away from me.

"I was only curious. Her necklace is so . . . unique."

He nodded. "What she means to say is that chokers aren't in style this season. Perhaps we could find you something else to wear."

"I don't care about any of that. It means a lot to me."

"I think she means the person who gave it to her means a lot," the princess said with a wink.

Goodness. This was going to be a long dinner.

"Vella, you troublemaker. You're making her blush." It sounded more like a compliment than a reprimand.

"It's almost time," the queen announced. She had changed into another stunning gown, this one spun from gold. On her chest rested a fat sapphire, one of the largest gems I had ever seen. She pulled the rope hanging from the ceiling, and a bell gonged in the adjoining room. "Vella, darling. I'm so glad you made it."

"Marigold convinced me," she said. "We are becoming fast friends like you wanted."

"Oh, that's wonderful. It warms my heart that you both are getting along. Maybe you'll stop hiding in that musty library. We could do an afternoon tea with your friends."

A glint sparkled in her wide eyes as she shook her head back and forth.

"Too soon, Mother," Prince Vian whispered.

"It has been plenty of time."

"Vella, you don't have to do anything you don't want to do." Prince Vian grabbed her hand, patting the top. She calmed at his touch.

"You heard what Father said. If you keep coddling her, she'll never get better," the crown prince said, suddenly taking an interest in us. Prince Vox resembled the king's side of the family with his crooked nose and large frame, towering over the rest of us. His gaze passed over me like I didn't exist.

"Nobody asked you," Prince Vian grumbled.

"Still sore about earlier, little brother? You are the sensitive one."

"And what does that make you?" Princess Emilia asked her husband. Dark circles hung under her eyes, her appearance more haggard since the last time I saw her when she visited Cadell a few years ago. As a princess of Glenton, her parents had hoped to match her to Prince Alexander, but his heart had already been spoken for. I wondered if she knew it was my sister who ruined her match.

"The handsome one, obviously. Don't ask stupid questions, my dear," Prince Vox replied haughtily.

I kept my face neutral, not wanting to get involved with their family spats. It seemed even royal families had their arguments.

"Marigold is looking for her sister too," Princess Vella said out of nowhere.

"Vella, this is not the time for one of your moods. The doors are opening any second. Smile on and hand up," the queen commanded.

As if transformed, a beautiful smile lit the princess's oval face. Her white teeth contrasted with her dark complexion, perhaps even more stunning than her mother's. She lifted her hand and wiggled her fingers. "Ready, Mother."

The queen stared at her a moment, her eyes narrowed.

"I'll behave," the princess added.

A side door opened, and a tall man with a high neck collar and wide shoulders sauntered out. This was the first time I had seen the king of Windcrest in person as he rarely left his castle. He adjusted his sleeves and nodded at each person in turn, pausing when his eyes met mine.

"Welcome, my lady." Turning away, he offered his arm to his queen, his attention now on the closed door. Standing by his side, she placed her hand over his. The crown prince and his wife queued behind them.

"Are you ready?" Prince Vian asked me.

I stared at the closed door. My eyes followed the golden swirls chiseled into the wood, as always overly extravagant. Why weren't we just walking in? Nerves ate at my insides, and my imagination ran rampant with what was on the other side of these doors.

"No," I whispered. "Can I eat in my room?"

"Where is the girl who would rather swim across a moat than marry me?"

"She is still here, and she wants to eat alone in her room."

The doors opened without any notice, revealing a stone path through a garden of tropical foliage. Sweet floral aromas washed over me. It was a relaxing scent, one I recognized from the expensive shops out in the Halberts quarter. Vine-covered pillars marked the edges of the room instead of walls so that the room was open to the elements and thick with humidity. No matter where a person stood, an amazing view stretched out before them. They could see either the expensive homes in the Breezeway quarter or the sea out in the far distance. Even the sun was putting on a show. Dipping lower to the horizon, its reflection glimmered across the ocean's surface.

At the center of the room stood a raised gazebo encircled by a pond. Flashes of colorful fish swam beneath the pond's clear water. Inside the gazebo was a lone table, elegantly adorned with a navy tablecloth and seven gleaming place settings that waited for its occupants.

A long horseshoe-shaped table lined the outer rim of the room closer to the pillars, taking up the majority of the area. Hundreds of strangers filled the seats, all their eyes on us as they waited. This was no small family gathering; every noble in the kingdom had come to dine with us.

And most of the ladies had their eye on the prince at my side.

"Too late now, my lady. They've all seen you," Prince Vian said and placed my limp hand on his. His fingers held on to mine with such a fierce grip that I scowled at him. "You're stuck with me just as I am with you."

I Stand with You

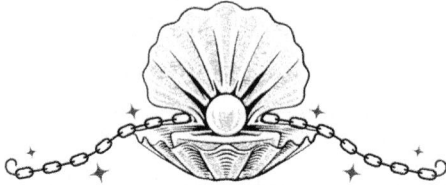

As we entered the double doors, the royal family waved at the full tables of nobility on either side of the dining hall. They applauded politely and bowed their heads as we passed. I bit my lip to keep my laugh from bursting out. Did they receive cheers every time they had a meal? I snorted at the absurdity of it. For a brief moment, I wished I could tell Rose. She would have laughed at the ridiculousness along with me.

Prince Vian sent me a sharp look, and I lifted my hand, mimicking the queen's and Princess Emilia's dainty waves in front of me.

I peered over my shoulder to Princess Vella walking in alone, her smile still in place and elegant. Why didn't Prince Vian escort his sister? The princess ranked higher than I did.

We climbed the steps of the white gazebo. Planters adorned the structure, filling the area with their fragrant blooms. Golden plates and silverware were placed at each seat, more settings than there were of us present. With precision, they sat in order of entry until it was my turn. Princess Vella waited patiently behind us.

King Galon narrowed his gaze in my direction like I had already made a mistake, his golden crown crafted to look like long pieces of coral.

Is it too late to run?

"Where am I to eat?" I asked, scanning the seating outside the gazebo for an empty spot.

The king sat at the head of the table, with his queen on his right and Prince Vox on his left. Princess Emilia sat beside her husband, her eyes locked on mine in mild interest as she fluffed out her napkin and set it on her lap.

"With us," Princess Vella said. The queen twisted toward us in her chair.

"Oh, I——" I squeaked. Eat with the royalty? There were too many utensils. Were the goblets made of crystal? I longed for the courage I had felt earlier. I shuffled away from the prince.

"I am honored, but it is well above my station. What would the nobles say?" I asked.

"As princess of Windcrest, third heir to the royal throne, I would tell them to mind their own business." She moved to stand behind the chair next to her sister-in-law.

"You are our guest, my lady. Of course we would invite you to dine with us. Isn't that right, Vian?" the queen pressed. She cleared her throat, drawing Prince Vian's attention. His spine stiffened as they continued to stare at each other in a silent argument. Her eyes flicked to the empty chair across from Vella and back to the rigid prince.

"Yes, Mother."

"Sit," the king commanded, rippling the water around the pond when he slammed his fist on the table.

"You heard him, brother," the crown prince said, his voice stilted. He smiled, an uneven line across his lips. It was as crooked as his nose. "Do as Father bids, eh?"

Prince Vian's grip tightened on mine as he guided me to the empty seat next to his. As soon as I sat, he scooted the chair in for me and slipped into the seat to my left.

"Blend into the wall as you always do, dearest brother. It makes mealtimes much more enjoyable," Prince Vian replied coolly.

"Do not start," the queen whispered from the corner of her mouth. "Your father is not in the mood for either of your antics."

"Marigold," Princess Vella whispered, distracting me from the squabble. Her eyes darted to something over my shoulder.

A female servant in a white gown held a bowl with wavy etchings around the middle.

I straightened. "Oh, I'm sorry. Were you waiting for me?"

"Yes, my lady. How many scoops?"

I'd never had quail before. Windcrest was known for its lighter dishes, always the most recent catch of fish and fresh produce. Now that I thought about it, quail was more common in Cadell, at least to the upper nobility. Vegetables with rabbit or squirrel were what graced our farm table. Maybe a hog if it was someone's birthday.

"Two?" Was that too much? Too little? Why did they ask me first?

"Do you not like quail?" the queen asked, her eyes drilling into me.

The servant scooped two hearty helpings into my bowl, the aroma a mouth-watering scent of spices and vegetables.

"I've never had it before. But it's not fish, which I'm thankful for."

"I'm sure you ate a lot of that while you were at sea," Princess Emilia, her seat diagonal from mine. She seemed shocked that she'd spoken at all, blushing.

"Actually, I didn't. I ate something called urchin. Do you serve that a lot here? It's quite good."

Prince Vian chuckled into his napkin.

"What?" I fidgeted in my seat. Even the princess was laughing behind her hand.

His lips trembled with mischief. "You know, sea urchin is an aphrodisiac. We don't serve it at family gatherings."

Mortified, a wave of heat coursed through my body. *Ryken! You sneaky merman . . .*

I shoved a bite of food in my mouth to avoid giving a response.

"I heard you are in search of your sister," King Galon said.

My spoon slipped from my fingers to clatter against the bowl. All heads swiveled to look at me, my face beyond overheating. I quickly swallowed the tough bite of meat.

"Yes, Your Majesty. I hope to see how she and my parents are faring. It has been some time since we last saw each other."

"A year is a long time to be parted from family," he said before slurping another mouthful of stew.

The air rushed from the room as if everyone held their breath.

I met Princess Vella's sympathetic eyes as she mouthed, "It was the truth."

So much for the hope that it was a lie. A whole year just vanished into thin air. When did that happen?

"Being lost at sea has made the days run together, it seems," I forced out, my breath picking up speed again.

"A small price to pay for the gift of survival. The ocean is fickle about who it lets escape its watery clutches. Not everyone is as lucky as you."

I thought of the man, the one Ryken had dropped into the sea when he was Collecting, and nodded in agreement.

"I understand this may be overwhelming for you. Wren has passed on your questions, and I want you to know that I offer my aid as a thank you to King Baxton. He was a good man and one I was lucky to call a friend. Cut from the same noble cloth as some of the great leaders before him, he was valiant and honorable, keeping our traditional values, unlike the current rulers of Cadell. Our kingdoms used to be close until his health started deteriorating. We lost contact and unity between our kingdoms."

"I never met him." I sent him a dubious glance at the kind words for Cadell's cold-hearted king.

He grunted. "It is no matter. I'm hoping you will be our connection back to Cadell. The Queen of Hearts is hot on your trail. The latest report was that she torched one of our farmlands searching for your whereabouts. War is coming, my lady."

More fire. More death. All because of me.

I placed the spoon on the table, my stomach hardening to stone. "What could I possibly have that she would kill for?"

"Who can say the reasoning of a tyrant when they are desperate for power? They say the curse has been broken, but her actions prove otherwise. They are still bent on destruction. I refuse to sit on my throne and watch my kingdom crumble because of their mistakes." He pointed his spoon at me. "If you leave here, we can't guarantee your safety beyond the walls of the castle."

The curse! How could I have forgotten? When I had eavesdropped on Prince Vian, he had asked if I was cursed like someone else. Someone who had also lost their memory. What was the old prophecy again? I'd

199

heard it so many times because we lived close to the forest border. . . something about the battle from hundreds of years ago . . . the Battle of the Bones. After Cadell's victory over Bressal, they thought Mistbrooke had betrayed their treaty, causing them to retaliate by burning their entire kingdom. But the Sorcerer survived and cursed the royal family. And now the royal family of Cadell would burn just like the lives they'd burned in Mistbrooke.

I couldn't breathe. *Rose.* Was that why the Queen of Hearts was searching for me? To kill my sister and possibly Prince Alexander to fulfill the curse? It made sense with the connection the Queen of Hearts had to Mistbrooke. I had to ask Ruah as soon as I was alone.

"What do you want from me?" I asked.

"For us to offer you aid, you must agree to an alliance with Windcrest. You will wear our colors so that the queen of Cadell knows that if she comes to take you, she declares war against our kingdom," he growled.

"Darling, you're getting worked up again." The queen placed a hand on top of the king's. Her jaw twitched when he snatched it back.

"I'm not one of your children, Ada. Don't coddle me."

I cleared my throat. "You would do that . . . for me?"

"I do it for many reasons, and one of them is in honor of my friendship with King Baxton. His son desperately loved your sister. The boy had always been a loose cannon on the verge of self-destruction. But at least he remained firm in keeping magic at bay. We will not stand by and let this tyrant destroy another kingdom. This is my home, and I want to keep it that way for future generations. Glenton is prepared to stand by our side, thanks to the union between Prince Vox and Princess Emilia. But it's not enough."

"Because of the curse of Cadell? You have to break it," I finished for him.

He raised a white brow. "Yes, the curse. You are so clever to have figured that out when it took us months."

"Father?" Prince Vox asked, looking between us.

"Not now," the king snapped. The prince frowned into his stew, mixing it as he watched the chunks of food float around.

"Not just anyone lasts a year out at sea and lives to tell about it. You have been blessed by the sea itself. And because of that, the Queen of Hearts wants you under her control."

I looked at my hands, confused. *Blessed?* If they only knew what had happened to me these last weeks—no, year. "She would be sorely disappointed if she met me."

"Whispers from her kingdom say she has gone mad in her search for you, claiming she sees you in visions. She will stop at nothing until she gets her hands on you. Stand with us, Marigold, and wear our navy colors. We will protect you and provide you with a safe haven until a new kingdom is created. A true king that will care about his people and restore order to how things were before. Over time, we may even consider you as family." His eyes shifted to Prince Vian, who picked at the edge of his napkin. "We take care of our own."

"I wasn't expecting such an offer. Can I think about it?"

"There's no time. A message arrived that troops have been spotted in Amille. She must be using magic to track you."

I froze. "She's in Amille? I know someone there. I can't just sit here and——"

"I already sent a guard to retrieve them," Prince Vian said, then turned to look at me. "We will right the wrong, and he will be returned to you."

"Thank you . . . I'm at a loss for words."

"We only ask for your allegiance, my lady," pressed the crown prince. His wife lifted her goblet, taking a long swallow.

"Of course, you have it."

"We will need something a little more . . . tangible," King Galon said, pressing his fingertips together. "Could you announce it publicly?"

"To whom?"

He waved a hand at the full tables outside our gazebo. "Nothing spreads faster than gossip. The Queen of Hearts will know by nightfall."

I swallowed. *Does he mean right now?*

He raised his hand, and a trumpet sounded from the entrance, silencing the room of chatter. "Stand."

With no other choice, I rose on shaky legs. A hundred pairs of eyes fixed on me, and I fumbled to find the words to speak.

"My humblest apologies, my lady." Prince Vian joined me at my side. "I forgot to introduce you."

"You did?" I croaked.

He inclined his head. "I am always forgetting my duties," he said with a hint of sarcasm. He held out his palm to me, ungloved as was the custom in Windcrest.

I hesitated only for a moment before placing my hand in his. He bowed over it, showing the nobles his respect for me. My face heated at the gesture. His fingers clamped on mine as I tried to pull away; instead, he pulled me around the edge of the gazebo, presenting me like a prized stallion.

"May I present our mystery guest, Lady Marigold Bellmond. The lost sister has been found."

A murmur followed by a round of applause rose from the outside tables, startling me so that I gripped his hand, my eyes wide.

"The Sea of Providence has protected her and has granted her favor. She has pledged her loyalty to navy, to the emblem of waves that marks our banners. Her presence offers our kingdom peace from the magic wielders in the south. We now have what the Queen of Hearts desires most."

"Uh, thank you, Your Highness, and to you all. I'm sorry that my presence has caused chaos and bloodshed. This is not the Cadell I left, but King Galon has promised to restore it to its former glory. I stand with the sea, the truth, and the kingdom that desires peace. I stand with you. I will wear your colors of navy with pride and thankfulness." I dipped into a curtsy.

The listeners erupted in applause again. Even the royal table joined in and clapped along. Hope-filled eyes turned to me. These strangers I had never met expected something I had no idea how to give.

As we walked back to our seats, the queen leaned in to whisper to her son, "Expertly done, Vian." Her lips cracked with a rare smile.

"As you wished, Mother."

"You will thank me one day."

"We shall see," the prince mumbled under his breath. He dropped my hand as soon as we were seated and turned to his sister-in-law to make light conversation.

"Prince Vian?" I said, and then repeated myself when he ignored me. I couldn't understand his mood swings. Did he still think I was an imposter? Or maybe he didn't like me, and he was better at hiding it than Prince Vox. I only wanted to thank him for coming to my aid. He seemed so natural at public speaking, probably from years of practice, charm oozing from his pores. I could only bumble out a few awkward words. If speeches were a common occurrence for meals, I would rather eat alone in my room.

"This is so exciting, Marigold. I have some blue dresses I could have you try on. We are almost the same size," said the princess. "We can have them hemmed, or you can hem them yourself. I heard you love to sew."

"That's servants' work," the crown prince pointed out.

"She may do as she pleases," Prince Vian countered.

"Mrs. Pretta will smooth out all the bumps in your upbringing," the queen said, ignoring her sons in the middle of an intense staring contest. "She already has a list of things you could work on. Perhaps tomorrow if you're free?"

"I'm taking her to her grandparents' shop tomorrow until midday as you requested," Prince Vian said.

"Oh, that's right. In the evening, then?"

"She promised to meet me in the library," Princess Vella chimed in.

As I opened my mouth to protest, she kicked me under the table. Prince Vian glanced between his sister and me, his eyes softening at his sister's smile.

"You can't avoid your responsibilities forever. Ask Prince Vian. He would know. Isn't that right, dear brother?" Prince Vox smirked.

"Maybe if you performed *your* responsibilities, we wouldn't be in this situation in the first place. Or aren't you man enough?" Prince Vian challenged.

Prince Vox's face contorted in rage, a vein pulsing in his neck. He gripped the spoon in his hand like a dagger. Everyone ignored the tension brewing between the princes and returned to their meal as if this were commonplace.

"I'm more man than you will ever be," the crown prince seethed. He grimaced at his wife, who had curled over her stew, her head bowed. "I'm doing the best with what I have. Mountain people are as infertile as the land they sow."

"That's not true. The royals in Glenton are known for their innumerable heirs," I said and then immediately regretted it when all eyes snapped to me. I clamped my mouth closed, shrinking to hide behind Prince Vian's form.

"No, please, *speak*. Enlighten us with your rudimentary education." He lifted his full goblet and downed it in an easy gulp.

Prince Vian's grip was almost tight enough to bend his spoon. "Vox, you're being a pompous——"

King Galon slammed his fist on the table. "Enough," he bellowed. The single word silenced not only the royal table but the tables on the floor as well. "She is our guest, Vox. I suggest you remain silent for the rest of the meal before you embarrass yourself further."

A friendly smile flashed on Prince Vian's face before it disappeared. He tilted sideways to whisper, "Ignore him. Everyone always does."

I chuckled despite myself.

Footsteps sounded in the distance, quick and urgent. They grew louder as the guard who had carried me into the castle raced across the dining hall toward us.

"Your Majesty, Your Majesty." Wren ran up the steps of the gazebo two at a time. His navy cape whipped around his shoulders, his eyes clear and his face cleanly shaven since the last time I had seen him.

"This better be urgent," King Galon said.

"It is, Your Majesty. Reports of a sighting in the moat have caused an uproar in the quarters. Two riots have already broken out, and neither took place in Pit, which alone is concerning."

The king chewed quickly, his eyes darting back and forth in thought. "Is it Cadell and their tricks?"

"We don't know, Your Majesty. It is some type of beast lurking in the depths of the water. There are whispers of——" his voice dropped to an inaudible whisper, well, inaudible to human ears "——Merfolk."

I smiled and resisted the urge to leap to my feet in joy.

Ryken is here . . .

Find Me

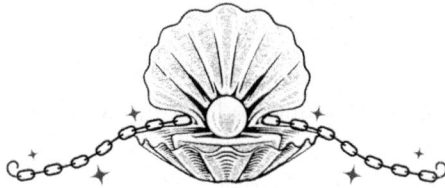

Upon hearing the news of Wren's report, King Galon paled. His eyes shifted warily to Princess Vella. She was the only person uninterested. She broke her bread into pieces, crumbling them in her stew as she hummed to herself.

"Vella?" the king called out.

Queen Ada did a double take at her daughter and sighed. "Manners, please. You are not a child."

The princess shrugged, crumbling another section of bread.

King Galon motioned to Wren before he spoke. "Make a public announcement on our behalf: Due to the potential threat, new safety precautions will be implemented immediately. For the safety of my people and for the kingdom, all entries to the castle will be closed and barred. Guards will be doubled—no, *tripled*—on the bridge, and all towers will be manned. Stay clear of the waters until further notice."

"Father, that seems a bit rash for a rumor, don't you think?" Prince Vox asked.

"Do you know what kind of leader ignores rumors?" the king replied, dabbing the corners of his mouth with his napkin before tossing it on the table.

"A wise one?"

"A dead one. Dinner is over," the king commanded, rising so

suddenly that a few of the goblets overturned. Red wine splattered across the table, causing Prince Vox to scramble from his seat to avoid the waterfall heading toward his lap.

"Darling, are you all right?" the queen asked, rising to join her husband. As soon as she stood, an echo of chairs scraped against the tile as the nobles also stood out of respect.

"I'm hoping Vella's pet hasn't escaped into the moat," King Galon whispered in his wife's ear.

Pet?

The queen gripped her husband's arm, mouthing words I couldn't hear.

I was so focused on their private conversation that I jolted when Princess Vella tapped my hand to get my attention.

"Marigold, are you ready to go to the library?" the princess asked, ignoring the harsh whispering of her parents.

The library? *Now?*

How could I read when Ryken was so close? I couldn't stop fidgeting with excitement at the thought of seeing him again. Prince Vian turned to stare at my finger tapping impatiently on the tablecloth.

"Are you frightened? There's no need to be. This castle is a fortress," he said. "We can have someone come sit with you in your room——"

I shook my head. "No, please, that's unnecessary. I'm only tired from the day's events, and I'm ready to return to my room."

"You don't look tired," Princess Vella said, eyeing me.

I tucked my nervous fingers under the table.

"Vella, don't be so pushy." The prince turned to me with an apologetic smile. "I'll escort you back."

"Oh, you don't need to. Can Trista take me?"

Prince Vian cleared his throat. "I still have to escort you out of the dining hall," he grumbled, mirroring his brother by helping me out of my chair.

The king and queen paraded by us, their faces neutral despite their heated whispers earlier. Prince Vox and his wife followed close behind. I accepted Prince Vian's hand, allowing him to lead me down the stairs and across the stone path to the double doors.

My name traveled on the whispers from the tables on the floor. Hushed murmurs of shock that I was still alive, hope that I could end a war, and doubt that I would survive the flames of the Queen of Hearts. One comment of suspicion had me turning to glance over my shoulder, but there were too many faces for me to pinpoint my accuser.

"What is it?" the prince asked from my side.

"Someone said I was a traitor. 'Blood is thicker than water.'"

"I'm sure you misheard. There's so much chatter in here, I can't even hear myself think."

I bit my tongue to restrain myself from arguing. With my sensitive hearing, I knew I hadn't misheard.

Instead, I focused on the thought of seeing Ryken again—which hopefully would be as soon as I returned to my chambers. I shook my head in disbelief. *He found me.* Somehow he had tracked me all the way from Amille. Was it our connection or some Merfolk ability? Whatever the method, I was thankful he arrived safely.

Would he be happy to see me?

Or . . . was he only here to retrieve me because he thought I had escaped? What lies had Jacek and Caitlyn fed him without me there to defend myself?

A tingle of dread shot down my spine. He had to know I wouldn't willfully leave without him. *Well* . . . I did purposely leave him at the beach during the storm. I bit my lip, remembering. And there was also the time he caught me cutting through my bindings to escape. He was so furious, almost to the point of biting me.

And then . . . he was devastated. His pain-filled words echoed in my mind. *Do you wish you were claimed by another?*

Nausea burned in my stomach. Of course I didn't want anyone but Ryken. A soft sigh escaped me. I had no idea what to expect when I saw him next.

No matter what mood he was in when he arrived, he still couldn't stay in the castle. There were too many guards lining the halls. He couldn't stay in my chamber either. Every time I made a peep, someone from the royal family barged in to investigate. We'd have to communicate with my collar and figure out the best way to sneak him out to my grandparents' shop. I could meet back up with him tomorrow when I was in Halberts.

But one key detail jolted me out of my thoughts.

"Your Highness, when the king said the doors would be barred, does that mean we can't leave either?"

"Unfortunately, yes. Until the threat has cleared, we are locked inside for our safety."

Squeezing my eyes shut, I held in a scream. Could one thing, just one, go right?

"I'll escort you back to your room if you're tired," Prince Vian offered.

"What about Trista?" I glanced around the hallway, but only two male guards were there, standing like statues. "Or anyone—oh, Princess Vella?"

In a swish of navy fabric, the princess raced by us. "I'm sorry, but I'm quite busy, and I have to return the library." Waving over her shoulder, she descended a spiral staircase.

Great. Alone with the prince again.

We walked the rest of the way in silence as I contemplated the different scenarios of what I would say when I saw Ryken. The more I deliberated, the more I worried he'd be furious at me for leaving without him.

"You seem deep in thought."

"Long day," I replied.

"About tomorrow . . ."

I turned to him, the subject catching my interest. "Can we go to my grandparents' shop?"

He grimaced. "I'll stop by in the morning to let you know whether the safety precautions have been lifted; otherwise, we will have to postpone the outing."

I stopped. "I really want to see them. I'm not worried at all."

"My father won't take a gamble with my life—or yours." He pressed his hand on my elbow, setting us in motion again. "I know Vella would enjoy the company if we are stuck inside. She already seems comfortable around you."

I nodded, not sure if I could agree that I felt comfortable around her.

"If we do go out, did you want to eat in one of the shops or have the cook make us a picnic?"

Why did both options sound like he was hinting at something romantic?

"Can I ask for a chaperone?"

He leaned his head back, laughing. "That was not the answer I was expecting."

"We really shouldn't be alone together. Like now." I glanced around dramatically. "Where is Mrs. Pretta when you need her?"

"*Oof.* You've said her name. If you say it three times, you'll summon the beast."

My lips twitched, but I refused to fall for his charm.

"Come on. That was a good one. It deserved at least a half-smile."

"No smile, Your Highness. You confuse me with my sister, who gives her smiles freely."

"Ahh, yes. Siblings. It's the same with Vox and me. You're more likely to get a kind word and smile from him than you would from me," he said with such a straight face I couldn't stop the laugh from bursting out. "There's the smile."

"Only one." Just as quickly as it came, it left. "Did you take us the long way?"

"You sound like you want to rid yourself of my company."

"Tired, remember?"

"How could I forget? You're just *bouncing* with sleepiness. Ahh, here's your room. See here? Look for the feather on the door," he said, pointing to the brass peacock feather.

"Thank you, Your Highness. I will see you in the morning," I said, secretly hoping I was wrong.

"Sweet dreams, my lady." He went to lift my hand to his lips, but I pulled it away, dipping into a rushed curtsy. Slipping into my room, I closed the door on his surprised face.

"Goodnight?" he mumbled through the wood.

As soon as I was positive he was gone, I kicked off my sandals and walked into the bath, the cool water as comforting as a hug. I paddled up to the window, lifting myself high enough to see the waters beyond.

Nothing. Only a few curious piranhas circled in front of the mesh of my window, their glassy eyes watching me.

I dropped back down into the pool, allowing myself to submerge below the surface until I sank to the bottom. I called out to Ryken the only way I knew how—with my song. It startled me at first, the high pitch of the melody. Up and down, the notes climbed in a soprano that I didn't think I could reach outside the water. I put all my worries, fears, and heart into each note, holding each one for a second before transitioning to the next. The new tune had me bursting with joy, shooting tingles over my skin. It was more than a song; it was a ballad. Feelings I was too afraid to admit or even think about soared up from my chest and formed into music, echoing from my lips and vibrating through the water.

Find me, Ryken.

I sang until my throat ached. Though he didn't come, I didn't give up on him. *Patience,* I reminded myself. I just needed to wait. Closing my eyes, I floated in peaceful silence, exhaustion from the day settling in. I thought of curses and flames and of an evil queen who was set upon destroying Cadell's royal lineage.

My dreams were of music. The notes of my song were bubbles floating around me. Each one I touched popped, releasing my voice as if it had been trapped inside. It felt like a puzzle. If I popped them in a particular order, Ryken would return to me. But the dream turned nightmarish when I couldn't solve the puzzle. The waters chilled, and notes turned into screams of pain—my screams, sending shivers down my spine.

Suddenly, I was jerked upright and out of the water, my head snapping back.

"Marigold!"

"Ryken?" I asked, blinking away the cobwebs of sleep. Had I somehow figured out the right combination of notes?

"Breathe. You're all right. I've got you."

Something whacked into my back, rattling my thoughts.

"You are blessed. How are you still alive?"

When my eyes focused on his dark skin and wide eyes, my heart dropped. It wasn't Ryken but Prince Vian. He had pulled me out of the water, holding me tight to his chest.

"What are you doing here?"

He froze, his eyes narrowing. "I just saved your life, and that's the first thing you want to say to me?"

My rebuttal would only cause more confusion. How could I explain to him that I was sleeping? The truth would only reveal who I was, and I wasn't sure if I could trust the prince with that.

"I'm so sorry, Your Highness. I was in shock. It was very heroic of you to save me again," I said, easing away from him.

"Marigold, this is not a joke. You were under the water for a concerning amount of time. You could have died," he said roughly, pinching the bridge of his nose.

Two soft taps sounded on the door.

"Everything okay in here? I heard screaming," Princess Vella whispered as she peeked through the crack of the door. "Marigold—*uh, Vian*? I can't believe what I'm seeing—are you in the bath again?"

"Would you believe me if I told you I was saving her life again?" But he didn't sound like his jovial self.

"No."

"Well, I tried." He raised a brow at me. "Do you want a summer wedding or an autumn wedding?"

"Neither."

He forced a laugh. "Winter it is."

Princess Vella hissed in a breath. "You have my permission to whack him. I'm beginning to think he keeps doing this on purpose."

"I'm not. I only came to see if she would be ready within the hour. The safety precautions have been removed. It seems they were only rumors."

"Oh," I said, my happiness deflating. "They searched everywhere?"

"Yes, but there was nothing out of place. So, we are back on schedule."

"Wonderful," I lied. The disappointment overshadowed the excitement of seeing my grandparents today. "I guess I better change so we can go."

"Come on, brother, before I tell Mother I caught you in the bath with our guest again."

He sent me a stern look and flicked a handful of droplets at me. "Stay out of the water until I return."

Prince Charming

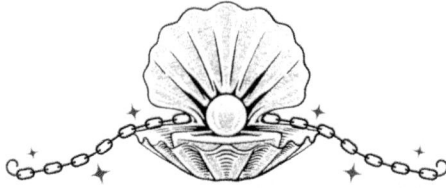

After I changed into dry clothes, I met the prince at the castle entrance. He had more gold accents on, Windcrest finery, the embroidery on his high collar sparkling in the sunlight. His good mood had returned too. Nibbling on his thumbnail, he smiled as he caught sight of me approaching in one of Princess Vella's navy dresses. The material was so light that it fluttered around my ankles, trailing behind me like a train. I left my hair loose in hopes of covering the small marks behind my ears. Not that anyone would be close enough to notice.

"Navy looks marvelous on you, my lady," Prince Vian said with a bow. When he stood, he did a double take of a section of my hair. "I love your enthusiasm. Adding it to your hair was a nice touch. I'm sure it will be all the rage soon."

"My hair?" I had quickly run a brush through it earlier while it was still damp, not paying it much attention. But on closer inspection, the curls hanging over my right shoulder matched the blue of my dress. Another sign that even though I was on dry land, my transformation hadn't stopped.

"Don't fret. Everyone will love it. Are you taking my arm today?"

"It's a little hot, don't you think?" I fanned myself as I stepped away.

"Right, right. Of course it is." He took a deep breath and let it go in a puff, bracing himself. "Before we leave, I just want to see how you are faring. I know these last couple of days—or even this year—has taken its toll on you. Are you . . . okay? Do you want to talk about earlier? Like why you were in the bath?"

I had hoped he wouldn't bring up the incident, but I guessed there were only so many times he could ignore my strange behavior.

"I'm quite well, Your Highness. When I'm overwhelmed, the silence of the water brings me peace. I didn't mean to frighten you."

He scanned my face. "Are you sure? I know my flirtatious personality makes it seem like I don't care—but I do. If you haven't noticed, nobody is perfect in our family. You don't have to pretend to be someone you're not."

Unable to take his intense stare, I glanced down at my clasped hands. His words struck a nerve, somehow piercing through the armor I wore around him. He didn't know how close to the truth he was.

Who am I? I plucked at the navy strands on my shoulder. *A human pretending not to be a mermaid? Or a mermaid in denial?*

When I didn't respond, he cleared his throat. "To be honest, I was frightened. Maybe more than that. I think my heart might have stopped when I saw you floating there. I haven't felt that way in a long time . . . not since my sister."

"Princess Vella? Or——" I thought of their other sister. The one the princess had mentioned yesterday.

"No, not Vella." He sighed, pained. "Verona. She is—or was—my youngest sister. It's been a little over two years since she left us."

My eyes widened. "I'm so sorry."

"It's not something any of us talk about. We all deal with her loss in our own way. Mother in her matchmaking and Vella in her books. *Oh, Vella.* It hurt her most of all. They were inseparable."

The prince's scent washed over me, reeking of a wounded heart that refused to heal. His feelings weighed heavily in the air, crushing me with his anguish. He had lived my worst fear.

My heart twisted painfully at the thought. "Losing a sister? I can't even imagine. I don't know what I would do if I lost Rosey."

"It's like losing a limb. You don't realize how much you need it until it's gone." Prince Vian squinted at the sky. "It seems I ruined a perfectly good sunny day. We don't have to go out. If you want to sit in the salon and talk, I promise I'm a good listener. I won't even try to hold your hand."

I sent him an encouraging smile and held out my hand. "No, I do want to go. If you still want to escort me."

Nodding, he smiled, and not his usual smirk or flirtatious grin, but a genuine smile that lit up his eyes. He took my offered hand, bowed over it, and then tucked it into the crook of his elbow.

"Shall we?" he said and led us across the bridge into town.

We waved at the people we passed. The streets were more crowded than usual, as if every citizen of Windcrest lined the pathways. Everyone was curious to catch a glimpse of the lost sister. They called out our names, waving and clapping, anything to get us to turn their way. All the noise and attention made me uncomfortable. I found myself tongue-tied as I stumbled over my responses. Luckily, the prince did most of the talking to anyone forward enough to approach us. One little girl commented on the blue streak in my hair and asked if it had fallen into an inkwell. The prince was still chuckling at that as we crossed into the Halberts quarter.

"You know, you don't need to prove your identity," he said, scratching the back of his head. "I wanted you to know before we got there that I believe you."

I glanced at him out of the corner of my eye. "Finally?"

"I think I always knew it was you. I had just hoped I was wrong. But it's as Mrs. Pretta said—stubborn people make poor decisions to prove their point."

"Is she meeting us in town or . . . ?"

"Oh. My parents said we were fine on our own. There are plenty of people about, so no chaperone is necessary."

"Well, it should be a quick trip."

"Why so quick? There is so much to do in town. We can go shopping afterward."

I started to protest, and the prince cut in. "Shopping isn't for us. It helps the people and the economy. Besides, it will be fun. Gives me a chance to show you around."

The prince chattered as we strolled down the path, pointing out bits of history hidden in plain sight. He greeted everyone that we passed, especially at the shops closest to Breezeway. When he noticed my fidgeting hands, he politely veered us away from the curious residents, picking up our pace so we could reach our destination sooner.

The shop was the same, and yet, it wasn't.

Countless times I had stood in this same spot, staring at the fine print marked on the shop window, "Sewn by the Sea," and not once had the windows been shrouded in darkness. Dirt and sand covered the steps leading to the entry, and dried sticks were all that remained of the potted plants lining the windowsill.

"Are you sure this is it?" Prince Vian questioned. He tilted his head back, looking up at my old window, the inside glass covered in cobwebs and dust.

"Yes, but I've never seen it like this." I raced up the steps and jiggled the doorknob, dread filling me.

"It's closed, dearie," said an elderly woman, not looking up as she swept the dirt from her steps. A wave of nostalgia hit me as I watched Ms. Celeste do the same task she'd always done every day before the afternoon crowd showed up. My grandparents' shop and hers worked together to provide stylish clothes and shoes at a fraction of the price compared to the fancier shops around the Halberts quarter. Our shop offered clothing, hats, and accessories, while Ms. Celeste's offered shoes, hand-crafted slippers, and sturdy boots.

"I hope the seas are treating you well, Ms. Celeste," I said, and she paused her work to turn to me.

"Little Goldie, is that you?"

"Goldie?" the prince repeated with delight.

"Yes, Ms. Celeste."

She tossed her broom aside, clomping her wide frame down the steps to bundle me up in a tight hug. "Oh, my poor girl. I thought you were dead for sure."

"No, I'm very much alive."

"And with—*oh my!*—you have a prince with you." She released me to dip into a wobbly curtsy. "Your Highness."

"It is nice to meet you, Ms. Celeste. I'm glad you were able to reunite with our Goldie here." The possessiveness in his sentence rubbed me the wrong way, and I took a sidestep away from him.

"Where are my grandparents? Their shop is never closed during the summer. It's their busiest time."

"They relocated to Cadell after you went missing. Perhaps a year or so since I saw either of them around here. Your parents came up and helped them pack up their things. Prince Alexander paid off the shop, so it just sits here, gathering dust. Such a shame too. Anyway, did you want to come inside for tea? It's getting close to lunchtime. We can catch up on everything we missed."

Blinking, I took in her words. Cadell. My family was in Cadell. I had hoped to avoid returning there, but if I wanted to make amends with Rose and say goodbye, I had to take the trip down one last time.

"Actually, we have to decline. She has a very busy day scheduled," Prince Vian said, gripping my arm.

"I'm sorry, Ms. Celeste. It was so good to see you," I said, still distracted by thoughts of Cadell. That was easily another week I might have to add to my trip. Would my transformation hold off that long?

"I completely understand. I'm always here if you want a chat. Don't you go leaving town without saying goodbye."

I smiled and patted her hand, knowing I couldn't agree to that.

The prince guided me away, and I didn't complain when he looped my arm through his. He purchased two kabobs from a merchant's stand and offered one to me. I nibbled as we walked, barely listening to his idle chatter, my eyes scanning the shops and activity around me.

While I was in the sea, time rushed on, and the memories I had in Windcrest, the people and places I used to visit, were long gone. I'd walked these streets many times, but today felt like the first time all over again. Something was off, an oddness settling into me like I was a stranger.

Like I didn't belong here.

"Are you all right? You look paler than usual."

"Just surprised. It's like everything has changed. Even I'm changing —and I can't stop it."

"Is change not a good thing? It allows you to grow as a person and have new experiences . . . maybe even open your eyes to something right in front of you."

But I didn't want what was right in front of me.

The sunlight winked off the water around the castle, and once again, Ryken's whereabouts consumed my thoughts.

"Can we sit by the moat?"

"You have an obsession with moats, don't you?" he teased, but there was a kernel of concern behind it.

"Please?"

"If you insist."

After discarding our trash, he walked me to the waist-high wall that bordered the moat. Piranhas swam past and circled back, suddenly interested in our arrival. I fanned out my dress before I sat on the stone, overwhelmed by the sudden desire to leap into the water.

"Don't fall in. I'm not going to jump in to save you like I did this morning," Prince Vian joked.

"That's okay. I wouldn't jump in to save you either."

"I could make you change your mind," he whispered in a low voice and picked up my hand to press a kiss against my knuckles.

I snatched it away. "Your Highness," I complained.

"Sorry." He sat next to me on the wall, sticking his lower lip out. "The fact that you don't find me charming is a terrible hit to my ego."

"I never said that."

"I'll have to be satisfied with that. You'll get there eventually, and I'll be waiting with open arms."

I frowned. "You'll be waiting a long time."

"Don't underestimate me."

I raised a brow at his confidence. A ripple on the surface caught my attention, and I turned to search for Ryken's face in the water. It wasn't the first time—I'd been searching for him in the crowds all day.

Prince Vian placed his hand on my shoulder. "Not so close. You don't need to test the theory if I will actually jump in after you. What if the beast still swims beneath the surface and is waiting for you to lean close enough to snatch you up?" His voice rose at the end, hoping to scare me.

Instead, I smiled. It was exactly what I wanted.

"That . . . was not the reaction I was hoping for."

"So sorry. Would this be better? Prince Vian, please help me. I'm so scared."

"I mean . . . you didn't ask me to hold your hand, but I'm enjoying the progress we're making together."

Laughing, I shook my head and went back to searching the moat. Doubt crept up my spine as I remembered what the king had whispered yesterday. Could it be Vella's pet in the moat and not Ryken? Was I so desperate to see him again that I had convinced myself of his reappearance?

"Does Princess Vella have some type of pet?"

The prince barked out a laugh. "*What?* Where did that question come from?"

"Just something I overheard at dinner. I've been meaning to ask you about it."

"Ah, more rumors. This kingdom is full of them—like the supposed beast that was in the moat. Don't believe everything you hear. Unless it's about me, then it's probably true."

Why would the king say that if it weren't true? Or was the royal family keeping secrets from one another? Even Rose had kept secrets from me. I sighed. Either way, it didn't explain why Ryken hadn't shown up yet.

Prince Vian cleared his throat. "In all seriousness, I'm sorry about your grandparents. I had no idea their shop had closed. I don't venture down this far in Halberts. Maybe I will from now on. Who knew they had rabbit kabobs?"

"I know these people would appreciate your business. Oh, speaking of which, can we stop by the apothecary around the corner? I was hoping to see what medicines were available."

"Are you unwell? Is it your head? You should have said something earlier."

"Actually, it's for my sister."

He froze. "Oh? Is she not well?"

"I can't tell you how I know, but yes, she is very sick. It's one of the reasons I'm so anxious to see her."

"Interesting." He rubbed his jaw, looking at me from under his lashes. "Say no more. We will buy whatever herbs or vials you might need. And don't quibble about the cost; I'll take care of that too. They can box it up and send it right to the castle."

"Thank you, Your Highness. I don't know what to make of you sometimes."

"You have such a way of humbling me."

"Oh, I didn't mean to offend you."

"Oddly enough, you didn't. It is rather refreshing. I like your honesty." His lips curved into a soft smile.

I took his offered hand, and he helped me to my feet. Just as I was about to reprimand him for his flirtatious behavior, something in his demeanor changed. He tilted his head, blinking as his thumb trailed over the back of my hand like he noticed something I did not.

His touch didn't cause my stomach to flutter or tingles to speed across my skin. Instead, it brought a keen sense of wrongness, my stomach twisting at his touch so that I snatched my hand back.

I knew in an instant what the problem was—he wasn't Ryken.

"What do you think of our kingdom? After a year at sea and surviving a shipwreck, Windcrest must be a pleasant change for you. The longer you live here, the more you will love the warmer weather. There is a Silver Moon Festival in a few months that I bet you'll enjoy. There's food and dancing." He laughed suddenly, his eyes lighting up. "It's the only time my brother lets loose and isn't a stuffy bore. He even sings."

"I'm not staying, Prince Vian. I've been upfront with you about this since I arrived." Though I couldn't lie and say I wasn't curious at the thought of the crown prince singing in public.

"Oh. I thought you might have changed your mind. You're wearing my—our colors."

"Yes, I said I would wear your colors because I believe in your cause. Peace must be restored to the territories in order to end the bloodshed. Magic, especially in the wrong hands, is dangerous. I'm thankful for your family's protection, but I only have a limited amount of time here until I have to return home."

"This could be your home."

"As wonderful as Windcrest and the familiarity of being back in Halberts has been, there is still a niggling feeling that I don't belong here."

He stopped me, looking serious for once. "What would make you feel like you could belong?"

The answer wasn't a what, but a who. Ryken's face appeared in my thoughts, his eyes the same calming turquoise of the sea. I had spent so much time pushing him away that, now that he was gone, I could feel the merman-shaped hole in my heart.

Right now, he was the only thing I wanted.

My breath shuddered out at the thought. "He's not here."

"Is he the name you said this morning? Ryken? Was he the one I sent the guards to fetch? Is there something between you two?"

"It's complicated." How could I describe how our hearts were connected without sounding like a lunatic?

His eyes narrowed. "Complicated? How so?"

"It's nothing you'd find interesting or would care about," I said nervously.

"Actually, I think I care more than I realized."

His eyes darkened as they held mine, and he shifted closer, oblivious to my discomfort. While my new senses told me his intentions were sincere, I threw my hand out to stop him. Charm radiated from him like a rope trying to draw me in, but all he did was make me miss Ryken more. If Prince Vian thought there could be something between us, I didn't want to give him the wrong impression. Pressing my fingers to my temple, I faked a headache.

He escorted me back to the castle, casting concerned glances my way until we reached my room, where I promptly hid, feeling unsociable.

I was too distracted to be pleasant company anyway. Ryken consumed my thoughts. I frequently checked the window, hoping he would swim by so I could see his face again. To touch him and hold him again, so I could stop worrying about him.

No. That wasn't true. I didn't need to use my new senses to know I was lying to myself. I missed him—so much my heart ached.

Sighing, I wrapped my arms around myself, wishing it was him I was holding instead. But it was more than that. I wanted to curl into the comfort of his embrace, listen to the soft rumbles of his voice, and laugh with him as only he could make me do. This wasn't a pull from the bond, it was *him*. Memories shuffled through my mind, sweet moments and endearing looks we shared as if he thought I was someone special.

Where is he? Even though the guards said the moat was clear, I didn't believe them. He was close, maybe not in the moat, but close enough that the pull of our connection increased as soon as I returned to my chambers. If only we could communicate without him touching my collar.

Pacing, I rubbed the tips of my blue hair between my fingers. I was running out of time on land. How many days did I have left before I woke up with a tail of my own? I turned to the window at my bath and bit my lip. Should I take my chances in the moat and find Ryken myself?

Trista knocked at the door again, the fourth time since I returned from my outing with the prince. Each time, I declined the royal summons for food or company, and especially to see Mrs. Pretta, letting them all know I'd be resting for the remainder of the evening. This time she dropped off a package from the apothecary along with a personal note from Prince Vian. The glass jars clinked inside the box as I set it on the bed, guilt eating at my conscience over my dishonesty. But this moment of solitude was just what I needed. Since I had arrived in Windcrest, I had been handed off from one royal family member to the next so that I hadn't had two seconds alone.

Plop.

Something splashed in the bath water, jolting me out of my thoughts. Or maybe it was a noise from outside? It reminded me of the sound a stone made after being chucked into a pond. I tilted my head, straining to hear it again as I surveyed the room.

I didn't have to wait long.

Plop, plop.

I spun back to the bath. Piranhas were tumbling from the window and into my bath. *Oh, goodness.* How did they get in here? Should I just toss them back through the window?

It sounded like a quick way to lose a hand.

Plop, plop, plop.

They weren't stopping. Another batch joined the first, swimming in my bath like they belonged there. Aware of my presence, they swam closer to the edge, their little mouths opening and closing like they were chewing on my toes already. I was so distracted with the fish and how to remove them that I wasn't prepared for the graceful arch of a merman diving through the window. My mouth hung open as a tidal wave of water slapped into me, soaking the front of my gown.

Too many emotions exploded, too difficult for me to focus on just one. Dazed, I entered into the bath one step at a time, too scared to blink that he might disappear again.

He found me.

Ryken swam under the water, magnificent in his merman form, the

221

tiny pool barely able to contain the long length of his silver tail. The piranhas huddled in the corner of the bath, afraid now that the real beast had arrived. My beautiful beast, who made my heart sigh in a way I knew I should be concerned about if I thought about it long enough.

Three things became absolutely clear as I jumped into the bath.

One: I was falling for Ryken whether I wanted to or not.

Two: I couldn't imagine a future without him.

Three: I was going to kiss him.

Trust Me

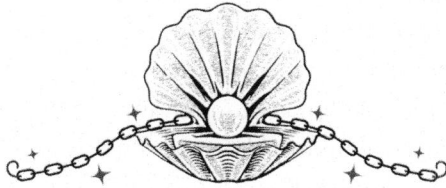

I needed to touch him. To hug him. Anything to prove he was real.

Ryken emerged halfway from the water, droplets sliding down his gray muscles in distracting lines. Impatient, he didn't wait for me to reach him, darting forward with a mewling sound. He plowed into me and knocked me into the water. His arms wrapped around my back and squeezed, his face burrowing into my neck.

Marigold...

Hearing the crack in his voice snapped my restraint, and I threw my arms around his neck, clinging to him as desperately as he was to me.

I didn't want to let go and be separated again. When he pulled away, I dug my nails into his shoulder blades and latched on tighter.

I want to see you. Please, he begged in my thoughts. *I need to see you're all right.*

How could I say no?

In his merform, his face hovered an inch from me, breathtakingly handsome, and I cupped his jaw. He leaned in, and I shut my eyes. The anticipation of his lips on mine jolted my heart into a frenzy of beats. But he only rested his forehead against mine, mumbling incoherent clicks and hums from his language.

I missed you, he said finally, sending a shiver down my spine at the deep rumble in his voice.

You're unharmed? I asked, scanning his features.

He nodded, inhaling my scent.

How did you find me?

I followed the beats of your heart, and when I was lost—your song called to me. Nothing would keep me from you.

More questions bubbled up, but I ignored them, desiring only to savor this reunion. Pressing my other hand to his cheek, he stroked my thumb along his skin and closed his eyes.

This . . . I have waited for this moment, he said.

Maybe I had too. My lips ached with want. The need to know how his mouth would feel on mine had my eyes fluttering closed.

Gathering what courage I had, I pressed my lips tentatively against his, hoping to show him what my words could not. A delicious warmth seeped into my veins, intoxicating and irresistible. Just like Ryken.

His hands clenched the fabric of my gown, and he pushed me away. Frowning, he squinted at me in confusion.

Oh, goodness. Not again. Was I a terrible kisser? Guessing by the way he held his fingers on his mouth, I had done it wrong. I bit my lower lip, hoping to stop the tingling sensation. Where he was disgusted, I wanted more. I kicked to the surface, embarrassed by another failed attempt at affection. Almost to the steps, I broke through the water, but Ryken yanked my foot, and I let out a surprised shriek before plunging back under.

Turquoise eyes scanned my face, hesitating over my mouth. His tail whipped up behind me, shoving my face to his. I stopped myself just before our faces collided. One of his hands splayed across my back, drawing me closer, as his other trailed across my mouth and down my jaw until it stopped at my collar.

Where are you going? he asked.

I wanted some fresh air.

Are you angry with me?

I held his stare. *I'm not angry.*

Then why did you try to bite me?

My eyes widened. *Bite you?* A flurry of bubbles escaped as I laughed. Was that what he thought I had done?

His nostrils flared. *I'm serious, Marigold.*

It was just a kiss. I won't do it again.

A kiss? His hand on my back tensed. *Explain.*

Warmth spread up my neck, my cheeks flushing. *Do you not know what a kiss is?*

They don't teach us everything about humans. Only—

Suddenly, he stiffened, his muscles tensing. Sniffing me, he jerked back, growling.

Now what is it? Could he sense how I was feeling? Like how I could smell his desire and . . . anger? But he was more than angry. He was practically vibrating with fury.

Your scent is different, he growled again in my thoughts, his tail whipping back and forth in wide strokes.

I smell? He was appalled with my hygiene? This was not the reunion I was hoping for.

Who is he? Ryken demanded.

My lips parted. *He? What are you talking about?*

Your scent. Ryken's lip curled, showing only the pointed tips of his teeth. He pulled my hair to his nose and released an animalistic roar. *He has marked you with his scent.*

Nobody has marked me. I pushed against his chest, but it was like pushing against a solid wall. Then I thought for a moment—was he talking about Prince Vian? *Ryken, this is just a misunderstanding. The prince rescued me because he thought I was drowning.*

You breathe underwater. His tone was flat and disbelieving.

Yes, but he doesn't know that. He was helping me. When he continued to stare, I added, *I don't care about him like that.*

And me?

I . . . care a lot about you, I admitted, looking away.

Is that why you tried to bite me? Ryken shifted closer.

Once again, it's called a kiss.

Do it again.

My skin heated, and my eyes dropped to his mouth. *Kiss you? Right now?*

Yes.

The single word echoed in my thoughts. I hesitated, but the alluring call of his scent had me ignoring the butterflies of nerves in my stomach, and I pressed my mouth to his. Three soft kisses, each one a little longer than the last. Relaxing, he pulled me closer, his thumb sliding along the edge of my collar and leaving a trail of flames across my skin.

I sank into him, lost in his touch. My thoughts and fears were wiped away, the room fading out of focus. It was just the two of us. His touch, his smell, and the heat of his skin made me want to surrender control. I wrapped my arms around his neck, wanting it all. I'd break every rule to be with him.

Love me, Ryken.

Startled at the thought, I pulled back, my lips tingling. I retreated, swimming to the steps, my head bobbing out of the water.

Like a predator locked on his prey, he broke through the surface and followed, pinning me on the stairs. His hands threaded into my hair. *Don't stop.* His mouth crashed back to mine a little too hard. *More. I want more.*

Too rough, Ry.

All at once, his grip gentled. His mouth sliding across mine sent sparks through me, and a soft moan escaped in the quiet of my room.

He jerked away, eyes scanning my face. *Did I hurt you?*

My insecurity had me mumbling into my chest. "No, I—uh . . . "

He raised my chin. *What?*

Trapped under him, I couldn't hide. But I still wasn't brave enough to admit it out loud. *I liked it.*

His lips captured mine, searing me with his heat. And I was falling again, consumed by his kiss.

Is kissing only for your mouth? Because I want to kiss your nose— which he did. *Your cheeks—* he nuzzled his way up my cheekbone. *Especially your beautiful eyes—* he pressed a tender kiss on each lid. *Anywhere you'll let me.*

I melted on the stairs.

My Marigold . . . Click, clickety-click, hummm, click.

A knock pounded on the door, and Ryken lifted his head, his pupils dilating as he scanned the room. He sniffed at the air. *Are we under attack?*

"No, there is just someone at the door. You have to hide," I said, catching my breath. My hands trembled as I tried to scoot from under him.

I'm not afraid. Let them see me. His tail slapped the water. *Then they will be full of fear.*

I rolled my eyes. "You're outnumbered. There is one of you and a castle inundated with guards. Jump back out through the window and wait for me where it's safe. I'll join you as soon as I send whoever it is away."

I'm not leaving you.

"I'm not asking you to. We have a better chance of sneaking out if we can escape undetected."

Good. We need to get back to the sea. His eyes darkened as he stared at me. *You need to complete your transformation.*

"I will . . . after we visit Cadell."

He twisted his lips into a scowl, not liking this plan at all. To soothe him, I leaned in to press a quick kiss on his mouth. Though he refused the quick part of the kiss and kept our lips connected even as I pulled away.

Another knock sounded at the door.

"Marigold," the prince called out, his voice high with panic. "If you don't answer, I'm coming in."

A low growl rumbled from Ryken's chest.

If he tries to take you, I will kill him.

The door rattled like someone was about to break through. "Final warning. I'm coming in."

"Your Highness, I'm indisposed. Please don't come in," I said. When Ryken didn't move from his protective stance over me, I pushed on his chest and mouthed, "Go."

Something thudded against the wood of the door. "Are you all right? You took your time responding."

"I was . . . distracted."

A look of heated possession crossed Ryken's face, and the urge to kiss him returned.

"Can we please talk?" the prince whispered urgently.

I blew out a breath of frustration and scooped my wet hair from my forehead. "I'll be right there."

Don't make me leave, Ryken said mournfully.

I placed my hand on his chest, raising my eyebrows at his racing heart. A calming wave rippled from my chest, down my arm, and into him.

Trust me, I said.

He sighed and pressed his hand over mine. *I do.*

Entranced, I watched as he drifted backward, his jaw ticking. He dove into the water, circling the perimeter of the bath over and over, picking up speed until water sloshed over the edges.

Mesmerized, I watched as he circled me and gasped when he launched into the air, droplets dripping from his body as he effortlessly dove through the window. His black tail appeared bluish in the light, scales shimmering like diamonds. I pressed a hand to my stomach, my insides melting all over again. How was he so attractive when he wasn't even trying?

Flashes of silver zipped closer, and I scrambled out of the water. Now that Ryken had left, the school of piranhas grew bolder, inching closer to my toes.

I climbed the stairs just in time. Pieces of my navy dress floated on the surface, the piranhas tearing them to shreds.

How was I going to reach the window with those menacing monsters in there?

"Marigold? Are you still there?"

"Yes, Your Highness." I rushed over to the door, watery footprints trailing behind me, and opened it a crack.

Prince Vian blinked at me, sighing when he saw I was soaked and shivering. "You know you don't have to wear your clothes to take a bath, right? Or is this a modesty custom in Cadell?"

"You said this was important, Your Highness."

"It is." He placed a hand on the door above my head and whispered, "Can I come in, please? I don't feel comfortable talking about this in the hall."

"Whatever you need to say to me can be said out here."

His jaw clenched. "Is this about requiring a chaperone for your reputation?" he asked. "Twice now we've been caught in a compromising situation. I think it's safe to say my mother is picking out fabric for your wedding gown as we speak."

"Goodbye, Prince Vian," I said flatly and shut the door.

His hand caught it before it closed, pushing it wide enough so he could slip in. I shot a worried glance at the water. Thankfully Ryken was still waiting outside.

"Goodbye? Don't you mean goodnight? Are you sure you're feeling well?"

"I'd feel a lot better if you'd let me rest."

"I'm worried about you. Your eyes are glassy, and your face is flushed. Even your lips are swollen. This looks worse than a headache. Did you take any of the medicine I brought you?" He reached out a hand for my forehead, and I batted it away.

I held up my hands, palms out. "I am fine, Your Highness. Please say whatever you came to say."

"It's about your sister."

My hands flopped to my side. "What about her?"

"Since you have arrived here—are you cold? You're shivering." He turned to the bed and snatched the top blanket.

"And? My sister?" I pressed, squeezing my hands together to keep from shaking the answer out of him.

"Yes, your sister. I don't want secrets between us." He shook open the blanket. "Would you rather have a thicker blanket? This one is too thin."

"*Vian*, I don't care about the stupid blanket."

He paused, his dark eyes meeting mine. "You called me Vian."

"I—yes, sorry, Your Highness. I didn't mean to be disrespectful. Sometimes I can be impatient when I'm worried."

"It's all right," he said quietly. He swung the blanket around my shoulders, bundling me tight, then rubbed my upper arms for warmth. "If it's just us, I don't mind."

Call him by his first name? That was madness. He was a prince!

I chanced another look at the bath and took a calming breath. "You were saying?"

"I know where she is."

I bit my fist to keep from screaming. Or mauling him. Or maybe both. If Ryken heard me, he would leap in here in a second. "You . . . have known all this time?" I kept my tone neutral.

"After we had that talk today about our sisters, I've felt sick inside that I didn't say anything. I came to apologize and . . . and . . . are those *piranhas* in your bath?" He thrust an arm in front of me like the

229

fish were going to charge us any minute. "What kind of sorcery is this?"

"I think there is a tear in the netting." *Big enough that a merman swam through.*

He spun to me. "You haven't tried to escape, have you? After I warned you?"

"I've been in my room the whole time."

He shook his head, frowning at himself. "Of course, of course. I'm sorry I accused you. Gather your things and come with me. We will move you to a new room."

"I'm all right—I'm sure we can scoop them out."

A look of absolute horror settled on his face. "They are *killer* fish. Nobody is going near them—especially you. I'll ring for a guard to remove them. Until then, we can wait in my chamber"—he stumbled over his words at my narrowed gaze—"uh, I mean, Vella's room."

"I wish to remain here."

His hands pressed into my back, ushering me out the door. "Don't be ridiculous. It's for your safety. Besides, you can dry off and change into one of Vella's dresses."

"But I'll be right back?" I shouted over my shoulder, hoping that Ryken heard the message before my door shut.

"Of course." He smiled, his hand rubbing my upper back. "I like that you're getting comfortable around the castle."

"Prince Vian . . . "

"Just Vian, remember? I've saved your life twice now. That should make us friends."

"Friends? And nothing else?" I guess I could handle being friends. Husband, I could not.

He nodded. "Your honesty is always bittersweet, my lady."

Knocking twice on the door, he led me into Vella's room. Clothing was strewn about the room as if a fabric shop had exploded. It reminded me of working in my grandmother's shop during the summer ball season. We'd have so many orders and not enough space to store them. But that was not the case here.

"My chamber would have been cleaner than this," he grumbled, the door clicking shut behind us.

The room was twice the size of mine, larger than the entire square footage of my family's cottage. The canopy bed was on a raised platform, blue buds of morning glory climbing up the frame and strangling the furniture with its roots. Unattended and forgotten, the vines knotted around the headboard in thick clusters, beautiful but wild. It matched Vella's personality perfectly.

Bookshelves lined the side wall, and what looked to be a chaise lounge was buried under a pile of garments. I stared at the books, wondering why these were allowed out of the library but not the one I had been interested in.

Light twinkled off the turquoise water of her bath, the beauty of it calling to me. When I took a step forward, the prince wrapped his arm around my waist, dragging me back to him.

"What is it with you and the water? I'm beginning to think you're as obsessed as Vella."

I shook my head, righting my thoughts. "We're not here to talk about your sister or me."

He sighed. "Promise you won't be angry with me."

"Please tell me already. Do you like torturing me? You know I'm worried sick about her."

"I know . . . I heard you singing. I'm sorry. The problem is that I took a vow to stay silent, and I can't break it."

"What vow? To the sea?"

Nodding, he squeezed my shoulders, and I realized he had been holding on to me this entire time.

"I can't say exactly what I want to say without breaking it. So, listen carefully. Your sister is looking for you, but due to her position, she can't leave her . . . home. Her husband is in Amille."

I blinked. "Prince Alexander is in Amille?"

"I never said Prince Alexander," he said, his eyes widening with a silent message.

"I don't understand."

He gave me a shake. "I didn't say Prince Alexander. Why wouldn't I say that?"

"Uh, because he's . . . not her . . . husband?"

He nodded. "Keep going. Finish the thought, Marigold."

"Prince Alexander would never have left her. And she loved him." Didn't she? A memory of Rosey screaming the day they became

231

engaged surfaced. Could she possibly not have gone through with the ceremony?

What had Vella said in the library? *If I were your sister, I would have run too.*

The squeal of metal grinding against metal snapped me out of my puzzling. I didn't have time to react before the prince tugged me to his chest with a squeak.

A piece of the wall slid open, and the princess walked in, her appearance disheveled. Her white hair hung loose around her shoulders in a tangled mess. She scowled at the two of us, an unnatural light in her eye. The prince angled me away, tucking me behind him.

"What are you doing here?"

"Thank the Seas. It's just you, Vella."

"Brother, this is an invasion of privacy. My room is not for your personal use. Take your little trollop and leave. Even Vox has some scruples."

"You don't understand. It's actually——" the prince started, but the princess knocked into his shoulder as she passed. He fell into me, and my footing slipped in the water that had pooled at my feet. The two of us tumbled to the tile, skidding away from each other.

The princess took a step back, surprised. "Marigold."

"Hi. Yes. We were here just looking for a dry dress."

"A dress?" Her eyes slid to the prince. "*Right.* And did you find it in his arms even though there are plenty scattered around my room?"

"He was trying to tell me something."

The princess crossed her arms, her lips pinched. "Tell you what?"

"The way her smile brightens a room," the prince answered before I could.

I sent him a look. Why was he lying?

"Vian, your level of desperation is appalling."

"You know I like a challenge." The prince rolled to his feet and offered me his hand.

"Your leg . . . " the princess said, pointing.

Oh, goodness. Heat burned from my neck to the tips of my ears, and I flipped my sopping wet gown back over my legs. Taking the prince's hand, I stood, keeping my eyes on the floor.

"Vian, leave us," Princess Vella commanded.

"I should go too," I mumbled, slinking to the door.

The princess's hand whipped out, gripping my upper arm in a painful hold. "I think you should stay. There is something I want to show you."

Her cool gaze held mine with an intensity that made my blood run cold. Shaking my arm, she squeezed tighter, her long nails digging into my skin.

"Vella, stop it. You're hurting her," the prince said.

"Why are you still here? I asked you to leave."

"Did you take your medicine today?" he whispered to her.

"That's none of your business," she snapped.

"It is my business when other people are involved."

She laughed, an off pitch sound that had me wincing. "We are friends. Isn't that right, Marigold?"

Her fingers burrowed deeper into my flesh, and I whimpered, unable to detach her before she yanked me closer.

"Vella, I know this isn't you. Whatever you want, it isn't worth forcing her. Please, release her. I don't want to make you do it."

They stared at each other for a moment before she shoved me forward. He easily caught me without breaking eye contact with his sister.

"I thought our little mermaid lover would be interested in what I found. I guess she will never know now."

I stiffened. Mermaid? What did she know?

"We aren't playing your games," the prince said, trying to guide me from the room.

I pulled from his hold, suddenly nervous. "What did you find?"

Her lips curled into the same smile I had seen on Prince Vox's face. "Let me show you."

Fear prickled across my skin, and my shiver had nothing to do with my wet clothes. "I'm not going anywhere without an explanation."

"This is lunacy. You aren't going with her at all when she is in one of her moods. Come on, Marigold." Prince Vian grabbed my hand.

I snatched it back.

The princess laughed again, tapping her lip. "Curious, aren't you?"

He moved between us. "Marigold, trust me. We shouldn't be with her when she is like this."

"Can't you take the hint, brother? She's not interested in you. You've embarrassed yourself enough." She tsk-tsked him.

Prince Vian ignored her. "I'm not leaving you alone with her."

"Why are you so devoted to *her* over your own sister? Especially when she hasn't been completely honest with us."

He shook his head. "We all have our secrets. She's allowed to have her own."

The princess walked to the expansive bookshelf against the wall, her index finger gliding along the worn spines. "There wasn't anything strange you noticed about her? Or were you too distracted by her pretty face?"

Turning to me, his eyes searched my face. My heartbeat thrummed in my throat as I caught a wave of his suspicion coating the air.

Whatever the princess wanted to show me, it wasn't worth getting caught up in. Not when each passing second filled me with dread. Ryken was waiting for me.

"I think I'd like to return to my room now," I said, drawing the blanket higher around my shoulders.

"It's too late for that," Princess Vella said with a sigh.

From my peripheral, a blur of white was my only warning before the princess slammed a vase into my skull.

Trapped

There wasn't enough time to scream. I crumbled on impact, the blow to my temple blinding me. Hazy images of Princess Vella's chamber warped into shadows, morphing into uneven blobs.

I braced for the floor, but strong arms scooped me up, cradling me like a child. Disoriented, I clung to the soft fabric. The smell of crisp linens and a masculine, spicy fragrance wafted from the material. I reeled back, knowing exactly who that was.

Prince Vian.

The sudden movement was too much. My neck prickled and the room spun just before the inky void snatched me under. A voice spoke in the darkness, the peaceful silence short-lived.

"Wake up, my child. There's work to be done."

Ruah? Exhausted, I struggled to collect my thoughts.

"Go, find the princess."

But hadn't she already found me?

Winds of a tornado pummeled my body, coated in a salty mist that commanded my eyes to open. I blinked the blurry shapes in the chamber into focus, narrowing in on the bright blood splatters on my sleeve. My blood. Another droplet dripped from my jaw to plop on my arm.

I glanced away from the grotesque stain, the kabob from earlier turning in my stomach. But I still couldn't escape the metallic odor, my sense of smell returning at an inopportune time.

The room pulsed, my ears struggling to translate the muffled voices. A scream? The call of my name? I couldn't tell. It was only by the barest shift in the air that I could detect the pressure of a sound wave even though I couldn't hear it.

The princess sneered as she spoke, spitting silent words. On either side of her were two grizzly sized guards, their larger stature similar to the citizens of Glenton more than the tall, lanky height of someone from here in Windcrest. They stood protectively, a silver scimitar gleaming in each guard's hand. The curved blade of a deadly weapon, one forged deep in the mountains. Alert, their cold eyes were trained on the prince holding me.

We shuffled backward, a reminder that he still carried me in his arms. Pieces of the vase crunched beneath the prince's sandals, startling me at the unexpected sound after the span of silence. Noises bombarded me as my hearing slowly adjusted.

"The guards are unnecessary. Would you really order them to stab your own brother?" Prince Vian said, his voice tight.

I stiffened. *Stab?*

"They wouldn't kill you. I mean, you are my favorite brother. Just a flesh wound or two. We only want her. Give her to Saban and there will be no quarrel between us."

Gasping, I sat up, my head still swimming. What would the princess need with me? I pushed against Prince Vian's chest, twisting to return to my feet.

The prince carefully placed me on the floor. "Careful, Marigold. There's glass everywhere."

"You're wasting my time, Vian. I'm on the cusp of a revolutionary discovery, and your misplaced chivalry is ruining everything. You almost had it right when you first met her, but you had one detail wrong. She isn't a spy for Cadell, but for the Merfolk in the sea."

My eyes widened as she locked her eyes on me. I didn't like where this was going one bit.

"Merfolk?" the prince repeated, oblivious to my panicked state. "Do you hear yourself?"

236

"Don't you dare call me crazy. I have proof. Bring her to me, and I'll show you."

"No, Vella. This has gone on long enough. You, Vox, Father—all of you have your own agenda, and you keep using me to achieve it. I'm done. Do you hear me? I won't be anyone else's puppet. She deserves the truth. Let her return to Cadell."

"You'd let her go? After what Father expects of you?"

"Yes," he said, meeting my gaze. "I'd let her go because of it. For her to be stuck with me for life? I don't want to see her face when she discovers the truth. She'll hate us—hate *me*."

"Your compassion makes you weak. If Father doesn't skin you alive, then you'll be fish food by morning because of your broken promise." She paused. "Well, maybe that would be a good thing. You can meet another mermaid to pine over."

"I'm not pining. I enjoyed her honesty for a change. Something our family wouldn't know anything about."

"Boo-hoo." She flicked an invisible tear away. "Are you finished yet?"

His breath caught. "What has happened to you? Since Verona died——"

Her hands balled into fists at her side. "She is *not* dead. I've told you over and over. You just won't listen to me."

"Stop living in a fantasy world, Vella. She's been gone for years without a trace. She is dead. It was hard to accept, but the sooner you come to terms with it, the sooner you can find closure. And maybe happiness."

I peeked over my shoulder and gauged the distance to the door. Could I outrun two armed guards?

"How can you say that? After Marigold disappeared for a year, she reappeared as if she'd never left. Did her family give up on her? No. Her sister never stopped searching—even when everyone called her crazy." She tilted her head, her eyes misting. "And what do you do in the same circumstance with our own beloved sister? You forget about her and move on."

"I never said forget. You are putting words in my mouth." The prince pointed at her, scowling.

"Verona isn't gone. I've *seen* her. You always think I'm the last to know something, but you underestimate me. Secrets are the lifeblood of this family, and I know everyone's. *Sweet little Vella,* you all say. *She's never paying attention.* But I am. I know Father and Vox haven't informed you about Windcrest's newest league of warriors." She leaned in and raised a brow. "They don't trust you."

A chill settled over me. What has Windcrest been up to?

Prince Vian shook his head. "I disagree. I'm aware of the new battle plans. We have our new warships in construction at the dockyard and archers training with poisoned arrows in the southern farmlands. Our informant has reported that our loyal soldiers in Cadell still wear our supportive band to show allegiance to Windcrest. Vox has already sent word for them to return home with as many weapons as they can carry. If it comes to war, I'm well versed on the situation, my sweet little sister."

"I meant the underwater soldiers."

He fumbled over his question. "Underwater?"

A chill raced down my spine, my feet rooted to the ground.

"Yes, but honestly, I don't care about the war. I just want Marigold's necklace so I can talk to my sister again."

I wanted to run, to be anywhere but here. But something in my gut told me to stay—to listen—because these details would be important later. Before, I had been worried about the Merfolk attacking the humans, but now I was fearful of the opposite.

Maybe I was a spy after all.

When the guards inched toward us, the prince stepped in front of me, holding out his hands to shield me.

"If I understand correctly, once you have her necklace, you'll release us?"

"Yes, I'll tell the guards to stand down. Her necklace has no clasp. You'll need to bring her down to my workroom so I can cut it off."

"Workroom? I thought it was the storage room."

She batted her eyelashes. "Father made a few adjustments for me."

He chewed on his lip, contemplating Princess Vella's request.

"Your Highness," I whisper-shouted, "I can't give her my necklace."

"It's just a piece of jewelry. I'll buy you another."

"This isn't something that is bought. It's——" I stopped myself before I said the word *magical* "——irreplaceable."

He glanced away, sighing. "Sometimes you have to make sacrifices. And I think your life is worth more than the gold around your neck."

Before I could respond, one guard sprang at us, swiping the prince aside in one stroke and snatching me around the waist. The other approached from behind, wrapping his meaty arms around the prince, restraining him so they could keep us separated.

"Unhand me this instant. This is treason," Prince Vian demanded, kicking when his feet left the floor.

"These are my personal guards Father gifted me, and they only obey our commands." She smirked, an odd look twisting her features. "Father doesn't want anyone interfering with my experiments—including you, brother."

Experiments?! A thick hand slapped over my mouth when I tried to scream.

"This is your fault, Marigold. You should have just traded your necklace with me in the library. Things would have been so much easier. Now we have to do it my way." A gleeful smile stretched across her face.

The guard carried me down the stairs, ignoring my screams of protest. Their footsteps echoed against the stones. The temperature chilled as we descended, the air becoming dank and stagnant. Water dripped in the distance, a constant splattering on the cement floor loud enough to hear over the constant humming.

"What . . . ?" Vian started, but his voice trailed off in disbelief, the fight leaving him when he saw the glass structure in the middle of the room.

The tall glass tube was filled to the brim, specks floating in the hazy water. I caught a glimpse of a girl through the claw marks in the green slime. Her long tail sparkled with a mix of aqua and hazel crystals. She tucked it underneath her, almost hugging it in comfort. Long white hair floated around her head, the ends tipped in blue fanning around her face so similar to the princess's bone structure. Her eyes were closed as if in slumber.

But I knew better. Merfolk didn't need sleep.

I didn't know what was more alarming, a mermaid here in Windcrest or the terrible state of her living conditions. She could swim vertically and turn around, but the confining space left room for little else.

The mermaid's arms were bony, her gray skin outlining each groove. She was not like the ones I had seen while I was in the sea.

Why were humans like this? The need to poke and prod to gain understanding. It became clear why Ryken urged me to stay in the safety of the sea. I sent her a pitying glance.

This might be my future.

"Restrain her on the table, Saban. I need to find my knife." The princess spoke as calmly as one would when asking about the weather. She walked past a golden harp to a table filled with stacks of books and notes, including the book I'd found in the library.

The guard slammed me onto a nearby table and tied me up with a thick piece of rope that had conveniently been resting there. Was this the princess's plan all along? To tie me up?

Stuttering, the prince's mouth opened and closed in shock. "What is that creature? Is that a—? No, it can't be possible——"

"Oh, her? It's what I've been telling you, but you didn't want to listen."

"Is that—a *mermaid*?" the prince asked, not sounding like himself.

"Not just any mermaid. It's Verona. I thought, of anyone, you'd recognize our sister."

"That thing is *not* my sister."

"It is, and it's all we have left of her. I'm trying to figure out how to communicate with her." She snatched a silver dagger from the table.

"Where did you find her?" he asked.

"For years, Father has been capturing Merfolk and trying to breed them into his unstoppable army. So far, it's been an expensive failure. But Marigold, a human turned mermaid, might save the experiment. We should document her changes and learn from her experience. Like, where is she getting the magic to change? It has to be in the necklace. Verona has the same one. That's how I knew."

I flinched when the princess approached and jammed her finger into my neck behind my ear.

"Do you see that mark there? Just below her ear here. Those are her gills. How do you think she lasted in the ocean for a year?"

He slowly spun to me, his shoulders hunched. "You can breathe underwater?"

I averted my eyes, unable to handle his betrayed expression.

240

"Did you not see her leg either? Patches of scales are already form-ing," Princess Vella added.

What?! My mind whirled with renewed panic. There weren't any scales the last time I checked when I changed. *Not yet, please, not yet. There is still so much I need to do before I transform.*

"You shouldn't get so attached to her. Eventually, Marigold will live in one of these glass cages."

"You said you'd let her go."

She shrugged. "I will, but Father may want to keep her around."

"No," he whispered softly.

"Come look at her future, brother." Princess Vella waved the guard over to the glass cage. As soon as they were a foot away, the mermaid's eyes snapped open. She threw herself forward, her rows of sharp teeth snarling at the glass. Startled, both royals jumped back, watching in horror as the mermaid clawed the glass between them, sending more green chunks into the water. I had no doubt that she would have torn them to shreds if she could.

"Isn't Verona amazing?" the princess said, sighing. "In life, she was sick and frail, but now look at her."

"I don't care how much she looks like her—that is *not* Verona."

"You'll see. Once we can explain who she is, she'll remember everything."

"What makes you think you can communicate with her?"

"Remember Marigold's song?"

"The sad one she sings at night?"

What about my song? I swallowed the fear in my throat.

"I was humming it when I came down here to feed Verona, and she reacted. It was only a few seconds, but it was more progress than I had made in the months she's been down here."

"Months?" His mouth dropped open.

"Father gave her to me in hopes it would improve my outbursts. I've made a genuine effort to change, haven't you noticed?"

"You just smashed a vase into a girl's head."

She sighed dramatically. "I'm allowed a setback or two."

"Vella . . ."

"Watch what happens when I play the song," the princess said, prac-tically skipping to the harp.

241

She fluffed her skirt as she sat on the stool and positioned her fingers on the harp strings. Her back was stiff, her arms posed as if she were in the drawing room ready to treat us with her performance. With grace from years of practice, she plucked at the strings, the notes mimicking my song but an octave higher.

Immediately, the mermaid stopped thrashing in the water, sinking down as she watched the princess play.

Abruptly, the princess stopped, throwing her head back with a frustrated sigh. "I don't know the rest of the song. I need to hear it again."

Something rattled around the corner out of sight, water sloshing onto the stone. Echoes of steady hammering had us all turning to look at the far end of the room hidden by a sheet.

"What was that?" I asked.

The princess sent me a knowing look. "As luck would have it, a merman. I filter the fish from the moat into a glass container, similar to Verona's. Earlier, when I was playing Marigold's song, he swam through."

"A what?" I bucked against the rope. *Did she mean Ryken? No, no, no.*

"He's a warrior of water just like the myths say. Huge and terrifying. I'm scared he will break the glass if he gets too agitated. So I covered it, hoping it would calm him. It's odd how the song soothes Verona, but it makes him volatile. Father has caught a few like him, but he's the biggest we've seen. Father will be so pleased. The merman will make a perfect addition to his new army."

Nobody was touching him if that merman was who I thought it was. I wouldn't let them.

"Let me up," I shouted, frantic.

The pounding in the distance grew louder, metal rattling.

"Marigold," the prince said, wheezing against the guard's hold. "Are you all right? I'm so sorry—I had no idea about any of this."

"Get us out of here," I begged, holding his stare.

The brute of a guard wrapped a forearm around the prince's head, craning it back at an unnatural angle. The curved edge of the sword fit perfectly around the prince's neck. His Adam's apple bobbed with each breath, a trickle of blood running down his dark skin.

The princess wagged her finger at him. "Uh-uh. She won't be released until I say so. It's time to hand over the necklace."

I bucked upward, fighting against the rope, but froze when the princess pressed a knife into my throat above my collar.

"I thought we could be friends. But I don't think I would be heart-broken if I never saw you again."

"Wait," I croaked out, wincing when the knife nicked me. "Let me try talking to her."

Princess Vella tilted her head, eyeing me suspiciously. "There is still another guard who will, at my command, run his blade through you if you think to double-cross me. I pay them extra for their continued loyalty, and they are itching for action."

The prince fought against the guard, drawing my attention. The hilt of the guard's blade cracked against his skull, and he sank into the guard's arms, blinking rapidly.

Panic pulsed through me, beating in tune with each of her laughs. "I'll help you. Release the merman in exchange."

"Oh, Marigold. You're such a delight. This isn't a barter. You either help me or I take what I want. The merman belongs to me now."

A possessive fury had me lashing out, snarling, "He is *mine*."

Wide-eyed, she sprung back, her hand clutching her chest. After a moment of staring at me, she smiled. "You are full of surprises. But so am I." She pointed the tip of her knife at me.

"Vella, this is outrageous. Stop before you go too far," the prince pleaded.

"Listen, brother. I can cut off your tongue or you can remain silent. The choice is yours, but I must concentrate as I slice the necklace off."

He ground his teeth as he turned to me. "I'm so sorry, Marigold."

In a flash, the princess was across the room, swinging her knife in a blinding rage. At the last second, the prince shrunk back, the blade slicing him from ear to mouth.

"Do not test me," she shrieked, her chest heaving. "I'm the one in charge."

His eyes softened as they trailed over her face, his brows scrunching together. "Did I lose you the same day I lost Verona?"

"Are you blind? We are both right here."

"You are no more my sister than that creature in the water is."

The princess arced her arm, winding it back with a twisted sneer on her face.

"I'll do it! I'll talk to her," I shouted, distracting the princess.

Glancing between us, doubt glistened in her eyes. She stomped back over to me. "You promise to tell her exactly what I say?"

Could I afford to make another promise? Not when I was prepared to do the opposite.

She held up a hand. "I have a better idea. I'll drop you in there with her, and you'll either figure it out and live, or you won't and she'll tear you to shreds. Since she arrived here, I have only lost four guards. I suggest you don't underestimate her tail."

She cut my bindings, but before I could even attempt to run, the guard swung me up and over his shoulder as if I weighed nothing. His grip on my thigh squeezed more painfully each time I pounded my fist into his spine. I was tired of being the damsel in distress.

The squeal of metal grinding against metal pierced my eardrums as he lifted the grate at the top of the cage high enough to throw me in. I plunged under the water, my skirt expanding in a poof as I submerged completely. The grate slammed shut, the noise muffled in the water. Kicking to the top, I pressed against the hard metal, shaking it to no avail.

An animalistic roar sounded beneath me, freezing me in place.

Oh, goodness. They trapped me inside with a feral mermaid. How was I ever going to survive this?

Aquamarine scales sparkled behind her, the beauty of her tail clashing with the sinister expression marring her face. In a flurry of bubbles, the mermaid pounced upward, her hands like claws, her teeth bared.

So many teeth.

I jerked back and screamed.

Touch Her, and You'll Lose a Hand

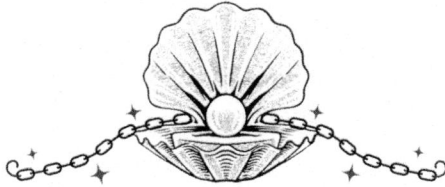

M ashing her pointed teeth together, the mermaid growled, approaching at an alarming speed. Hunger reflected in her glassy eyes.

I couldn't watch another second and spun away. My scream shifted, dropping an octave to form my song. Haunting notes tore from me, burning my throat. Fear twisted in my chest as I braced myself, the oily water swirling around me.

Clicking sounded, followed by a long hum.

The mermaid hovered beneath me, the cage too tight for the two of us to be side by side. Her features relaxed, the time spent in captivity hollowing her once-beautiful face. Up close, she was wasting away. Her head tilted as she communicated in a language I didn't understand.

I shook my head and shrugged. Body language was the best I could do.

The mermaid mimicked me, shaking her head and whipping her long white hair around her face. A ghost of a smile pulled at her lips. She flicked her tail and leaned forward, inhaling my scent.

Unable to stop myself, I did the same on instinct. Basic facts filled my mind. She was a female about my age, curious, and a tart aftertaste of her nervousness coated my tongue.

My scent must have revealed something because her eyes widened.

Excited, she chittered noises and hums, her hands flailing about as if she were telling a grand story. Not that I minded since a story was better than her trying to eat me.

Pointing to my ear, I grimaced and shrugged.

Her tail sagged. She glanced down and became distracted by my dress. She grabbed the material, lifting it closer to sniff the ripped hemline. Catching sight of my feet, she made a high-pitched squeal and crowded in closer to investigate.

Wedged between her and the glass, I reached for the grate above me and lifted my face out into the tiny sliver of air. Voices echoed in the room, loud compared to the muted sounds I heard in the water. The baritone of Prince Vian's voice rose above the others as he barked commands and threats.

Looping my fingers through the metal holes, I shook the grate. It rattled but didn't open. "Help," I screamed.

Glass shattered from somewhere in the room. Liquid splattered on the floor, sloshing, followed by a frenzied roar. *Ryken?*

The mermaid grabbed my ankle, dragging me back under. Eyes narrowed, she reprimanded me in clicks as she yanked me farther down to the bottom of the cage. She appeared disinterested in the ruckus on the other side of the glass, but when another roar vibrated through the water, she froze and threw a protective hand across my legs.

I wiped the filth from the glass, searching for Ryken in the fray. I didn't see him among the others. A swell of relief coursed through me. Not only for him, but for Prince Vian too. Somewhere along the way, the charming prince had worn me down. I didn't blame him for what Vella had done. Those were her actions alone. If only I had listened when he'd tried to warn me. He had stayed to protect me, and now he suffered the princess's wrath.

I really should be nicer to him.

My thoughts of the prince vanished as Ryken slid into view, riding in on a wave of water. His tail flicked, launching him in the air and plowing into the first guard, his teeth bared as they sunk into the man's neck. Even though they were matched in size, Ryken overpowered him in seconds and slammed his head into the floor.

I gasped, having forgotten he was a wild creature. I remembered him

246

talking about his daily training sessions. He was a warrior, not just when he was in his armor, but all the time.

It was a side of him I had never seen . . . until now.

He slammed the next guard's arm on the empty table, the bone bending at an odd angle. In rapid succession, he banged the man's forehead on the table until he flopped limply to the floor.

Shocked, I couldn't tear my eyes away. He was lost in his animalistic instinct, reminding me of his true nature. To defend and protect. I knew he preferred peace, so something must have snapped his restraint.

Click, clickety-click, hummm, click, he cried, loud enough that I heard it crystal clear in the water. His chest rose and fell in desperate pants as he scanned the room.

Me. He's searching for me.

Ryken locked on the prince as another threat. Princess Vella cowered behind her brother, sobbing into her fingers.

Nobody else needed to die.

I banged on the glass. *Here I am.*

Ryken's head whipped toward me, his mouth covered in blood. When he saw me locked up, his eyes narrowed. Growling, he skidded across the inch of water, his arms windmilling claws, building up speed as he slid straight toward me.

Prince Vian ran past him for the ladder, just missing the swipe of his hand. The princess wasn't as lucky. She flew back into a stack of crates with a plume of dust.

A hand gripped my gown, and the mermaid squeezed me to her. Her bright tail curled around me, her eyes on the grate above us. She let out a series of warning clicks in the back of her throat.

"Marigold?" the prince called out through the grate above us. "I don't know if you can hear me, but if you lure her to the top of the water, I can pry her off of you with my dagger."

The mermaid hissed, squeezing me tighter. I doubted the prince realized she understood every word he said. Distrust leaked into the water as she growled up at him.

Ryken's fist punched into the glass, a hairline fracture appearing where the blow landed.

The mermaid squealed, tossing me up and out of the way as she clawed at the glass, speaking rapidly in their language.

He tilted his head, responding.

I didn't waste my freedom and kicked straight to the top where the prince waited with the grate open and his hand outstretched in the water. He reeled me out, his muscles trembling.

"Are you all right? I always seem to be asking you this," he said.

"I am," I wheezed, grunting as I climbed out onto the platform. My gown refused to cooperate, and I was panting by the time I was completely out of the water. I pushed my wet hair from my eyes as I caught my breath.

A crazed look glinted in the prince's eyes. "We have to figure out how to get this mermaid out of here. I think she is the key to all this. That merman won't stop until he gets his wife back. Perhaps he will spare us if we give him what he wants."

Another thud sounded as Ryken punched the glass again.

"Wife?" My heart clenched at the thought. *Ryken with Verona?* I suddenly felt murderous. I couldn't even fathom how I would feel if it had been her scent on him like Vian's had been on me. "Ryken is here for *me*."

The prince swayed, his eyebrows high. "*Ryken?* The one you left in Amille? *Wait*—the merman is the one you have feelings for?"

The room was eerily silent as if it, too, waited for my answer.

"Yes," I said, my cheeks flushing. I hadn't admitted that to anyone aloud before.

He covered his mouth with his hand, thinking. "Your song . . . it wasn't for your sister."

"No, it wasn't." I scooted to the edge of the platform.

"You called him here to you. The necklace is from him, isn't it?"

I smiled and placed my hand on it. "It is a symbol of our bond."

He looked skyward with a gruff laugh. "It's all making sense now: the piranhas in your bath, why you kept checking the moat, your obsession with water, *ugh*—why didn't I see it earlier? You're in love."

My lips parted. *Love Ryken?* I leaned over the platform, my heart quickening. *Dare I?* Ryken stood by a guard, fiddling with the buttons of his stolen pants.

"There's no point in denying it. I mean, look at him. What's . . . uh . . . is he . . . standing? On legs?" He whipped me to face him. "Can you shift between forms too?"

"No, I'm still human. Mostly. Can you release me? I *need* to see him."

The prince let go so I could rush down. Before I reached the bottom rung, Ryken ripped me from the ladder and gathered me into his arms. He made a mewling sound and buried his face in the crook of my neck.

I didn't resist. I snuggled closer, his skin softer in human form. His heart thudded against my hand, and I spread my fingers wide, thankful to feel each beat.

"Marigold," he whispered in my hair. His hands flexed on my back, pulling us flush together. "I feel so many things. It's confusing."

As I held him, his body relaxed into mine. The heat of his breath on my skin scrambled my thoughts, and I took a step back to collect myself.

He brushed his hands across my wet skin, starting at my face and across my shoulders, then down my arms to my hands, inspecting every inch of my exposed skin. "Are you hurt?"

"I'm all right. What about you? It's hard to tell when you're covered in blood," I said.

"None of it is mine."

I used my sleeve to wipe his face, my lip curling in disgust at the metallic smell.

"I heard your song," he said between wipes. "The woman trapped me. I didn't like it."

"I know. I didn't like it either."

"The other man is approaching. Do you want me to kill him for you?"

I flinched at his indifferent tone. "No more killing. That's the prince."

His nostrils flared, and he ground his teeth. "The one who marked you?"

"He helped me. Where did you get these pants?"

"I took them from the big man." Ryken jerked his thumb over his shoulder at the unconscious body.

I quickly glanced away, my face heating at the guard's naked legs. "You can't take things that don't belong to you."

Ryken huffed. "So I have to give them back? But I finally figured out the buttons." He moved to unbutton the top one.

I averted my gaze. "No, keep them for now. The princess said they had plenty of garments to spare."

He nodded and tensed, his eyes sliding to something over my shoulder.

The prince stepped around me. "Ryken, is it? I don't think we've been introduced——"

Ryken growled a low, guttural sound a moment before his fist whipped out, producing a sickening crunch as it collided with Prince Vian's face. Stumbling from the impact, the prince's head snapped back, and blood dripped over his lips. He cradled his nose, hissing in pain.

"Ryken," I barked, furiously throwing my hands in the air. "Was that necessary?"

The merman shrugged one shoulder without an ounce of regret.

"I'm so sorry, Your Highness. He shouldn't have done that."

The prince pulled his hands away and moaned at his ruby-colored fingers.

I slapped my hand over my mouth, hoping to cover up my horrified gasp. It was more than a small nick. Blood covered the lower half of his face, the slice on his cheek oozing and swollen.

"Is this a Merfolk greeting or something?" the prince asked nasally, squinting through the pain.

"No," Ryken said, crossing his arms. "I just don't like you."

Stunned, I hissed his name again. He ignored me, his eyes still locked on the prince. This was a dreadful introduction.

"Merfolk are territorial by nature. He's still not happy that you——" I took a breath, knowing how odd my next words would sound "——marked me with your scent."

The prince blinked at me, lost for words.

"Don't take it personally. He doesn't like a lot of things."

Ryken nodded. "That is true. And I especially don't like you."

"He is . . . not what I expected," the prince whispered to me.

"You're only alive because my mate wishes it," Ryken added bluntly.

I groaned. Why did Ryken keep saying all the wrong things?

The prince dabbed his nose with the back of his sleeve, deep in thought. "Your mate, you say?" He sent me a wry look. "You weren't jesting when you said it was complicated."

I cleared my throat. The heat from Ryken's gaze sent goosebumps up my spine. "Anyway, he's really quite sweet once you get to know him."

Their faces twisted in disgust, neither of them interested in that suggestion. At least they agreed on one subject.

The mermaid slammed her tail into the glass, drawing our attention.

"Liora!" Ryken said, taking a few steps toward her, his stride more confident than when I last saw him. "I didn't recognize her at first."

The mermaid straightened, her tail swishing in excitement. She nodded, then rattled off a range of clicks and hums.

"You know her?" I asked.

"I do."

An unreasonable stab of jealousy coursed through me, and I wanted to shove her across the room. Instead, I tucked close to Ryken's side, a subtle gesture he didn't miss. He chuckled and combed his hand through my hair. Inhaling my scent, he tilted my chin, his turquoise eyes darkening as they held mine.

Jealous? he asked through our connection, his thumb resting on my collar.

Maybe. I glanced away.

His breath shuddered out. *You shouldn't be. Nobody can compare to you.* His thumb slid to the pulse in my neck, the corner of his mouth ticking up at the irregular beats.

Prince Vian cleared his throat. "You knew Verona?"

"Verona? This is Liora. Last time I saw her was over a year ago. We assumed she'd been killed. The mating bond must have kept her alive."

"You should take her back to the sea," the prince said. "I don't know what plans my family has for her, but I think it's best to keep her away from Vella."

"What is Vella?" Ryken asked.

"His sister," I explained.

"Oh." Ryken's shoulder touched mine in comfort.

"She's the one you knocked into the crates," the prince added harshly.

He scowled.

"Have you checked on her?" I asked before Ryken could say anything else.

"Yes, she's bruised but otherwise fine." He touched the gash on his cheek. "She needs to rest. I'll fetch help for her as soon as you all leave since this place will be swarming with people."

"Thank you for all you've done for me. For all of us. I won't forget it."

"Take this," the prince said, offering me his silver dagger, sapphires twinkling on the hilt. Waves were etched along the sheath, and above the crest of the waves was his name in a swirling script. "For your protection."

I held up my palms, refusing to be indebted. "It's too much, Your Highness."

"Consider it a loan. You can give it back to me the next time we meet."

I frowned.

"It's nothing compared to what you've done for me. For years, I thought I was broken. Verona's death had left a mark on me, too, and for the first time, you made me realize I could open my heart again. I'm thankful for that."

"You will find someone."

"Friendship, then?" He lifted his hand to my shoulder.

Ryken's chest pressed against my back. "Touch her, and you'll lose a hand."

Startled, the prince snatched it back. "He doesn't mean that . . . does he?"

"He better not." I jabbed Ryken in the ribs.

Cautiously, Prince Vian offered me his dagger again. "Please, take it as a token of our friendship. Only friendship, I promise."

I hesitated for a moment, then tucked it into one of the gown's many pockets. "Thank you."

The prince turned to Ryken. "Do you want to rescue the mermaid or should I?"

Ryken shifted from one foot to the other. "Could you? I can't figure out how to get up there."

The prince swallowed and glanced back at the mermaid. "All right, I'll lower her down to you, but could you please tell her not to rip me apart in the process?"

While Ryken and Prince Vian fished Liora out of the cage, I knelt by the princess. Her pulse thumped weakly, and her right eye was swollen

252

shut. I almost pitied her. Had nobody noticed the darkness eating away at her? Or had they ignored the problem until it disappeared? But it didn't, really. It festered until she snapped.

I placed a hand on her arm. "May you find peace." I stood and found the prince by my side.

Still crusted in blood, he peered down at his sister. "I'll find out about the other mermen my father is hiding. They don't deserve to be locked up any more than Vero—I mean, Liora does. I promise you, I had no idea of these plans or that my sister's mind had warped beyond recognition. Some masks are invisible."

"I believe you."

"She wasn't always this way. It's disheartening to think that this is how she will be remembered." He scooped his sister into his arms. "We will get help for her."

We followed him up the stairs, Ryken ahead of me with Liora. I went to offer him help, but he surprised me, climbing up on his own. When did he become so steady on his feet? He almost seemed . . . human.

Prince Vian rested Vella on her bed, drawing the quilt over her. Sighing, he walked back to us with his head hung low. "Again, I'm sorry for all the trouble she caused . . . for what my family has caused. Think about what I told you earlier about your sister. I know you can figure it out."

I nodded.

"Stay off the main roads. Soldiers and scouts from all the territories are hunting for you. Don't give anyone your real name," the prince said. "Blend in if you can."

I nodded again.

He lifted a hand as if to touch me but then thought better of it, turning it into an awkward wave.

"Keep on course, Marigold."

"May the wind be at your back, the waters be clear as glass, and——"

"——and your *true* home be on the horizon. There is salt in your veins."

I smiled. "I know."

"Just don't forget it."

"I won't."

His eyes landed on Liora clinging to Ryken's shoulders. He opened his mouth as if he had something else to say but scraped a hand through his frosty strands instead, ducking back and out of the way. "I don't know if Vella was right, if she was my sister or not, but take care of her for me, will you?"

"She will be better when she returns to her mate. Keeping them apart is killing them," Ryken said. "Mates aren't meant to be separated."

"I see," Prince Vian said, glancing between us. "You better hurry. There's no doubt someone from my family has been informed about all the racket going on here. Escape to the moat from Vella's window."

"Thank you, Your Highness," I said.

Even Ryken mumbled a word of gratitude.

Not waiting a second longer, Ryken tossed Liora up, and she dove through the window, her splash sounding like she had made it safely outside. Next, he placed me on the window ledge. His hand rested on my thigh when I leaned out. "We will jump together."

"Wait," the prince called out, joining us in the bath. He reached behind his neck and grabbed the fabric of his tunic, pulling it over his head. Bare-chested, he offered it to Ryken. "You can't go out there half naked."

Begrudgingly, Ryken took it and slipped it on. The linen stretched taut over his muscles. "Thank you for this and for watching over Marigold." He climbed into the opening, squeezing next to me.

"Always." The prince sent me a half-smile. "Until we meet again."

Ryken entwined our fingers and fell out the window, pulling me behind him. We splashed into the moat, and he kicked his legs to mimic his tail, keeping us afloat as Liora chomped through the mesh.

When the hole was big enough for us to swim through, Ryken placed a hand on my collar.

Are we going to Cadell or back home? he asked.

Both. Cadell first and then home.

He squeezed our linked hands in agreement. *I hope your sister is nicer than his.*

She is.

And I couldn't wait to see her again.

Turn Back

T oo slow to keep up, I lagged behind, my gown tangling with my feet as I kicked. Ryken turned around, oddly still in human form, motioning for me to hurry.

With a cautious smile, Liora glided over. She grabbed the fabric at my back and dragged me through the moat, clicking and humming to Ryken along the way.

I had never felt more useless in my life.

She pulled me through a long tunnel under the bridge, the end of it spewing us out into the river outside the kingdom. The water wasn't as deep as the moat and I stood, feeling less like a sack of sugar being carted around.

It was quieter here, the water clearer and crisp. To my left, the hum of the ocean called me. To my right, the river twisted into the unknown. The quickest way back to Cadell was to the right. Though most of it required traveling on foot.

Liora placed a hand on my cheek, drawing my face to her. With a shy smile, she reached into the tangles of her hair and pulled out a coin-sized cowry shell. It was coral pink with a stripe of violet, but the sun gave it a rainbow sheen. She presented it to me, her eyes hopeful. Humming and clicking, she nodded to Ryken.

"She wants to show her gratitude by giving you this," he translated.

"Oh, thank you. It's beautiful." I took it and held it closer to view the different colors.

"She wants you to wear it."

"Wear it?"

Liora pointed to her head and then mine. Plucking the shell from my fingers, she looped my hair through the hole in the shell and braided it in place, knotting the ends. A grin spread across her face, her tail swishing in excitement.

"She approves," Ryken said.

My laugh bubbled out. "I can tell."

The mermaid swam around me in a flurry of bubbles and then jetted off downstream toward the setting sun without a backward glance, eager to return to her mate.

I'd probably do the same thing if I were her. I stole a peek at Ryken through my eyelashes, and his sappy smile surprised me.

"What?" I asked, rubbing the back of my neck.

"The shell looks pretty on you. We will have to get you some more. Maybe yellow ones like the flowers you like."

My heart swelled at his thoughtfulness.

Grasping my hand, he pulled me eastward and away from the call of home. When Windcrest was far enough behind us, we took the rest of the journey by foot and headed south.

Ryken kept pace with me, his long legs making up for his slower gait. It allowed us time to catch up on what we had missed the last few days apart. Him following my trail and searching the river to the castle, and me with my abduction by a royal family full of secrets. After the dead-end at my grandparents' shop, my last lead to my family was to return to Cadell.

If we'd eventually get there. After Ryken had shot us up the river in minutes, the hours of walking seemed tedious . . . and painfully slow.

Unfortunately, we lost what little sun we had, and the chill in my wet clothes had me shivering. The brisk wind from the mountains in the east pushed against us, howling angrily.

"I think we need to stop," I said finally, my arms around my chest.

He scanned the empty terrain. Scattered trees dotted the barren land, leaving us vulnerable out in the open. This strip of land was on the outskirts of Bressal. If we continued south, we'd be lost in the bogs and marshlands of their ruined kingdom. The land of illusion was not one I cared to wander into. Before, I had thought of illusions as fables whispered by the fire to scare young children away from the deadly marsh.

But maybe I was wrong, as I had been about everything else. It could be made of magic, and we were just too blind to see it . . . or too scared to want to see it.

"Why stop now?" Ryken asked, sticking close to my side.

"I'm cold and tired. I think we need a fire."

"Walk faster. It will warm you." He took two steps, expecting me to follow, and spun back to face me when I didn't. "Are you hurt?"

"No, but I'm hungry." A shiver raked over my body.

"I can get some fish for you."

"That's in the opposite direction. I think I can wait and eat tomorrow. I'm just exhausted. Can you help me gather sticks from the trees?"

"Sticks," he repeated, nodding but looking clueless.

Shaking my head, I went about making camp. Ryken was a fast learner and gathered more wood while I tended the fire. We picked a spot hidden by a thicket of bushes and kept the flames low enough so only a small tendril of smoke spiraled up that the wind blew away.

Ryken didn't get too close, eyeing the fire with apprehension.

When I leaned in closer to warm my hands, he placed a concerned hand on my back.

"It's all right," I soothed.

"I don't trust it."

Darkness surrounded us, leaving us with just the light from the flames. I stared at the blanket of clouds. The bushes provided some privacy, but they couldn't protect us if the skies opened up.

"I hope it doesn't rain. I'm feeling dry for once."

"Dry or wet, it's all the same." He shrugged, scooting closer to the fire. The orange glow highlighted his features, so devastatingly handsome that I found myself staring longer than necessary. That strange sensation of wanting to trace his cheekbone returned.

As if he could read my thoughts, his eyes snapped to mine.

Quickly, I said the first thing that came to mind. "Tell me about Alara."

A broad smile uncurled on his face, brightening his teeth in firelight. "It's the main kingdom under the sea. Most of the unattached mermen dwell there to protect the treasure buried beneath the city. Most of the Collectors live there, too, since it's where we train. Well, everyone is there but me."

"How did you know you wanted to be a Collector?"

"Ruah marks the tails of the worthy." He glanced down as if it were there. "We don't need the bright colors to tempt a mate. Instead, we are created for battle."

"Have you been in a battle before?"

"No, but one is foretold, so I must keep training."

"And what about me? What will I do when we return?" I didn't think tailoring was a necessary skill set for the Merfolk.

"Gatherer?" He blushed. "Breeder?"

I snapped straight. "Oh."

"There isn't any rush for the last one if you aren't interested. I only recently thought of it myself when I said goodbye to Mattis."

"You were thinking about children?" My chest warmed at the thought. I had never been opposed to having children. Most young women knew that their number one role was to provide an heir. But my mind had trouble grasping that I had leapfrogged over a husband and gone straight to producing offspring. It made me wonder if that was all I was to him—a breeder.

I frowned.

"What's wrong?" He crawled a few feet to reach me. "Do you not like younglings?"

"No, it's not that."

His hand tangled in my hair, distracting me.

I debated on how honest I should be. "You said your people are dying."

"Yes." His lips firmed. "Without being able to produce sirens, there are fewer of us each year. Soon there will be none left."

"And you think I'm a siren? Because of my voice?"

"Maybe not right now. But when you transform—I do."

"And I will be the one to save the Merfolk?"

"If Ruah wills it, then yes."

Silently, I watched the fire crackle. A weight of obligation to be everything they wanted settled on my chest. I could hardly breathe.

"We don't have to if you're not interested."

258

"I never said I wasn't. It's just that my life feels out of order and I'm going in reverse." It was supposed to be love, marriage, and then children, but I guessed I could start with children first. I threw another stick on the fire, the red flames gobbling up the tinder.

"Why does order matter to you so much?"

"Stability? Comfort? I don't know, but things just need to be in their place."

"And your place? Is with me, yes?" He leaned in, his breath heating my ear. "As my place is with you."

I shifted away as worry burned in my gut. "What if I'm not who you think I am? What if I'm just like the others when I transform?" I glanced at my hands. Everything was out of my control, and I hated it.

He pulled back the curtain of my hair that shielded my face. "It would change nothing. You are perfect the way you are. I put too much pressure on you, didn't I?"

The pressure of being perfect would end up shattering me into pieces.

"I think I'm going to get some sleep." I avoided the problem as I always did and tucked into a ball on the hard ground.

The heat of Ryken's gaze burned into my back, hotter than the blazing fire. Eventually, exhaustion claimed me, and my heavy lids closed.

I woke up sometime in the night, faintly aware that Ryken's spot was now empty. Blinking, I sat up, searching the gray shadows around me, and tingles of worry prickled along my skin through the haze of sleep.

"Ryken?" I whispered.

A stick snapped, catching my attention. Ryken stumbled into view, his hair tousled and dripping wet. Not just his hair, but all of him was soaked through. Where had he gone to be near water? The closest river was miles from here back in Windcrest. Or had he ventured ahead to the river that cut through Mistbrooke Forest?

"Ryken?" I repeated, concerned when he plopped next to me as if his legs had given out.

"Hmm?" He rolled on his side, facing me.

"Where were you?" I asked groggily, one eye open.

His eyes fluttered closed. "I don't know. Collecting. Too tired to talk."

"Where were you Collecting?"

When he didn't respond, I leaned closer to study his sleeping face in the twilight. His chest rose and fell in steady breaths of sleep. Not only that, but the salty brine of the ocean wafted up from his clothes and skin. Nostalgia crashed into me. Memories of the sea awakened a desire to be submerged in those cool depths again. I wanted to go home.

You are going the wrong way. The voice was so quiet, I almost missed it. The power from Ruah's presence sent goosebumps down my arms.

"This has always been my plan. My family—my sister needs me." I yawned, my eyes heavy again.

I told you Roselyn of Mistbrooke is as strong as ever. There are others that need you far more. My people need you, Ruah said calmly. *Turn back to the sea. Follow the princess.*

The last command hung on the wind, echoing away from me.

Vella? Liora? My mind was too muddled with sleep to comprehend. Perhaps I had imagined the entire conversation. I curled into ball in the dirt with a frustrated sigh.

I'd think about it in the morning.

Deep in sleep, Ryken stretched out his hand to rest on my side. Normally I would have pushed it off, abiding by the rules of etiquette, but I was too tired to care. I rested my head on my curled arm, content that he slept an arm's length away from me. His presence brought a peace I didn't know I'd been missing. My eyes drifted closed as I allowed myself to relax enough to slumber.

Questions were for tomorrow. But tomorrow came faster than I liked.

Instinct

T he morning sun burned the back of my eyelids a fiery shade of red. I rolled to my side, hoping to burrow under my arm for a few more minutes of sleep, but a weight held me in place.

I blinked awake, confused and disoriented. Caked in dirt from sleeping on the ground, I was hidden behind a briar thicket. I rubbed a hand down my face, bumping into Ryken's tan arm that looped across my torso, his hand relaxed on my shoulder.

Immediately, I tensed at such an intimate position.

Always aware of my emotions, he tightened his arm in response.

Since I'd first met him, Ryken had never understood the concept of personal space. His nose rested on my neck, and with each breath, he swayed loose strands of my hair. It was a steady rhythm, oddly comforting, and the tension eased out of me as quickly as it had come.

I shouldn't be lying here in his arms. But the voice of reason and my mother's stern rules were overtaken by a new emotion.

For the first time, I felt safe.

I didn't want to move away. I wanted to snuggle into his embrace and fall back asleep.

I sighed, struggling with my conscience.

Propriety won, as it always did. I leaned forward only to be jerked back against the wall of Ryken's chest. His forearm muscle rippled. Even in sleep, he was protective. No matter how much I wiggled or pushed, his arm didn't budge.

Long, jagged slices marked his forearm where his sleeve had rolled up to his elbow. I used a finger to trace the red lines, following them down to his bruised knuckles. Not as terrible as what could have been if he had been in his human form when he rescued me. The corner of my mouth ticked up as I remembered. He had come back for me—to save me.

I had hoped to let him sleep, but it seemed waking him was the only way to break out of his iron grip.

"Ryken," I said gently.

He let out an incoherent noise and pressed his nose to the ticklish spot at the nape of my neck. An involuntary shiver raced through me.

Inhaling deeply, his hand flexed on my shoulder. He whispered my name, husky from sleep.

"Can you wake up, please?" I asked.

"Up?" He inhaled again, completely distracted and lost in my scent.

"Ryken," I scolded as another shiver shot through me.

"Marigold," he purred back.

"I need to get up." Somehow my tone didn't match my words, so I tried again, forcing myself to sound like I meant it. Because I did . . . didn't I?

A mournful whimper sounded in my ear.

"We have to get moving or we'll lose daylight."

He sighed, wrestling internally before he released me. "Why are all my emotions mixed up when I am human? Just inhaling your scent has my mind flooded with thoughts and feelings. You consume me until I can think of nothing else."

I fought a smile as I stood and dusted the dirt off my wrinkled gown. "You make it sound like I'm a disease."

"Disease?" He flopped his head to the side.

"Like something that is killing you."

"You are killing me—in a good way."

Shaking my head, I placed my fists on my hips. "Then stay away from me if it's so torturous to be close."

"You misunderstand. Torturous isn't the correct word. You're tantalizing, like a delicious morsel of food dangling in front of me.

But no matter how close I get, it swims out of reach." His head whipped back to me, his eyes a dark teal that glittered with heat. "It's part of the mating ritual. You're participating in it whether you realize it or not."

What? My breath hitched. *I am not.*

He hadn't moved an inch, but I felt pursued, as if his stillness was intentional and any sudden movement would cause him to pounce.

"Don't . . . move." His voice was low. Pained.

I swallowed at his intensity. Not in fear, but from the rush of adrenaline. I was ashamed to admit I wasn't frightened at all, even when I should be. Instead, I wanted to push him to find out what would happen.

Goodness. Where had that thought come from? I didn't trust myself to speak.

"Don't look at me like that." Slowly, he rose to his knees.

The urge to run, not to evade but to lure him closer, startled me. It was the opposite of my usual thoughts. One I absolutely planned on ignoring.

My toes curled. I wouldn't run.

At least, I think I won't.

My pinky twitched at my side as I wondered how far I could get before he would catch me. Or was he even fast enough on foot? I raised a brow in challenge.

"Marigold, if you run, I will chase you. It's my instinct. I suggest we wait this out," he grumbled. "We must wait . . . always wait."

I peeled my eyes from his in silent agreement. To distract myself, I listened to the whistling of the wind through the leaves of the trees. The twittering of the birds sounded laughing, as if they mocked our plight. A lone yellow bird was braver than the rest and swooped to a lower branch. It watched me with its beady eyes, ruffling its feathers.

Ugh, birds.

I cringed away from its pointy beak, knowing from experience what it felt like to be pecked at. Crows from our orchard used to torment me. At least until Rosey shooed them away. She was always better with animals than I was.

Thankfully, the distraction worked. The unexplainable urges disappeared and morphed into shame. I covered my face, spinning away. I still wanted to run away, but more to distance myself from my wanton behavior. Why had I acted like that?

"Don't be embarrassed," he said, coming up behind me.

Oh, goodness. Can't he just let me be?

"Please, don't hide——" he pried my fingers from my face and hunched down to peer into my eyes "——especially from me."

"I'm sorry."

He grimaced, his lips twisting. "Don't apologize either."

"What should I do then?"

"Stay with me. Talk to me. We are both experiencing new feelings, and I know it's confusing. You helped me through mine, and I can help you through yours. And . . ."

With a quick intake of breath, he lifted a strand—*oh my*—more like a clump of my hair tipped in blue. "Your hair is changing." He met my eyes. "You're changing."

"Yes."

Unable to stay contained, his grin blossomed across his face like a child who received an unexpected prize. He brought the ends up to sniff them one last time before letting them fall into place.

"Soon, Marigold. *Soon.*" A promise more than words.

"This is why we need to hurry. I need to make it to Cadell."

He nodded. "Is there . . . anything else that is changing?"

My neck flushed to my cheeks. *"Ryken."*

"You can talk to me about it—if you want to."

"I have nothing else to talk about." I spun away, fanning my face.

He marched past me, his shoulders stiff. "Why do you bother lying to me? I always know when you do."

Sprinting, I caught up to him. "You do not."

He turned to me, his jaw clenching. "My body is so attuned to yours that I notice even the tiniest of changes. I can feel when your temperature rises or when you fidget from nerves. Each of your sighs has a different meaning." He stepped toward me, crowding me. "I can smell the sweat beading on your palms. Now, your heartbeat is picking up, and I see it pulsing in the vein of your neck. But your green eyes give you away. They always tell me the truth even when your mouth does not. It's not just our hearts that are connected—we are connected." His jaw ticked again. "So do not tell me I don't know you when *I do.*"

264

"But do you *know* me? What do I like? What don't I like? There is more to me than physical attributes." *More to me than breeding,* I wished I could say.

He blinked at me as his anger drained. "No. But I would like to."

I threw my hands in the air. "Then ask me."

"Why do you hide? Are you afraid of me?"

I had been expecting a question about my favorite color or my childhood, so his blunt questions blindsided me.

"I'm not afraid. I'm . . . not used to being honest about my feelings. Young women are not supposed to talk about these things with someone who isn't their husband."

"Their husband?"

"When a man and woman marry, he becomes her husband."

Ryken hummed and clicked as he thought. "Mattis talked about this. How does a person do that? A quest? A ritual? No—he said a ceremony. How do we do it?"

"We?" I fumbled for words.

"Then you can be honest and say what you mean."

"That's not why you get married." He wouldn't understand. What would a merman know of love? I walked away in frustration.

"You're running again."

"I'm hungry." It wasn't a lie if it was half true.

He sighed, ducking his head in resignation.

I foraged sandy mushrooms, a common and edible brown top fungus that poked through the weeds of the trail. It wasn't much, but I didn't feel like catching and preparing one of the birds in the trees. Ryken complained of the rubbery texture and refused to eat another bite. He also found out that the grass on land was not as delicious as the seagrass he was used to. But watching his sour face while he ate broke some of the tension between us.

We traveled most of the day, and I filled the silence by talking about growing up in Cadell. Most words I had to translate since he didn't understand. I still wondered if he completely understood what a cow was.

The smoke of a distant chimney signaled the first sign of civilization since we left Windcrest. At least we were heading in the right direction.

My feet were aching from the walk, the royal sandals more for show than functionality.

"Thank goodness. There is an inn of some sort up ahead," I said, walking faster despite the blisters.

"What's an inn?"

"A place we can get hot food and rest for the night."

His eyes lit up. "Will they have the squishy things we lay on? I like those."

"Beds? Yes, they should if they have any space available." Now that we were closer, I could make out the sign: The Boar's Inn. I squealed and turned to Ryken, bouncing on my toes.

"What?" He tilted his head and squinted one eye in confusion.

"I'm excited," I singsonged. I grabbed his hand to pull him faster down the path. "This is the inn that sits between Cadell and Windcrest. If we continue this way, we will run into the outskirts of Mistbrooke Forest, which is close to where I grew up."

"I don't understand. What is Mistbrooke?"

I shook his hand, laughing. "It just means we're almost there. We can rest here tonight and then trek the last leg to my family cottage. I will get to see my family tomorrow!"

He frowned. "And then back to the sea?"

"Yes, of course. But there is so much I want to show you first. You have to try one of the apples from our orchard—it tastes best right off the tree. And my mother's strawberry jam. We make it every summer together. It's so good you'll want to eat it right out of the jar."

"I will? What's a strawberry?"

The more I rambled on with excitement, the sulkier Ryken became.

"Are you listening?"

"Yes. I heard everything," he replied, quieter than usual.

"When we get inside, let me do the talking. It will already be strange that we are two unwed traveling companions."

"Unwed?"

I pulled him up to the door and spun back around to add quickly, "Don't attack anyone inside—no matter what they say to you."

He rose to his full height, and I had to crane my head back. "What will they say?"

266

"I don't know, but I just don't want you to bite or punch anyone because they were talking to me."

"Some instincts are difficult to control. Protecting you is like breathing."

"Nobody is trying to hurt me. I'm going to take Prince Vian's advice and go by an alias. If they don't know I'm Marigold, I can be just another patron of the inn."

Ryken grumbled at the prince's name and crossed his arms. "I don't like this."

"It's one night, and then we'll leave in the morning."

Pinching his lips, he held my gaze. "We should stay away from humans. Look at what trouble they caused in Windcrest." He held up his arm as proof. The sleeves were still rolled up to his elbows, displaying the tanned forearm.

I blinked in confusion as my eyes trailed over the ridges of muscles, my insides warming. Then it occurred to me that it wasn't his muscular physique he was showing off, but the slices from when he escaped the glass cage.

Oh.

His scent changed to his alluring fragrance of masculinity. A unique smell that was all Ryken. I breathed it in again, enjoying the sensation of butterflies dancing in my stomach.

He whispered my name and leaned forward, his lips parting in surprise. Or was it me leaning in to kiss him? I stretched up on my tiptoes, vaguely aware that he hadn't actually moved at all.

The door to the inn swung open. Gasping, I jumped away and wrapped my arms around my chest. A young blonde woman in a plain-styled gown walked outside, nearly running into us. Completely distracted, she jerked to a stop at the sight of us.

Ryken shifted closer to me, the back of his hand brushing mine.

"I'm sorry to startle you," the woman said, rolling her r's. "We rarely have customers this early. Please, come in. You might have an hour of peace and quiet before the evening crowd rolls in. A rowdy lot they are."

"Is there lodging available for tonight?"

"I'd have to ask Miss Opal. This is her place, and she allows Ean and me to stay . . ." her voice trailed off, her eyes locked on the high collar of my borrowed dress. Her eyes flicked to Ryken's clothes. "One moment . . . I need to—uh—see to something." She went to dash back in but pivoted around to add, "Don't go anywhere. I'll be right back."

Leaving the front door wide open, she raced to the back of the inn and barreled through the double doors like the Sorcerer himself was hot on her heels.

Ryken and I stood in confusion at her hasty retreat.

"Now I really don't feel good about this," Ryken said flatly.

I had to agree with him. Nothing about this was normal.

"Let's sneak away before she gets back," I whispered from the corner of my mouth.

But we weren't fast enough.

Earning Our Keep

Before we could escape, a sweet old lady bounded up to the door, her brown skirt stitched in thick velvet despite the scorching summer temperature. "Good evening to you both. My name is Opal, and I am the owner of this humble establishment. I'm honored to be at your service." She dipped into a curtsy so low she struggled to rise back to her feet. It was a curtsy too deep for a mere noblewoman.

Ryken stepped back and grabbed a handful of my skirt, ready to whisk me to safety if necessary.

"Do you need help?" I asked, offering her a hand as she wobbled upright.

Chuckling, she brushed my assistance away. "It's supposed to be me inquiring the same of you. Anjali said you were interested in a room. Our blue room is our most luxurious and is fit for a queen. Please, come in, Your Highness."

Goodness. First, they called me a lady back in Windcrest, and now they thought I was royalty in Cadell.

"Highness means royalty, yes? Then you are misinformed. There is only one king worthy of the title, Ruah's Chosen One," Ryken said.

Opal's brow crinkled, adding even more wrinkles to her forehead. Her mouth hung open.

"*Ahem.* What he means is that we are not royalty. I'm sorry for the confusion with our attire. They are . . . castoffs for the poor."

"With a necklace like yours?"

I placed a hand on my collar. The weight of it had become unnoticeable as if it were a second layer of skin. "It's all I have left to my name."

"Oh." The old woman's lips puckered in disappointment. "Beggars."

"We have no crowns to trade, but we are hard workers. Do you have chores you need completed in exchange for food and a night of sleep?"

"Ean and Anjali do most of the things I need. I took them in a year ago and can't seem to get rid of them."

The blonde woman swooped into view and looped an arm through the old woman's. "Oh, don't let her fool you. Opal has a soft heart for strays. I'm sure there is something around here you could do."

I grinned, excited about the prospect of a hot meal. "Thank you so much, miss. We're weary from traveling. After a small bite to eat, we'll be ready to work." I bobbed a curtsy, which Ryken quickly mimicked.

The old woman lifted a brow at him. "An odd fellow you have with you. Large enough to help with wood chopping and barn repairs, though. What's your name?"

"You may call me Ryken."

"And you're from Windcrest?"

His lips puckered in a sour expression. "No. I would never claim thieves as my own."

I cleared my throat, stepping in front of him. "We are roaming travelers just passing through Cadell."

"And you are?"

"Uh——" My mind emptied.

"Her name is Alice." Ryken lied more smoothly than I thought possible.

"Alice, is it? You look familiar." The younger woman squinted as her eyes trailed over my features.

A nervous laugh bubbled out of me. "I get that a lot. I must have a common face."

"Perhaps. I do see so many faces each day that they start to blur together. My name is Anjali. I do the gardening, cleaning, and laundering. If you need anything mended, I can do that too."

"Actually, I'm quite skilled with a needle," I said.

"What we could use is an extra hand during the dinner rush. They are a spirited bunch, especially after one too many ales."

I nodded.

Opal huffed at Anjali. "So, it's decided, is it? You run the inn now, young miss?"

"Think of it as a night off your feet. I attend the kitchen, and Alice will serve up the dishes."

"Nobody cooks in my kitchen but me," Opal snapped, her jowls flapping. She gave me a sharp look. "What else can you do?"

In a panicked moment, I said the first thing I could think of. "I can sing."

The old woman's eyes widened. "Entertainment? My customers might like that. Sing me a few notes so I can see if you can carry a tune."

"Right now?"

"Did you think I meant another day? Of course right now."

"I don't have an instrument or sheet music . . ." My fingers twisted together.

"A true musician needs nothing but the music in their heart." She smirked.

I sent a pleading look to Ryken, but he only shrugged.

Both women stared blankly as I scoured my memory for any song at all. Even my mermaid song I had sung so many times had conveniently disappeared. Then the comforting melody of a song my mother sang to Rose and me broke through my thoughts. Every night, she sang this lullaby to us as she tucked us in bed. When we were too old for good-night kisses and songs, Rosey sang it into the darkness of our shared room, knowing it brought me comfort as I fell asleep.

> *Sleep is calling your name, my little one.*
> *Watch as the starry blanket covers the sky,*
> *For even the toiling sun needs his rest.*
> *Shining all day—*

Opal lifted a weathered hand. "Enough. Do you want to put my patrons to sleep? Though your voice and pitch are easy on the ear, lullabies aren't tavern songs. Can you learn a new song by tonight?"

"I don't see why not."

"Then you have yourself a deal. You can serve, clean, and perform, and your husband can chop wood and assist with the barn repairs."

"Oh, he's not my husband," I corrected, my cheeks heating.

"But I want to be. I'm wooing her," Ryken added proudly.

Humiliation had my response frozen on my tongue.

Anjali bit her lip to keep from giggling.

"Well, then," Opal said, staring up at him. "A man who is honest about his emotions. You could teach Ean a thing or two."

"Teach me what?" A man shuffled from around the corner of the inn, his white linen shirt covered in hay. A few loose pieces were stuck in his brown curls. He approached in boots plastered with what I hoped was mud, his stance stiffening at the sight of Ryken.

"It's nothing for you to worry about. These are our new day workers Opal just hired," Anjali said, rushing to his side. "I was coming out earlier to let you know that the second step on the stairs is loose again."

"I'll fix it." He flexed his gloved fingers.

"And the chimney in the dining hall needs to be cleaned. I tried to put a kettle on, and now the room is full of smoke."

He sighed. "It's probably the birds again."

"Just be careful and don't hurt them this time."

Glancing away, he massaged his neck as he strode off, mumbling under his breath. "You'd think she would be more worried about my safety on the roof than a few feathered pests."

"Ean, wait. I wasn't finished. There are a few more tasks." Anjali lifted the hem of her skirt and jogged after him.

"Are you going to stand out here all day? Come in already," Opal said, moving with the agility of someone half her age.

Inside, I could barely make out the inn's details through the thick gray cloud. Logs sat unlit in the fireplace, yet gray plumes still wafted from the chimney and poured into the room, just as Anjali had said. Through the smoky haze, I could make out three large circular tables and the curve of the staircase leading to the second landing. After the grandiose style of the Windcrest castle, these wooden walls and floors were plain. The only spots of color were the burgundy curtains over windows opened to allow fresh air inside.

Open windows? Could they have heard everything we said outside?

We followed Opal to the back of the room, weaving around the tables and chairs. They were carved from birch and polished for the evening customers.

Ryken uselessly swatted the smoke away from his face. His nostrils flared at the acidic smell.

"Excuse the smoke. No matter how many times we evict them, those sparrows keep returning. Sir, could you please help Ean with removing the nest?"

Ryken coughed. His fingers grazed the back of my neck, resting on my collar before his voice entered my thoughts. *Do you think it's wise for me to leave you alone with this stranger?*

Do we have a choice? Nothing is free. If we want to eat and have a place to sleep tonight, then we have to earn it.

I'd be less worried if I kept you in eyesight.

My eyes darted to Opal and back. *She's a little old woman. What danger am I in?*

Anyone with a weapon can be a threat, no matter their age, Ryken countered.

Immediately, Princess Vella's contorted face flashed in my memory. The crazed glint in her eyes sent a shudder down my spine—a reminder that not everyone was who they appeared to be.

"Sir? Are you able to help Ean?" Opal asked again, her eyes darting between us.

You're right. Trust me, I'll be cautious, I assured him.

I do trust you. His thumb swiped across my neck, sending a sizzle of tingles down my spine. *I just hate being separated from you.*

I glanced over my shoulder to meet his eyes. *Me too.*

The corner of his mouth twitched.

Opal cleared her throat politely.

"Yes. I will go offer him my assistance."

He shot me one last glance before he walked out, a silent message that I need only scream and he would tear this place down to get to me. At least, I thought that was what it meant. It could have also meant that I not do anything stupid while he was gone.

"Oh, that boy is wooing you, indeed. Reminds me of my late

husband, Davy. He knew what he wanted and wouldn't give up until he won me over."

As soon as we walked through the doors of the kitchen, the air cleared, and Opal pinned her narrowed eyes on me. "All right now, Miss Alice. Look me straight in the eyes. So you know, I have a knack for catching a fib, so don't think because I'm old you can pull the wool over my eyes. Did you steal the clothes and jewelry you're wearing? I pride myself on keeping everything on the up and up. I will not have a fugitive tarnish our well-established reputation. It's taken months to earn the trust of our patrons."

"I promise, my lady. These were both given to me."

She held my stare for another second. "Good. We want no trouble with Windcrest or Cadell. Now, this is the kitchen. You can help us cut vegetables for my famous potato soup. It's the best in the five kingdoms —even the queen herself said so, and you know that's high praise indeed with all the fancy chefs she has at her disposal."

"The Queen of Hearts visits here?" I swallowed the lump in my throat. My eyes searched the opened windows and half door leading out into the garden, expecting to see an evil witch cackling with delight.

"Oh, goodness, no. One could wish, right? She's such a sweet thing and has been through so much this last year. I don't know how she bears all the weight on her shoulders, but she does. Normally, I'm not one for gossip, but——" she leaned in to whisper "——she has herself locked up in the castle most days. Rarely even visits her people in the forest. Mark my words, something is afoot."

"What are you whispering about in here?" Anjali said, leaning her elbows on the half door.

"Oh, you know me. I never gossip." Opal pulled a clean potato from a basket and started to peel the skin in a long curl.

Anjali shook her head with a laugh. "Say it as much as you want. It doesn't make it true."

"Oh? And what do you know, my sassy girl?"

They bickered the way families do, but I couldn't get Opal's words out of my head. *Sweet? The Queen of Hearts?* Were they talking about the same queen who murdered the innocent hoping to fulfill the Sorcerer's curse? The woman who wanted to kill my sister?

Maybe Opal's old age distorted her memory.

274

"Alice?" Anjali said, snapping her fingers to catch my attention.

Alice. I had to remember this new name.

"Yes, that is me." I blinked at Anjali's outstretched hand. "Could you repeat what you said?"

"I asked if you could hand me that basket and join me in the garden. We need some carrots."

"Carrots? Isn't it late in the season?" I grabbed the basket from the worktable and followed her into the sweet summer air.

This was no ordinary garden. Rows and rows of plants were boxed in by bushes full of berries of all colors. The size of the strawberries was nearly double what grew back home. Greenery sprouted down the line, displaying off-season crops like broccoli, beets, and even pumpkins ripe for the picking. Peach trees, apple trees, orange trees, and olive trees lined the outside border, their branches sagging from the weight of the produce.

The sweet aromas mixed together and my stomach growled, desperate for a taste.

"This way." Anjali took the basket and led the way while I gawked behind her. "You sound like you lived on a farm? But your accent isn't Windcrest or Glenton. Are you originally from Cadell? I know some local farmers out there."

I ignored her, unable to believe the utopia of produce hidden behind the inn. "How is this possible?"

"You've been in Windcrest too long and it shows," she joked, swinging her basket as she walked down one of the long rows past the twisted pumpkin vines. "Magic, of course."

"Magic," I stammered, the one word stopping me in my tracks. I was surrounded by black magic. Though I had heard of it, I never thought I would see the effects of the Sorcerer's magic in broad daylight. "But those who use it will be put to death."

"Maybe under the old king, but now His Majesty has taught us the benefit of magic. Encourages us to use it to help others. Not me personally. I'm not an Enchanter." She did a double take when she saw I was rooted to the ground as much as the plants surrounding me. Sighing, she walked back to me to drag me along behind her. "It's okay, Alice. I'm from Windcrest too. I know it's hard to believe, but everything they told us was to cast Windcrest in a good light. King Galon wants nothing more than to get his hands on Cadell's throne so he can rule all the territories."

"How do I know they're lying and not you?"

"Look at you, covered in navy to the point that even your hair is dyed blue. Open your eyes. What is the harm of magic soil if it provides food and peace of mind for the people? Are these vegetables hurting anyone?"

Realizing she was actually waiting for me to answer, I shook my head.

"Exactly. Windcrest is twisting the truth in hopes of starting another war."

"Windcrest?" I sputtered, agitated at her ignorance. She knew *nothing*. Innocent lives had already been sacrificed, and their blood was on Cadell's hands. "You are misinformed. It was the Queen of Hearts who declared war. She's burning the farmlands around the castle and growing her army of Enchanters in Mistbrooke Forest."

Anjali stomped her foot, almost crushing an oversized cucumber. "That is an outrageous lie, and I will not have you spreading rumors about my king and queen."

"So, you stand with Cadell," I said, crossing my arms.

She frowned in disappointment. "And you stand with Windcrest."

Trapped in a silent stalemate, we were both too stubborn to back down. One thing was for certain: I had to take extra precautions to keep my true identity hidden from Anjali and Opal. I expected to encounter Cadell loyalists as I traveled closer to my family's home, but all the way up here at the border? Cadell's reach was farther than I thought.

After a few moments, she added, "You know, I once believed the lies too. I thought magic was wrong because I didn't understand it, and the unknown frightened me. Then a dear friend opened my eyes and taught me differently." She sent me a determined look. "Maybe it's time I returned the favor and educated you in what nobody in Windcrest will teach you—*the truth* about magic."

A Bad Influence

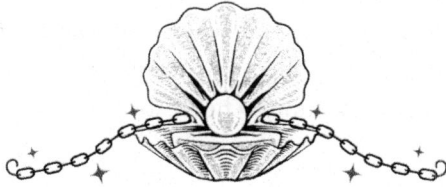

"**Y**ou think I'm frightened of magic?" I gestured to the thick foliage of plants sprouting in neat rows around us, their stems full of unnaturally ripe fruits and vegetables. "While this garden is magnificent, it's a façade hiding the wielder's true intentions. Magic doesn't scare me. The person wielding it does. The Queen of Hearts is a killer. I wouldn't trust anything created with her black magic on my lips." My traitorous stomach gurgled in protest, and I gave a glossy red apple a lustful glance. The apple's color reminded me of the ones from home, so it was too easy to recall the sweet yet tart, mouth-watering flavor.

How did I know the apple wasn't poisoned or spelled? All these delights and I couldn't eat a single bite.

"My queen is not a killer." Her eyes widened a fraction. "Unless . . . are you talking about King Alexander? His death was ruled an accident, and . . ."

My breath left in a rush, her continued ramblings like white noise in the background. *No. I must have misheard.* He couldn't be. *Impossible.* He had always been around, a staple in my life. I could barely get the word out; it clung to the back of my throat. "D-dead?"

Anjali pinched her lips and nodded. "I didn't think anyone would miss him."

"He was still a person," I said, aghast. How could anyone be that uncaring about a person's life? Yes, the prince was stern and hot-tempered, but he had to be assertive because of his position. He had a kingdom to rule. Didn't all royals act like that to hide their weaknesses?

Without realizing it, my hand snuck into the pocket of my dress, grasping the hilt of the borrowed dagger. Prince Vian hadn't acted that way. What had he tried to tell me yesterday? Rose hadn't married Prince Alexander—no, *King Alexander*? When had that happened? Had the queen killed his father too? Then that would mean Rose had no ties to the crown. Why were they hunting her if she had nothing to do with the curse?

Or did she?

Nothing made sense. Confused, I rubbed my temple. It was hard to keep track when everything felt like a riddle. Or maybe Ryken's brutal honesty was rubbing off on me. Why couldn't people just say what they meant?

"I'm sorry to have offended you. It was so long ago, and the king I knew wasn't known for his kindness."

"Well, he was with me." I wouldn't call him a friend, but he had always been friendly. "What about——?" I clamped my lips shut before I slipped and mentioned my sister's name.

She placed a reassuring hand on my shoulder. "We don't have to talk about it if it's upsetting you, Alice."

"Let's just finish what we came out to do. I don't want to argue anymore."

"Me either. Truce?"

I nodded.

Anjali set off down the row of waist-high tomato plants, the fruit growing in reds, yellows, and greens. My stomach rumbled again. Eventually, I had to eat. But what if this was how the queen enchanted her people? By bespelling their food so they mindlessly did her bidding?

"Here they are," she said, dropping to her knees in the dirt. "I hope you feel comfortable getting your hands in the soil. Do you have experience in the garden? These carrots are larger than normal, so you'll have to dig them out some before you can pull them free."

I laughed. "I grew up with a constant layer of dirt ingrained in my skin and stuck under my nails from weeding. I'm surprised I've been able to scrub it all off since leaving Cadell. We grew carrots back home, among other things."

Joining her on the ground, I used an old family trick passed down through generations. Instead of pulling it straight up, I pushed it deeper into the ground, twisting it just a bit before easily yanking the large carrot out of the soil.

While Anjali still wrestled with her first one, I pulled three more out of the ground. "Did you grow up on a farm?"

She grunted, clawing at the dirt. "No. My family runs an apothecary shop in the Halberts quarter in Windcrest. I'm used to clipping herbs and spices."

"Really? I think I strolled by the shop the other day. There is only one in town, right?" I added two more carrots to the basket.

Her mouth dropped open, and she leaned away to stare at me. "Did you see any young girls running around? I haven't seen my family in years, but my sister Pippa sends me letters every so often. My youngest sister should be walking now. Did you happen to see a toddler stumbling about?"

"Oh, I'm so sorry. Prince Vian went inside, not me. I don't remember seeing them outside. The streets were crowded when we went shopping that day."

The air shifted, Anjali's surprise overpowering the fragrance of the vegetables. I held my breath, afraid I had said too much. *I shouldn't have mentioned the prince.*

"You are friends with Prince Vian?" she whispered, leaning forward. "He greeted me once, and I nearly fainted."

I groaned, rolling my eyes skyward. "Don't tell him that. He already has a high opinion of himself."

"Don't they all? Who can blame them when that's all they've ever known? You must have held a position inside the castle—me too. Even Ean worked as a guard in Cadell."

"So, you really were in the thick of it." I itched to ask if she knew my sister, but I reminded myself that, despite her friendly demeanor, Anjali was still a Cadell loyalist.

"Too much so if you ask me. That's why we had to escape. It didn't sit right with me the way things were changing, so I left and eventually wound up here with Ean. We were snowed in during the winter months, and when everything melted in the spring, we just stayed." She brushed the dirt from the tops of the carrots. "I can't explain it, but it felt like I was already home."

"No, I understand. There's a feeling you get, and when you're not there, it's like the ocean calling me back home."

"Oh, the sea has captured your heart? Well, you'll never be happy in Cadell."

Her words struck a chord in me. "I know. I'm traveling through more to say goodbye."

"Is that where your family is? Or are they in Windcrest?"

"Both." I dug into the soil, the grainy texture reminding me of my youth. The rich earthy smell transported me to endless days sweating in the fields and climbing trees to harvest apples. I plucked another carrot from the ground, the stringy roots dangling from the tip.

"That explains your Cadell accent. How did you manage to get a position in the Windcrest castle? It's almost unheard of." Anjali let out a squeal after finally pulling up one carrot.

"There was a carriage accident, and one of the guards brought me to the castle to recuperate."

"We are so similar! The guard that saved me was Ean. Was yours Ryken? He looks like he has had some training. You're lucky to have some protection while you travel. The roads these days are quite dangerous. I mean, just south of here is where the lost sister was taken. You need to be watchful through those parts."

My hands trembled with the memory, and I pushed my fingers into the warm dirt. "I don't plan to go that way. We're staying off the roads and sticking close to Mistbrooke Forest."

"It's faster if you cut through."

I blinked. "Nobody goes into Mistbrooke Forest."

"The Sorcerer removed the barrier so the king and queen could see each other before the wedding. Isn't that romantic?" She sighed.

Goodness. The Sorcerer is a romantic? That's one phrase I never thought I would hear.

"Do you think this is enough carrots? The basket is overflowing." I patted the pile of carrots.

"*Oh.* You're good at this." She rose to her feet, snatching the full basket up with ease. "This is plenty. Let's bring them inside to clean them. Don't worry about chopping. You should bathe before the customers arrive. You look a little dusty from travel."

The thought of the cool water over my skin made my legs itch. "That would be wonderful."

"Opal will still put you in the blue room, so you're in for a treat. It's too fancy for any paying customer to afford anyway."

As we headed toward the inn, I shielded my eyes from the setting sun, the bright orange rays slanting across the side of Anjali's face. Neither Ryken nor Ean were in eyesight, and worry bubbled in my chest. "Should we check on the men?"

"Check on them? Whatever for? Ean has been on the roof more times than I can count."

"I'm sure, but Ryken——"

"You are worrying for nothing. They will fetch us if they need anything," Anjali said. She unlatched the half door, whisked us inside, and placed the basket on the table.

"That was quick," Opal said.

"Two pairs of hands are better than one. It helps that she has worked on a farm before."

Opal sprinkled some seasoning and herbs into the bubbling liquid. "Oh? Maybe you can learn a thing or two before she leaves."

"Remember, I can leave at any time," Anjali joked.

"You'd leave a poor, defenseless, elderly woman all by herself?"

Anjali laughed. "You are none of those things. You could probably beat me in a game of strength."

Opal waved her wooden spoon in her direction. "And don't you forget it."

I cleared my throat. "Would you both excuse me for a moment? I have to tell Ryken something. I'll only be a moment."

Anjali raised a knowing brow, but I scampered out before they could deter me.

Once I heard the low rumbling of conversation, I stopped and listened.

"Wooing, you say?" Ean asked, his voice slightly higher than Ryken's. "I'm not the expert on this subject. As you can see, I'm still unwed."

"As am I. Human ways of courtship are confusing. I gave her a flower, yet she still refuses to be my wife. Why?"

"I—uh—don't know where to begin. You gave her flowers?"

"Yes, one. Plus, I complimented her. She doesn't like that at all."

"Are you eavesdropping?" Anjali whispered over my shoulder.

I whipped around with a muffled cry. "I—uh—yes."

"What are they talking about?" She tilted her head, listening.

"Well, do you love her?" Ean asked.

Anjali's eyes went wide, and she pressed closer to my shoulder to listen.

"That word . . . I don't know what it means," Ryken grumbled.

"You *what*? Where are you from again?"

"Across the sea."

"Oh, a sailor. That explains a lot. Can you hand me the board by your foot? To your right—uh, your other right. Thanks." The sound of a hammer echoed off the side of the inn. "That looks straight. What do you think? One more board?"

"Explain love," Ryken demanded.

Ean sighed. "I told you, I'm not the one to be asking. If I knew how it worked, don't you think I would have confessed my feelings to the girl I love?"

Anjali's back stiffened.

"Feelings? I have a lot of those."

Ean barked a laugh. "Don't we all." Something thudded on the ground. "Look, I'll tell you what I know, but it isn't much——"

"What are you two ninnies doing?" Opal hissed.

Anjali and I spun around, bumping into each other in our haste.

"Oh my stars, you gave me a fright," Anjali said, her hand over her heart.

"Are you both eavesdropping? You——" Opal pointed a weathered finger at me "——are a bad influence. We don't have time for this. Both of you scamper back into the kitchen. Those carrots won't chop themselves. I'll stay here and let you know if I hear any good tidbits." She wiggled her gray eyebrows.

Anjali looped an arm through each of ours, smiling sweetly at the old woman. "Remember? You aren't one to gossip."

Opal frowned at her. "I'm not gossiping. I'm out for my daily turn around the garden."

"You hate walking." She tugged us both back through the kitchen door. "If we can't all listen, then none of us should."

"Haven't you heard about respecting your elders?" Opal huffed.

Anjali released me and placed both hands on Opal's shoulders. "There's no one I respect more than you."

"Ah, there you go. You're making me well up again."

My heart grew heavy watching their exchange, and I missed my family more than ever. When I was home, I had longed to get away, sick of the labor and family drama. But now, that was what I missed the most. Listening to Mother harp on Father about his muddy boots or when he snuck a bite off the plates before dinner was served. Roselyn's constant positivity normally grated on my nerves, but I'd give anything for us to dance around our room again, laughing and singing together.

I'd do anything to have those moments again. Father's hugs. Mother's herbal teas. Rose's outlandish stories of talking to animals.

My throat tightened as I turned away.

Soon, we fell into a routine: scrubbing, chopping, and then tossing the ingredients into the big pot. Opal was not one for silence, prattling along about this and that.

"A lot of sailors stop here for supper when they haul their shipments to Cadell. Usually, they want a break from the fish and dried meats from travel. I think one of their songs would be good to start with. Do you know *To the Sea*? The chorus always gets stuck in my head, so it should be something easy for you to learn that you won't forget." Opal added the last of the potatoes to the pot, the water bubbling.

"I think that's a great choice," Anjali agreed, wiping her starch-covered hands on her apron.

"I'll have to trust you on this since I've not heard that song before. I know pieces of *Warriors of Water*, mostly the tune and the part about the golden treasure. My grandmother hummed it a lot," I said.

"Yes, that's a good one too. Maybe you can sing that one after this one. Trust me. This song will get everyone's attention," Anjali said.

"Do you sing too?" Perhaps Anjali and I could perform a duet.

"A few times, but my voice isn't nearly as good as yours. I think they were just desperate to hear something besides the sound of their own chewing," Anjali said with a laugh.

"So, I just stand there and sing?" I leaned against the table, my fingers twisting together.

"Well, the more into the song you are, the more the crowd will respond." Anjali's eyes flicked to my hands. "Since you're so nervous, maybe you should take my tambourine up there. It will give you something to hold on to. You're going to do great," Anjali encouraged.

Opal added two pinches of salt to the pot. "With the whispers of war lately, nobody wants to get too close to the border. I'm hoping that the mysterious woman with the voice of a siren will drum up some interest—and profits."

I swallowed. "I'll try my best."

While we cooked, Anjali munched on scraps and I listened to her instruction. She repeated the lines of the song, clapping her hands to the beat. Soon, I wasn't stumbling through them, the tune catchy enough I was singing earnestly as I kneaded the bread.

Even Opal hummed along, swaying her hips as she sprinkled some seasoning into the large pot over the crackling fire.

I had run out of time to bathe, only able to wash my face and hands and change into another borrowed gown with the promise of a warm bath after my performance. I braided my hair as I rushed down the stairs.

A roomful of eyes turned to me and stopped me in my tracks. It was only a second before they returned to their drinks and demanded their meals.

Tables had filled fast, mostly of men, their accents a mix of the territories. Anjali and I shuffled in and out of the kitchen, balancing large trays full of hot bowls of soup. Some sent me curious glances, but most were starved, devouring the contents of their bowl before I had set it on the table.

"Did you eat?" Opal asked, wiping the sweat from her brow. "Ryken is on his third bowl. Thank goodness you are only staying a day. I didn't think I would meet someone who could surpass Ean."

I whipped my head to Ryken, fearful that he had eaten the vegetables from the garden.

He leaned against the wall, his bowl tipped back so he could slurp

284

the juices. Sensing my distress, he glanced over at me, swallowing his last bite. "What?"

"You had three bowls already?"

"It would have been three, but she hit me with the big utensil. The soup is good. Not as good as fish, but better than grass."

"I'm going to paddle you with this spoon again, young man," Opal threatened.

"I want no war with you, elder woman. I only meant to say I like the food."

I sent Opal an apologetic look before she could thump his head with her spoon. "Ryken," I said, inspecting his features. The nerves from my performance became a second thought to my concern for Ryken. "Are you feeling all right?" I pressed a hand to his cheek, but the temperature was normal.

He shrugged. "Tired. I saw a horse and chickens out back."

"That's nice. Your stomach doesn't feel weird? Are you lightheaded?" I checked his eyes, but the color of his face was its normal tan.

"No, I'm the same. The chickens leave these balls. Ean said we could eat them for breakfast. The balls, not the chickens. Or can we eat the chickens too?"

I shook my head, trying to stay on topic. "You can eat both. But I want to make sure you're all right before I leave to sing. Do you want to wait in the blue room until I'm done?"

He flinched as if I had struck him. "I'm not leaving you unprotected in a room of men."

"You can't attack them. Listen to them out there. They're already riled up."

"As long as they aren't marking you or hurting you, I should be able to control myself. Besides, I want to hear you sing—"

Anjali burst through the door with a tray full of dirty bowls, the pottery clattering from the movement. "Actually, now would be great to start, Alice. They are getting restless. Ryken, would you put these in the bucket of water for me?"

I gave him a subtle gesture to the wooden bucket on the counter.

He sent me a grateful look and grabbed the tray from her outstretched arms.

With a nervous exhale, I left the safety of the kitchen and entered the dining hall, the voices talking over one another. One table was in the middle of a card game, a pile of gold crowns stacked between the players, more crowns than I had ever seen. Obnoxious laughter echoed across the room, and someone slammed their tankard of ale on the table to get my attention.

"Wench, stop standing around. We need refills."

"Speak for yourself, Abe. She can stand by me if she wants," a balding man next to me said, giving me a wink. He slapped his thigh with a hearty laugh. "Or you can sit, too, if you like."

I cringed, sidestepping away.

More laughter broke out, hands slamming on the tables as I made my way to the fireplace to grab Anjali's tambourine from the mantel. Slowly, I turned back to the unruly crowd, my confidence leaking from me with each passing second.

The grumbles of the patrons made me want to dive under a table and forget this ridiculous idea. I hid behind the tambourine, trembling with nerves so that the bells jingled. Taking a breath, I spied Ryken through the circle of bells, the only encouraging face in the room.

He leaned against the back wall, his eyes narrowed at the table of hecklers.

Ryken, I thought. *I'll sing for him.*

The melody of the song strummed in my mind.

I can do this. Be brave.

A portly man with a bulbous nose pounded on his table, rattling the steins of ale. "Sing or fetch me another drink, *wench.*"

Baring his teeth, Ryken pushed away from the wall, his hands balled into fists.

Sing, now.

My Song

"Look at her, Milo. She'll faint before one note comes out."

"This was a wasted trip," another man complained. He tipped his ale back, guzzling noisily. The foamy froth drizzled down his beard.

"What did you expect from a scrawny wench? She's a nobody. Lower your standards, my friends," a skinny man taunted with a sneer. He was more finely dressed, the clothing style similar to the royal court in Cadell. "Or maybe we can make her dance for a crown." His table hooted and laughed in agreement.

Squeezing the tambourine, I narrowed my gaze on the rude man. Rage burned through my veins, filling me with a need to prove him wrong. More than that really—to sing better than he had ever heard before. Then he'd feel foolish for assuming the worst of me.

I was *not* a nobody.

I tapped the tambourine to my hip once, twice, and by the third chime the crowd was deathly silent. Soups and jokes forgotten, all eyes locked on me.

> *She is a beauty, a temptress so fair.*
> *When I'm not with her,*
> *My thoughts always stray there.*

I detest when we are parted, I count down the days,
For my soul is torn, the other half you carry
Deep in your waves.

A few men broke out into smiles, their blackened and crooked teeth more appealing than when they were heckling. I swayed my hips, the music overtaking me. The chords played in my mind. The verses were slow at first, swaying up and down like the crest of a wave.

The ocean's melody has captured my heart.
I'm tangled in your net,
And I don't want to depart.
There is no one so lovely, no one that compares,
Mother, wife, daughter—it's only the call of the siren,
To my utter despair.

The more I sang, the easier it became. Notes slipped off my tongue and melded into one another more beautifully than I had ever heard before. I shook the instrument above my head, ramping up the excitement for the chorus when the song picked up tempo.

Oh, oooh,
To the sea, to the sea,
Where my heart longs to be.
The turquoise blue waters keep calling to me.
To the sea, to the sea,
Yes, I'm caught on your hook.
You reeled me back in,
Somehow it happened, despite all the precautions I took.

I stared at their entranced faces, surprised they had joined in at the chorus, echoing the lyrics. They beat their fists on the table, keeping the beat.

I'd give up everything, yes, all I possess.
Because even treasure is worthless,
Without your bubbly caress.

288

Oh, my sweet enchantress, I'll sneak out at night,
To race to your shore, never to be parted,
So you're forever in sight.

With confidence I didn't know I had, I danced around the room, tapping the tambourine to the beat. I twirled around the tables, smiling more as the customers joined in and sang along with me. Another spin and I stopped, catching Ryken's intense expression. I focused on him, letting the others fade from my mind. *You.* He was the only one I wanted to sing for.

I tapped the tambourine on my palm, taking three steps toward him with each tap. I wasn't a nobody—I was *powerful.* My voice and my dance could convey what I was too afraid to speak aloud.

That he was the ocean I wanted to lose myself in.

Swallowing, he sank into a lone chair against the wall as if his legs couldn't support him anymore. Now I was the predator, and he was my prey. Danger pulsed with each step I took, and I knew I was venturing into uncharted waters. His chest rose and fell as he struggled for air.

Your kisses are salty but perfectly sweet.
I love your warm, frothy waves
That lap at my feet.
However did I leave you? I couldn't again.
You're my heartbeat, the breath in my lungs,
My beginning and end.

An electric current sizzled in the air as I sang to him. It was tangible enough that I could hook it around him and reel him in closer should I choose to. Similar to the tension just before a kiss, it tempted and lured me until the pull between us left me as breathless as the song.

Ryken gripped the seat, the wood splintering from his desperate hold.

Twirling away, I focused on the lyrics and not his smoldering gaze. The heat of it sent a wave of tingles down my spine like a caress of his hand, calling to me as much as I called to him. I shook my head, desperate to finish the last line of the chorus before I leapt into his arms.

Oh, oooh,
To the sea, to the sea,
Where my heart longs to be.
The turquoise blue waters keep calling to me.
To the sea, to the sea,
You're the only place I find rest.
Submerged in your love,
We'll never be parted, not even in death.

Eyes closed, I held the last note, low and haunting—the sound of it reminding me of my song from the sea. Goosebumps sprinkled over my arms, something not of this world hanging in the air.

Magic?

For a moment, the room was silent, then an uproar of applause broke through. Unprepared for whistles and cheers, my eyes shot open at the ferocity of them. But I didn't care what they thought. I sent a shy smile to Ryken, but my heart plummeted to my stomach when I noticed his chair was empty.

"Another," a man shouted.

"Sing *Nightingale of the Sea*."

"No, *My Tavern Girl*."

"Ah, yes. Sing *My Tavern Girl*."

"Don't listen to them. Sing *Warriors of Water*."

Sounds were muffled, my heartbeat pumping more loudly in my ears the longer I stared at Ryken's empty seat. Was my singing so terrible that he left during my performance? My eyes heated, my vision blurring.

It was just a silly song. Why was I getting so worked up about it?

Ignoring the rest of the song requests, I placed the tambourine on the closest table, ready to race upstairs to hide in my room before I lost control and the tears came. Just as I did, someone spun me around by my shoulders, his cologne a mix of sea salt and—*Ryken*.

Tilting my head back, I met his eyes, hooded and darker than usual. His hands tensed as he grappled with his thoughts.

"You didn't leave," I murmured.

"Leave?" he said with a sigh, and he pulled me closer, wrapping his arms around my back. *"Never."*

"Come on, lad. Kiss the girl," a customer shouted.

A predatory grin curled the side of his mouth, scrambling my thoughts. My song had called for a merman, for my mate—and that was who was standing before me. Gone were the human mannerisms, leaving only the merman behind. He leaned in, inhaling my scent as one who savored the flavors of wine before taking a sip. He ripped the tie from my braid, throwing it on the floor as if it insulted him. Then he unwound my hair and combed his fingers through the loose strands, tugging the ends so I lifted my face upward.

I couldn't peel my eyes away. Nor did I want to.

"Kiss the girl," the room chanted until it faded into the background.

Ryken took their command to heart, his lips crashing into mine with pent-up desire. Not a sweet, delicate kiss as he had the first time. His mouth was possessive, claiming mine as he growled.

Dizzy, I eased back, gulping air through my tingling lips. He rested his forehead against mine, panting as well.

"The song you sang . . . is how I feel about you," he said with a throaty hum. His thumb brushed over my cheek. "You're my beginning and end."

My insides melted to liquid. This time it was me dragging his lips to mine, hungry for more. He didn't resist. Though I was on my tiptoes to reach him, I wasn't close enough, so he lifted me off the floor, hugging me against him.

"Marigold," he whispered reverently between kisses. Then I felt the vibration of his words in his other language—*Click, clickety-click, hummm, click.*

One moment I was lost in the haze of his kisses, the next I was snatched from his arms. He snarled like a wild animal, his complexion draining of color.

"Ryken," I shouted, panicked that he was going to transform completely.

He roared, the words unrecognizable but dripping with fury.

Ean held me by the arm, angling his body in front of mine, and squared his shoulders. "I doubt this is the type of entertainment Opal had in mind when she hired her to sing. She is a lady and deserves your respect."

Ryken's chest was heaving, and his eyes flicked to the rowdy crowd hooting and hollering over the outburst. Coins exchanged hands as men placed bets on what would happen next.

Oh, my goodness. Suddenly lightheaded, I placed a hand on Ean's arm to steady myself. Had I been kissing Ryken in front of all these people? My body radiated enough heat I was sure I would dissolve into a mortified pile of dust.

"Strike him down," someone hollered.

"No, kiss her again! I have a week's pay riding on this."

"Or maybe he's not man enough. If you don't kiss her, I will!" Drunk laughter rippled across the room.

At that, Ryken flipped the nearby table, flinging the cups in the air, ale spilling on the shirts of the men. Enraged shouts from the patrons filled the room. The men shot to their feet, wiping the liquid from their stylish tunics.

"Touch her, and I'll rip you into two," Ryken snarled at a well-dressed man.

"Do you not know who I am, stable boy? I have the power to ruin you with the snap of my fingers."

"And I can snap your neck with mine." Ready to accept the challenge, Ryken released a roar, animalistic in pitch. A sharp-toothed grin spread across his face, displaying all his teeth in their full glory.

Terror lit the room. Patrons stumbled over their chairs, bowls of soups overturning and silverware clanging to the ground as the once fearless men frantically rushed to the door to escape. Too many for one little door, they bottlenecked, shoving at each other to get through. A few smaller men were trampled in the rush.

Ean pulled me closer, his eyes widening behind his stray curls. "A monster in Cadell?"

"*No*, he's not. Please, release me. I'm the only one who can calm him." I fought his hold, unable to shake him off.

Instead, he scanned my features. "How did I not see it? You—you are . . . *no*, I have to protect you. Get back to the safety of the kitchen."

Did Ean know I was a mermaid? Surely he couldn't tell with just one look . . . could he?

"Release my mate," Ryken screamed, vaulting over a broken table. He bared his teeth, the tips as sharp as razors. Crouching, he spread his fingers wide like claws. "Last warning."

I winced, knowing what I had to do. "I'm sorry, Ean." My elbow collided with his face, the adrenaline making the impact more forceful than I planned. Blood spurted out, and he released me with a howl, his gloved hands catching the ruby splatters.

Ryken's lethal smile stretched in approval.

"Alice? What in the seas is going on in here?" Anjali cried out as she entered from the kitchen. She screamed when she saw Ean's hunched form, blood trickling down his arms.

Not to waste the distraction, I raced to Ryken and cradled his face in my palms. "Look at me."

At the sound of my voice, he relaxed, the peachy color rising back up his neck. He sagged into me, gripping me tight. "Help me, Marigold. Too many . . . feelings."

"Come," I commanded. Grabbing his hand, I pulled him up the stairs and into the blue room, slamming the door shut against the chaos of the dining hall.

His body trembled, his eyes downcast. "I lost control."

"You didn't hurt anyone . . . unlike me." I wiped my hand across my face. *Poor Ean.* What had come over me?

"But I was going to if you hadn't stopped me." He sucked in a breath, expelling it slowly. "I'm lost in your world, like an outcast who doesn't belong . . . and I don't want to live in a world where we can't be together."

"It doesn't matter what they think. You aren't an outcast to me." I threaded our fingers together, holding them up between us. The rightness of it stole my breath away as easily as his kisses had.

He tilted his head, eyeing our fingers before wiggling out of my grip.

"You don't want to hold my hand?" I asked, embarrassed by another rejection.

"Let me show you. This is more. Rest your palm on mine."

I placed my palm on his, his large hand dwarfing my own.

"To my people, this is a sign of respect. Of trust. We are equals. We do not lead each other but swim side by side. And I trust you. To my core, I trust you. You are free to come and go. I hope with that freedom you will choose to stay with me."

My heart soared, fluttering in my chest.

"Please stay with me," he repeated, his voice cracking. "Bond or no bond, I don't think I could survive without you."

My hand fell to my side. "Why would I want to leave you when I just fought off a crazed princess to get back to you in Windcrest? Did you not hear my song? My feelings for you have changed since I've gotten to know you—the real you. It doesn't matter which form you take, I never want to be parted from you."

"You are mine," he promised, bending forward to capture my lips.

Leaning away, I dodged his kiss. "Don't say that."

His shoulders drooped. "I don't understand."

"I'm not yours."

He flinched.

"I'm not an object to be collected and stored in a ship," I said, begging for it not to be true. "I want someone who will love me—not own me."

"Own you?" he sputtered. "I didn't say that. Did I not translate correctly?"

"It's a common phrase."

"It's *not* common to us. It's a sacred oath and a pledging of hearts. Whatever human word expresses when two things become one. Everything that comprises you is now within me. Your fears are my fears, your joy is my joy, and your tears are my tears. Our hearts beat as one for all eternity. You are mine to provide for, to protect, and to treasure."

There was a human word for what he described, and I had been waiting for him to say it.

"You love me?" I crumbled into his embrace, burrowing into his chest, his heart thudding in my ear.

Ryken kissed the top of my head. "With all I am and all I will be."

"Why didn't you tell me earlier?"

"If I didn't say—I thought I showed it. I would never have left the sea if I didn't love you. I want you to be happy."

I smiled into his tunic. "I am."

His arms tightened, his chin resting on my head. "My feelings are too much when I am a human. Especially when it comes to you."

"I have to admit, the connection between us is strong—almost tangible like rope I could have tugged you closer with if I had desired."

Or wanted to control you was the more apt phrase, but it didn't sit right with me. Why would I want to do that to Ryken?

He sighed, stirring my hair. "I don't think I should hear you sing again."

Surprised, I pulled back, my breath caught in my throat. "Oh."

Then I was right after all—he did hate my song.

"Or if I do, I don't think anyone should be around me." He licked his lips, a possessive gleam in his eyes. "I meant what I said. Mermen do not like to share."

No More Lies

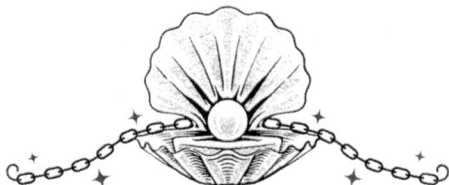

"You'll never have to share me. I'm yours alone," I whispered, cupping his cheek.

Ryken bowed his head. His jaw twitched as he fought with his emotions. "You do not know how long I've waited to hear you say that. Say it again. Please."

I leaned into his embrace, entranced by his desire for me.

"I am yours. *Forever.*" My promise echoed in my heart.

His eyes fluttered closed just as a tear escaped down his cheek. He pressed our foreheads together.

Then I repeated it in his language the best way I knew how. *Click, clickety-click, hummm, click.*

I placed my hand on his chest, and my heart sped up, matching his pace.

"Forever," he repeated.

Suddenly, he pulled away and exclaimed, "My eyes are leaking, but I'm not sad. What did I do wrong?"

I burst into laughter. He had such a way of catching me off guard. "Nothing. Sometimes we cry when we are overflowing with joy. Those are called happy tears."

"Happy tears," he repeated. "I like those."

Ryken's red-rimmed eyes trailed over me. Eventually, they landed on my hair, loose about my shoulders.

"I also like your hair down and free—not bound with a string," he said. "Every part of you is beautiful. You shouldn't hide it away."

I scooped my hair behind my ear, glancing away. "It's not that I'm hiding it. It tangles and gets in the way."

"In Alara, having long hair shows status. Golden hair like yours?" He teased a curl with blue ends. "You are someone special."

"And the shells the mermaids wear?" I pulled the one Liora had given me from the pocket of my dress.

Ryken plucked it from my hand and looped it through my hair. "They can mean many things depending on the reason behind the gift. Gratitude, friendship, love—and sometimes a combination of all three. For you, it's also a sign of acceptance into our community. Though it seems like just a shell to you, we see much more."

"Oh, I had no idea. Should I have offered her something in return?"

"No, it dilutes the gift if you do. The best thing you could do is say this: *Hum, whooooop, click, looo-do, click-click.* It means, 'I will wear it with honor.'"

I blinked at the strange sounds. "You might have to remind me the next time someone gives me a gift."

Ryken nodded. "I had hoped to be your first, but watching you—"

A fist knocked on the door.

"Alice? Are you in there?" Anjali called out.

I bit my lip, knowing we had to explain the situation downstairs. Ryken placed one hand on my collar and the other on my cheek, turning my face toward him.

You smell of fear. Do you think we are in danger?

I don't know. You were between forms in the dining room, which I didn't realize you could do.

I didn't either. Should we prepare for an attack?

My eyes widened. *Oh, no. I don't want anyone else to get hurt.*

"Alice? Ryken? Are you in there?" The handle jiggled, but the steel lock held the door in place.

Or maybe we could sneak out? I suggested, pointing to the window.

I'm not sure if I can. Climbing is still difficult for me.

Footsteps stomped up the stairs, immediately followed by pounding on the door, sending my heartbeat into a frenzy.

"Alice," the old woman barked, "you open the door this instant. I have a destroyed dining room downstairs, and I want answers."

If you say jump, I'll jump. If you say fight, I'll fight. Ryken's thumb caressed my cheek. *Tell me what to do to make you feel better.*

I think we need to apologize.

He frowned at the boring choice.

"Opal," I started tentatively, sliding the lock and opening the door. "I'm sorry—"

The elderly woman pushed the door open and barged in, cupping my cheeks in her wrinkled hands. "Are you all right? Did those men hurt you?"

All my thoughts scattered at her concern. "I—what?"

"Those men can be a handful, especially after they've been drinking. I'm wondering if I sent a lamb out to the wolves."

"Once I started singing, they were more manageable."

"It was my fault," Ryken admitted. "Nobody talks to my mate that way and lives to speak about it."

Opal spun toward him, her lips pinched. "*You.* Jealous suitors need to stay in the kitchen if they can't control their tempers."

"Suitor?" Ryken asked, turning to me.

"He's just protective," I blurted, hoping this would be the last time I had to cover for his merman instincts. "When Ryken gets worked up, he needs to be removed from the situation. The patrons were taunting him, and the incident spiraled out of control. I'm thankful nobody was hurt in the process."

"I promise, I did try to suppress it." Ryken bowed his head.

Both Opal and Anjali sent him a suspicious look, shuffling away.

"He's relaxed now."

Opal cleared her throat. "I know I promised you a night of sleep, but I don't feel safe with him staying in the inn. He didn't seem like himself—"

"He didn't seem human," Anjali stated crisply.

Silence floated between us, thick with tension.

An awkward chuckle bubbled out of me as I tried to think of a good reason behind Ryken's change in demeanor. What could I say to explain the animalistic sounds, his inhuman strength, and a mouth full of sharp teeth? A trick of the light? A side effect of moldy food?

"Good. We don't have to lie anymore," Ryken blurted before I could respond.

"Ryken," I gasped.

Anjali drew the older woman to her side.

"Lies are for humans. My kind prefers honesty."

"Y-your kind?" Opal stammered, her hand resting on her chest.

"What he means is—" I started, but he cut me off.

"No more lies," he said to me, placing a supportive hand on my shoulder and turning to Opal. "There is nothing for you to be frightened of. I will not forget that you provided us shelter and offered us food when others did not. For that, I am thankful."

"While I appreciate your gratitude, that won't fix my broken table downstairs. Customers will arrive at morning light wanting a hot meal."

"I will fix it. Ean can show me how."

"Is he around? I need to apologize to him," I asked.

"Ean is out in the barn. He took off after the crowd dispersed, mumbling incoherently. You gave him a good scare and a fat lip." She placed her fists on her hips, scowling at me.

"I'm sorry," I said again, my hands in the air. "Please don't kick us out because of me."

"I did make you a deal, but how do I know he won't snap again?" Opal accused. "Windcrest, Glenton, or the moon—wherever you're from, I do not tolerate violence in my inn."

I nodded. "Understood. It won't happen again."

Just when I thought the matter was settled, Ryken spoke.

"Actually, violence is a human trait. We are known for our peacefulness, but due to our bond—" he gestured between us, and I hid my flaming face behind my hands "—other males, whether human or mermen, can force me to overreact. I am sorry to cause you to worry."

"Did you just say—?"

"Anjali, tell me my hearing isn't going as well as my eyesight. Did he just say *mermen*?"

"I did," Ryken agreed.

"Mermen?" Anjali clarified again.

"Yes, mermen," he said, tilting his head.

"I'm sorry if I sound skeptical. It's just—ah—you aren't what I pictured," Opal said.

Oh, goodness. They didn't believe him.

"He is," I said at the same time Ryken grumbled, "And how did you expect me to look?"

Anjali and Opal sent each other a quick glance.

"Well, I thought you'd be more fishlike," Anjali said, almost sounding disappointed.

"I'm blending in. M—Alice thought I would scare everyone in my other form. Plus, I only have one pair of pants. I suppose I could take them off . . ." He trailed off, reaching for his top button.

"No!" the three of us shouted in unison, stopping his hand from further movement.

"We will just have to take your word for it," Opal said, her eyes wide.

"You have seen him like this?" Anjali said, a thread of doubt woven through her words.

"Yes, it's truly magnificent to see." As soon as the words left my mouth, I wanted to snatch them back.

Ryken's head whipped toward me, and I struggled to keep my focus on Anjali's confused expression. Heat radiated just from his stare, his unique aroma of interest teasing my senses. His hand slid an inch along my shoulder, his finger grazing my collar.

Magnificent? he purred into my thoughts.

Oh, goodness. Pretend I didn't say that.

But you did.

Ignoring his smirk, I stepped to the side, needing a moment to catch my breath.

"Fine, we will continue with our agreement. Ryken can sleep in the barn with Ean. Alice may sleep here. You will be up bright and early to fix my table downstairs, young man—merman?—whatever you are."

"I would prefer not to leave her," he stated. "She makes me calm."

Opal sighed. "All right. You may sleep in here but on the floor. I don't know what the rules are in the sea, but I run a tight ship here. Nothing untoward, you understand?"

"Uh, I—" He sent me a desperate look, his mind still stuck in translation.

"He will."

Opal raised a brow at him until he agreed too.

When we were alone, he winked at me. "I want to hear more about how you think I'm magnificent."

I groaned. "How do you know that word but not untoward?"

He shrugged innocently.

During the night, I couldn't find rest. I tossed and turned despite the luxurious comfort of the bed. A slight itch on my legs turned unbearable. Pinpricks from my foot to hip poked all night long, never ceasing. I scratched them in frustration, which only fueled the pain more.

It had to be a reaction from something in the magical garden. Either a plant that touched my skin or the soil when I dug up the carrots.

I flopped to my side and moaned into my pillow.

"Marigold?" Ryken whispered from beside the bed. "Is something wrong?"

Another wave of tingles had my right leg kicking out.

He scooped my hair to the side to lean over me.

"I don't feel well," I mumbled into the pillow. "Would you . . . lie with me? Until I fall asleep?"

Even with my eyes squeezed shut, I could sense his smile, his pleasure rippling through the air. The mattress dipped as he crawled in next to me, his arm curling around my waist as it had the night before. Immediately, the comfort of his presence allowed my body to relax, the pain lessening.

I sighed in relief.

His breath tickled the back of my neck. "My sweet Marigold. I'd do anything for you."

I pressed my hand over his, hugging him to me before I nodded off. The peaceful rumble of his contented hum was the last thing I heard.

I woke alone, chilled without Ryken next to me. Slipping from the bed, I splashed water from the basin on my face, washing the sleep from my eyes. The few hours of rest I did end up catching were not enough.

Luckily, my legs no longer itched or stung, and I hoped the magic had run its course.

I pulled up my skirt expecting to see swollen calves or hives dotting my skin. Instead, shiny patches of colors glittered up at me. My hand jerked in surprise, releasing the fabric.

My pulse picked up as I gasped for air. *Shiny. Colored. Scales.* I didn't even have time to recognize the color. The jolt of seeing anything besides skin had my vision spinning.

Scales. I have scales.

Princess Vella had said she saw patches of scales, but I hadn't seen any the last two times I checked. Not that I had time to inspect thoroughly with Ryken always present. I assumed the princess's delusions had her seeing what she wanted—but I was wrong. They were hidden, spreading from a small patch behind my knees where I hadn't noticed.

My hand shook as I forced myself to grab the hem of my gown, raising it inch by inch. A flash of light caught my shin, a silver gleam reminding me of Ryken's tail blended with a translucent shade of jade the same color as my eyes. Similar to the beautiful green sea glass my grandmother collected from the beach.

On a deeper scan, the patches weren't as big as I originally thought. They were smaller than my palm and in only a few spots on each leg. I still had time. Not much, but hopefully enough to make it to Cadell and see my family one last time.

Would they accept this new version of me? Or would they try to place me in a cage like Princess Vella had done to Liora? Though I hoped for acceptance, fear of the unknown could turn them against me. I should keep up with the lie. It was never wise to be different. I was taught to go through life with my head down, following all the rules to blend in.

Now look at me. I was sparkling like a jewel in the sunlight.

Unable to resist, I rubbed a scale. It was smooth in one direction and bristled in the other. Overly sensitive, my nerves exploded at the single touch. It was best to leave it alone. I didn't want the pain from last night to return.

I blew out a breath. *A tail . . . I am actually growing a tail.* I knew it was coming, but seeing it close up was a different story. It made it seem more real.

Today was already full of surprises, and I had only just awakened. Combing my fingers through my hair, I rushed out of the room and jogged downstairs, freezing halfway.

The dining room was crammed with customers. All the chairs were occupied with an assortment of men, women, and even a few small children. Most were gobbling down large stacks of syrupy pancakes. People stood along the wall, chatting with each other while they waited for a spot to open up. Outside the window, the blur of more silhouettes walked by. A few patrons glanced inside, eyeing the wait.

This was more than triple the number of people that were here last night. Anjali breezed into the room, nonplussed by the enormously packed room. She squeezed through the cluster of bodies, holding her tray of food above her head as she tried to reach the nearest table.

A low growl came from the kitchen door, and the men closest to her jumped away, allowing her room to walk. Eyes narrowed, Ryken followed behind her with two pitchers in hand and began filling up drinks as she slid the plated dishes to hungry customers.

Like they had done this before.

Anjali patted Ryken's arm as she passed him and headed back into the kitchen.

"She's here," a man said from somewhere in the crowded room.

Ryken caught my eye, more at ease than I had ever seen him. Dropping the pitchers on the table, he crossed the room in two steps and leapt up to the backside of the banister to be face-to-face with me.

"Are you feeling better?" he asked.

I tried to ignore the ogling stares.

"I am. Uh, what is going on in here?" I looked over his shoulder, everyone watching us like we were this morning's entertainment.

"Is she going to sing?" a man who looked slightly familiar asked.

"She better. I waited an hour outside to make sure I got a good seat."

"Sing *To the Sea* again," another person demanded in a gruff tone.

"Careful, Abe. You frighten her, and her husband will box your ears in."

My wide eyes swung to Ryken, who was smiling like a satisfied cat.

"They call me your husband," he said, beaming at me. "I like it—wait, no—I *love* it."

"Ryken," I whispered, "it doesn't work that way."

"It works for me." He leaned in for a quick kiss, the room erupting in hoots and whistles. He laughed at their excitement. "They make the sound of how I feel when I kiss you."

"Ryken," Opal hollered from the kitchen doorway.

303

He ducked away.

"Are you trying to break something else, like your head? Get down and come help us." She turned around and walked back into the kitchen. "And don't bite anyone."

"Bite?" I repeated in utter shock. He better not have.

"Just once. It slipped." He shrugged a shoulder before hopping down. The men parted to let him through, giving him more than ample space.

What was going on? Had I fallen into another world while I was sleeping?

In a daze, I continued down the stairs and forced my way through the customers. Unlike Ryken, they did not make it easy for me. Hands reached out, grazing my gown and hair, whispering words of awe. The stench of sweat and body odor stifled me, trapping me in place as much as the people were. I pushed another hand away, revolted.

"Excuse yourself," I snapped.

"The lost sister has returned," a woman whispered.

What?! I stared at her dumbly.

"The queen will be so pleased," her companion agreed.

"I heard Windcrest is sending an army to bring her back," a man wearing blue added.

"Good luck to them. My king will burn them to a crisp."

I stumbled backward, somehow still stuck in a war I wanted nothing to do with.

"Sing a song for us, my lady," a little girl pleaded from my side.

Surprised at her appearance, I jumped back, my elbow hitting a mug of water and knocking it across the table.

"Oh my. I'm terribly sorry," I said quickly, using a cloth napkin to soak up the spill.

A man stared open-mouthed, starstruck at my nearness. He spoke in a garble of words that made no sense.

Forcing a smile, I sidestepped the rest of the way to the kitchen, doing my best to avoid the pawing hands.

"Ryken?" I pushed through the door.

The casual scene before me had me stumbling to a stop. The eerie calm was just as jarring as the chaos in the dining room.

Ankles crossed, Ryken leaned against the table next to Anjali, snatching chunks of ham off the cutting board before Anjali slapped him away. With sad eyes, he rubbed his hand, looking wounded.

Anjali rolled her eyes. "Just one more piece. You've had enough as it is."

He grinned before he scooped up a handful and barely avoided her second swat.

"Morning, Marigold," Opal said from her stance by the fire.

"Good morni—*wait*, what did you call me?"

Did everyone know our true identities? If so, we had to leave immediately. They wouldn't hesitate to hand us over to the Queen of Hearts.

Ryken stiffened, eyeing me with concern.

Anjali whipped around, her smile lighting up the room. "Marigold, you're here."

Before I could gather my thoughts, she wrapped her arms around me and twirled us around in a circle. "How did I not see it? You look just like your sister."

Some of the tension eased from my shoulders. "Rose? You know Rose?"

"Of course, you silly girl. Haven't you been listening?" Anjali laughed, squeezing me again in a friendly manner. "She's my friend."

Ryken took the moment of distraction to grab another handful of meat. He almost got away with it, too, except Opal shook her spoon at him.

"I don't care if you're not human. I'll still beat you with my ladle if you eat any more. You can eat whatever leftovers we have, but not another morsel until then."

"What about the yellow thing? Can I eat that?" Ryken asked. "What is it called again?"

"A bird," Anjali answered. "This one is called Tiny."

A yellow bird chirped from the half door, hopping along the top. It watched me with its dark eyes. It tweeted a few notes, but the melody was lost under Opal's commands to take the next batch of plates out.

All the noise left me disoriented, and the room whirled before me. I pressed my fingers to my temples. "Stop, stop! Can everyone just be quiet for one moment and explain to me what is going on?"

Because of You

Ryken pressed a comforting hand to my shoulder, his touch calming my nerves. I placed my hand on his, thankful he always knew when I needed him.

"Marigold?" Opal asked, ladling porridge into a wooden bowl. "Are you well? If you are nervous about performing—don't be. You don't have to sing if you don't want to. Had I known who you were, I would have gladly offered you a place to stay for free."

Had someone arrived from Windcrest and revealed my true identity? Or had someone recognized me from last night's performance?

"No, it's not that," I responded. "How did you know I'm Marigold?"

Both ladies turned to stare at Ryken.

"You couldn't make it *one* day?" I whipped around to glare at him.

He tilted his head. "I thought we said no more lies."

"*You* said that, not me," I snapped.

Anjali chimed in. "Why keep it a secret at all? We should be celebrating. The lost sister has returned. Everyone has been tearing across the countryside looking for you. Your family won't give up their search for you."

Surprised, I turned to her. "You've talked to them? Recently? My sister is unwell. It's the reason I came back—I'm worried for her."

306

"I received a similar letter a few months ago——" Anjali started, but then Opal jabbed her elbow in her side, silencing her.

They held each other's stare, communicating with looks alone.

"What is it?" I asked, my eyes darting between them. "Please. I've come all this way to see her."

Lips pinched, Opal shook her head.

Anjali sighed and crossed her arms, not pleased with the result of their silent conversation.

"We don't want her to worry her when we don't know the truth ourselves," Opal reminded Anjali.

"Is she dying?" My stomach dropped as if the ground had disappeared beneath me. Air refused to leave my lungs.

I couldn't lose her. My sister. My first friend and protector.

Roselyn.

Arms gathered me close. Tears blurred my vision, but I knew Ryken's scent like my own, and I burrowed into his chest.

"Sad tears this time?" he whispered into my hair.

I nodded, the coarse material of his tunic scratching my cheek. I breathed in his salty musk and soaked in his comfort.

"I like the happy ones better." He squeezed me tighter.

"Sweet child, she isn't dying. It's just bouts of sickness that come quickly. There's no need to cry," Opal said kindly. She snatched up a dry dishcloth and offered it to me.

I stared at it, forcing myself to leave the protection of Ryken's arms so I could grab it. When we untangled, his hands clung on a second longer, as if he struggled with releasing me too.

After thanking her, I took the offered cloth and wiped my tear-stained cheeks. "I saw her in a—you wouldn't believe me if I told you—but I've never seen her look so unwell."

"Opal," Anjali whined. She gestured at me. "Look at her. She's distraught."

"Nobody's seen her. She hasn't left the castle in a few months," Opal hissed under her breath.

"Are my parents with her at least? Are they all safe? Is Rose safe? After I learned about Prince Alexander . . ."

"Oh my, yes. She has plenty of people surrounding her each day. She is beloved by all. Not that I wish ill of the dead, but it's been better for everyone now that he's gone. Your sister has blossomed."

"But she loved him," I stated.

Anjali jerked at that, her back stiff. "How could you possibly think that? He was a manipulator."

"No, that's not true—he spoiled her and provided for her every whim." Dread pulsed under my skin. Anjali couldn't be right.

Anjali's cheeks pinked, fury radiating off her. "He nearly killed her. Chained her to him in front of the entire kingdom so that she sat at his feet. I saw it with my own two eyes. His love was poison."

"Poison?" Ryken asked.

"It's something that can kill you," I mumbled, still in shock.

"Love can kill? Explain," Ryken said, taking a step toward Anjali.

"It was too much."

"Too much?" he repeated, his voice spiking.

"He gave her the world and whispered his sweet lies until she believed them. He bought her everything and even threw a ball in her honor. His love crowded her until she couldn't breathe. The only thing she asked for, he couldn't give—*her freedom.*"

I pressed my trembling fingertips over my mouth. Anjali's words blared through my thoughts and mixed with the memories of the last time I saw Rose. Her chilling scream as she denied the prince's proposal. Then her defeated collapse onto the floor.

How did I not see what was happening? Not hear her cries for help? She hid her misery behind her smiles—her way of protecting me as she always did. What had it cost her?

"She didn't love him," I said, blinking at my fingers. "And he wouldn't let her be with anyone but him."

Ryken frowned.

"Yes," Anjali agreed. "I was trying to explain that out in the garden —but you seemed so upset. For what it's worth, she is happy now."

I glanced away, lost in my memories. Her smiles, laughs, and mannerisms were all dissected again in my mind's eye. What else had I missed?

"Thank you for the truth. I've been in the dark about most things," I said, my voice a faint whisper.

"Oh, don't be upset. This is a day to rejoice. You have returned home. She will be ecstatic to have you back in Cadell. She has scoured the territories looking for you."

Opal clicked her tongue at me. "Speaking of which—where have you been all this time?"

"She was with me," Ryken said, his eyes softening as he smiled down at me.

I smiled back, thankful he had been there that fateful day when I was thrown into the sea. So thankful that he heard my song.

"Well, not the whole time I was sleeping. See, I had this chain——"

"No. I was there the whole time."

"—attached to my . . ." I stopped, my heart stuttering. His ocean eyes held mine. "You stayed?"

"From the moment you plunged into the water, I've been with you. Your heart struggled with each beat, you were so weak. So many times I thought I had lost you to the sea. But I couldn't let you go. On those days, I used our bond and had my heart beat for you to boost your strength."

My mouth hung open in what I knew was an unladylike expression. How was I only learning this? He had stayed with me the entire time I was asleep? Why hadn't he said anything?

"A whole year? Ryken . . ." I murmured.

Movement distracted me from the corner of my eye. Anjali and Opal placed their hands on their hearts with dreamy sighs.

"You seem shocked." He tilted his head.

"Of course, I am. Every day? *For a year?* I assumed you hadn't stopped by often or at all. The other caves were empty when we passed. You were so surprised to see me."

Ryken chuckled at that, a giant grin on his face. "Because I *was* surprised. Months I had been with you and now you were finally awake. I was . . . I don't know—nervous? I already knew you so well. The curves of your face, the texture of your hair, your scent, your sighs—I spent a lot of time waiting for you to wake. I wanted it to be perfect."

"I think I'm swooning," Anjali whispered to Opal.

"Me too. If she doesn't marry the man, I will," Opal added.

"But—you weren't there when I woke up," I said.

He ducked his head. "And I regret that too. I still had my duties and had to train with the others."

"Others?"

"The other Collectors: Egon, Jayco, and Pike. They had hoped to meet you at the ceremony, but you fainted. To be honest, it was a relief. It allowed us to leave early so we could be alone again."

The corner of my mouth pulled up as the warmth of his words filled me.

"What's a collector?" Anjali whispered again to Opal.

Opal shushed her. "*Quiet.* I'm listening."

"Ry, I had no idea."

"I was never sure if I'd get to keep you. You hovered on the edge of death so many times, and I'd have to snatch you back." He placed a hand over my heart. Immediately, our beats synchronized. "Now your heart is stronger. Each beat that vibrates in your chest brings me peace. I know you're safe."

"Because of you," I whispered. I stood up on my tiptoes, my fingers threading through his silky hair at the nape of his neck. Angling his head down, I pressed my forehead to his and closed my eyes.

He gripped my hips, pulling me closer. "You know . . ."

When he didn't continue, my eyes fluttered open to catch him staring at me.

"I think I prefer the kisses." Ryken pouted.

I laughed. "Were you hoping I was going to kiss you?"

He nodded enthusiastically, shaking my head with his.

I laughed again. "You are incorrigible."

"I don't know what that means, but I'll translate it as 'kiss me.'"

"That's not what it——"

His lips pressed softly against mine, cutting off my sentence before sinking deeper, his hands sliding up my back. The urge to run and for him to chase caught me off guard and startled me back, but his grip was like iron, only allowing me an inch of movement.

A range of emotions shifted across his face as he breathed in my scent, so quickly I couldn't catch them all, but the last one—the predatory gaze—burned to my core.

"Are you going to run?" he asked, his voice deep.

"If I did, would you catch me?" I challenged.

"Always." A low growl rumbled in his chest as his fingers tightened on the back of my gown. "You wouldn't make it far."

I leaned in, watching his pupils dilate. "I guess we will have to find out."

Opal clapped her hands, snapping us out of our bubble. "My goodness. We couldn't get through to you two. I thought we'd have to douse you with a bucket of water."

"If he's a merman, wouldn't he like it if we threw water on him?" Anjali asked. She tapped a finger to her lip in thought.

Opal gave her a side eye and cleared her throat. "You don't have time to dilly dally. Your family is coming to fetch you."

I jerked upright. "All of them are coming? Here?"

"The note said just Cedrick . . . I think?" Anjali checked the pockets of her gown, then her apron, before lifting bowls and plates on the table. "Oh, no."

"Did you lose it?" The elderly woman joined in the search.

Anjali squatted down, peering under the table. "Maybe."

Opal rolled her eyes. "You'd lose your head if it wasn't attached."

"I know, I know." Anjali sent me a pained smile. "I'm so sorry."

"Who's Cedrick?" I asked.

"Her husband," Opal responded, squinting at me.

"Whose husband?"

"Your sister's," Opal and Anjali answered at the same time.

"He's coming here? How does he even know I'm here?"

"Ean left last night to fetch him. They sent Tiny today with a note," Anjali said.

The forgotten bird cooed, startling me.

"Not a fan of birds?" Anjali asked with a laugh.

I took another step away, eyeing the bird's beak. "Not really."

"I didn't like him either when we first met. He's very intelligent— maybe more so than a dog. He's probably listening to us right now."

His glassy black eyes drilled through me. I shivered. I didn't like the idea of anyone spying on me, not when there was a queen chasing me. I angled away from the bird and wrapped my arms around myself.

Voices hollered through the door from the dining room. Fists thundered on tabletops, vibrating the floorboards beneath our feet. Impatient for their meals.

"They're going to revolt. You two, deliver the next batch," Opal said, pointing at Ryken and Anjali. She lifted a gray brow at him.

"With the amount of food you're eating, you need to earn your keep."

"So, I can have more?" He smirked as he went to the door and opened it for Anjali.

She followed close behind and maneuvered the tray far away from him as she walked into the dining room. "Don't even think about it. Grab the pitchers you left on the table and help me refill cups."

"Then I can have another bite?" Ryken asked.

"No," Opal shouted before he even finished his sentence.

Crestfallen, he eyed the stacks of pancakes on the tables.

Before he took off, I grabbed his hand and placed it on my collar. *I'll give you mine,* I thought with a conspiratorial wink.

Suddenly, the dining hall went silent.

My spike of worry immediately had my other senses scanning the room. To the human ear, it was eerily quiet, but I could hear the customers' breathing accelerate. Like a tidal wave, the smell of shock and excitement coated the air and slammed into me.

Ryken stretched out an arm in front of my chest, his nostrils flaring as he inhaled deeply.

"As I live and breathe . . ." a woman said, fluttering herself with a napkin.

Distracted by the hushed silence of the customers, I had missed the man standing in the open doorway. A breeze from outside ruffled his black hair, thick and straight, the ends stopping at his neck. He wore a stylish green tunic with silver embroidery along his collar that shimmered in the sunlight. I supposed he would be handsome if he wasn't scowling at the packed room. Cool, dark eyes darted from one face to the next, his strong jaw ticking in a broody way. An aristocratic snob by the looks of it, but there was a mysterious air about him.

Not enough to tempt me closer.

I didn't recognize him and couldn't understand why everyone had gone quiet at his arrival. Part of the royal court if I had to guess from the fabric. Whoever he was, this man wasn't my brother-in-law. Roselyn would never marry such a pretentious lord. He looked like he'd never smiled a day in his life.

"Is she here?" he demanded as if he was used to commanding people with the snap of his fingers.

She? Did he mean me? I tucked into Ryken's side.

As quickly as the noises had muted, the inn roared back to life, the patrons shooting to their feet and calling him by many names: Your Majesty. My king.

Then one that made me clutch Ryken's tunic—*the Keeper of Flames.*

His jaw ticked, his eyes roaming over the boisterous crowd. His boots thudded against the wooden planks as he entered the inn.

My throat went dry. They had found us after all.

On the Run

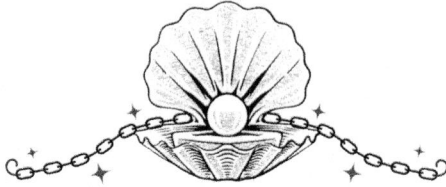

King Galon was right—nothing spreads news faster than gossip. How else had the king of Mistbrooke found me so quickly? Was the Queen of Hearts outside in her carriage?

I wasn't staying to find out.

Marigold? Ryken asked through our connection. *You smell of fear.*

Shut the door, I thought.

He didn't hesitate. Heavy-handed, he slammed the kitchen door closed with a crack, the wooden frame rattling.

As quickly as it had shut, it swung open, the king's arm outstretched toward us from across the dining room. His amber eyes flicked to me, his eyebrows rising in recognition and . . . *relief?*

Did I appear to be an easy target?

I reached into my pocket and clasped the handle of the dagger. I would not go willingly. I'd spend my last breath slicing him to pieces if he so much as touched me.

This time I kicked the door shut so he got the message.

"Hey now," Opal scolded. "I already had to repair a table today. I don't want to add a door to my list."

The three of us jumped as the door flew open again, crashing into the wall with such force that the top hinge snapped off. Wood splintered off the door as it sagged sideways, sliding slowly to the ground.

Opal screamed, her porridge-covered ladle clattering to the floor.

Hoots and cheers erupted around the room. The customers applauded at the morning entertainment.

"I'm coming here every day," a woman said from the table closest to us. "Such a gripping performance."

The king pushed against the crowd, his focus locked on me.

"Give him space," Anjali shouted to the masses. "He's trying to get through."

Now can we attack? A low rumble sounded from Ryken's chest.

We run.

"Run?" he repeated, disappointed.

I shushed him, my eyes flicking to the feathered spy on the back door. I placed his hand on my choker again and held his gaze.

We need to sneak out the door.

Who is that man?

Someone—a voice I didn't recognize—shouted my name. I ignored it.

He's one of the people we've been hiding from. We don't have time to discuss it—run. Out of patience, I didn't wait for him to understand and bolted for the half door.

"What has gotten into you two?" Opal screeched as we zipped by her.

"Don't let him follow us," I shouted at her over my shoulder. "He's trying to take me."

"*What?* Who?" She picked up her ladle and brandished it like a weapon. "I'll box his ears in."

The bird took flight as we approached, wing wide, coasting out into the garden on a long squawk. We dashed outside and turned sharply for the barn.

"Should we hide?" I asked between pants.

"I never hide from a fight. Let me transform. He's only a man, and men are weak."

I changed my mind and veered left, avoiding the building at the last second. "*Water.* We need water. You're faster there."

"This way," Ryken said, taking the lead. "I can smell it."

I pumped my arms as I ran, keeping pace with him. Though I couldn't smell it myself, I trusted he knew where we were going. We

315

faced a long stretch of land with no place to hide or tree to climb. Not unless we went southwest toward Mistbrooke Forest.

The enchanted forest where the Sorcerer lived and the homeland of the king that chased us. But as I scanned our surroundings, I realized it was the only place we could go.

We couldn't outrun anyone if they had a carriage or horse. Already I was winded, a crackled wheeze rattling in my throat with each inhale. Ryken pulled ahead of me as I stumbled on a rock, a painful cramp in my waist slowing my stride. With the back of my hand, I wiped a layer of sweat from my forehead and squinted. The hot sun held no mercy as we ran.

Maybe traveling through the woods would be a good thing. Anjali had mentioned it was a faster route to Cadell. So much had changed since I was taken. Perhaps this was our best chance at escape.

"We need to go into the woods," I shouted at Ryken.

We crossed through the wildflower fields and ran toward Mist-brooke Forest.

"There it is," Ryken yelled back at me, his face dripping with sweat.

A river stretched out before us and wound like a snake from the copper mountains of Glenton to disappear through a wall of trees. A wooden bridge arched over the clear waters, wide enough that a carriage or wagon could cross. The glorious sound of gurgling water called to me, beckoning me closer, and my dry throat tingled in anticipation.

"Marigold," the voice cried out somewhere behind us.

A flutter of wings sounded in my ear just before a bird landed on my shoulder. Panic seized me and I screamed, swatting wildly at anything and everything to get it off of me.

It dodged my swings only to land on my head. Its sharp talons gripped my hair for purchase. It cawed, sounding like an alarm.

With one menacing step in my direction, Ryken opened his mouth and released an enraged roar that echoed across the field. His fury resonated all the way to my bones.

He was forever my beast and protector.

The yellow bird darted up and away in a flurry of feathers, letting out frightened chirps. He circled us once before zooming back in the direction we'd come from, swooping down to fly beside the king who was racing toward us.

Oh, goodness.

"Hurry. Get in the water," I shrieked.

Ryken glanced up from removing his boots. "I have to take off my pants."

"No time," I countered, giving his shoulder a push.

It didn't take much to set him off balance. Arms flailing, he grabbed my skirt as he tipped backward into the river, dragging me with him into the cool liquid.

Deeper than I thought, the water was well over my head. I sank toward the rocky riverbed, my blue gown bubbling up around me. I pushed it down in annoyance.

My eyes easily adjusted to the hazy water, a school of minnows scattering as I kicked my legs. It wasn't dark enough to hide, but it could buy us some time if the king wasn't a good swimmer. Or maybe fire and water simply didn't mix?

Ryken's boots floated next to me, and I batted them away just in time to see the flash of silver from Ryken's tail, the water rippling as he swam closer. He pressed a ball of fabric into my arms, humming and clicking like I could understand him. *His pants?* I grasped them to my chest just before he grabbed my upper arm and dove off.

Everything was blurry, and I couldn't figure out what direction we were heading, but whichever way it was, we were swimming faster than we ever had before. The water pulled at my skin and gown the faster we went like invisible hands refusing to relinquish their hold.

Sunlight dimmed, the water darkening as the scent of pine grew stronger. My shoulders tingled as goosebumps trailed down my arms. We were going too fast for me to see, but I didn't want to keep swimming if this river dumped us off at Mistbrooke castle . . . if there even was a castle. I had thought it was destroyed in the fire in the Battle of the Bones, but how could there be a king without a castle?

I placed a hand on Ryken's, squeezing his fingers.

He slowed our pace until we came to a complete stop. The water here wasn't as deep, and my feet touched the bottom so that I could peek out over the waterline.

Ryken's hand cupped the back of my neck, pulling me into his soggy tunic. From the waist up, he seemed human, but below his tunic, his long silver tail swooshed back and forth in distracting swipes.

Something is not right here, he said through his thoughts.

It's the woods. They're haunted.

His eyes scanned the trees. *Keep swimming?*

No, I don't want to swim into their kingdom by accident. I need to go south to Cadell. Can you tell which direction we are facing?

Ryken spun in a circle, careful not to make too much noise. *No. Those things are blocking the sky.*

The trees? We could climb one. It would give us a better view.

I swim. You climb.

I agreed and kicked off for the edge of the river.

He tightened his grip, pulling me back. *Give me my pants first. I'll change while you climb.*

My eyes widened. I nodded again, somehow overheated in the water. He took his pants from my weak grip and winked as if he could read my thoughts.

Don't think about it, I scolded myself. *Stay focused on the task.*

Another odd tickle at the nape of my neck had my attention snapping to the row of pines. I eyed the trees as an odd feeling crept up my spine. Tall pines and red oaks grew on either side of the river with no clear path to walk. Each direction was eerily similar.

There is no reason to be frightened. They are just trees.

It would be just like when I climbed apple trees back home.

I paddled to the river's edge where a long, twisted branch dipped into the current, the water rippling around it. I grabbed on, hoping to use it as leverage to pull myself up.

As I held onto the branch, the bark moved, pulsing like it was alive.

Unprepared, I screamed at the movement, letting go to fall back into the gushing water with a splash.

The current whisked me away and carried me in its frothy waves. Before, the water was a calm trickle as it moved downstream, but now it was more like rapids, spinning me downstream with increasing speed. I was barely able to snatch hold of some muddy roots to keep from drifting farther down the river. With what strength I had left, I crawled onto the grass and flopped onto my back, panting.

What *was* that? Or had I imagined the river's flow speeding up?

Something touched my foot, causing me to scream again.

"Quiet, Marigold," Ryken said. "It's just me."

I threw an arm over my eyes. All the magic and superstitions were messing with my mind. We needed to get out of these woods.

Fully human, he stood next to me and offered a hand, helping me to my feet. He scooped my tangled hair behind my ears and tilted my face up to his.

"Are you all right?" He pressed a kiss to my forehead. "You scared me."

"I—yes. These woods are creeping me out."

"They are plants. There is nothing to fear."

"I know." I sighed. "I'm just imagining things." Though I said it more to convince myself than him.

I kept repeating that phrase as I climbed the nearest oak. Even though it had been years since I'd climbed an apple tree, once I started, it was like my body remembered. The farther up I went, the skinnier the limbs were, and I realized I wouldn't be able to reach the top without the branches snapping.

My gown didn't help matters. It doubled my weight and snagged on the branches and bark.

I placed my foot on a higher branch, and the limb bowed with the lightest of pressure. This was the highest I could go.

It still wasn't high enough.

Slowly, I made my way back down, but my dress caught a pointed stem and threw me off balance. Then I was falling, the branches slapping my arms and legs until something grabbed my ankle and jerked me to a stop.

"Marigold," Ryken screamed. He spoke in his language, a rattling of noises and clicks. "Don't move."

My heart raced like it wanted to leap from my chest. My hair hung down, and my gown was tangled in my legs. Whatever held me pulled upward, surprising a shriek out of me.

Like it came out of nowhere, another branch appeared at eye level. I grabbed onto it, and the pressure from my ankle released. But now instead of going up, I was going down, not a quick drop but a gradual descent to the ground.

Is the tree . . . moving on its own?

I clearly must have hit my head in the fall. A tree didn't lower a person to the ground. Yet, it was happening.

As soon as I got close to Ryken, he snatched me from the branch, his eyes wide.

"Not a plant, not a plant . . ." he repeated, concerned. He wrapped his arms around me, his hand holding my head to his chest.

"We shouldn't have come in here. I don't know how to get out," I said.

A wolf howled in the distance, and I stiffened against Ryken. And now we were going to be lunch for some furry beast.

"That noise—it's familiar."

"It's a wolf, and if it's in these woods, it's wild and will eat us."

He blinked, listening to the howl again. "No."

I jerked back to see if he had hit his head too. "Since when do you know about wolves?"

"She said to go east."

"*She?*" I stammered.

"She said the way home is east."

"No, no. We are not listening to a wolf."

"Do you have a better idea besides falling out of a tree?"

I narrowed my eyes and pulled from his grip. "It's not like I've done this before."

Another howl sounded, ending with a few barks. Ryken met my gaze. "She said she is coming."

"*Go*, then. East. I don't want to meet a wolf."

We took off, jogging in our wet attire and weaving through the trees. Soon the river was far behind us, a thick canopy of trees surrounding us.

"Are we still going east?" I asked, spinning around. Had we backtracked?

"Yes? I think," Ryken said, sounding just as confused.

I groaned.

"Maybe we should go back?" he suggested.

"Which way is back?"

He scratched his head. "I don't know. That way?" He pointed to our right.

We set off in that direction, the grass and weeds growing higher.

Vines dangled down from the branches, shadows playing tricks so their forms reminded me of snakes.

"No, we're going the wrong way," I grumbled.

"Turn back?"

"Is back even backward? Or is going forward going backward?" I said. My face twisted in confusion at my own words, and I wondered if I was descending into madness.

The look Ryken gave me said he thought I was mad too.

"Let's just turn around."

When we turned, we froze at the open field now in front of us. I grabbed Ryken's hand, fear making my legs tremble.

"This . . . was not here before," I whispered.

"No, it was not," he agreed. "The sea is not like this."

"It's like a maze, but I——"

Through the silence, a beautiful voice began to sing, knocking the air from my lungs. Entranced, I listened to the high-pitched chorus of the lullaby my mother used to sing to me as a child. I took a step toward the voice.

Ryken anchored me in place. "What is it? Do you know the song?"

"It's the lullaby . . . but the voice . . . it cannot be . . ." I couldn't get my thoughts together. My emotions tumbled inside me until I was light-headed. I pulled from Ryken's grip to cover my face, using my senses to hear each note clearly. The desperate need to be closer so I could verify if my assumptions were right nearly overtook me. That voice, I'd heard it so many times, every night before I fell asleep.

Roselyn?

Why would she be in the woods when she was ill and in bed? It had to be a trap. Someone hoped to lure me to them and was using my sister as bait. Or worse, it was the forest warping my mind with more illusions, teasing me with the person I wanted to see most.

My fingers tapped the sides of my legs as I thought. I had to resist the urge.

I shouldn't go. The pieces don't add up. It can't be her.

It wasn't her.

But what if I was wrong? I couldn't take the chance that I was so close and didn't at least try to see if it was her.

"Marigold?" Ryken asked, reaching for me.

I bolted before he could touch me, making a snap decision. Listening to the notes, I followed the melody like a trail of breadcrumbs and ventured deeper into the forest.

Please. Lead me to Rose.

Where Have You Been

I jogged across the tiny field through the blue forget-me-nots
sprinkled in the grass. The woods around me pulsed, the air
tingling and thick. Leaves shook on the trees as I passed them. So
odd, since there wasn't even a light gust of wind.

When the song stopped, I did too. Doubled over, I panted for air as
I strained to hear the next note.

"Don't run off," Ryken said, jogging up to my side with a wheeze.
"The paths are changing every time we turn around. We shouldn't separate or the trees will keep us apart. I don't want to lose you." He inhaled
quickly and pointed in the distance.

One of the tall oaks swayed back and forth as if dancing to a mysterious tune. Branches snapped, sending the leaves fluttering down. Each
sway bent the trunk closer to the ground until it curved over completely.
The bushy treetop now rested on the ground to create a wooden arch, a
doorway of sorts. Branches from the neighboring trees beckoned us
over, their leaves swishing with noise.

I questioned my sanity again as I stared at the animated trees. Years I
had lived by Mistbrooke Forest, and I had never seen it move on its own
before. Or ever had it try to communicate with me. Perhaps I was quite
mad if I thought to follow instructions from a tree. What sane person
listened to trees?

"Are these trees good or bad?" Ryken asked.

"I don't know. The one did save me when I fell. So, maybe good?" I lifted my shoulders, still not confident in my answer.

A hard object poked into my back and shoved me in the direction of the arch. I stumbled forward, warily peeking behind me for the culprit, but all the trees appeared the same. Nothing out of the ordinary—just some skinny saplings with sparse bits of greenery.

The lullaby started again, more of a hum this time. My sister sounded distracted, half-heartedly keeping the tune. It echoed in the distance from the direction of the strange arch, the music ricocheting off the trunks of the trees.

"I think that's my sister singing," I told Ryken as I moved toward the voice.

"Are you sure? This place is full of trickery."

I placed my hand over my heart. The pull of her song called to me. "I can't explain it, but it feels like her. It's a strange bond we have."

"Then I believe you. Wherever you go, I will follow. Just stay close this time," he said. Palm out, he gestured for me to lead the way.

The soothing notes helped calm the bubbles of nerves in my stomach. I rubbed my hands down the fabric of my gown and crossed the field to the arch, hoping desperately that it wasn't another trap or illusion.

The more I longed for something, the deeper the ache when it slipped through my fingers. My heart couldn't take another disappointment.

My breath left in a whoosh at the lone figure. I gripped the gnarled bark to steady myself before I darted across the clearing. I had to be sure it was really her and not another dream or figment of my imagination.

But I could smell her floral scent and hear the faint thuds of her heart. She was real.

Rose.

She sat amidst the wildflowers, a mix of white and blue forget-me-nots. Her head tilted down, she was lost in thought as she twirled one of the white blooms between her fingers. Red curls were half pinned up, shining in the sunlight, the other half flowing over her shoulders and down the back of her cloak.

Sweet relief coursed through me. The weight of stress around my shoulders ebbed away, melting the crippling fear I carried about her health. I pressed a palm over my chest and inhaled the first calming breath I'd taken in days. Ruah had been right all along—*Rose is well*. More than well. She was just as beautiful as I remembered and practically glowing. The forest scenery suited her. As long as I'd known her, she'd been drawn to the outdoors and could be found running barefoot in the grass with some small animal trailing close behind. Relaxed, she hummed a few more notes, still unaware of my arrival.

Had what I seen in the mirror only been an illusion? Another magical trick to lure me out of the sea? Yes, I was thankful to see her again, but I couldn't help but be wary. Was this part of Ruah's plan? Or someone else's?

In my rush to get here, I never thought to practice what I would say, and I was too nervous to approach. Would she be angry? Demand an apology for my hurtful words?

Or maybe she would scream at me to leave her alone as I had done to her.

Ryken's shoulder pressed into mine, offering me silent comfort.

As if by magic, a dark figure stepped out from the trees some feet away from her, appearing out of thin air. It was the king who had been chasing us, his face flushed and glistening. He frowned as he stomped through the flowers, destroying the buds under his boots with each step. The tranquil moment shattered as I realized he had his sights set not on me, but on Rose.

I stiffened. What did he want with my sister?

A protective instinct took over, shrouding my vision in red. I reached into my pocket and pulled out the silver dagger, unsheathing the blade with a quick swipe.

If he touched her . . . hurt her . . .

I'd kill him.

Oblivious to the dangerous man creeping up behind her, she continued to hum, always one to daydream. She lowered the flower she had been holding to a speckled rabbit. The creature nibbled on the offering. It rested a paw on her knee and stretched up on its hind legs for the bloom.

Sunlight reflected from the metal of my dagger, the beam of light on my chest shaking with my trembling hand. The best chance I had of success was the element of surprise. I rocked onto the balls of my feet, waiting for the king to turn around and give me an opening.

"When I find your sister, I'm going to lock her in the castle so she stays in one place," he growled. "I'm weary of this game of chase she is playing."

Beside me, Ryken bared his teeth at the king, crouched, ready to pounce. I gripped my dagger tighter, my thoughts matching his. I had no idea what I was doing, but the concern for my sister outweighed any thoughts of my safety.

Rose's head whipped around, horrified. "I'd never let you lock her up—*ever*."

He scrubbed a hand down his face. "I didn't mean it like that."

She struggled to her feet, wobbling with the weight of her enlarged stomach. When the king gripped her elbow, she slapped it away. "Don't."

I gasped, staring at the taut fabric over her abdomen. *Pregnant? Is it Prince Alexander's?*

My noise drew their attention, and they spun to face us, Rose teetering awkwardly to a stop. She took a step toward me, mouthing my name, but the king threw an arm out in front of her to stop her.

"Don't get any closer," he said to her, his eyes on my dagger.

"Let her go and we will leave peacefully," I demanded. My heart pounded frantically, a mixture of adrenaline and fear pulsing through me.

"I—what?" the king asked. He leaned over to Rose.

"Step back," I screamed. "Hands where I can see them."

The king tilted his head, calculating my words. "Is . . . your sister trying to rob us?"

"Marigold? Is it really you?" Rose asked, her voice full of hope. She took another step, but the king sidestepped in front of her and blocked her path.

"Red, no. She is wearing Windcrest's colors. And so is he."

"She's my sister," Rose insisted, pushing against him. "She would never hurt me."

My hand holding the weapon dropped an inch. I had heard that she was searching for me, but it tugged at my heart to hear it from her own lips. She still cared about me.

"Rose," I called out. "I'm here to rescue you."

"Rescue?" My sister's eyes widened. "From whom?"

"The Queen of Hearts and him."

The king threw his arms in the air in exasperation. "I thought you said she was the serious one."

"She usually is," she murmured to the king.

Why did they almost seem . . . friendly?

"Enough talk," Ryken barked.

"Who are you again?" the king asked, then asked Rose, "Am I supposed to know him?"

"I am her mate."

"Your what?" Rose choked on her words. She met my eyes to verify his claims.

My face flushed as I nodded. She would have discovered it eventually, but shouting it across the forest in front of the enemy wasn't my first preference.

The king crossed his arms, eyeing Ryken. "There is something different about you."

"We are only here for her." Ryken dipped his head to Rose. "We've traveled a long distance so we can say goodbye and return home."

"Goodbye?" Rose exclaimed. A determined look crossed her face. "You aren't taking my sister anywhere."

Ryken stiffened. "She *will* return with me."

"She will *not*," Rose countered.

A rumble sounded in Ryken's chest, the coloring of his face darkening. He growled, "She is mine, and nobody will take her from me." He flashed his sharp teeth as a warning. "We belong to the sea."

"Ryken." I breathed out his name in shock.

"What are you?" Rose shrieked. She covered her stomach with her arms.

The air crackled just before a wall of flames burst up in a straight line between us. High enough that we couldn't pass, but low enough that I could still see the amber eyes of the king. Fire coiled down his outstretched arm, but it didn't set his clothes ablaze.

"Black magic," I whispered.

"Don't hurt her. Don't you dare hurt her," Rose threatened and shoved past the king, running.

The king called out, frantic. Rose didn't make it far before he snatched her from behind. She wrestled in his fire-covered arms.

An animalistic roar echoed in the clearing, the sound coming from my own lips. Ryken joined in the battle cry. The noise scared the birds fluttering from the treetops. Weapon drawn, I charged forward, sprinting for the flames.

Rose kicked up her feet, fighting his embrace. "She is going to catch fire. Help me stop her."

"I will protect you foremost. I don't know what I would do if anything happened to you—either of you," the king said. "You have to stay here."

"Please," she begged. "I can't lose her again."

Molten heat from the flames warmed my skin. The air sizzled, my flesh itching as it dried. I stopped at the flames and glanced both ways to calculate which direction was the fastest. Or perhaps I could go through the fire. My dress still dripped with river water, and I contemplated whether it would burn in its drenched state.

From the sky, the caw of a bird rang out, and the same yellow bird from before swooped down.

Ryken swiped, his reflexes faster than I had ever seen. In a blur of motion, he knocked the bird sideways. It spiraled a few feet before it gained control again, flapping its wings for high ground.

"Tiny," the king cried out.

Suddenly, the king burst through the flames, scowling at Ryken. A golden crown of entwined twigs rested on his head, the authority of his domain and magic not to be questioned. He swung his arms in a circle, the fiery rope windmilling around his biceps. Orange light highlighted the angles of his face, his sharp cheekbones, and his straight nose. His eyebrows slanted in fury over his unnatural eyes.

"Nobody touches my bird."

Baring his teeth, Ryken snapped aggressively as his body spasmed. A blazing white light rippled from Ryken's head to his toes, his Collector's armor now in place and a liquid sword forming in his right hand. Turquoise water churned through the clear pieces, the air heavy with the brine of the sea.

The king leapt back and morphed his flames into a fiery shield, the surface crackling with heat. A shadow of fear reflected in his eyes, and he braced himself for the oncoming attack.

Ryken bowed his head, his eyes a flat bluish color. No, not Ryken, but someone else, like before. "Do not be afraid, Chosen One."

"Who are you? How do you know of me?" the king demanded. He raised his fire shield higher.

"I am Tzedek, a warrior of truth, mercy, faithfulness, and justice. I am one of four whom Ruah sent."

The flames coiled back into the king, the smoky remnants smoldering in the charred ash of the flowers. "Ruah sent you?"

"The merman followed the siren, but I have come to deliver a message."

"Merman? Siren?" Rose asked, stepping through the ash-covered brush.

The king angled his body in front of her and kept his focus on Tzedek. "What are you talking about? Why isn't Ruah speaking directly to me?"

"If you do not listen, then Ruah will not speak. It is a privilege earned through obedience. Did Ruah not command you to stay in Cadell? To prepare your people?"

"Yes, but——" the king started, but Tzedek continued, turning to me with a look of disappointment.

"Were you not commanded to follow the princess?"

I swallowed my guilt. "Yes."

One mistake after another. Ruah had every right to claim me immediately, drag me down into the sea's depths. But they allowed me to stay. *Why?*

"Only the worthy may hear the words of Ruah."

"You speak with Ruah?" Rose asked me.

"I have. If not for Ruah, I'd probably still be dead." I touched the cool metal of my choker. "Although Ryken helped too."

"Of which princess does he speak?" Rose asked, slowly edging closer to me.

"I'm not sure. It's one of the princesses of Windcrest. When I stayed at their castle, I thought it was Princess Vella, but after spending time with her, I think Ruah means Liora."

The king grumbled. "Windcrest is the bane of my existence. Did you hear? Marigold pledged her loyalty to them too. It's all everyone is gossiping about. Who knows what else the traitor has agreed to?" The king frowned at me and pulled my sister back to his side.

"Careful, my king," Rose said, her tone dangerously low. "That's my sister you're speaking of."

Glaring at the royal, I balled my hands into fists. "I'm the traitor? How can you say that when you're the one building a magical army and controlling people's minds for your cause? Burning up innocent lives for what? The use of black magic?"

He sputtered. "Are you listening to her? She might as well be carrying their navy banner. They have corrupted her mind and turned her against us. Look at her weapon—it's marked for royalty."

"I am no foe." I met my sister's eyes, begging her to believe me. "In fact, I don't wish to be part of the battle at all. I just wanted to see my family and fix the mistakes of the past before I ran out of time."

Rose pressed her fingers to her lips.

"You must choose a side," Tzedek said, catching me off guard. "The battle comes whether you want it to or not."

"Then I choose Ruah," I said.

His patience long gone, the king thundered, "Who do you think I serve? Myself? The magic I have been blessed with is a gift from Ruah and is to be used for *protection* of their people, not to control them."

I blinked, almost unable to breathe.

Was this man the Chosen One Ryken had mentioned? The one that will bring peace to all the lands? How had I not seen it earlier? Or put the pieces together faster?

Maybe Windcrest had skewed my judgment after all.

"He speaks the truth and does as Ruah commands," Tzedek agreed.

I ducked my head, sick at my accusations. Prince Vian's dagger dropped to the forest floor. *What have I done?*

"Come, let's bring you back home," my sister said, holding out her hand. The same olive branch she had extended the last time I saw her. This time I wouldn't refuse it. "We will get this all straightened out."

The king's head swung to Rose. "*Home?* After everything she said, how could you think that wise?"

"I know my sister. She is loyal to a fault. I trust her with my

330

life———" she pressed a hand on her rounded stomach "—and my child's."

My lips trembled at her honesty.

"It's true. You stood up to who you thought was a murderous king to save me. I didn't need it, but you rushed to protect me all the same. This is only a misunderstanding, one we can easily fix without finger-pointing or weapons. Let's not let the rift between us grow any wider. I'm thankful for this moment and that Ruah has guided you back to me. Having you back in my life is all I've wanted since you went missing."

"How?" I blurted, my eyes misting. "How could you forgive me after what I said to you long ago? After everything that has happened, what I have put you through? I'm the reason you returned to Prince Alexander, aren't I? All those terrible things he did to you . . . it's my fault. Please tell me that you knew I didn't mean it, that I didn't hate you. Yes, we fight, but in the end, you are my sister. Nothing could ever change that. I want to right this wrong, but I don't know how. An apology would never be enough for you to forgive me for what I made you go through. If I knew the truth about the prince—or—or———" my throat clenched as the salty tears slid down my face. I had come all this way, and I couldn't muster the strength to get the words out.

Rose rushed to my side, gathering me in a hug that stole my breath away. "Forgive you? What is there to forgive? We both said things in anger. I should have been honest with you from the beginning. For that —I'm sorry. I didn't want to expose you to that darkness of my life. For you to know the truth: that I was weak, and Xander's friendship was killing me on the inside. I feared how you would react. You always looked at me like I was someone special."

"You are special."

"Goldilocks," she said into my hair, her fingers combing through the wet strands.

"Rosey-posey." I whimpered her nickname, clinging to her shoulders as if I were a child again.

"I got you," she murmured.

"And I got you."

The frustration of traveling the territories, believing all the force-fed lies, and being traded to royals melted away at her touch. While I knew our time together wouldn't last long, the fact that she cared and forgave me made all the troubles of my second chance worth it.

"What a fright you gave me. I thought I'd lost you." She sniffed and squeezed me tighter.

"I know. I'm sorry."

She pulled back and wiped my damp cheeks with a swipe of her thumb. "No apologies, remember? It's in the past. Everything that has happened has led me to the man I love, a sweet babe in my womb, and a part of a kingdom—no, two kingdoms—that want to bring peace and prosperity to the territories."

I turned my head to whisper in her ear. "And you are sure this king is to be trusted? I've heard terrible things."

Rose pulled back with a smirk. "Of course I trust him. He's done so much for me, his people—*you* in particular. If you only knew what lengths he's gone to find you."

"King Galon said he torched villages in his pursuit."

The king sliced his hand through the air. "That is a lie. He has been trying to get me to cross into his kingdom so he can declare war. Nothing has tempted me over the border, well, except to find you. But you are like a ghost. One moment you are here, the next over there, and when I finally arrive there, you're gone again."

"Where have you been, Goldie?" Rose asked.

"I tried to tell you in the dream—*in the sea*."

"I knew it," she ground out, pumping her fist. "Everyone called me crazy."

"I've seen crazy—you're not crazy." The image of Princess Vella and her knife to my throat returned.

"Glad to know my mental state is intact. Many have called it into question." She leaned back to cradle my cheeks, turning my face this way and that. "Let me look at you. Goodness, you're all wet. Are you harmed? Cedrick can heal you if so." She paused for a moment. "My word, you seem so grown up. When did that happen?"

"Cedrick?" I asked, glancing around for her husband in the woods behind her. "Where is he?"

The king cleared his throat. "That would be me."

"Oh." My eyes widened. *Oh. My. Goodness.* Had I threatened him earlier? I hissed inwardly. "*Oooh.*"

"He doesn't do well with first impressions. I should tell you about the first time we met," Rose said with a laugh, her eyes twinkling as she stared at the king—Cedrick.

My sister married the king of Mistbrooke.

He crossed his arms. "If you tell her that story, then I get to tell her about you climbing through my window."

If my sister married the king, that would make her a queen. Queen of what?

I stiffened.

Rose wrapped an arm around my shoulders, chattering nonstop while I stood immobile, holding the king's—my brother-in-law's—stare. I could feel my carefully constructed theories toppling over like a house of cards. Every decision I had made was based on lies. Had everyone in Windcrest been lying to me? *Prince Vian?* My chest constricted at the thought of his betrayal . . . but he did try to tell me something. Was this it?

My heart rate picked up as I grasped for the truth. Facts. I needed order and rules. Something concrete to hold on to before I spiraled out of control.

The king of Mistbrooke had married my sister. He controlled fire, a magic that had been outlawed since before I was born. Now he was campaigning to normalize it, using it to protect his kingdoms.

No, their kingdoms. The Queen of Hearts who sat on the throne in Cadell.

I glanced at my sister laughing at something her husband said. She tucked a strand of hair behind her ear, a ruby ring catching the light on her middle finger. On the gem was an engraving of the royal insignia. The same one I had seen torched on the carriage so long ago.

"You? All this time it was you?"

"Me?" She tilted her head.

"You are the Queen of Hearts."

"Oh, that silly nickname? Yes, everyone knows it. Did you . . . not?"

"Nobody told me it was you. They said you were a killer. That you stole the crown."

She flinched, her eyes downcast.

"Tell me it's not true," I begged.

Her lips pinched.

"She didn't hurt anyone. Who told you these lies?" Jaw tensing, the king restrained himself from saying more.

"Everyone in Windcrest believes it. They warned me you were searching for me, both of you, and that King Galon was the only one who could protect me. Only Prince Vian——"

"I've heard enough. Forget whatever he told you. Their family is hoping to take Red's crown for themselves," the king spat. "I'll never let that happen."

"Red?" The word halted my thoughts, stirring a chuckle from me. I turned to my sister, her cheeks pinking. "How many names do you go by?"

"Funny coming from you, Ms. *Alice*," Cedrick said, lifting his brow.

Before I could snap back, my sister jumped in. "He'll grow on you over time like he did for me."

I huffed, doubting her words. It was strange to see anyone besides Prince Alexander next to her.

"It's amazing what can happen in a year. You are a queen. It's hard to comprehend." I rubbed my temple.

"Nothing will change for you—I've always bossed you around."

"I missed all the important moments of your life."

"We can catch up over tea and cake. You can tell me all about your new friend here," she said. Her eyes flicked over to Ryken and winked. "He's very handsome."

Ryken . . . I glanced at the familiar features under the circlet. Bored, he stared between us as if we were wasting his time. No wonder he had been quiet this whole time.

"He is, but that's not him. I mean, it is, and yet it isn't."

Her features scrunched together like I had grown two heads. "*What?*"

"This is Tzedek who controls Ryken when he's Collecting." The longer I stared at the imposter, the hotter the anger flowed through my veins. I marched over to him and rose on my toes to poke his chest. "Why are you still here? You're not Collecting anyone," I snapped at him.

"You are bold," he replied coolly. His clouded eyes lacked emotion and chilled me to my core.

"Are you going to put me to sleep again?"

The corner of his mouth tipped up, and I hated that he looked like my Ryken when he did it. "If you are disobedient."

"Bring back Ryken," I demanded.

"Stop, now. You are upsetting him."

"Well, you are upsetting *me* by controlling him at all," I retorted.

A bright glow shimmered around his shell-shaped circlet. "Don't tempt me."

Cedrick stepped close, drawing Tzedek's gaze, and changed the subject. "What do you collect?"

"Broken vows." Tzedek narrowed his gaze at me.

"Vows of what? To whom? I've never heard of this."

"I have," Rose said, her mouth hanging open. "It's a Windcrest custom. I mean, people do it there all the time. What happens when the vows are broken?"

"The sea will come to claim you for judgment. But this is not the reason I have come today. I have come with a message."

To my surprise, he turned to me.

"Your voice will herald the war—call Ruah's people to take up arms and fight, and set the Merfolk free."

"Me?" I glanced at the shocked faces around me but doubted they could match the skepticism of my own features. "There must be some mistake."

"Ruah does not make mistakes. The darkness is coming, and it's time for you to sing."

Do Not Be Late

I blinked up at the treetops over Tzedek's head, trying to catch my breath, and focused on what I could control.

Inhale.

My sister was the Queen of Hearts—the queen of Cadell.

Exhale.

She had married the king of Mistbrooke, a man that wielded fire at the flick of his fingers as easily as one would a sword.

Inhale.

Ruah wanted to use my voice to . . . *what*? Start a war? Save the Merfolk? From what I remembered being in a room surrounded by them for Ryken's ceremony, they wanted nothing to do with me. Orion had suggested killing me because of my abnormal transformation.

Exhale.

"Sing?" Roselyn asked me, placing a hand on my shoulder. "What is he talking about? Sing what?"

"Really? You ask about the singing? Not about the ominous darkness?" the king countered.

"I want to ask about all of it. Like how do you know Ruah? And where did——" Rose pointed at Tzedek "—this man come from? Is he an Enchanter? Or an Illusionist?"

336

"We are neither. I have done what was requested, and now there is nothing more to say. Remember your promise."

I didn't dare sneak a glance at my sister. I was sure she had another batch of questions to ask me. "I will do as Ruah commands after I say goodbye."

"You don't have much time left on land."

Rose's grip on my shoulder tightened.

"I know," I whispered. "Let me do this one last thing."

"You don't have to convince me of your selfish reasons. Speak to Ruah." As soon as the words were out of his mouth, he spun around, his sword slicing through the air with a zing. "Whoever you are, show yourself, and I may grant you mercy."

A white wolf, twice the normal size, stalked out from behind a tree, the fluff of its tail whipping behind it. It prowled around, its golden eyes flicking between us. When its gaze landed on me, its muzzle peeled back, revealing a row of sharp teeth.

Instinct had me reaching for Ryken, and I placed a hand on his free arm. Tzedek frowned down at me, not pleased by my touch, and I scrambled back, having forgotten it was him and not Ryken.

"Stand down, Mallak. She is with me. Ruah has sent for her," Tzedek announced with an air of authority.

Without breaking eye contact with me, the wolf sat on its haunches, wrapping its tail across its oversized paws. Ears pulled back, it sniffed the air with deep huffs.

"She knows," Tzedek replied as if someone had spoken.

"Knows what?" I asked, confused.

"She says you don't belong here," Rose said, tilting her head. "Why would she say that? My sister doesn't mean any harm." She moved in front of me like a human shield.

"She?" Was Rose talking about the wolf? My sister always had a special connection to animals . . . but speaking to them? Or was this another secret she had kept from me?

Tzedek raised a hand. "There is no quarrel here, human queen. The siren is under my protection, and she must return home."

Rose grabbed my hand, linking our fingers. "She is home. I haven't even had a day with her, and you want to take her away again? I will not allow it."

A wind roared from the trees, barreling out of the forest with such ferocity that the wolf's white fur was ruffled about. Brightly colored leaves ripped from the trees and danced in flurries. The gale shoved into my chest as strong as a human hand, surprising me. I stumbled backward, knocked from my sister's grip. The forest spun in my vision until Tzedek snatched my bicep to lift me upright, bringing me back to his side.

"Marigold," Rose screeched.

"I'm all right."

"Darling, don't fret. It's not good for either of you," the king said. He wrapped his arm around her shoulders and tucked her into himself. "Whatever is happening, it's all part of Ruah's plan. We may not understand now, and we may not even understand when it comes to fruition, but we have to put our faith in Ruah. Remember my sword and vow: *May Ruah guide you always*. We have to trust their decision."

"But it's my sister. I can't lose her again." Her emerald-green eyes held mine as they misted over.

"You won't, Rosey," I said. "If I have to make a promise to the sea, I will. Things are changing . . . even me . . . but that doesn't alter who I am inside. You will still be my family and dearest friend. We will discover a way to stay connected."

"Changing?"

The king gasped, his eyes wide. "Siren? You?"

The corner of my mouth ticked up as I shrugged. "So they think."

"Siren? As in those creatures that live in the sea? The ones grandfather goes on and on about?" Rose asked. "I don't believe it."

"It's true," I pressed. Now that she knew the truth—would she accept me?

With a tilt of his head, the king asked, "Earlier, in the river—did you shift? You both just vanished as you fell into the water."

"He did." I jerked my thumb at Ryken but remembered it was still Tzedek. His attention was locked on the wolf. "Well, Ryken did."

"I'm lost," Rose said. She rubbed her temple.

"I'm glad it's not just me in the dark." I laughed. "It's complicated. How about I explain everything to everyone, Mother and Father, all at once? From the beginning so there are no more secrets."

"I'm sure we could all use some answers. Like why you dyed half of your hair," my sister said.

"Really, Red? That's the first question you have?" The king laughed.

"I'll leave the boring questions to you, my dear," she said, then leaned in to kiss his cheek.

I teased the ends of my hair, wondering how to explain all the changes I'd been going through. The list was long: my vision, my sense of smell, gills, scales, the never-ending call of the ocean, and my dyed hair—which was the least exciting part of my transformation.

"She is marked with honor as all the Merfolk are," Tzedek answered for me.

The blue of the strands was bolder than before, easily noticeable from a distance, like watching the sands in an hourglass slip through. I sighed and turned to Tzedek. "How much time do I have left on land?"

"Days. You should return directly to the sea."

"And if I don't?"

"Merfolk don't last long on land. Only Collectors have the gift of both, though most prefer the sea. Your merman prefers wherever you are."

"Ryken," I whispered, my heart clenching. "Can I please have him back now?"

"My message has been delivered. It is up to you to do the rest."

"I will. I made a promise to Ruah, and I intend to keep it."

"Good answer. I will see you at the battle line. Do not be late."

A sad howl sounded from the forgotten wolf, its eyes closed and head angled up. Without glancing back, it dashed into the woods, stirring puffs of dirt in its haste.

"I still don't know how to feel about her when she says things like that," the king said, a frown creasing his cheeks.

No, not the king. *Cedrick.* I had to change my mindset of how I thought about him.

"Who said what?" I asked. Once again, I felt like the odd man out.

"She said, 'Death rides swiftly on the fins of justice.'"

I spun, surprised to hear Ryken's cadence back in his voice and see his eyes clear again. "Ryken?" I didn't wait for him to answer because I sensed in my soul it was him. Arms wide, I pounced and gathered him tight. "You left me."

As if expecting it, his arms encircled me, lifting me off the ground so my feet dangled midair. "Never." He pressed his nose into my neck, the pressure of a single kiss heating my skin.

How did his touch have such power over me?

The urge to drag him back to the sea drowned any other thought I had. My fingers clasped his tunic, ready to obey. It didn't help that he smiled on my skin, his scent heavy with desire.

Soon, he said through the touch of my collar.

"Were we like this?" Cedrick's voice shattered my musings.

"When you weren't annoying me," my sister said, chuckling.

"*Me?* I think the curse may have jumbled a few of your memories. I was dashing, daring, and the most romantic man you'd ever met. We might need to kiss again to make sure all your memories are restored correctly." He swooped in for a kiss.

Curse? Rose's curse?

She spun away at the last second, her red hair flying about her shoulders. "This is not the time, Your Majesty. More pressing issues are at hand than *your* spotty memories. My parents are waiting for my sister's arrival."

"You may win this round, my queen, but I know the secret to your heart—chocolate."

"Chocolate? Explain," Ryken asked.

"Has he not had chocolate before?" Rose asked, horrified. "This poor man."

"Merman," Ryken corrected, his lips twisted in disgust.

"He hasn't been on land long and is still adjusting to the human world." I wiggled from his hold until he set me back on my feet. "Chocolate is a sweet food people eat. Like the apple you ate in the inn, but better."

"Yes. I would like to try some." Ryken nodded. He held out his hand to my sister and added, "Please."

"She doesn't carry any on her," Cedrick said.

"But maybe I should," Rose said, batting her lashes at her husband.

He lifted a brow at her.

She sighed. "All this talk of chocolate, and now I fear the baby demands a chunk. Shall we return to Cadell? Mother and Pa are there waiting for us. Grandmother and Grandfather are staying at the farm, but we can summon them to the castle for dinner."

"But the woods—they're enchanted. We couldn't escape them."

"Ah, your sister has a way with the trees. What would take me a half day of travel takes her mere minutes. It's quite unfair."

"He's just jealous," she said. They turned to each other like they would be cross, but only tenderness shone in their eyes.

"Perhaps," Cedrick whispered.

"I, too, don't like to share my mate," Ryken blurted.

My sister shot me a look, her eyebrows high and lips parted in surprise.

But I wasn't ashamed. Ryken was himself. Honest, even if it meant being blunt at times, but always kindhearted in his intentions. Watching him try to find common ground with my sister sent a golden warmth through me. My smile softened as my heartbeat picked up with the shocking realization.

As if he sensed my change, he ducked to whisper, "What is it?"

I love you.

I blinked at him, awestruck at how right that one phrase was and how intense my feelings for him had grown in just a short time. That it wasn't just the mermaid inside me, but all of me had fallen for him. I had fallen for a merman with sharp teeth and gray skin, who preferred swimming to walking, who found the beauty in the small things like a button or chicken egg, who was always the first to notice when I needed him, even before I realized it, who always told me the truth and was so curious about my thoughts, wants, and wishes that he left the only place he had ever known to follow me to the place he hated most.

He was my protector, refusing to let me give up on myself. His heart had beat for me when mine couldn't. And now, my heart would forever be his.

Human. Merman. Whatever his form—I loved him.

My lips trembled, and the words I wanted to say were too inadequate to describe the blinding light that pulsed through me as I beheld his turquoise eyes. Nothing I could say would ever express what he meant to me—what he had done for me when I had done nothing but complain the entire time.

How did I not ruin this moment? Every time I said something, it always came out wrong. Overwhelmed, I closed my eyes and tried to focus my scattered thoughts.

What should I do, Ruah?

I never expected an answer, but I received one anyway.

Ask him—you know what he desires.

"Marigold? Are you hurt?" Ryken cupped my jaw. "Tell me what to do."

The chatter of the background faded, and the noises in the forest muted. It was just him and me.

Of course I knew what to ask.

It went against society's rules—and I didn't care that it did. With everything he had sacrificed to be with me, with his endless supply of patience as he waited for my heart to catch up to his, my being the one to ask made it even more meaningful.

Since I'd met him, my life had flipped upside down, and I couldn't be happier. I wanted to share that with him.

When I smiled, he squinted at me. Then I confused him more when I reached out and placed my palm on his heart. The rush from our bond and our synchronized beats was pure bliss.

Even he couldn't stop a contented sigh from slipping out. His hand covered mine as if he never wanted us to be separated.

And neither did I.

"Ryken," I breathed, barely able to get the words out, "will you marry me?"

Don't Make Me Tell Mother

A grin lit up Ryken's face, and he pulled me closer, resting his forehead against mine. "And if I say yes, then I would be your husband?"

"Well, we have to attend a ceremony first. After that, then we would be married, and I would be your wife."

His eyes closed, a gentle smile teasing the corners of his mouth as he savored the moment. He inhaled deeply, his muscles twitching on his face.

I continued to wait, as he seemed in no rush. Unlike his usual quizzical self, he was quiet as he thought. The shimmer of confidence I had began to wane. Had he changed his mind? I pulled away and studied his handsome face.

"Ryken?" I whispered, fidgeting.

"Hmm?" He opened one eye.

"You never responded to my question."

"I know. I wanted to be calm before I answered. I could scream it across the seas—oh, trees? Is that right? Woods? I just wanted this moment to be perfect for you. We have nothing like it back home. I'm ready now." He blew out a jittery breath. "My answer is yes."

"Yes?" Even though I was expecting him to agree, the sound of it still sent a thrill of excitement through me.

343

"Did you expect a different response? *Yes* to being your husband and mate. *Yes* to loving you more with each breath I take. *Yes* to a future of possibilities and new adventures. You are my heart, Marigold."

"You are mine, Ryken."

He sucked in a breath at my choice of words.

"You've had such patience waiting for me to decide on my own."

"I was also an expert at wooing."

"Expert is a strong word. How about persuasive?"

"You can use any word you want as long as we get married."

"I hate to break up this lovely moment," my sister interjected, "but do you really know this man?"

"Merman," Ryken corrected, frowning.

"A second ago, he appeared to be someone else," Rose complained, shaking her head so her ringlets swayed. "I'm confused."

"It's not for you to understand. I know what's in my heart." Holding Ryken's stare, I said, "I've never understood a person more. He's honest, loyal, sweet, and thoughtful. When I was unwell, he took care of me. He let me leave the safety of the water to come here to see you because I wanted it. And after each disaster happened on our journey, he still didn't force me to abandon my search for you. Equals, he called us. There is a connection between us that you wouldn't understand even if I had all the words to explain it. He is my destiny."

Ryken's cheeks pinked as a broad grin stretched across his face.

"But . . . he's a stranger, Marigold," Rose persisted.

"Red," Cedrick said.

"Wouldn't you like Pa to meet him first? And Mother? Can you really know someone after so little time? I mean—I thought I knew Alex . . ."

"*Red*, look at me."

"How will I know he will take care of you like I would?" Her voice cracked with emotion.

Cedrick stepped in front of Rose, grabbing both her hands. "Darling, take a breath. You're getting worked up over what is supposed to be a special moment for your sister."

Blinking, she glanced down at their clasped hands.

"I'm not trying to ruin her moment . . . again. I worry about her.

Someone has to protect her. I wish someone had done so for me." Rose's mouth pinched in the corner. "I want her to be happy."

"And I am happy," I stressed. "He makes me smile and laugh. He accepts me for who I am, all my rules, my obsession with structure."

"You say that now, but how do you know he won't change?"

"Can I say something?" Ryken asked, stepping forward.

"You may," she said with a nod.

"You don't have to worry about Marigold."

"Because you will protect her? I've heard that before."

"Of course I will protect her, but that's not what I meant." Ryken grabbed my hand and pulled me to his side. "She doesn't need my protection or yours. I had the same impression when I first met her. That she was tiny, therefore she was weak. But I was wrong—and so are you. She is fierce enough to fight her own battles. Each trial she's endured has only made her stronger. The fact that she is standing before you today is proof of that. She was not meant to hide meekly in the shadows. Sirens are warriors. And when a battle comes our way, I will be next to her, fighting alongside her."

Cedrick smiled and wrapped an arm around his wife. "See? Feel better?"

"No," Rose muttered. "He's still a stranger to me."

"Roselyn," I snapped, my hands balling into fists at my sides.

Ryken cut in before I could unleash my anger. "Would it ease your concerns if we learned more about each other? You can ask me any question you like, but I will warn you, some of your human words are unknown to me. You are a big part of Marigold's past, and I know you mean a lot to her—so you should mean a lot to me too. I am willing if you are."

Cedrick whispered, "Red, it's okay to lower your guard and trust him. Trust that your sister can make her own decisions. This is who she's chosen."

"I'll try." She sighed and walked over to me. "You know I love you, don't you, Goldie?"

"I do, and I hope you know I love you too," I said.

Her eyes misted as she nodded. "I'm sorry. I don't mean to be difficult. So much has happened while you were missing, and it's taking longer than I realized for these old wounds to heal. It has made me more cautious and protective of those I care about. The baby hasn't helped matters either. My emotions are in flux most days. Strangely enough, the chocolate helps." She turned to Ryken, dipping her head gracefully. "Thank you for the heartfelt appeal. I accept and look forward to getting to know you more."

Cedrick picked up her hand and pressed a kiss to her knuckles. "Well said, my queen. Now, let's get you back to the castle to rest. Go work your magic and convince these trees to lead us home."

"Convince the trees?" I asked. "You can talk to them?"

Cedrick only smirked.

Rose's hem rustled in the grass as she crossed the distance to the closest tree and pressed her hand to the worn bark. Her lips moved as if she were conversing with an invisible person.

"My sister speaks to trees," I mumbled under my breath.

"And animals," Cedrick added.

He stood at my side with a sappy smile as he watched my sister at her task. Is this what love looked like from the outside? Almost as if it were contagious, my heart softened at his adoration.

"You really love her, don't you?" I asked.

"How could I not? She is my wildfire. My light in the darkness."

"I'm glad she found someone who understands her instead of——"

"King Alexander?" he growled. "She will probably talk to you about it later, but it was a bleak time after she lost her childhood friend. Even after everything he did to her, she still mourned his loss. Who does that? Who has a heart that forgiving? I still can't comprehend it."

"I'm thankful she forgave me," I said.

Cedrick turned to me, his eyes reminding me of storm clouds. "She'd do anything for you. The news of your death nearly crushed her, leaving her a lifeless doll on her throne. I don't know what magic brought the vision of you in the sea, but from that moment she started to live again. I'm not going to lie—I'm worried about what will happen when you leave."

"We can't stay here," Ryken said.

"I understand. I only ask that you tread lightly on the topic. Maybe she will be better now that she has seen you and knows you are in excellent hands," Cedrick said.

"The sea isn't far from Cadell. Maybe you could journey out to the coast occasionally and visit us."

"Her advisors hound her when she leaves the castle what with Windcrest pressing against the border. She shouldn't even be in Mistbrooke today."

"But she is queen. She can do what she wants."

"Can she? If she wants to be a good monarch to her people, she has to do what is best for them. She wanted to traverse the countryside to look under every rock and behind every tree for you, but her people needed her. I can only guess what lies King Galon has told you, but the Queen of Hearts is a nickname given to her because her people love her. For her kindness, her sacrifice, her leadership that they desperately needed."

"Why are you telling me this?"

"I didn't want the lies to cloud your judgment."

"I had no idea Rose was the Queen of Hearts or I would never have believed them. She's brave and smart—I wish I could be more like her."

"I believe I've heard her say that exact phrase about you," he said.

"Really?" I whispered.

He winked. "Really."

"Everyone, we need to go this way," Rose called. She marched through the trees ahead, her fingertips skimming the top of her round stomach.

Cedrick sprinted after her, leaving Ryken and me to trail behind.

As we followed behind them, Ryken leaned in to whisper, "Your sister seems nice. Not like she would try to murder us at all."

I shook my head, laughing. "No, she wouldn't do that."

"Why was that other kingdom so worried then?"

"I think they had their own agenda." I frowned. "I hope that doesn't include the prince. I thought we were becoming friends."

Ryken glanced away. "I sensed his honesty when he was talking to you. Not that I care to speak positively about him."

"You can't hate him that much. He didn't mean to mark me."

He grabbed my hand, jerking me to a stop. "That's the thing. He can only mark you if he's interested."

"Interested?" I pulled my hand free.

"He wants to be your mate. A merman would know better than to touch the mermaid he was interested in. Everyone would know."

"Ryken, you're being ridiculous. Prince Vian is a flirt, but he has no intentions other than that."

Crossing his arms, he huffed.

"You're wrong," I said.

"I've never wanted to be more wrong in my life," Ryken said. "But I'm not."

"Lovebirds," Cedrick called from a distance away. "You're going to get lost if you don't pick up the pace. The trees are whispering about you."

The tall pines shook, their leaves swishing. A reminder that this was probably not the best location for an argument. Grabbing my skirt, I waded through the high weeds after them. But I couldn't help myself from saying one last thing.

"It doesn't matter how he feels when I'm in love with you."

Ryken's arms encircled me from behind, halting us in place. "You are?"

I spun around. "I wouldn't have asked you to marry me if I weren't."

He leaned down, hovering an inch away. "My Marigold."

I grabbed his tunic to close the gap between us. His warm lips sunk into mine, eagerly claiming them. Heat coursed through my veins, waves of tingling delight that seemed to grow more potent with each kiss.

"I like kissing you," he whispered against my lips. "We should continue this human tradition when we return to the sea."

"Marigold," my sister shouted, "don't make me tell Mother the real reason we were late."

I groaned in frustration, tipping my head back to stare at the dusty blue sky between the branches. "I'm coming."

"I'm standing right here until I see your feet moving," Rose stated, sounding like Mother.

Your sister won't be there when we return to the sea. It will be just you and me, he said through our connection then kissed my nose. *Oh, the possibilities.*

I chuckled, untangling myself.

"Now, stop distracting me or she will never like me," Ryken reprimanded.

"How could she not like you?"

As we started to walk, I looped my arm through his. He gave me an odd look at the gesture, and in response, I rested my head on his shoulder, and his chest rumbled in contentment.

We followed them farther into a thicker part of the forest, the path lined with strange flowers the color of blood. As we drew closer, the blooms unfurled, revealing a yellow middle that swayed back and forth. I thought nothing of it until those yellow pieces traced my movement, watching me in an eerie way.

"Uh, Rose?" I asked.

Up ahead, larger patches of red flowers awoke, all of them turning to face me. Were they alive like the trees?

"Don't touch them," Cedrick said. "They're poisonous."

I grimaced. "I hadn't planned on it. How much farther?"

A breeze whistled through the branches, veering off to the left, and we changed our course to follow it. After a few more stops to talk to the trees, we finally arrived at the edge of the forest, the meadows of our home on the other side.

A spike of dread hit me, so urgent that I shuddered.

"Stop," I screamed.

Immediately, Rose and Cedrick whipped around, eyes wide.

"What is it?" Ryken asked, his turquoise eyes scanning my face.

"I don't know," I mumbled. "A feeling."

"A feeling?" Rose asked.

Not just a feeling but my senses sending me warnings of danger. Pine and metal drifted on the wind, followed by a distinct odor of men. A group of them, moving on horseback, the ground rumbling beneath my feet.

"I smell them too," Ryken said.

The hairs on the back of my neck rose with each ragged breath I took. My prey instinct took over, and I jogged to a nearby tree, hiding behind it as I scanned the meadow beyond the woods. I waved the others over in a panic.

"Why is she acting like this?" Rose asked.

"Someone is coming—men on horseback. They smell of fear and guilt . . . and anger."

Rose glanced around me. "Where?"

"The main road," I said.

"Oh," Rose said, straightening. "Those are just our guards. They're probably out on a routine perimeter check."

"No, Marigold is right," Ryken said, his voice low.

Eight guards barreled down the road on horseback, their heads low on their steeds, making haste for the northbound road. They were all clad in red uniforms, marking them from Cadell. But my eyes remained locked on the blue bands around their left biceps.

"The bands on their arms," I said.

"Bands?" Cedrick glanced around the tree.

Metal clanked with each gallop from the many swords tied to their belts.

"They're stealing our weapons," Rose exclaimed.

The air crackled with heat, and twin ropes of fire spiraled down Cedrick's arms. His eyes glowed amber, narrowed in determination.

"I will go get them back," Cedrick said. "Windcrest has gone too far."

"I shall go with you," Ryken said.

Cedrick nodded. "Stay clear of the flames."

"You don't have a weapon," I blurted in a panic when the two of them took off into the clearing. "Rose, we have to stop——"

I froze at the sound of my sister's song. Eyes closed, she hummed a lighthearted melody. Was she trying to soothe herself by singing?

A caw rang out from the trees, followed by another and another. Soon a flock of ravens circled us, their pitch high, outraged. Rose's green eyes snapped open, shining with fury.

"Stay here, Marigold." And she ran, as best she could with her extended stomach, with the ravens following her in the shape of a V.

What could I do? I couldn't fight. I couldn't control animals. I frowned at my uselessness.

At the sound of Ryken's roar, I bolted from the tree, refusing to wait while the others did all the work. Orange flames danced along the road, a barrier keeping the guards from escaping.

"Lay down your weapons," Cedrick demanded.

350

"My king, there has been some mistake," one guard said, his hands up.

"Treason is a deadly mistake," the king said.

"We were only checking the perimeter," another guard said.

The air rippled with a sour stench.

"Liar," I spat.

The guards turned at my voice, their eyes suddenly filling with hope.

"Are you here to save us?" a guard asked.

"Nobody is here to aid you," my sister said, her voice sharp like a spear.

"King Galon sent word that the lost sister stands with Windcrest."

"Does it look like my sister stands with anyone but me?" Rose drawled.

"But my lady wears our colors." One guard took a step toward me— a mistake.

In a few steps, Ryken had his fingers curled around his throat, lifting him in the air. He yanked both swords from his hip and his dagger after that, flinging them behind him before chucking the guard back to the ground like trash.

"Good thinking, Ryken," Cedrick said. "Take back our stolen weapons."

Ryken needed no more prodding. One by one, he ripped the weapons from their belts and added each guard to the heap of men. If a guard moved an inch, a raven dove, flapping and pecking at his head.

One of the older guards with a bushy beard spat in my direction. "*Traitor*. The sea would never choose the likes——"

Ryken's fist slammed into his face before he could finish his sentence. The others huddled together.

"Are you going to kill us?"

"No one is dying today," my sister said. "We will take back what is ours—the weapons, armor, and horses. Then you are free to leave and never return. Give King Galon a message for me. If it is a war you want, then it is a war you shall have. I'll see him at the border in seven days. I expect him to fight with honor."

"Fighting with magic isn't fighting with honor," the bearded guard shouted.

"Then you've learned nothing about us during your time in Cadell."

"You heard the queen. Return the armor," the king ordered.

Ryken gathered all the chain mail, adding them to the growing pile of metal.

"Now leave my kingdom. If we catch you in Cadell again, I won't be as understanding. Be gone," Rose shouted, pointing to the road.

The flames fizzled out, coiling back to Cedrick like fiery serpents.

In only their undergarments, the men ran off, never turning to look behind them.

"How did you know?" Rose asked me.

"Know what?"

"That they were coming. Or that they were lying."

I shrugged. "Instinct, I guess."

"Are you all right?" Cedrick asked Rose. He was at her side in an instant, pressing a hand on her stomach.

"Just tired." She shook her head at the pile on the ground. "What was Windcrest thinking?"

"They are eager for battle, just as you said."

Rose sighed. "Why must everything lead to bloodshed?"

"The Merfolk also prefer peace," Ryken said, his eyes still tracking the men in the distance.

"The Merfolk," I whispered, remembering. "Windcrest has an underwater army."

"What?" Rose stuttered.

"They are abducting mermen to fight for their cause. I have no idea how they are doing it, but I overheard the princes speaking about it."

"Merfolk have been disappearing for a few years now," Ryken said.

Rose placed a hand on her chest and gasped. "I told them to meet us at the border. We'll be right next to the sea and unprepared for a side attack."

"Unless," Ryken started, his eyes landing on me, "we call the rest of the Merfolk for aid."

"We can do that?" Rose asked.

"He can." Ryken pointed at Cedrick. "He is Ruah's Chosen One. They would honor your request."

"How can I lead them and the Enchanters? They are your people. Can you ask?"

"If you request I should, then I will." Ryken bowed his head.

"Wouldn't that be a surprise for Windcrest?" Rose said and snorted at the thought. "Beat them at their own game."

"Seven days isn't a lot of time," I said, my nerves already tingling.

Rose clasped her hands and rested them on her stomach. "We aren't giving them seven. We will be there in four. After those traitors nearly stole weapons from under our noses? I don't trust them."

"Why not sooner?" I asked.

She wrapped her arm around my shoulder. "Apparently, we have a wedding to plan and not much time to do it. Speaking of which, how would you like to get married tomorrow?"

My head snapped back. "Tomorrow?"

"Tomorrow is perfect," Ryken blurted.

"We could use the ballroom," Rose suggested. She tugged on my shoulders, guiding us back to Cadell.

"Or your garden is nice with all the flowers in bloom," Cedrick added.

"Tomorrow?" I repeated, still in shock.

"Mother will want to help. I have plenty of dresses you can pick from. Cook makes delightful cakes and pastries. Oh, we can have a sampling with tea when we get back. I wonder if Zarek could officiate on such short notice. He's the one who married Cedrick and me."

"Red, maybe your sister would like a say in the details of her wedding," Cedrick said, holding in a laugh.

"Of course, I was only making suggestions. Where do you want the ceremony?" Rose asked.

I thought for a moment. "By the cliffs near the sea. The border between our lands."

"As close to the sea as possible," Ryken agreed. "Then it will feel like home."

"Then it's settled." Rose bounced on her toes and clapped her hands.

Butterflies fluttered in my stomach at how quickly everything was happening. *I am getting married tomorrow.*

The Reunion

With her arm linked through mine, Rose prattled on about wedding details as we walked down the dusty road toward the main gate. She had whisked me away from the men, putting them some distance behind us so she could have me to herself. It was strange how, after so much time had passed, it felt like none had passed at all. We fell into the old ways of things, Rose with her fanciful ideas and me with my realistic expectations.

I grimaced at her latest suggestion. "No throwing birdseed after the ceremony. You know I don't care for birds."

"Oh, come now. That was so long ago. You should meet Tiny. He's so sweet. Once he hears you sing, he'll be begging you to sing with him all the time."

"I met Tiny. He tried to claw my head off. I'm just not a bird person."

"Pity." Suddenly, a mischievous smile twisted her lips. She leaned in to whisper in my ear, "Perhaps you are more of a fish person. Speaking of which, what does he look like when he is a merman? Is he more fish or more man? And what of his tail? Is it like a snake or fish—*oh my*—have you touched it?"

"*Goodness*, Rosey," I said. A blush crept up my neck to the tips of my ears, the heat of it burning my skin.

She burst into a fit of giggles.

"What are you two whispering about up there?" Cedrick asked from behind us. "It better not be about me, Red."

"It's not. Your wife wants to see my tail. So you know, Marigold said it was magnificent," Ryken said, sticking his chest out.

"Ryken," I stammered. I could only imagine what my sister's husband thought of me now. My blush deepened, the urge to run and hide overwhelming me.

Rose spun around, aghast. "You heard me? From back there?"

"Merfolk have excellent hearing," Ryken stated.

"Interesting," Rose said.

Cedrick frowned at his wife, crossing his arms. "Since when are you so curious about mermen?"

"Since one is about to marry my sister." Rose turned back to stare at me, her eyes bulging as she mouthed, "Magnificent?"

Laughing, I nodded.

She blinked for a moment, sobering. "And you will have a tail too? Instead of legs?"

The image of the jade scales on my legs returned. "I will."

"How long do you think you have? You keep saying it's soon. How do you know?"

"Because I'm already changing."

She touched the ends of my hair. "Really? You seem the same to me. Perhaps paler with bits of blue in your hair, but still human. Not very fishy."

"A lot of it is internal and is difficult for me to show you. My vision is clearer, I can see farther and in dark places. I can hear even the faintest of whispers, even the beating of your heart. My sense of smell is annoyingly problematic—your lavender perfume is . . . eye-wateringly strong."

Rose huffed. "It's not perfume. I add petals to my bath water. You can smell that?" She sniffed her sleeve. "Is it terrible?"

"Cedrick's scent helps dampen it."

"His *what*?" she said, sniffing her clothes again.

"Do I even want to know why she is sniffing herself?" Cedrick mumbled.

"Marigold said she smells of flowers, but you've marked her with your scent, so it dilutes the fragrance."

"She smells like me?" Cedrick asked, laughing.

"It's so nobody else will claim her. It's permanent after the mating process."

"Good."

Rose sent her husband a scowl over her shoulder. "He looks so proud of himself."

I stole a glance too. "He looks besotted to me."

"Indeed. As he should be." She winked at him.

Ryken asked Cedrick, "What is besotted?"

Sighing, Cedrick responded, "A sickness of the heart for which there is no cure. Best to avoid it if you can."

Before I could jump in and correct him, Rose bombarded me with more questions. "You said you were in the sea for months. How is that possible? Without you being fully . . . transformed—is that the right term? Did you have to come up for air? Or did you use magic?"

I scooped back my hair to reveal the mark behind my ears.

Roselyn gasped. "Are those . . . ?"

"Gills? Yes."

"Perhaps I should be more shocked, but I can still remember the many times I had to drag you out of the pond back home. Your favorite place to hide."

I glanced down, pleased she had remembered such a minor detail.

"I guess the water has always called to me. My new home."

"We both have new homes now," Rose said. She stared off into the distance, the stone walls of Cadell closer with each step.

The air seemed lighter and more pleasant than before. Laughter flowed from the gates, and the few travelers and merchants we passed nearly fainted at the sight of the king and queen leisurely strolling into the kingdom.

Or it could have been the haggard state of my appearance in Windcrest's colors. My wrinkled dress was splotched with mud and grime, and my hair had dried into a tangled mess.

Miles of green farmland stretched out, flanking the stone walls of the kingdom. Cornstalks in rows upon rows on my left and a pasture with a herd of sheep on my right. A shepherd boy sat on a grassy mound playing his fife. His comforting song drifted on the wind and instilled a sense of peace deep within me.

How could this be the same Cadell I had left?

Our cottage wasn't far, and my feet itched to travel the path to our orchard. What else had changed? Was my room still the same?

"The land is so fertile. Are you using magic? Like at Opal's?"

"No magic. This is the result of hard work and determination." Rose squeezed my arm to her side. "I didn't realize you met Opal. Did you meet Anjali too? They are so dear to me. We should invite them to the ceremony tomorrow."

"I liked them. And they were kind to Ryken and me . . . after everything." I clenched my teeth, inhaling sharply. "I owe them a new door."

"A door?"

I filled her in from the moment I arrived at the inn to the moment I met her in the forest. Out of everything, she was still stuck on the fact that I had sung in front of a crowd.

"Goodness, I can't believe I missed that. My dear sister who prefers to blend into the wall gave a musical performance. What did I tell you? You always were the brave one."

"What does that make you?"

"The fun one." She laughed, leading me through the gates. "We better enjoy our time now. As soon as my advisors discover my little adventure in the forest, they will schedule a council meeting to discuss my reckless ways. There are so many rules when you are queen. It's worth it though . . . for them." She nodded to the townspeople, their faces alight with joy at her acknowledgment.

"If I remember correctly, you weren't very good with rules," I said.

"I'm not perfect, but I try my best. The people seemed desperate for kindness. For a ruler to finally care about them as individuals. It's easy for me to know what they need—I've been in their shoes."

The excitement of the people escalated as we moved closer to the castle. "My queen," they said, bowing and dipping into curtsies. Hoots and waves spread throughout the crowd, unable to contain their excitement at the king and queen's arrival. Children ran through the street, laughing with long ribbons attached to sticks fluttering behind them.

"I don't even recognize this place."

Gone were their bleak looks. They walked with purpose, upright, without the fear of a tyrant lashing out.

We climbed the steps, and Ryken called out my name in wonder. He watched the commotion of the town, spinning to make sure he didn't miss a thing.

"Is this his first time in town?"

I thought for a moment. "It is. He's very curious about things he hasn't seen before."

"You know what Pa always says. Curiosity is a sign of intelligence."

"He catches on quick," I said.

Ryken took the offered stick from a small girl and sniffed it.

"Should I be worried? He won't try to attack anyone, will he? I forgot he's not human." Rose bit her lip, watching him shake the stick to make the ribbon dance.

"No, he likes younglings—I mean children."

My sister fought a smile. "I can see."

Ryken led a line of kids, all of them running with their sticks outstretched, the red ribbons flying like tiny flags. After a quick lap, he returned the stick to the young girl. She stared at him, charmed as much as I was.

Was it possible to fall deeper in love? The urge to kiss him nearly stole my breath away.

"Come on now, let's go find Mother and Pa. They've waited long enough to see you."

She didn't think it strange when the door opened as we approached, nor when a servant collected her cloak and handed her a diadem to place on her head. My sister with a crown on her head was an odd sight to see. Or maybe it was the fact that she seemed so natural at it. With grace I didn't know she had, she led me through a maze of corridors and into an empty sitting room.

"Wait here," Rose commanded. "I'll go find them."

I tried my best not to gawk at the paintings on the wall or the fancy vases lining the fireplace mantle. A golden chandelier hung above our heads, dripping with diamonds. So much finery, but still not as lavish as Windcrest. To think this castle had been here my whole life, and I never thought I would step foot in it.

Ryken tapped at his reflection in the mirror, drawing me out of my musings. "I look strange as a human."

"Hmm." I moved to his side, admiring the two of us in the glass. "I think you are quite handsome."

My mouth dropped. *Had I really said that?*

"Do you?" he purred.

I turned to flee, but he snatched my wrist, tugging me closer.

"No hiding, remember? I like when you are honest."

The door opened, startling us apart. Mother and Father strolled in, laughing at something my sister had said, unaware of us in the corner of the room.

"I thought you had a surprise for us. I don't see any . . . " Mother's voice trailed off as her eyes met mine.

"Hello," I said, suddenly unsure of what one should say at such a grandiose moment.

It must have been the wrong thing to say. No sooner than I said it, my mother crumbled into the mounds of her skirt, leaving her a sobbing mess on the floor. Father was the opposite—a statue, unblinking, staring at me as if I were a ghost that had appeared out of thin air.

"Mother," Rose said, kneeling next to her. "This is good news. Marigold has returned to us."

"My girl, my baby, my Goldie . . . " she wailed into her fingers. "I cannot look. If this is a jest, it is a cold-hearted one. My heart cannot take losing her a second time."

Rubbing Mother's back, Rose sent me a pleading glance.

I knelt down in front of my mother and gently pried her hands from her face. The agony twisting her features was a punch to my gut. "Please don't cry. It's me."

She sprang forward to wrap her arms around me, the smell of soap eliciting memories from my youth. Usually, it was me clinging to her for comfort, but now our positions had reversed.

The relief in my heart at being here again, having her close when for so long I had thought it was impossible. Her damp cheek pressed against mine, and my tears mingled with hers. The combination of the joy of seeing her again mixed with the realization that our time together was temporary.

I closed my eyes, breathing in her scent. The comfort of her skin on mine. The weight of her arms around me. I tucked it all away in my mind to remember on the days I missed her most.

"My Goldie," she whimpered. She leaned back and offered a watery smile. "How do you look so much older? Oh, my gracious, your hair. It's blue. Honey, look."

She held out the strands for my father to see, still sniffling.

"I see . . . but I can hardly believe it," Father said slowly, blinking at me.

I was too afraid that one false move and I'd wake up and discover this had all been a dream. But how could I imagine such fine details like the stiff lace on the neck of my mother's gown or Father's mustache peppered with more gray than when I had seen him last?

He quickly snatched my outstretched hand with both of his and pressed a light kiss on my knuckles. "My ray of sunshine."

After a moment, Rose joined in, throwing an arm around my shoulder and leaning her head against mine. "I'm thankful, so thankful I found you."

My heart clenched at the emotion behind her words, and a slow ache pulsed with each beat. How could I leave them again? The joy on my parents' faces, the contentment in the air radiating from them.

Ryken cleared his throat, shifting from one foot to the other. "Hello."

"Oh, goodness," Mother said and dashed away her tears. "I didn't realize we had company." She stood and dusted her skirt. Blinking at Ryken, her eyebrows lifted in confusion. "I'm sorry, but I don't think I know you. Have we met?"

"No. You may call me Ryken. I'm Marigold's husband."

Color drained from my parents' faces.

"Husband," my father mumbled, returning to his statue-like state.

My mother couldn't speak, her mouth hanging open.

"He's not my husband," I amended as I stood. "Yet."

"Yet," my parents repeated.

"She asked me to marry her today," Ryken said, standing taller.

"Today," they repeated.

My parents stared at each other, communicating as couples do, before turning back to me.

"We had hoped to conduct their ceremony tomorrow," Rose added calmly.

Mother grabbed my father for support. Her eyes dipped to my stomach. "Are you——?"

My face burned as hot as the sun. "Mother—*no*."

"We hope soon though," Ryken said without missing a beat. "I've been thinking about it for a while. But it would be wise to wait until after the battle. Mermen are protective of their young."

Father's left eye twitched.

"Ryken, stop talking," I hissed.

"Did I say something wrong?" he whispered. He inclined his head respectfully. "I'm still learning human customs. Was I supposed to hug them?"

Rose jumped in front of them before he dared try. "This is just a bit of miscommunication. Nobody panic."

"Panic? How could I not? He said he wants Marigold to have his baby," my mother shrieked. She fanned her rosy cheeks.

"What did he mean by 'human customs'?" Father finally sputtered.

"He must be a madman, dear."

"Mother," I said, astonished. "That is positively rude."

"Marigold, get away from him this instant. Quick, now," Mother pressed, waving me over like one would call a small child.

I stepped closer to Ryken and crossed my arms.

"Is she bewitched? Don't underwater creatures lure humans to their deaths?" Father's chest rose and fell rapidly.

"To their deaths?" Mother screeched.

"I said not to panic," Rose repeated. Her skirt swished as she placed a calming hand on Father's chest.

"Where is Cedrick? He needs to break the spell."

"There is no spell. He's actually quite sweet," I said.

Ryken sputtered, "*Sweet?* I'm a Collector—a mighty warrior."

"A collector of what?" Father asked. "People?"

"And what is that thing around your neck?" Mother inquired. "It looks like an animal collar."

"It's what binds our hearts and——" Ryken said, but suddenly everyone started shouting at once.

"I did not allow this," Father barked.

"Are you holding her against her will?" Mother asked.

"I think he seems kind," Rose interjected.

The air stirred and became coated in an unfamiliar smell. A salty musk that distracted me from our argument. I turned to the source—to Ryken.

Back hunched, he stared at the floor like a wounded animal.

"Ryken." I placed a hand on his arm.

He stiffened at my touch.

"I don't belong here," he mumbled.

I tightened my hold. "That's not true. Don't listen to them."

The chatter in the room fizzled out, the weight of silence pressing us closer together as if the room had shrunk in size.

His long lashes fluttered. "I've thought about this day since the moment we arrived on land. What would your family think of me? Would they see me as all humans do—a monster?" His turquoise eyes met mine, shimmering with hope. "Or would they accept me as you have? Would I become part of your family?"

"You are part of my family. They just need time to get to know you, to see you for who you truly are," I said.

"We don't have time for that," he ground out.

Rose rubbed a hand down her face, sighing. "Today has been a shocking day for us all. Perhaps we could sit down, drink a cup of tea, and start our introductions over."

"But it will never change the fact that I'm a merman. Or that Marigold is a siren," Ryken bit out.

Mother sucked in a breath, her fingertips pressed to her mouth. She swayed on her feet, and Father caught her about the waist and walked her toward the closest chair.

"Everything my father—your grandfather—said was true?" my mother asked, her eyes wide.

At that moment, the door swung open. Cedrick stepped into the room and froze, his smile drooping as his eyes bounced from person to person. He backpedaled, slinking back through the wooden arch to the safety of the hallway.

"I believe I left something . . . important in my chambers. I'll just go and fetch——"

"Cedrick, don't even think about it. Get back in here," Rose demanded.

He shuffled into the room with a frown. "I'm not good at these things, Red."

"Family is family. Even in the difficult moments, we need to be there for each other," Rose stated. Then she looked at Ryken. "That includes you too."

A faint smile pulled at Ryken's mouth, loosening the tightness in my chest. I looped my arm through his and rested my head on his arm.

"Decorum, Marigold," my mother reprimanded.

Years of habit had my back stiffening, demanding to follow the rules. But my heart overruled it.

"No." I held her gaze.

She coughed, choking on her tongue.

"What is the meaning of this, Goldie?" Father said, his hands outstretched. "This isn't like you."

Leaning back, I stared up into Ryken's eyes. "I love him, and I am marrying him tomorrow. Can't you be happy that I found someone who loves me as I am? Just as I love him because of who he is? Trust that I know my own heart. Fins or feet—he's the same person on the inside."

Ryken took a step forward. "I know you don't know me or understand my kind. But what she said is true. I love her—with everything inside of me. I will spend the rest of my life proving that to her."

A hushed silence fell over the room.

"I apologize for my outburst," Mother said. "It's hard enough to gain our daughter only to find we have another son too. We want her to be happy, and if she says that you are what she wants, then that's what we want too. I look forward to getting to know you . . . and learning more about the Merfolk."

"Her mother is right, as usual. It might take some getting used to. It feels like just yesterday she was our little girl."

I threw my arms around him, hugging him tightly. "Thank you, Father."

He pressed a kiss to my forehead and pulled away. "I think I need a walk to clear my head. Maybe work in the garden for an hour." He shook his head, mumbling to himself as he snuck out the door.

"That's a good idea," Rose said, dabbing her eyes. "Let's have a moment with just us girls. I'm sure Mother has tons of questions. I know I do."

I sat on the settee with Rose and Mother on either side of me. It still felt like a dream having them at arm's length.

Mother placed both her hands on mine. "I'm just delighted to be in the same room as you."

"I think that's our cue, Ryken," Cedrick said.

"We're leaving?" Ryken asked, staring over his shoulder at me as Cedrick guided him to the door.

"Yes, they're evicting us to discuss . . . lady things."

"And we don't want to do that?" Ryken asked.

Cedrick opened the door. "We most certainly do not. Not that we'd have any say in the matter if we did."

"That is correct," Rose agreed.

Eyes downcast, Ryken headed out the door. "What will we do to pass the time?"

"Do you read?"

"No."

"Horseback riding?"

"No, again." Ryken sent me a forlorn glance from the hall.

"Chess?"

"What is chess?"

"I'll take that as another no. We'll figure something out." Wide-eyed, Cedrick forced an overly bright smile at us and reached to pull the door closed. "It will be great . . . so great."

Just before the door clicked shut, I heard Ryken grumbling, "I can tell you're lying."

Rose and Mother turned to me expectantly.

"What?"

"How on earth did you meet such a strange creature?" Mother asked.

My fists balled into my skirt as a wave of anger rolled over me.

"Mother," Rose reprimanded.

"I didn't mean to be rude," she said, pressing a hand on her heart. "I was only curious."

So I told them everything that happened that fateful day when I was stolen from the carriage. The days of mistreatment. I stumbled over my words, embarrassed by the sickening details I had hoped to forget that so easily rose to the surface.

"I should have those men sent to the gallows," Rose seethed. Her hand squeezed mine in solidarity.

"Leaving them to rot in the dungeon is a better form of punishment." A shiver coursed through me at the thought of their close proximity.

"I can decide their fate later. I'd rather hear what happened after you fell into the sea."

"It was the strangest thing. It was like my voice sounded different underwater. Instead of screaming, it was a song."

"A song?" my mother and sister said together.

A knock sounded on the door, and a servant entered.

"Your Majesty, we have an unexpected guest. He demands an audience. I wasn't sure where to send him. The morning room is too plain for his rank, and the Evergreen parlor is too frilly. It was the first time——" The servant blathered on until my sister cut him off.

"Andrews? What are you going on about? A visitor?"

"Yes, Your Majesty. He says he's the prince from Windcrest. In my stress of getting him settled into a room, I forgot his name. V— something . . ."

I was surprised to find myself standing, and I quickly flopped back onto the stiff settee, my hands trembling. What could he possibly want? And which prince was gracing us with his presence?

"Isn't that bold of him? But King Galon couldn't have received my message yet. Did the prince state the reason for his visit?" Rose asked, resting her clasped hands on her stomach.

Andrews cleared his throat and turned to me. "Actually, he's here to see you, my lady."

A Royal Guest

"**M**e?" I stammered.

"You know the prince of Windcrest? Why would he travel all this way to see you?" Mother whispered to me, her hand gripping mine.

"It depends on which prince it is. This might not be a social visit."

If it was Prince Vox, he might be here with his own demands, or he could be upset about the health of his sister.

The servant took a step toward me. "I have him waiting in the morning room. Are you accepting visitors today, my lady?"

"I suppose so?" I turned to Rose with a shrug. Was there special etiquette for entertaining royalty? "What do you think, Rosey?"

Rose's lips pinched, and she shifted straighter in her chair. "I don't trust them. But he didn't ask me—he asked for you, so it's your choice. I only request that you take my guards with you if you accept. Who knows what other underhanded plans Windcrest has concocted? They had spies in our castles for who knows how long. I'm guessing Cedrick is inspecting the armory to see what else those thieves stole."

"Should I wait until he gets back?" I'd also feel better if Ryken were here too. I was worried he'd be more prone to strike first and ask questions later if he stumbled into Prince Vian down a hallway.

Andrews cleared his throat. "He said the matter was urgent, my lady."

I have to see him right now?

"Give me one moment . . ."

I grimaced at my tattered and dirty gown, knowing my hair was probably even worse. Fidgeting in my seat, I quickly set to braiding my hair, the navy strands twisting with the gold.

"Do not rush her," Rose ordered, her voice like steel. "She's had a most tiresome journey and needs to catch her breath." She met my eyes, waiting for my direction.

Help, I pleaded silently. I was in no state for entertaining.

Rose nodded back and stood with an air of authority. "She is not presentable for company. If he wishes to wait, you can escort him to the throne room. After we freshen up, we will meet him there."

"Yes, Your Majesty. I will inform him immediately." He bowed at the waist and dashed from the room.

My sister pulled me up to her side. "Come. I have plenty of dresses I can share. It's not like I can fit into any of them for a few more months." She bit her lip. "May I suggest something a little less . . . blue? It might help him see that your allegiance has shifted."

"I still can't believe they didn't tell me you were the Queen of Hearts. I wouldn't have sided with Windcrest if I'd known."

She patted my hand. "I know, and I'm not upset in the slightest. You're home and safe. That's all that matters."

Mother rose to her feet, picking nervously at the lace on her sleeve. "I'll let your sister handle this. She's had more training in these types of situations than I've had. I'd be more of a hindrance than a help."

"Me too," I said. The thought of running off with my mother sounded so tempting.

Mother leaned in to kiss Rose's cheek and then mine. She paused to tuck a loose curl behind my ear. "I'm so happy to have you back, Goldie." Her eyes raked over my misshapen braid. "Though you seem more blue than gold now. I might have to call you something else soon."

"I'll always be your Goldie, no matter what I look like."

"Yes, my sweet girl. *Agh,* you're going to make me cry again. Go with your sister now. I need to find your father. Last time I left him alone, he got into a shouting match with the head gardener."

"We'll see you at dinner," Rose said to Mother before looping our arms together. She led me out the door, with Mother's hawk eyes watching our every step.

"She won't do well when you leave," Rose said, worry lacing her words. She swallowed, squeezing my arm to her side.

I returned the hold, knowing she was speaking about herself as much as Mother.

Perhaps even more so.

"We will figure out a way to see each other. I want to see my little niece or nephew."

"It's still hard. I missed you—even before you were abducted, I missed you. I hated not being close when we were fighting. I wrote you letters every day. You never replied, which, I understand——"

I pulled us to a stop. "What letters?"

Rose squinted at me. "I sent you a letter every day before the wedding. I even mailed them to you when you left for Windcrest."

"I didn't receive any letters."

"Not one?"

"No," I seethed. "Was it King Alexander?"

She ground her teeth. "I wish I could say no, but he became obsessed with keeping me in the castle. I don't wish to talk about it. It makes me feel not like myself. Like I was weak and stupid."

"Roselyn Bellmond, you are neither of those things," I chided.

"I thought I was doing the right thing, but I was making things much worse. You probably don't know what that's like. You always seem so put together."

"Me?" A delirious laugh exploded from my lips, and I doubled over at her assumption. "If you only knew how wrong you were."

"My word," Rose said, joining in laughter with me. "I guess we are more alike than I thought."

Giggling, we compared our mistakes all the way to the queen's chamber. This was one competition I was sure to be the victor.

As soon as I stepped through the double doors, my breath whooshed out of my lungs. Larger than Princess Vella's room, this room was filled with bookcases and so many plants, like a smaller version of Mistbrooke Forest in decorative pots scattered around the room. Three large windows overlooked the town, the sun shining in a soft light slanting across the tiled floor.

Where a bed should be was a small sitting area. Balls of yarn rested on most of the seats. Piles of knitted baby clothes, shoes, and hats were stacked on the table in a rainbow of colors.

"Uh, I wasn't expecting company," Rose admitted sheepishly. "But you're used to my messy habits."

"Don't you have a maid?" I picked up a pair of baby booties, my heart melting at their teeny size.

"I do. Her name is Clara. She helps me get dressed and prepare my baths, but otherwise, I do everything myself. I don't need more people underfoot than I already have. We have servants for the smallest of tasks —did you know we have one that just lights candles? Apparently, he takes all night to light them and all day to extinguish them. Don't even get me started on chamber pots." She made a face.

"I won't! Goodness, if Mother even knew you were talking about such things."

Chuckling, she opened one of her wardrobes and held up a red dress of expensive velvet. "Mother stays out of the castle most days. She prefers the cottage where it feels like home. She's only here for you." Rose smiled, but it didn't quite reach her eyes. "Here, what do you think of this? I've never worn it."

"Is that Windcrest fabric?"

"No, it's from one of the traders' ships. Feel how soft it is."

My fingers sunk into the buttery soft texture. "Oh, it's splendid." I couldn't stop myself from caressing the sleeve one more time.

"Take it. It's yours." Rose offered it to me.

"It's too much." I refused it even as I wanted to run my hand over the gown again.

"What's the point of being queen if I can't spoil you every now and again? Please," she begged. She pushed it back into my arms.

How could I say no? This would be the last dress I wore before my wedding gown. Just the thought sent me into a daze of nerves and excitement. Rose tied up my corset and buttoned the gown before I realized that the queen of Cadell was acting as my lady's maid.

"Rose, you shouldn't be doing this," I said.

Ignoring me, she pressed me into her vanity chair to brush out my tangles. "Why not?"

"You're a queen."

"I'm also your sister. I've been helping you dress and braid your hair since you were learning to walk." She leaned in to whisper in my ear. "Also, as queen, I get to make the rules."

I met her eyes in the mirror. "You are terrible at following the rules. I guess it makes sense that you make them now."

"Not all of us can be such strict rule followers like you. You make us mere mortals look bad." She pinned the last section of my braid across my head. "There we are. What do you think? It's a new style where the braid looks like a tiara."

"It's so pretty. Let's see how long it lasts. Ryken likes my hair down and free."

"He is quite smitten with you, isn't he?" Concern flickered in her eyes. "Is he kind to you? I don't know how mermen usually behave to their—what did he call you?—mates."

I spun around in my chair to grab her hands. "Rosey, he is the sweetest. You don't have to worry about that. Truthfully, I couldn't be more fortunate to find someone who is so gentle and patient with me. I love him."

Rose's lips wobbled as one side of her mouth perked up. "Good. I'm glad you found someone that captured your heart. You tell him to take care of you, or I'll send my soldiers to bring you back home."

I stood and threw my arms around her, pulling her into an affectionate embrace. "Thank you."

She pulled back, her green eyes misting. "You don't have to thank me for being your sister. But I will say, after we meet this prince, you are having a bath. You smell fishy."

"I do not. I've been in the bath almost daily."

She wrinkled her nose and nodded. She grabbed a bottle of perfume from her table and dabbed a few drops behind my ears. "Better, but you still need a bath."

"If you insist. But keep the water on the cooler side."

She took a moment to straighten her attire and adjust the crown on her head. "Ready?"

I nodded.

370

She led us back out of the winding stone corridors. A few maids curtsied as we passed, their eyes on the floor.

She wouldn't let me stop to gawk at the pillars or vaulted ceilings. Not even a second to marvel at the stained glass windows or the strange mural on the ceiling. She dragged me down the red carpet to the two thrones up on the dais. One was occupied by her husband. He tapped his fingers on the armchair, looking bored.

"Why have I been summoned here?" he asked.

He seemed to not enjoy being bossed around either.

"We have guests, and I thought you'd want to be here when they arrive." She yanked me up the stairs to stand by her throne.

"More mermen?" His brows shot up.

"No, dear." She leaned in to kiss his cheek, but he turned at the last second so her lips met his. Laughing, she jumped back and sat on the throne beside him. "You scoundrel. You're going to scramble my thoughts."

A predatory smile spread across his face, and he leaned over his armrest. "I like it when your thoughts are scrambled. You are less dangerous."

I fidgeted in place. "*Ahem.* The prince of Windcrest is here to see me."

The king nearly fell out of his chair. "What? Here? Now?"

He didn't have a moment to right himself before the double doors opened and Andrews led Prince Vian down the carpet.

I sighed in relief. This prince I could handle. At least, I thought I could.

He wore a blue tunic with a golden belt around his waist. Brown leather breeches were tucked into knee-high boots that thudded with each step toward us. His head swiveled back and forth, scanning the room, and his hand rested on the hilt of a sword strapped to his hip, the metal jingling with his movement.

A deep frown pinched the corners of his mouth. It enhanced the puckered scar from the right side of his lips and curved it up to his hairline like a permanent smile. I took a step toward him, trying to see it better.

Rose's hand shot out, keeping me at my post by her side.

The sudden movement caught his attention. His eyes swung to

371

mine and instantly filled with relief. Tension eased from him, and despite his scar, his usual charming smile dangled from his lips.

"Marigold, I was so worried about you," he said. He moved to pass the servant, and the guards lining the bottom step tensed and placed their hands on the hilts of their swords.

"How dare you address my sister so," Rose snapped.

"We are well acquainted, Your Majesty. Or has she not told you?" He glanced around the room again, scratching his head. "Where is the merman? Gone?"

I frowned at the hope in his voice. "No. He's here. Did you wish to speak with him?"

"No, thanks. I'm still healing from our last conversation."

"Prince Vian, is it?" Cedrick said, his words clipped. "Excuse us if we aren't feeling too hospitable. We caught your spies stealing our weapons when we returned from Mistbrooke."

Prince Vian closed his eyes, sighing. "I was hoping to arrive before that would happen. Those guards were placed by my brother, not me. Are you all right? Did they hurt you?" His gaze fixed on me as he waited for my answer.

"I am well," I said.

Rose argued, "But that doesn't change the fact that you have broken our treaty. War has been declared, Prince Vian, so I suggest you return home and prepare for battle. Five days will be here sooner than you realize. If you have come to change my mind and beg for forgiveness, you're wasting your time. My decision is final." Her words echoed across the throne room, burning with fury.

"I'm not here to change your mind—I'm here to help."

"Help yourself, you mean? You've come ill prepared. Why would a prince travel alone?" Cedrick asked.

"I'm no longer a prince," Prince Vian said.

"Excuse me if I don't believe another one of your lies," Rose spat.

"My lies?" the prince asked, tilting his head.

Rose shot to her feet, her eyes glittering with distrust. "Have you and your people not been spreading lies about Enchanters and Cadell's intentions? That I am a murderer, killing innocent people in my quest for power? That my people are to be attacked on sight—despite the treaty between our kingdoms? Why should we trust you after your kingdom has betrayed us at every opportunity?"

"Everything you said is true. But you are placing blame on the wrong person. I'm not responsible for the actions of my family, yet I am here out of responsibility and guilt. I don't want more bloodshed in either kingdom. I'm hoping that if I take a stand against it, my father will see reason and end this madness."

"More lies," Rose hissed.

"Wait," I said, breathing deeply. "He's telling the truth."

"Thank you, Marigold," Prince Vian said, bowing his head.

"Did you not hear me? Please show her some respect. She is a betrothed woman and doesn't need you tarnishing her good name."

His mouth fell open. "Betrothed? When is the wedding?"

"It's not any of your business," my sister said at the same time I said, "Tomorrow."

"Oh," the prince mumbled, appearing momentarily lost.

"I almost feel bad for him," Cedrick whispered to his wife.

"Don't," the prince said. "If she doesn't get married, my father will force our union. It's why he sent me—to bring back my wife."

"She will not marry you," Rose shrieked. "Nor would I allow it. Nobody will be forced to wed under my rule."

Cedrick placed his hand over hers. "I stand by her ruling."

"Let me speak, please, uh, Your Majesty," I said, making a face at the oddity of referring to my sister as my queen.

"You'll get used to it," she said softly so only I could hear. "Go on, say what you need to say so he will leave."

"I've already told the prince I wouldn't marry him," I said, then turned to Prince Vian. "You said we were friends."

"Friends," my sister repeated.

"I did come as a friend. I have no plans to marry you. I was only shocked to learn that you were indeed . . . marrying. But it doesn't stop me from the true purpose of my visit."

"Which is?"

"Change is coming, and this is the side I choose. I want to pledge my allegiance to you. My family has no just cause for bloodshed, nor will they listen to reason. This has to stop."

The three of us stood awkwardly, unprepared for his suggestion.

"You pledge your allegiance to Cadell?" Rose asked, her pitch high in confusion.

"Actually, no." The prince held my gaze and kneeled. "I pledge it to you."

"Me?" I pressed my hand to my heart.

He smiled at my response.

"But she is queen," I pointed out.

"She is. I still choose you."

"Cedrick is the Chosen One—pick him instead."

His smile grew, and he shook his head, declining.

"Marigold," my sister whispered behind her hand, "it's not a terrible idea to have one of their own standing with us. If you trust that he is telling the truth, then why not have an extra ally?"

"What do I do with him?" I asked, panicked.

"Nothing. Just have him show up and fight. And you are sure he's trustworthy?"

I nodded. "He's the one that helped Ryken, Liora, and me escape."

"Then trust your instinct." Rose shifted back into her chair and jerked her chin toward the prince kneeling on the floor.

What did my instinct say? I took a deep breath, holding it in and releasing it.

"I accept," I said.

When the prince didn't move from his spot, my sister pointed at him. "He is waiting for you to approach him."

Slowly, I descended the stairs, my red gown trailing behind me until I stopped before him.

He pulled out his sword and offered it to me above his head. "My sword is yours to wield. No matter the chaos of the storm or whatever this battle may bring—I will stand with you until the end has claimed me."

"Um, thank you?"

He lifted his head, chuckling. "That will do." He rose to his full height. "I see you're in red. Do you have any tunics in my size?"

A roar sounded from outside the throne room, animalistic and furious enough that the hair rose on the back of my neck.

"Stay behind me, my lady," the prince commanded.

"Guards," my sister ordered.

But I knew who it was based on his smell alone. "It's Ryken."

The prince spun around, shielding me just as the doors flew open and cracked against the wall. The long, ornate mirror fell to the floor, the bottom corner cracking.

Ryken's nostrils flared with each breath, and he bared his sharp teeth.

"You," he seethed, his frosty eyes on the prince.

Dangerous Games

Ryken stalked into the room, a hunter ready to pounce on his prey. As if in a trance, he didn't respond when I shouted his name. His eyes remained fixed on the prince.

"I don't remember the teeth," Prince Vian murmured, stepping back until he bumped into me. "Has it gone feral?"

My top lip curled at his assumption, and I shoved at his back. No one spoke about my mate that way.

The prince stumbled away from me, noticeably more worried about my response than Ryken's approach.

The king shot up from his throne, his voice a royal command. "Halt."

Ryken's feet rooted to the carpet, his lower half stopping before his torso, jerking him to a stop as he swayed in place.

"He is not worth it," the king said, pointing to Prince Vian. "Violence will not win her over. Trust me."

Chest heaving, Ryken fought with his inner beast, his hands clenched into fists at his side. His eyes trailed around the room, sliding from Cedrick to my sister until they finally landed on me. His eyebrows slanted together in pain, and his lips trembled over his pointed teeth.

The need to soothe the creases on his brow and whisk him from the castle set me in motion. I raced past the prince's outstretched arm, growling at him when he tried to whip me behind him to safety. Scowling, I snapped at the air close to his skin, a not-so-subtle reminder that I didn't need him or his protection when it came to my mate.

The prince jerked back and held his arm against his chest.

"Marigold," the prince sputtered in dismay. He flexed his arm, checking for injuries. "Did you . . . try to bite me? You're behaving no better than this—this monster."

My eyes widened as the truth of his words struck me speechless. What had come over me? Shame replaced my anger, and I ducked my head, a blush covering me from head to toe.

"Hold your tongue, prince," Rose said, squeezing the armrests on her throne in a death grip. "Marigold doesn't owe you an apology for who she is. The fact that you are still here is because of her kindness, and you are wearing out your welcome. Ally or not, this is your last warning. The next insolent remark and you'll be escorted to the border in shackles."

The prince bowed at the waist, too low for his rank and a sign of submission more than respect. "No, you are correct in your commands, Your Majesty. I had forgotten she isn't exactly human—even though she looks it." He spun to me, bowing again. "My apologies, my lady. You had warned me before about your complicated relationship, or I guess it's an engagement now. I take my new oath to heart. He is not the enemy."

"I am not a monster either," Ryken bellowed, not very convincing with his glower and sharp teeth on display.

The prince nodded dutifully, edging away from him. "Of course. How ungentlemanly of me to have mentioned it. Mrs. Pretta would be sure to scold me with just a single look alone. She's cranky in her old age, but she has the best of intentions in keeping me in line."

"What is he saying?" Ryken asked, his anger increasing with his confusion.

The prince rubbed the back of his neck. "It's nothing. I'm sorry to have brought it up, as it seems to have made matters worse. I was only trying to protect her."

The king's dark eyes glowed with an amber glint. "Do you think our guards cannot perform their duties?"

"Pardon, I meant no insult. As I said, when a beast comes barreling at you, you react first and think later. Her safety, after everything she had been through, should be of the utmost importance. Most of the territories are searching for her as we speak."

"Like you?" Rose questioned.

"Marigold has resilience and a stubborn streak, and I knew she would make it here eventually. She traveled faster than I expected." He peered over his shoulder at me and sent me a friendly smile. "You always surprise me."

A keening wail ripped through the air, jarring me from the discussion. So broken, it pierced my heart, and I turned toward Ryken as he bounded from the room.

Like a string connected us, I took off after him, ignoring the calls of my sister and the prince.

Instinct took control. Arrows of his scent guided me through the maze of corridors, dark stone lit in the glow of the flickering torches. He knocked a vase in his haste, blue ceramic shattering like a river between us. I lifted the hem of my gown, leaping over the jagged fragments. I sprinted after him around the corner to find him trapped at a dead end.

Frustrated, he ripped a tapestry off the wall, crumpling it in his hands. But he froze, spreading it out again as his eyes raked over the fabric's design.

"Ryken," I called out, slowing as I reached his hunched form.

His thumb traced the stitched couple. An unknown queen and king stood side by side, her hand resting on his offered arm and the other holding her skirt. Ryken turned toward me, shaking the tapestry at me as if this were the sum of all his problems.

"This . . . this should be you." He glared at it again.

"Me?" I walked up, worried about his ramblings. "But I'm not a queen."

"No, with him—*the prince*. All these human things I don't understand, he does. All the rules that you love, names of objects, and appropriate behavior. It makes no sense to me. When he talks to people, they don't show fear or confusion. I do not belong in this world, but you do. Anjali said love could be like poison. What if she is right? What if my love is killing you? It nearly killed the prince." He gathered my hands and pressed them to his chest. "You want your freedom and to stay on land, to be with all the things you love, especially your family. Everything that brings you happiness is here." Glancing down, he mumbled to himself, "Am I being selfish? Keeping her for my own desires?"

"What are you talking about?" A sickening panic clawed my chest. Why did it sound like he was leaving me?

"With each passing day, I've realized how much you belong in this world and not mine. How you shine with joy and laugh without restraint. Even your face lights up when you talk about your favorite things."

I tugged at his tunic, desperate to keep him with me. "Ryken, my face lights up because of you. The thought of showing you my world, my interests, and the things I care about brings me such happiness. I don't care where I am as long as we're together."

"But he can give you everything I can't. It was stupid to think I could. Our ship, months of me collecting treasures——" He leaned back to groan up at the ceiling. "Junk—it's all useless. No wonder you weren't impressed."

"You're not listening. All I want is *you*."

He blinked, and my words finally soaked in.

"Really?" He expelled a pent-up breath.

"Of course, you silly merman." I whacked his arm playfully, and his eyes dilated at the gesture.

He lifted me up by my waist to bring us eye to eye. Tension crackled between us, static electricity that sizzled at his nearness. I could sense his restraint, that he wanted to devour me with more than just his eyes.

My lips parted, desperate for his touch.

He breathed in my scent, sighing as if he could taste it.

"You don't want the prince?" he asked.

"No."

"He's everything a human could want. Power, beauty, wealth, legs that work——"

I blew on his lips and apparently blew the rest of his thought away too. "I don't want those things," I whispered.

"You make conversation difficult." His eyes dipped to my mouth.

"Then stop talking."

"Why can't I resist you?" It was a desperate plea ending with his mouth on mine. A thrilling warmth spread from my lips and ignited like fire across my skin. Similar to a man starved, his lips slid across mine with a need that left me breathless.

How could I want anyone but him?

I nipped at his lower lip, still upset at his suggestion. But what was supposed to be a reprimand sent him into a frenzy, and I found myself trapped between him and the wall.

He reared back, momentarily surprised at himself, then immediately captured my lips again.

"You bit me," he said against my jaw, kissing his way to my neck. He nuzzled my neck, and the heat of his breath sparked my nerves until I was putty in his hands. "I liked that a lot. Maybe too much . . . I don't want to let you go."

I grunted. Why was he talking at all?

His mouth glided to the spot on my shoulder, the same spot he had bitten me when I first met him. "Does this mean I'm allowed to bite you too? New rules?"

Oh my. I couldn't find my voice to speak, so lost was I in his touch.

"Marigold . . . this is a dangerous game, and I'm losing control," he growled in my ear. Reluctantly, he released me, his eyes pained. His nostrils flared with each heaving breath until he finally stepped away.

My legs quaked, and I slid down the rough stones before he pulled me upright again with a smug smile.

"I'd carry you, but I think I should wait before we are so close again."

"All right," I said dumbly, trying to remember my name and what I was doing in this hallway.

"Unless . . . you've changed your mind?"

"About what?" What were we talking about?

"We could return to the sea right now," he suggested.

"Now?" There was a reason I wanted to stay. "Uh—wait, no, the ceremony." I shook my head and righted my thoughts, ignoring Ryken's chuckles. I pointed at him. "No more kisses for you."

The smile slid from his face. "*What?!* B-but I like those. If you're worried about me biting you, I promise I won't."

"I need to keep my wits about me. And you have a way of clouding my thoughts and reasoning."

"What if it's just a little kiss?" He pinched his thumb and index finger together with just a sliver of a gap between them.

"No kisses until after the wedding."

Ryken pressed a hand over his heart and sucked in a breath. "So long?"

"You went your whole life not even knowing what a kiss was. One day won't kill you."

"It could. We don't know."

"I know, and you'll be fine." I patted his cheek and turned to walk down the hall.

He sighed, following behind me, muttering, "If I had known that was the last one, I would have made it last longer."

I laughed, looping my arm through his. "Come on. You're probably just hungry. Once you've eaten something, you'll feel better. Rose said she was holding a family feast in honor of our wedding."

"Feast?"

"Food."

His eyes lit up, and he picked up his pace around a corner. "What kind of food? Ham? I liked that."

"I think she said fish," I joked.

Ryken frowned. "But we have that back home."

Laughing, I squeezed his arm. "I'm jesting. I don't know what she's serving."

"Can we eat now?" He glanced down at me and then groaned at my expression. "You're going to say we have to wait again."

"They have to cook it. Plus the wait will make it even more delicious."

He sent me a look from the corner of his eye, and a sensual smile twisted his lips.

I quickly pressed a hand over his mouth to silence him. "No. Don't say it. You only need to behave one day. You've barely made it ten minutes."

His hand brushed over my shoulder until it rested on my collar. Holding my stare, his words echoed through our connection.

I've waited for you for a very, very long time. So, how delicious will you taste?

Ryken, I scolded, heating all over again.

I didn't say it. He winked.

I wished his words didn't affect me so. But they had a way of jumbling my thoughts as much as his kisses. My hands dropped to my side, tingling from his touch.

"Let's find this feast." He led us down a well-lit corridor. "Will I have to use silverware? Those seem so useless when you already have hands and teeth that do that same thing."

"Yes, you'll have to use your manners. The prince will probably be dining with us because of his rank."

He growled, but he caught himself.

"What is it about him that bothers you so much?"

"The way he stares at you—I don't like it."

"People are going to look at me. You can't react like that every time someone does."

He scrubbed a hand down his face. "I know. I'm trying. His persistence claws at my patience, and there is a longing in his gaze—I'm getting angry just thinking about it." He huffed and balled his hands into fists.

I stopped and turned his head toward me. "Whenever you catch him looking at me, remember that my eyes will only be on you."

He pressed his forehead against mine, sighing. "That helps."

"There you two are," Rose shouted from down the hall, startling us apart. She picked up her skirt to rush over to us. "I was so worried about you, Ryken."

"Me?" he said.

"Yes, you." She placed a comforting hand on his arm, then jerked it back. "Oh, is it all right if I touch you? I'm not sure what Merfolk customs are. We want to make sure you feel welcome here."

"Yes, uh——" He fumbled over his words and ended up settling with, "Thank you."

Rose inclined her head, a graceful gesture that seemed so natural. Gone was the girl that ran barefoot through the flowers and climbed trees for apples. She truly was every bit as royal as the Windcrest family.

"What?" she asked. "You're staring at me funny. Is something on my face? I sneaked some chocolate while I was searching for you."

"I'm only amazed at how much you've changed since I saw you last."

Rose wrinkled her nose. "I wasn't much to look at then."

"I never thought that. I've always admired you."

"Agh, don't be sentimental. It doesn't take much for me to break down into tears. Are you hungry, or should we wait to eat?"

"I'm ready to eat," Ryken said. "Do you have ham? Or chocolate?"

"I'm sure we can arrange something for you. I mean, it is your celebration." She clapped her hands together. "Follow me. Somehow you've found the part of the castle that I haven't explored yet."

A burning sensation rippled up my legs like fire ants. I latched onto Ryken's arm, holding him for support as another wave of pain flowed over me.

"Oh, Goldie?" Rose grabbed my hand. "What's the matter?"

"My legs . . . they hurt sometimes."

"Like before?" Ryken asked. "Do you want to sit and relax?"

"Yes, if you both don't mind."

Ryken scooped me up into his arms with ease. "Why would I mind? I'd do anything for you."

Roselyn fought a smile, shooting me a knowing look. She'd want all the details later when we were alone. "This way, I'll show you to her room."

Even as I tried my best to hide it the rest of the evening, the pain didn't let up. Not through dinner, not during my dress fitting, not during my bath, not even now while I lay in the darkness waiting for the new day to dawn.

I should be excited, bursting with butterflies. But everything seemed distant like I was in a long tunnel and the world around me was miles away. Only this blasted pain was my constant companion.

Please, make it stop.

Another wave of pain struck me, and a cry slipped from my lips before I muffled it in my silk pillow. Earlier, my legs had stung, but now they were ablaze with an internal fire that had me kicking the bedding away and scrambling for the cool bath water still sitting in my room.

The door cracked open, Ryken peeking his head in. "Marigold?"

I pinched my lips, trying to hide the pain again. "Yes? Do you need something?"

He slunk into the room and closed the door behind him. "Why did you not ask for me? Like before? You are in pain—I can feel it."

"It's not so terrible," I said, wincing as another heat wave hit me.

"Let me look at it. If it's a wound, perhaps I can heal it." He marched over to me, clear as daylight with my new senses despite not having a candle lit.

I shifted, keeping the tub between us. "I'm not injured. Go back to bed."

"You don't have to pretend." He moved right the same time I did. "Let me examine it."

"No. You can't just look at my legs."

"Why not? You've seen mine. They're hairy and pale. It's nothing like my tail, which . . ." he trailed off, his back straightening, and his eyes softened in the darkness. "*Marigold.*"

Shaking my head, I kept the tub between us as he tried to sneak around from the left. "No, Ryken."

"Is it what I think it is?" He faked right, then darted left, nearly catching the sleeve of my borrowed white nightgown.

"We are not talking about this. It's improper." I almost added that just the two of us alone in my room was frowned upon, but the urgency of following rules at this moment seemed less . . . important. I wanted him to stay.

My jaw dropped at my blatant disregard for structure. I'd never not cared before.

Ryken was too fast, vaulting over the tub to gather me in his arms. "Mine," he whispered in my ear, spinning me in a circle. The air was coated with his happiness, a sweet taste that had me giggling at his excitement.

"You're making my head spin," I said.

"I know. It's a distraction from the pain. I could think of other things, but you said I had to wait." He pouted. "Did you want to lie in the water?"

"I was going to before you showed up, but I feel better now that you're here."

His thumb rubbed my cheek. "Good."

Ryken didn't ask. His intense stare did the task for him until I finally crumbled.

"One look," I said begrudgingly.

Squealing, he set me on the bed and kneeled at my feet to grab my skirt.

"I'll do it. Only a quick glance," I said.

He ignored me completely, flipping up the hem to cradle my leg in his hands. Green with flecks of silver flashed, more than I remembered, covering the majority of my skin.

"Finally," he said, a slow smile spreading across his lips. "Your tail is forming. I've been imagining you in all the colors. It's kept me up at night." He glanced up through his lashes. "Now, I know to dream of you in green. It's magnificent, as you would say."

He dreams of me? As a mermaid?

His fingertips trailed over top the shiny scales, and my breath shuddered. Like he had scratched an itch I didn't know I had. A heat that melted my thoughts and made my insides quiver . . . I wanted more.

"It's sensitive," he said, breathless. "It will be until you get used to it. Though you have a lot more to go. I can still see your toes."

As if he couldn't stop himself, his fingers brushed across my scales again.

I trembled, my lips parting.

"I should go," he whispered.

Go where? I couldn't think properly as his thumb torturously swiped down my calf.

"Are you in pain?"

"No. Not right now."

His fingers moved again as he studied my reaction.

I placed my hand on his, halting the movement. "Dangerous games, remember?"

"I know," he agreed and lowered my nightgown back to the floor. "Can I stay tonight? To sleep? If the pain comes back, I can be here to help. I can sneak out before the sun rises. I just want to be close to you right now."

He placed my hand on his heart, our beats synchronizing. Turquoise eyes, so blue and clear, broke through any argument I could muster.

"Sleep only," I said, keeping my voice stern.

He nodded as we both climbed under the covers, his arm wrapping around me as it always did. Right before the pull of slumber won me over, Ryken pressed a single kiss to the nape of my neck. His lips curved upward against my skin.

"Green," he whispered to the night.

Sighing, I fell into a blissful sleep, safely wrapped in his arms.

A Wedding to Remember

True to his word, I woke alone and already missing him. A soft smile tugged at my lips as my fingers slid over the chilled sheet where he had slept. He came when I needed him, like he somehow always knew when I was hurting.

Our nights for cuddling were at a minimum because once I transformed, I wouldn't require sleep as I had as a human. So I planned to appreciate these moments while I had them. Maybe I'd have until after the battle before I transformed, but after the excruciating pain from last night, I wasn't so sure.

The silence only lasted a second before the door flew open and a handful of maids marched in, their arms full of buckets of water. My mother sailed in behind them, my dress resting over her arms. Not far behind, Roselyn entered, holding a small wooden box carved with daisies.

"Wake up, sleepyhead." Rose laughed, opening the curtains wide to let the blinding light pour in. "You're going to sleep through your wedding."

Mother pressed a gentle kiss between my brows. "Good morning, my sunshine. How are you feeling today? Better?"

Rose eagerly waited for my response, laying out the oils for my bath on the table.

"Yes, the bath and night of rest helped."

"Wonderful," Mother exclaimed, then ripped the covers off me. "Then there is no reason to laze all day in bed. Up, up, up! We have quite a morning before us."

I quickly tucked my legs under my nightgown, not wanting to frighten them.

"Do I get a say in the matter?" I asked, rolling to my knees on the bed.

"No," Mother and Rose said in unison.

Pouting, I crawled out of my comfortable bed.

Mother nodded to the maids, watching them fill the tub with hot water. Ribbons of steam drifted up, and I shivered at the thought of climbing into a boiling cooking pot.

"Don't fret," Rose whispered at my side. "I exchanged half the buckets with cold water for your sensitive skin."

I threw my arms around her, so appreciative that she always noticed the minor details. "Thank you."

She wrapped her arms around my shoulders, her round stomach pressing against me. A sudden thump kicked me in my rib.

"Oh my," I said, leaning back. "Was that the baby?"

Rose fumbled for words. "I mean . . . yes, but . . . never has it been so strong before. Even Cedrick hasn't felt it." She blinked at me, her slow smile spreading as she thought. "Give me your hand."

She pressed my palm firmly against her stomach, sliding it along the top until she reached a hardened mound.

"Is that its head?"

"Actually, it might be their bottom," she said, laughing when her whole stomach wiggled. "It still surprises me that they have room to summersault. My poor ribs are taking a beating. Mother said I only have about a month left, so things will start getting even more cramped as they continue to grow."

"You're gonna get bigger than that?"

"I'll try not to take offense at that," Rose said dryly.

"My turn," Mother demanded, practically shoving me to the side so that I stumbled to stay afoot. "Hello, my little darling. Grandmama is knitting you a special blank—*ooh my!* What a kick you have!"

Rose stepped back, a protective hand over the top. "Excuse me for

388

one moment. I need to find Cedrick while this little one is still kicking around. He'll be distraught if he missed out. He's tried so many times but has felt nothing." As soon as she bolted out the door, she was shouting his name down the hallway.

Mother tsk-tsked. "A queen screaming down the halls. What am I to do with her?"

"She's happy though," I said.

Mother raised a brow as soon as we were alone in the room. "You will not get clean outside the water. Come now, let's take these off and get you into the bathtub."

I fiddled my fingers together, worried about my scales.

Mother walked over to the table with the wooden crate. "Say what you will about the brutes in Glenton, but they make the most delightful bath oils." She held up an amber vial to read the label. "Sunflowers? Who has even heard of such a flower?" She grabbed another in purple. "Ah, here we are. You still love lavender, right?"

She turned to me and sputtered. "You're still dressed. Do you need me to help you unbutton?"

"Mother," I squeaked when she grabbed the shoulders of my nightgown.

"No need to be shy, and time is of the essence. You already slept too long."

I jumped away, holding out a hand to keep her at bay. "*Stop.*"

Her eyebrows slanted up, and she glanced away toward the door. "If you'd rather I not be here, I understand."

"No, that's not it." I took a calming breath and hated that the air was laced with my mother's disappointment. "It's me. I've changed, and I don't want you to look at me differently."

Her eyes welled up. "Goldie, that is utter nonsense. I would never love you less because you were different. Do you hear me? Scales, teeth, fins, gills—whatever happens, you are still my little ray of sunshine."

I opened my mouth but was hit by a wave of emotion. How lucky I was to have a family so loving. So accepting. Tears brimmed over my lashes as the sobs raked through me.

Here I thought I was so unlucky because of one terrible event after another. But in perspective, those were trivial. For when it came to the things that mattered most, I was blessed beyond measure.

389

Mother gathered me close, her hand running through my hair. "Now, now. Don't you start crying or we will both be in tears."

Sniffling, I pulled away, wiping my eyes with the sleeve of my gown.

With a deep breath, I lifted my nightgown over my head in a quick movement, my scales sparkling and glorious in the light.

Mother sucked in a breath and her eyes lit up. "Your tail is beautiful. I was afraid it'd be fishier, but your scales are truly magical, like they are glowing. Now in the tub and no more fussing."

I washed, dried, and then laced up into a creamy gown of silks, a buttery yellow sash at my waist. A maid worked at my hair, a high bun of curls on top of my head.

Mother sipped her tea on the couch, trying her best not to rush us out the door. Her gown was of a sky blue satin with yellow accents along the neck and sleeves, highlighting the blue in her eyes.

Dressed in a golden gown that matched my sash, Rose crossed around the couch to the vanity, holding a tiara out for me.

"Do you want to wear one?" Rose asked.

"Um," I said, thinking. "That may not be wise. I'm not royalty."

"Yeah, but——" she placed one with diamonds on my head "——they are fun to wear."

I took it off and handed it back to her, laughing. "Yes, but I want to be myself. No playing dress-up today."

Rose nodded. "I understand. No tiara."

The door opened, and Ryken walked in unannounced, yanking at the collar of his high-neck tunic. It was black and yellow, the stitching glittering like actual gold. "Marigold, do we——?"

Rose and Mother screamed, waving their arms about in a frenzy.

"Out, out," Mother screamed.

"It's bad luck," Rose said, grabbing a confused Ryken by the shoulders.

"Bad luck—explain," he said. He glanced at me over his shoulder, fear in his eyes.

"You're scaring him." I stood, shaking out the length of my skirt. "There is no such thing, Ryken. Ignore them."

But he wasn't paying attention, his eyes softening the longer he stared.

"My Marigold," he whispered. "So beautiful."

Cedrick jogged into the room, out of breath. "So sorry. I was only distracted for a moment, and I lost him." He put a hand on his shoulder, dragging him out of the room. "We have to leave now if we want to beat the afternoon heat."

"I want to stay," Ryken complained from down the hall.

"I know. I think it's part of the torture they make us endure to get to the wedding night."

"What happens tonight?" Ryken asked.

"Oh, uh . . . "

Their voices trailed off down the hallway, eventually fading out. Unable to contain it any longer, the three of us burst into laughter.

"All right," Mother said, breathless. "I like him. He's so sweet."

"Yes. I feel horrid that I gave him such a hard time earlier," Rose agreed.

"He won't hold it against you. He knows what it's like to be protective of me."

Mother pinned my veil in place, fluffing the long lace that stopped before it reached the ground. "I've never made one so short before, but it is just stunning on you."

Grandmother and Grandfather snuck in next, kissing my cheeks and offering well wishes before it was time to rush out the door.

Rose led us out through the secret door in her garden, holding my hand as we walked toward the cliffs. My mind was a flurry of excitement and nerves, and I prayed that the pain in my legs wouldn't flare up again.

More people met up with us along the walk. Anjali, Opal, and Ean had traveled from the inn, so thankful to be included in the celebration. Even Prince Vian showed up, walking by himself, his head down. Guards marched along the outskirts of the procession, their sharp eyes scanning the distance in all directions.

An elderly man strolled out of the woods, leaning heavily on his staff. Perhaps gossip had spread about our wedding after all. I had hoped to keep the attendance to family and friends, but I supposed one old man wouldn't hurt things.

When we reached the wooden platform by the cliffs, I stood off to the side, overheating already. My legs tingled, a slow ache starting at my ankles that drifted up to my knees. I plastered on a smile, hoping no one would notice the pain settling in like it had yesterday.

As the old man walked past me, he stumbled, his staff slipping from his fingers, and he tumbled into the wildflowers.

Picking up my skirt, I rushed to his aid and offered him a supporting hand under his elbow. "Are you all right? Those sneaky tree roots are hidden in the thicker parts of the grass. Are you able to walk? I'm sure I could find someone to escort you back to the castle if you need it."

A smile stretched across his wrinkled face, and he rose to his feet. "My word, it's the young bride herself. Hello, Marigold."

"Hello," I replied, nodding my head. "And you are?"

"How rude of me. I'm Zarek, a friend of the family, so to speak. Your sister requested I perform the ceremony. Is my presence still required?"

"Yes, yes." I squeezed his arm and led him closer to the platform. "Sorry about that. I'm a little distracted by everything going on today. Thank you for helping us out on such short notice."

He bowed his head, revealing his thinning hairline. "I'm honored, my lady."

"Zarek," Rose said, rushing to gather his hands. "I see you met my sister. Goldie, this is the Sor——"

He quickly held up a hand to cut her off. "The title isn't necessary. It's about time it was dropped from my name anyway. It's a part of my past I'm not proud of. Perhaps we should make our way to the platform? It will be midday soon, and we will all roast in our finery."

Ryken watched me from the other side of the crowd, his eyes narrowing at the old man. He was at my side before I could take my next breath. "Can we start the wedding now? I don't like waiting, and Cedrick speaks of things I don't understand. He's nice but confusing."

"Yes, we only need to inform——" I explained.

"The wedding is starting," Ryken yelled to the crowd of people, halting all side conversations.

"That's one way to do it." Opal chuckled behind her hand.

As we walked arm in arm parting the guests, Mother wept loudly into her handkerchief.

Ryken sent me a sidelong glance, leaning in to ask, "Happy tears, I hope?"

I laughed. "Yes. She thinks you're sweet."

His neck reddened, and he was at a loss for words as he helped me up onto the platform.

"Thank you all for gathering together to celebrate this union between man and woman," Zarek said, his voice strangely amplified.

"Merman," Ryken corrected.

Zarek stuttered, "Merman? You?"

"Yes."

"It's just you don't look——"

"He is, I promise," I cut in, feeling a similar pattern of questions starting. "Could we possibly speed this along? I need to get off my feet."

"Is it your legs again?" Ryken asked, concerned. "Lean on me. I can help hold you upright should you need it. You once did the same for me."

I smiled, having forgotten what it was like when he was first human. "Now look at you."

"I can't. I'm too busy looking at you." He leaned down as if to press a kiss on my nose.

Zarek cleared his throat, startling Ryken back. "I can see this will be similar to my last ceremony. No kissing till the end."

Ryken grumbled under his breath.

We turned to one another, and his lips twisted in a goofy smile. Zarek rushed us through, removing most of the flowery description and frills. He nodded for me to start my vows.

"I have never met anyone like you before. Anyone that made me feel so special, so loved. You broke through my armor and found a way into my heart when I wasn't looking—and I'm so glad you did. You make me happy and give my life new meaning. I promise to love you more with each breath I take. To cherish, honor, and never part from—on land or sea, forever and always," I whispered, holding his gaze. "You are mine."

He shut his eyes.

"These human emotions . . . they are strong. But what I feel for you has always been." He opened his turquoise eyes, filled with love and adoration. "From the moment I saw you, I knew. You were my everything. I promise to love you more with each beat of my heart. To cherish, honor, and never part from—on land or sea, forever and always," he said, his voice dropping to a bare whisper. "You are mine."

"Oh, Ryken." I pressed my hand to his heart, the heart that had

393

once beat for mine. The touch sent tingles down my arm, our thumps synchronizing. "Thank you for saving me. For hearing my song and staying by side while I recovered. For never giving up on me despite how stubborn I was. Our bond may be of magic, but my love for you is a choice. No magic could make me feel this way—only you. And I will keep choosing you and loving you, as long as my heart is beating."

His eyes misted and he covered my hand. "My Marigold . . . "

Lost in each other's eyes, time ceased to exist. There was only me and him, and the steady drum of our hearts.

"May Ruah guide you always," Zarek ended, the crowd sounding in applause.

Ryken didn't wait a second after Zarek declared he could kiss me. His lips descended on mine in a sweet kiss, his hands cradling the back of my head. He nipped playfully at my lip as he pulled back an inch, surprising me.

"Are you my wife now?"

"Yes," I breathed, and his lips were back on mine.

"Ahem . . . I said *ahem*," Zarek said before separating us. "And don't growl at me, merman."

Ryken ducked his head sheepishly, stepping away from me.

A gust of salty wind swirled around us, sending my curls into a dance.

Marigold, my child.

"Ruah," I said, looking skyward.

"What is it?" Ryken asked.

It's time to come home, my child.

I felt it as well as heard my bones snapping, followed by an intense pain as my legs gave out. I crumbled to the ground, blacking out for a few seconds.

I gasped through the pain. *Everything* hurt all at once. Is that what it felt like when he shifted? How did he survive it?

"I'm here. Hold on to me." His hand found mine. "Squeeze my hand when it—*ouch*."

I didn't need to wait for the pain. It was already here and unbearable. The air turned uncomfortably hot, my skin dry and stiff, parched for water. All I could do was focus on my next breath and try not to be sick.

"Water," I begged, my voice brittle.

"Anything you need." Ryken stood, glancing around us in a panic. "She needs water. Someone get us water."

"There isn't any. The best we can do is return to the castle," Cedrick said.

The pain ebbed away, only the memory aching my muscles and bones. Swallowing, I winced. My throat felt covered in sand, sending me into a coughing fit. My last hack, so loud, shot my legs forward. *No*, not my legs, but a jeweled tail of jade mixed with silver hues, unfurling from under my wedding gown.

Opal screamed, the pitch so high I roared in pain, covering my ears.

"Marigold," Rose shouted. She took two steps toward me before Ryken leapt in front to block her from getting any closer.

"Stop," he commanded. He held up his arms, blocking anyone who got too close. "More than her body has changed. I don't want anyone to get hurt, and I'm sure she would regret it later when her senses returned. Keep your distance."

Hurt them? Why would I do that?

I opened my mouth to call his name. But I sounded more froglike than human.

"At least let us make sure she's all right," Rose said.

"She would never attack me," my mother said. "I'll talk to her."

I blinked up at him, but the sunlight stabbed at my eyes, and I wrapped my arms around Ryken, pressing my cheek into his calf. The aching intensified, not just around my legs, but every inch of me.

And I was so thirsty.

I whimpered, turning my head away from the loud arguments.

Ryken placed a hand on top of my head, clicking and humming at me. The sound of it was soothing. "She might not remember you at all, so prepare yourself if that is the case."

"Not remember me?" Rose squeaked. "Have all her memories been erased?"

"Red, give him a moment. Don't get too close to her," Cedrick said.

"I need to see her—to see if she remembers me."

"Red, it's all right."

"Is it? Because the thought of her not knowing who I am would make the whole situation worse. What if she doesn't come back?"

"I'll bring her back," Ryken blurted out. "And I'll make sure she knows who you are. All of you. Family was very important to her."

I turned from his pant leg, trying to see the bright, fuzzy halos that were people. I tried to speak, to say something, but my throat was so dry. Air passed through it and sent me into another coughing fit.

I wanted to tell them I could remember them, but I couldn't speak. My tail flicked up in frustration, the weight of it odd. I repeated it a few more times, my scales shimmering and distracting me.

"Marigold," my mother shouted, drawing my attention. "Remember what I told you. I love you no matter what."

"And you all called me crazy," Grandfather said, laughing during the chaos. "I'm related to Merfolk. I never imagined the sea ran that deep in my veins."

"Uh, Red? The prince fainted." Cedrick's voice rose louder than the rest.

"What—? Oh, come on. Can you do something to wake him up?" Rose asked.

"Slap him?" Cedrick suggested.

"There has to be a less violent option. Anjali knows potions. What do you suggest?" Rose asked.

"You can slap him, gently, of course," Anjali said.

"I get first dibs," Cedrick said.

The crowd of people turned their attention to him so that they didn't notice when Ryken scooped me up, my tail flopping over his arm. He pressed a kiss to my temple. "Are you all right?"

I pointed to my throat and croaked.

"Water. You need water."

I nodded my head eagerly.

He held me tight, walking away from the racket. The salty breeze tickled the wisps of hair framing my face, beckoning me closer and whispering of home. I reached out a hand toward the direction of the sea, wishing I was in the cool water already.

"I'm hurrying," Ryken huffed, jogging through the grass.

"Ryken," someone screamed in the distance.

"Remember, hold on to me," he whispered in my ear just as the ground dropped out and we were plummeting down.

My hair broke free of the ribbons, snapping wildly around my face.

Air slammed into my nose and mouth, choking me, my eyes watering from the assault. Down we fell, my stomach flipping in circles as we picked up speed.

There was no fear because I knew where I was going and how wonderful it would feel when I got there.

The impact of the water was a painful blow, slowing everything down in a finger snap. Sound muted, light darkened, and the sweet echo of the sea soothed my soul. Saltwater wrapped around me, releasing the tension in my skin.

I twisted, my tail pushing me forward, but I didn't get far before it tangled in the hem of my dress. The fabric buoyed, pulling me back to the surface, and I fought against it, wanting to swim lower.

I breathed in, refreshing my mouth and gills from their dry state. Hints of Ryken's scent flowed in the water, and I turned to him, hoping to catch his reaction to my changed form.

It was then that I realized I was alone.

"Ryken," I cried, my voice garbled with bubbles. I switched to the phrase I had heard so many times. *Click, clickety-click, hummm, click,* I called out for him.

Had he left me? Was I supposed to follow him somewhere, and I didn't hear him?

Then I saw him, my insides chilling at his lifeless form. Eyes shut, his arms floated upward as he sank lower into the darker waters, still in his human form.

Sick with fear, I dove after him.

A Kingdom of Gold

I was furious at myself. Why hadn't I listened to his instructions on how to swim earlier? I had been foolish in trying to avoid my fate. Now I was inching through the water no faster than the plankton floating around me.

Arching my back, I let the movement snap all the way to my fins, but my tail kept tangling in my wedding dress. I didn't hesitate, shredding the fabric with my long nails until I was free, and I snapped my tail again, finally moving downward.

Fins. I have fins.

I didn't even have a second to waste on that realization.

Faster, I picked up speed until it felt less like steps and more like instinct propelling me into the darker water.

Perhaps too fast, as I slammed into Ryken, not knowing how to stop. Wrapping my arms around him, I held him close, remembering his last words to me. This time I wouldn't let go.

I placed a hand on his heart, his beats a faint whisper.

He is still alive.

I growled at him, a throaty sound that scattered the neon fish around me.

You will not leave me. Not now. Not after everything we have been through.

398

Our hearts synced—or tried to—mine slowing as it drained my strength to speed his up.

I placed his hand on my collar. *Don't give up, Ryken. You made me a promise—forever and always.*

He didn't wake, but his heartbeat picked up, still too weak for my liking. We sank down together to the seabed, where I cradled him in my arms. I searched around me for anyone that could help us.

I froze at the large stone ahead of me.

This rock . . . I'd been here before. It was the cave entrance. The one where the humans changed into mermaids. Had I been so close to my family this whole time and never knew? These caves must be under Mistbrooke Forest.

It seemed so long ago that I had awoken to a strange merman who had chained me in a cavern and forced those disgusting pearls into my mouth.

My breath bubbled out.

The purple pearls. The medicine he said healed me.

I have to get one.

Gently, I rested Ryken in the sand, placing a rock on his chest to keep him from floating away. I pressed a kiss to his forehead as a promise that I'd be right back.

I clawed at the stone, rocking it back and forth until I could squeeze in the tiny opening. It rolled back as soon as I entered, closing me in.

Ryken, I thought, pressing my palms to the rough stone. I didn't like having a barrier between us. But I had to keep going—the faster I grabbed the pearl, the faster I could return to him.

Darkness weighed down on me, casting gray outlines along the cavern walls. The passageways were eerily quiet. I swam through the shadows, my eyes adjusting. Mermaids slept safely in their caverns, their golden chains twinkling in the dim light. Soon, they would awaken to a new life and their own second chance. I dared not disturb them, just in case their mates lurked nearby.

Wiggling my fins, I swam down the tunnel, tasting the water to know which way to go. Above me pulsed with a purple glow from the crystals embedded in the ceiling, almost like a heartbeat, and I continued down the left path, following a flickering pattern. Entering the cavern, I inhaled in wonder, the floor and ceiling full of jagged amethyst crystals.

They shimmered like flames burning from the inside to emit colorful light on the rocky walls.

The largest crystals grew down from the ceiling, tangled in thick roots. White dots of clams hid beneath the sandy surface. I snatched a shell up, warm to the touch. As I went to open it, I hesitated at my claw-like nails, longer than when I had woken up this morning.

Ryken, I reminded myself and returned to my task.

Almost too easily, I wedged my nail into the seam of the clam and popped it open with a loud crack. The sour taste still haunted my mouth, and I tried not to think of the sickening flavor as I swam back to Ryken.

Eyes closed, he was still resting where I'd left him. I slipped the pearl between his lips, and his eyelashes fluttered.

I lifted him into my arms, holding him tight while I waited. This had to work.

Please wake up.

When his arms wrapped around me, I sagged into his chest with relief, listening to his heartbeat even out. His hands glided up my back, tangling in my hair.

Breathing in my scent, he whimpered.

Where are your clothes? he whispered through our connection.

Really? I batted his arm, holding back my tears. *Of all things, you want to ask me about my attire?*

I'm still not sure if this is a dream or a reality. If it's a dream, don't wake me up.

He nuzzled into my neck, the bubbles tickling my skin.

I pushed against his chest, almost forgetting what I was about to say.

His hands tightened. *Wait, you remember your past?*

Of course I do.

The tension eased out of his shoulders.

You didn't transform, I yelled at him. *Why?*

I was terrified for you and filled with too many emotions. I did what you said and focused on one at a time—getting you into the ocean. So I just . . . jumped. Once I was falling, sensations overwhelmed me again. It took everything to not let go of you. That part was important or you'd crash into the rocks. I'd do anything to keep you safe.

His lips pressed into the curve of my neck, kissing a trail around my collar, my insides melting. But I refused to be distracted and flicked my tail in anger.

This is serious, Ryken, I growled.

He pulled back, tilting his head at my furious reaction.

Don't you ever do that again. Do you hear me? Ever. I thought . . . I thought I had lost you. My face crumpled. The sickening ache returned at just the thought of his lifeless form. What would I have done without him? I truly understood what he meant when he said a mate could die of heartbreak.

I burrowed back into his embrace, never wanting to leave it again.

My Marigold, he said, *it would take more than that to separate us. Now let me see you.*

Leaning back from his chest, I peered up into his hooded eyes. Did my face look that different? His skin appeared so soft in contrast, his dark hair floating around him.

How odd that we had switched places. He as a human and I as a mermaid.

Not just your face. I mean all of you.

Oh.

Human propriety had me crossing my arms over my chest despite the fact that there wasn't anything to see. Silver scales crisscrossed from my hips and covered my chest in glittering emeralds. My skin was paler, grayish in tint but not as dramatically changed as I expected. My tail swished without a thought, keeping me steady as a school of neon fish zipped by.

Ryken tapped his lip with his finger, pondering my transformation as one would a new gown. And just before my insecurities could twist into a painful knot, he sent me a teasing wink.

I shot up through the water, my hands balling into fists at my side. My hair fanned out, still golden with the ends dipped in blue. I scowled at him, ready to give him a piece of my mind, when I realized what he had done.

I was no longer cowering, floating over him so he could get an eyeful of my new appearance. He grinned, kicking to reach for me.

My tail swung forward, and a bubbly current sent him tumbling backward, flipping him head over heels. When he caught his balance, he sent me a predatory look, his teal eyes narrowing into slits.

For once, I was the stronger of the two of us.

And I rather liked it.

I floated on my back, drifting away, and waved my fin like I was saying goodbye. A large, gloating smile had me wincing. The sharp tips of my teeth poked uncomfortably against my lower lip. I ran my fingers over it and checked for blood. But my skin was thicker there, too, and hadn't broken.

Using my distraction to his favor, Ryken plowed into me with enough speed that a surprised squeak erupted from me. We swirled underwater like a tornado, his arms looped around me. The silver of his tail and the way our colors blended together caught my eye.

It was like I was made for him.

We spun to a stop, my hair encircling us and cocooning our heads together. He had transformed when I wasn't looking, his broad shoulders more relaxed now that he was back to normal. Next to me, he was bigger, his tail a few feet longer than mine.

He snagged my wrists, lifting my arms away so he could study me. He spoke in his language, still gibberish to my ears.

I shrugged a shoulder.

When he reached for my fins, I slapped his hand away.

He growled, his arms wrapping around me so our chests were flush.

Why do you like torturing me? he barked through our connection.

It had become second nature to fight him, and I suddenly realized that there wasn't a reason to anymore. Ryken was my husband, after all.

I didn't mean to.

You're still skittish. It's understandable. He sighed. *You don't know what you're doing.*

Embarrassed, I ducked my head. *I'm sorry.*

Why are you sorry? You're doing all the right things, but I want you to be aware versus acting on instinct.

I am aware.

Are you? he asked, the corner of his mouth lifting. *Of me?*

His scent saturated the water. I breathed it in, tasting his attraction.

You are my husband. Why shouldn't I be?

A grin stretched across his face, delighted that I referred to him as that.

And what of you? You have so many names. What should I call you? Wife, mate, Marigold?

I pressed my hand on his heart. *How about 'my love'?*

He hummed in contentment, his tail curling around mine.

A high-pitched note echoed on the waves in the distance. I covered my ears, wincing at the frequency. Ryken shouted something in his language, something suspiciously close to a curse.

What is it? I asked when the noise stopped.

It's Orion. He's calling the Merfolk to gather. He frowned as his thumb caressed my cheek. *We must go when we are called. Even if we really, really don't want to go.*

We need to anyway. Ruah called me back for a reason.

He nodded, untangling us. *I know, I had just hoped for more time with you.*

Soon, I said. I grabbed his hand, linking our fingers. He made a face at the human gesture, so I added, *So we can swim together.*

Ryken perked up. *Let's see how fast you can go.*

It took me a minute to get my body into an easy rhythm, that up and down motion, before I was gliding through the water next to him. It came naturally to me, and soon I was swimming so fast the coral reefs around me blurred and the feeling of flying returned.

I flicked my tail, soaring past Ryken, and his hand became an anchor holding me in place. He squeezed my hand, his hair combed back from our speed, and he pointed with his other hand off to the left.

Nestled between the volcano rocks, the kingdom was a beauty hidden within the blackened wall. It shone with a calming light, an underwater castle made entirely of gold. Twisting spiral turrets pointed like arrows to the surface. Open holes led straight into the castle, with Merfolk coming from all directions to enter inside.

Ryken guided us through a larger opening, the inside made of gold as well. The sparkle caught my attention, the sapphire jewels lining the edges of the windows. Floors were made of black marble, glossy, similar to the marble I had seen at Windcrest.

The snails from the caverns crawled along the ceiling, illuminating each room in a soft glow. We stopped in an open room with golden columns and seashells decorating the walls.

Panting, a goofy grin split his face, and he shook his head, chuckling.

What? I mouthed.

You're fast, he mouthed back, his hand mimicking the swimming motion.

The hairs on the back of my neck tingled a warning. I turned in time to see another merman launching to attack Ryken from behind, a spear in his hand. There wasn't time to think as I dove over Ryken's shoulder, baring my teeth, knowing I had lost control. Nothing would stop me until the threat was eliminated.

The attacker's eyes widened just before I slammed into his chest. The loud wail that escaped my lips switched to my haunting melody, each note like a punch in the water rippling around me.

Then I felt it, like I had in the inn, the rope forming with my song. It was tangible enough that I wrapped it around the attacker, pulling it snug with a high note, and his body relaxed. His hands dropped to his side, his eyes clouding over. Somehow a connection between us had formed.

You will do as I command you, I said, my voice echoing even to myself.

I didn't break my stare, and neither did he. If he so much as moved a muscle, he would regret it.

Do not touch Ryken. I spoke into his mind, holding his gaze as I continued my song.

He nodded weakly.

A hand slapped over my mouth, and the water turned unnaturally quiet. Ryken's smell enveloped me in a hug, the only reason I didn't bite through the muzzle. *Release Egon,* Ryken asked. *He means us no harm.*

I blinked, breaking whatever spell I had over the other merman.

Egon shot back, fear in his eyes. He pointed his spear at me, shouting in clicks and hums.

You can't use your gifts for personal reasons, Marigold. Even for me. Only dark magic forces free will. It's like thick sludge, spreading within you the more you disobey, eventually decaying you from the inside out.

I—I didn't know...

He tilted my head up, holding my gaze with a deliberate intensity. *On land, they called us warriors of water, but actually we are peacekeepers. The Merfolk have taken an oath to never use our gifts for destruction*

404

or selfish purposes, only to protect our kind and defend Ruah's name. You must fight the temptation to control with your song.

I realized then that we were surrounded. Merfolk gaped at me, murmuring words I didn't understand. Ryken snapped back, pulling me close, his tail curling protectively around mine.

What are they saying? I asked.

They are upset with me, Ryken said after a moment. *A siren should have been offered to someone else besides a Collector.* He took a long breath, the water swishing through his gills. *I told them I would kill anyone that tried to take my mate from me.*

Orion parted the crowd, swimming through. As he spoke, a voice entered my thoughts, a calm reminder of why I was there.

Listen, my child. Tell them to follow you and set my people free.

Do you mean for me to tell Ryken to translate?

No, I mean you.

My eyebrows raised. *But how? I don't speak their language.*

You can't . . . but I can. Listen closely.

The external noises warped. The hums and clicks, all their sounds stretched into letters, words, and then phrases until I understood. It happened so quickly all the words collided together.

"She is the last of her kind and you didn't think to tell us? Why do you think you are the worthy one?" I caught the ending of Orion berating Ryken.

"I chose him," I blurted in their language, interrupting his tirade.

Ryken whipped me around, cupping my cheeks. "You understand us? Since when?"

"Just now," I said.

Orion's tail slashed through the water, doubtful. "This human girl has been nothing but trouble. Everything about her transformation has been abnormal. I do not trust her."

"She used her song against me," Egon accused.

"You attacked my mate," I growled back, straining against Ryken's hold to tear into him again.

Listen. The word repeated in my head like a command.

I closed my eyes, trying to calm my animalistic instincts. The gnawing need to argue and protect had forced my actions. The Merfolk wouldn't listen to someone that didn't have control of themselves.

I opened my eyes and turned to Orion.

"The discussion about who I belong to is irrelevant. Ryken is my mate and my husband. On land or on sea, we are one. Nothing can change that."

Murmurs broke out around us. Outraged that we had left the sea, confusion over the unfamiliar word *husband*, but the majority were shocked that we had returned from the surface and mysteriously survived.

I continued on, keeping my voice even. "Please continue to the reason you have called us here."

"The sea turtles carry a message. Chaos is spreading across the land. Ships are coming along the coast. We must double the protection of Alara and our people before more of us are taken."

Fear spread like a tidal wave among them.

"It's Windcrest, and they aren't coming here. They are preparing for battle against Cadell—where my sister and my family live."

"That life is long gone. This is your family now, here in Alara. Let the humans burn and destroy the gifts Ruah has given them. We will stay here and protect our own."

The Merfolk nodded in agreement.

"No, that's not what Ruah wants."

Orion circled me, crossing his arms. "And what does Ruah want?"

"For you to follow me. The Merfolk are being held captive, and we need to set them free."

"Captive?" Orion glanced at Ryken over my shoulder.

"All she said is true," Ryken added. "Listen to her."

High-pitched murmurs burst out from the crowd.

Orion waved his hands, silencing the Merfolk. "We will not listen to this outsider. Ryken's bond has clouded his judgment."

"I know her. Let me speak," a female voice rang out from the masses.

Liora swam out into the open, her jaw set.

"Speak your piece," Orion said.

"I wouldn't be alive if it weren't for her. She saved me from imprisonment. The humans listened to her, and one even helped me escape. I owe her my life and gratitude. I will follow her to the end of the seas."

She swam up to me, the seashells in her hair tapping together. Hand up, she offered her palm to me—a gesture of trust.

"Thank you," I said.

I placed my palm on hers, and a smile lit her face.

"I trust Ryken. If he says follow her, then I will too," a silver-tailed merman said. He was one of the mermen from Ryken's ceremony.

He nodded in my direction.

"Me too," another silver-tailed merman added.

The two mermen sent a blistering stare at the last Collector, Egon . . . the one I had attacked.

Egon made a face, but he mumbled, "I place my trust in Ryken. I will follow the siren."

Echoes of agreements sounded, one after another. Strangers I had never met before were agreeing to trust and follow me. I pressed a hand over my heart, in awe of their acceptance. They didn't even know where they would go but trusted me all the same.

Just as Ruah planned.

Orion's eyes flicked to Ryken like he wanted to continue the argument, but he settled on a nod. "Congratulations, it seems you have won the vote."

"No, Marigold won it." Ryken squeezed my shoulder.

Orion asked, "All right, siren. Where do you want us to follow you?"

More eyes than I could count landed on me. I straightened my back, my tail flicking nervously.

"To war."

The Unexpected

The tartness from the Merfolk's shock rippled across the water.

Orion waved a hand, silencing the surrounding murmurs. "You are mistaken about our purpose, siren. We are made for peace—not war."

"They have taken your own people—Ruah's people. We must bring them back, as you said, and protect our people."

The Merfolk hummed in agreement.

"Windcrest is forcing them to use their gifts in order to benefit their kingdom."

Orion jerked, swimming upward in surprise. "They are forcing them to fight?" His tail thrashed angrily.

"Yes," Ryken growled.

Tell them it is my command. They need to go now. Ruah's voice echoed into my thoughts, sending a chill down my spine.

"We must go now," I shouted.

"Now?" Ryken asked from my side. "I thought we——"

"Ruah said now," I said.

"Then we leave now," Orion agreed. "Come. Gather your weapons and meet at the edge of Seahorse Grove." He turned to me before he swam off. "All this rests on your shoulders. Do not let your emotions dictate your actions. Leave your ties to humanity where they belong—in the past."

"My ties are what make me stronger. I fight for them."

"Then you'll send us to our deaths."

"We aren't in this battle alone. Ruah will be there too."

"Then I put my faith in Ruah. You have yet to prove yourself to me." Orion nodded farewell, swimming off into another part of the castle.

"Ignore him," Ryken said. "He prefers to be the one in control."

"Don't we all . . ."

He gave me a soft smile. "I trust you."

I smiled back, my stomach fluttering. "Thank you."

"Hello," a voice said over my shoulder. A silver-tailed merman studied me as I turned, narrowing in on my face. "It's nice to finally meet you."

He was handsome, as most of the Merfolk were, but not even close to my Ryken. His brown hair still had the jagged cuts from the ceremony, giving him a wild look.

When he swam closer, Ryken let out a low warning growl.

"I'm not going to take her. I just want to see her. We've only heard about her nonstop for an entire year."

Wide-eyed, I glanced at Ryken.

"He's exaggerating," Ryken said, his tail flicking quickly.

"No, he's not." The other silver-tailed merman swam up, a jagged scar across his chest. "I'm Pike and this is Jayco. You've met Egon already."

Egon huffed in annoyance off to the side.

"Don't listen to the crab. He's sore you bested him without a weapon," Pike said, smiling.

"She used her song—it wasn't fair. I demand a rematch," Egon said, swimming upward.

"She has nothing to prove to you," Ryken said, swimming in front of me.

"I never thought I'd see my colors on a mermaid's tail," Jayco whispered in awe.

The dreamy quality of his tone unnerved me, and I spun sideways as he moved closer.

I didn't need to say anything. As usual, Ryken sensed the swing in my mood and whipped around with a menacing growl. "*Jayco.*"

Transfixed on my tail, the merman sniffed the water. His eyebrows shot up, and his turquoise eyes dilated. "The bond is still incomplete."

I flicked my tail hoping to distance myself, but instead I escalated the situation, my glittering scales drawing him closer.

Frustration rippled out of Ryken in a murderous roar. He shot forward, his hand gripping Jayco's throat, his fingers squeezing his gills.

"She is claimed, and we will complete the mating bond when we are ready." His voice was as sharp as a knife. "Collector or not, I will remove your head from your body if you so much as lay a finger on her. Understand?"

Bug-eyed, Jayco nodded, his mouth opening and closing, unable to get a word out.

Ryken threw him a few feet and swam back to my side as if that settled the matter. His tail curled around mine as he circled me, winding us together. He stopped in front of me with a huff.

"Did he hurt you?" he asked, holding my hand to his chest.

"No, he didn't touch me."

His eyes drifted shut. "Good."

"I thought I smelled like you."

Ryken brushed my hair from my face. "Not enough, but you will soon. Until then, I have to let them know there are consequences should they try to claim you for themselves."

"Aren't they your friends? Why would they take your wife?"

"They don't know that word. We've gone so long thinking we'd never have a mate that when one is close at hand, well, it's hard to resist." He closed the distance between us, pressing his lips on mine. Before I could sink in and enjoy it, he pulled back with a smirk. "Now look at them."

The three Collectors watched us with horrified expressions.

"They don't know what kissing is, do they?" I asked, chuckling.

"No, and I'm sure they think there is something wrong with me and I tried to eat you."

"I don't care what they think. You can kiss me whenever you want."

"Whenever?" His eyes twinkled. "I will remember that."

I cupped his cheek. "I was hoping you would."

"My heart," Ryken whispered, "are you sure we don't have one day to relax? We have to leave now?"

"Ruah's command, not mine."

He nodded, his brow furrowing.

"Alice?"

I turned, surprised at the name. "What——?"

Jayco approached with his head bowed and eyes averted. "I wanted to apologize."

"Alice?" I repeated.

"This is Marigold," Ryken corrected.

"Why are they calling me that?" Did an Alice actually exist? I bared my teeth, demanding an answer.

"Calm down," Ryken rushed to say. "I can see you trying to figure it out. Most mermaids wake up having forgotten their past. Their mate names them. I had selected Alice for you . . . but you didn't need it. You never forgot."

"Marigold," Egon said. "I've never heard that word before."

"It's a flower that grows on land. Sometimes it comes in the color of my hair."

Pike reached out a hand to touch a floating strand. "It looks soft."

Ryken growled and narrowed his eyes. "No. Touching."

The water hummed, the current's temperature dipping into frigid levels. It called to me like a song, beckoning me to follow.

This way, my child.

"We need to leave now," I whispered.

I didn't wait for anyone's response before diving off into the cool current. I knew my mate would be close behind, so I pushed myself, swimming until I felt free, soaring through the water.

"Too fast, Marigold," Ryken called out, panicked.

"I got her," Pike reassured him as he matched my speed. "Sirens are too fast for merman—me being the exception. Go as fast as you want. I'll protect you until the others catch up to us."

"Really?" I said. "Ryken doesn't like me to be too far away."

"It's good for him. He has to trust others around you, or he might not leave you in battle."

"But what about . . . before?"

411

"We didn't know you were unmarked. I promise not to touch you. Now go, follow the current's call."

So I did. Arms at my sides, I glided through the water like an arrow, my fins pushing me faster and faster. Colors swirled around me, and dots of silverfish scurried out of my way. It was peaceful and exhilarating at the same time.

Pike was true to his word and stayed at my side but not close enough to touch me. He grinned and, at one point, closed his eyes in pure bliss.

"Marigold," Ryken shouted, stopping in a rush of bubbles inches in front of me. "You left me."

"I felt Ruah calling. I had to follow," I reasoned.

Jayco and Egon swam up behind him. "See? She's fine. Pike had her."

Ryken's jaw ticked, not liking that statement at all.

"Remember what you told my sister? I am not weak."

"She bested Egon," Jayco reminded him.

"Could we stop bringing that up?" Egon grumbled, crossing his arms. "It was an unfair match."

I placed Ryken's hand on my collar and spoke privately. *You said you trusted me.*

He glanced down then back up, then leaned in to place his forehead on mine. *I do.*

"The current is pulling us to the right, close to land," I said. "I think we should keep following it."

"But we have to meet everyone at Seahorse Grove," Pike said. "We need to go the other way."

"I can track her with our bond," Ryken said, holding my gaze. "I will bring the others to her."

"Split up?" Jayco asked. "Do you want one of us to stay with her?"

"Not you," Ryken said, narrowing his eyes. "You."

Ryken pointed to Egon's shocked face.

"Me? I don't know if I even like her."

"That's what makes you the perfect choice."

Egon's lips curled in distaste. "Don't be long."

"Oh, I won't," Ryken said. Swimming closer, he brushed the hair floating in front of my face. He breathed in my scent, holding it for a beat before expelling it. "I'll find you."

"I know."

Ryken glanced one more time over his shoulder and frowned, then swam off with Pike and Jayco flanking him. Egon jutted his chin at me, the front of his hair longer on the left than the right.

"Lead the way, siren," he said sarcastically. "It's not like I have a say in the matter."

"You don't have to stay with me."

He made a choking, gurgling noise. "And lose the only siren we've had in a century? I'm staying by your side, so keep a realistic pace for us slow swimmers."

I dove back into the current, forcing myself not to ride it at my maximum speed like my instincts begged. A few times I caught myself pulling ahead and had to slow down to let Egon catch up. He squinted at me, probably not enjoying that I was faster than him.

The seabed met us as we continued closer to shore. When I snapped my fin to rise to the surface, Egon screamed, jerking me back under.

"What are you doing?" he scolded.

"I'm checking to see where we are." I shook him off.

"You aren't human anymore. If we fight, it will have to be underwater."

"I understand. But I need to see what's going on. You stay down here if you are scared."

He growled, his teeth mashing together. "I'm not scared."

I made a high-pitched noise in disbelief, then swam to the surface, smirking when Egon stayed by my side. Where I broke through the surface with a splash, though, he stealthily rose to eye level, scanning for danger.

Trees lined a clearing, what I'd guess to be the edge of Mistbrooke Forest. Its mysterious fog rolled between the tree trunks. About a mile north, the trees ended at the sandy shore, the border of Windcrest and Mistbrooke. Where Rose had said to meet.

I was three days early, but Ruah insisted I move quickly. For what? There was no one here.

Egon had his entire head out of the water when I turned to him. "We need to make it to the clearing."

I swam across the surface, no boats in the distance or people within view. The closer I drifted to shore, the more flustered Egon became.

413

"Aren't you a Collector? You've gone on land before."

"I don't remember it—and I'd like to keep it that way. Humans are . . ." He swallowed the rest of his sentence like it tasted bitter.

"We are what?"

"You're not human."

"You could transform if you wanted to," I said.

"What? That's insanity."

I laughed. "Ryken did it."

"He'd do anything for his mate. You're not worth leaving the sea for."

"Well, I could go and see if there is anyone around."

His hand shot out like a snake, curling around my forearm. "No."

Goodness, this would be a lot easier if Ryken had stayed with me.

"And don't even try to sing me into submission. We wait here where it is safe." Suddenly, his entire body went stiff, and he pulled me under until we were practically flat on the seabed. "There was a man."

"Where?" I went to swim up, but he squeezed tighter.

"In the tall green things."

My spirits soared. "From the forest? Oh, he's one of us."

Still, Egon didn't release me.

"Let go. I need to see him. It will only take a second."

"Why did they leave me with you?" Egon grumbled as I wiggled free.

"One man can't possibly cause any trouble," I coaxed, swimming higher to the sunlight. "Come on."

He grumbled but still followed me above water.

A lone man stood motionless, eyeing the sandy stretch of land in front of him. He leaned heavily on his cane, his mannerisms familiar as he walked.

Wait. That's the old man from my wedding.

I whistled a long note that echoed among the rocks and trees.

Egon pulled me back underwater, his scowling face inches from mine. "Are you trying to kill us?"

"I know him," I shouted. I slammed my tail into his side, gaining enough space to swim as fast as I could to the shoreline.

I surfaced just before the tumbling waves, knowing the rip current would be too strong if I went much closer.

The old man, Zarek, stumbled at the sight of me.

414

"Marigold, is that you?"

"It is. I've come to tell you——" At his pursed lips, I realized I was still speaking in hums and clicks. I started again, barely getting a few words out before Egon wrapped his arms around my torso to drag me back underwater.

"No talking to humans," he said in a frenzy. "We'll stay down here until Ryken gets back."

"You are being ridiculous. It's an old man with a cane. He's not going to hurt a fly."

He tilted his head in confusion.

"Uh, he's not going to hurt a . . . seahorse."

"I'm not taking any chances."

"Egon, not all humans are terrible."

His tail whipped back and forth.

"Ryken would let me do it—and you trust him, right?"

Crossing his arms, he glared are me, unmoved by my plea.

"Allow me to prove you can trust me too."

He huffed, his hair ruffling over his brow. "You have one minute to say what you need to say."

"I'll take it."

I broke through the water again, surprised to find Zarek in the surf.

"There you are," he said, sighing. "Everyone is worried sick about you."

"I'm all right. I want you to pass a word to my sister. The Merfolk are coming."

"Oh, that is good news. Are they here now?"

I shook my head. "Ryken is bringing them."

"Then who's that?" He pointed with his cane over my shoulder.

Egon hissed.

"My babysitter, and he's not liking it one bit."

Suppressing a smile, Zarek leaned heavily on his staff. "We don't always get the duties or responsibilities we think we've earned. But whatever Ruah has planned will be even better."

"I hope there is a plan for this battle. Where is everyone?"

"They returned to the castle to gather their soldiers. I came here to keep them from entering the forest."

"You?" I tried not to laugh.

415

"I've lost some of my strength this last year, but there is still enough in me to do some damage. Besides, the trees said they'd help, so I'm not alone."

These trees could do more than the impossible. Their bony limbs stretched out like a fence around the forest, barring anyone who dared to enter.

The sound of horses thudded in the distance, the pebbles on the beach shaking and rattling with the shells. Horses and soldiers clad in navy galloped toward the forest.

"Excuse me a moment," Zarek said, bowing slightly.

"What is he doing?" Egon asked.

"I don't know, but it makes no sense why they left him by himself."

We dipped lower in the water, watching Windcrest's army arrive. King Galon was a sight, his golden crown resting on his white hair, each point adorned in sapphire. It matched his golden armor, looking more appropriate for a banquet than for battle. The horses fell into a line and marched in step behind the king.

Prince Vox, sitting atop a white stallion, wore a similar golden armor. Behind him was a girl, dirty and unkempt. Her arms were bound, the rope wrapped around the prince's hand.

Who was she? Was she someone important to Cadell?

Did they hope to trade her?

I tried to swim closer to see her face, see if I could recognize her, but Egon held fast.

"We should go," Egon whispered. "Something doesn't smell right."

The prince cantered forward, moving past the king.

"You are not welcome here," Zarek called out. "You can avoid bloodshed today by returning to Windcrest."

The horse trotted in a circle, not wanting to stop.

"We have a gift for the queen," Prince Vox sneered.

I tensed, my fingers curling into claws, itching to wrap around his royal neck.

He dismounted, an odd strategic move, to pull at the rope. The girl tumbled off her horse, flopping into his arms like dead weight. He set her on her feet, her black gown torn to knee length, revealing open slices down her legs. The prince ripped the rope from her wrists and discarded it in the sand.

"Walk," Prince Vox barked at her.

And she limped three steps, her face void of emotion. Ebony hair hung in knotted clumps down her back, crusted with an unknown substance. She eyed the old man cooly before lifting her hands above her head, displaying a black marking on her wrist.

"That's close enough," Zarek called out. He held up a hand, his fingers trembling. "I don't want to hurt you."

In one quick motion, her hands dropped, the air around her shifting, changing until it was no longer the woman but an old man with a bored expression and elongated jowls.

An exact replica of Zarek.

"Take the old man and put Tifa in his place," King Galon commanded.

I jerked back into Egon's chest. This time it was me yanking him underwater.

"What? What is it?"

"She can glamour—change the appearance of things and summon illusions."

Lightning cracked in the distance, an ominous sound that rattled my bones. Windcrest had more up their sleeve than we realized.

Shape Up

Glamour magic disappeared when Bressal was vanquished in the Battle of the Bones. I should have known that if the tales of the Merfolk were true, then so were warnings of Illusionists in the misty bogs in the east. Their power to alter physical appearances and their surroundings was considered the vilest of magic because it was mental manipulation. Magic should never affect free will.

So how did this woman exist? And were there more like her?

Egon pushed me away, distancing himself. "She changed herself? Why?"

"It's a trap."

Another rumble of thunder sounded, followed by a flash of lightning. It blinded me to the point I saw spots. Egon cried out, shielding his face.

Then the storm was gone.

Water gurgled, a peaceful sound of the waves drifting closer to shore.

Zarek. I panicked.

Egon was still rubbing his eyes as I darted back up to the surface, peeking over the foamy crests to scan the shoreline. If Zarek needed me, what could I do? I didn't have any legs.

I was too late. Prince Vox stood a few feet away, his sword aimed at Zarek's head.

A cry erupted from me, a beacon that rippled out across the ocean to signal for help. An ability I had no idea I had.

Zarek rolled his head to the side, meeting my gaze.

My fear for him stirred me forward. Maybe I could distract the prince and give the old man a chance to escape.

Sand and coral scraped against my scales as I entered the shallower water. The waves crashed into my back, trying to drag me back underwater to safety.

The prince strutted forward, laughing with each step. "Look at you —you can barely stand. What kind of queen would send a frail man against an army? A murderer. Already she's sacrificing the innocent. Your loyalty is ill-placed, Enchanter. You were the sacrificial goat."

"Appearances can deceive, boy," the old man said, hate dripping from his words. "Do not speak of my queen that way."

"When I kill her, I will pass along your undying devotion."

My scream was off pitch, more of a screech that was painful even to myself. Multiple Windcrest soldiers hunkered down, covering their ears.

At the same moment, Zarek reached out, and lightning extended from his fingers like a battering ram, slamming into the prince's chest with enough force he flipped Prince Vox backward. Light gleamed off the prince's golden armor with each somersault as he rolled past the fake Zarek who didn't spare him a fleeting glance. Eventually, he stopped on his back. A charred mark of spiderwebs marred the armor's pristine surface.

Fake Zarek met my eyes across the sandy dunes. Her eyes widened and her lips parted in surprise—almost as if she had never seen a mermaid before.

I hissed, showing my teeth as a warning.

"First wave," the king bellowed from on top of his horse, not showing an ounce of concern over his eldest's unconscious body, "take no prisoners."

It was an unfair match. Fifty soldiers with swords drawn to one old man who could barely stand without a cane. But what could I do here in the ocean? I fought the water, clawing at the air angrily.

Zarek grinned, catching me by surprise, his lips turning an icy blue.

His body illuminated with energy, his skin blinding white and pulsing with neon veins. The air around him crackled with static.

His voice rose, a battle cry loud enough to be heard for miles. "For Mistbrooke. For Cadell. In Ruah's name." Then he charged, running without his cane and heading straight for the king. Any soldier he touched seized from the electric current and slumped instantly to their knees.

Piles of soldiers dropped in Zarek's wake, his amber eyes so determined and locked on his target he didn't see the arrow that pierced his shoulder. It didn't even slow him. Neither did the second arrow in his thigh.

When the third plunged into his heart, he stumbled to a stop, teetering in place.

"Ruah?" he whispered through bloodied lips. "I . . . hear you now."

Sick to my stomach, I dove below the surface and swallowed my screams of anguish. Was I truly meant for war? I had no training . . . no strength. Doubt plagued my thoughts, my tail drooping as I sunk lower to where Egon kept watch.

One look at me and he was by my side, unsure what to do. He reached out a hand and then snatched it back, confused. "What happened? You're . . . sad. Did we lose?"

"The old man is gone." *Zarek.* I didn't even know him, but my heart still ached at the loss of an innocent Enchanter. He fought for my sister and for Ruah with more courage than I had in my entire body.

I felt small and useless in comparison.

"What do you want me to do? You smell salty."

"I want Ryken," I whimpered. I wanted someone to hold me. To protect me.

"He's not here, so you have me. If the battle isn't over, then *shape up*." He snapped the last part, my tail stiffening. "You don't give up until your last breath. Do you understand? Merfolk are not quitters. You are blessed by Ruah. I may not be the fastest or strongest, but I'm clever. Rely on your strengths, and Ruah will provide the rest."

I nodded.

"And fix your face. The Merfolk will look to you for encouragement, and if you appear defeated, then they will give up too."

I forced a smile.

420

"Better. No more whining."

Maybe Egon was exactly what I needed after all.

Periodically, I covertly scanned the shoreline. The moon was high in the sky, the starlight twinkling along the water's reflection. In the few hours that passed, tents were erected and bonfires danced skyward, leaving a smoky trail to the clouds.

Fake Zarek had not informed the others of my arrival. She hadn't forgotten about me either. Her face turned toward the ocean breeze. Hands tied on her lap, she made it look like Zarek was a prisoner in enemy territory.

A molten rage sizzled in my blood at the cruelness of her still wearing his face after what they did to him. His body and the soldiers' bodies were dragged from the beach. The only evidence left were the footprints in the sand.

Egon tapped my hand, reminding me I hit my time limit, and we swam down to the seabed to wait for the others. He ate, tearing through a sunrise perch, scales and all, munching noisily as tiny morsels floated around him. He stopped when he caught me staring and offered me his fish.

My stomach churned, still not ready for food. I shook my head, letting him continue with his meal.

I missed the luxury of sleep, being able to close my eyes and fast forward the world to the time I wanted. Instead of having to be patient and wait.

I sighed.

Egon flashed me an annoyed look.

When I heard Ryken's call on the water, my heart sputtered, beating double time in my chest. *He's back.*

I echoed the call, a note that dropped an octave. As soon as I heard him again, I shot off.

"Marigold——" Egon cried, but I was already gone.

Swimming full speed, I didn't slow, not even when I saw him break from the pack of hundreds of Merfolk.

He caught me around the waist, chuckling at my enthusiasm. My momentum had us spinning, my tail wrapping around him, and I held on tight in desperation. When I was silent, tucked snug under his chin, his scent turned worrisome. He tipped my head up, sniffing me.

"What is wrong?" he asked.

"Zarek is gone."

"The man who married us? Where did he go? Back to Cadell?"

"No . . . he's dead."

"Oh," he whispered into my hair. "You can stay here as long as you want."

"No, Egon was right." I pulled back to Ryken's frown. "He said I need to shape up. I asked your people——"

"Your people now too," he added.

"Yes, I asked them to follow me. I have to be brave, even when I don't feel it."

"You are brave. Pre-battle nerves get even the most seasoned warrior. And, so you know, Egon has told me to shape up a few times too."

I smiled. "I missed you."

He pulled me back to him, cradling me like he never wanted to let go. "Stay with me. I want every last second with you before I have to put my armor on." So we stayed, whispering to one another promises of the future we hoped to have.

Though I drew the line at twenty younglings.

Maybe three.

Later.

When we were both ready for the next stage in our life. Right now, I just wanted to survive.

It wasn't long before the current tugged at my fins again, demanding we return to the shore. Egon wasn't pleased to see me and hissed at me as a greeting.

"You left," he accused.

"To see Ryken."

"There are others here besides him. You must protect everyone, not just your mate. I was unguarded and alone."

Ryken growled, not appreciating Egon's tone.

I placed a hand on Ryken's shoulder, shaking my head. "Let me do this." I swam over to Egon. "I'm sorry. You're right. I should have waited and kept to my post. I care about you and all the Merfolk here. I'll do a better job proving it."

He sighed. "It's the bond. I've heard it's strong."

"Still. I promise to be more careful."

"Good. And I promise to be . . . more understanding. Truce?"

"Truce," I agreed.

Sometime in the early hours, our lookout swam down, reporting movement from the forest. I flicked my tail, rising to the surface with the Merfolk following my lead.

Two men in flowing beige robes stepped out from the forest, their hands tucked into their oversized sleeves. Not here to fight, the Chronicle Weavers had taken a sacred oath of truth and silence until death, dedicating their lives to documenting historical events between the kingdoms. A violet rope looped around their waists, a reminder they were neutral parties there for observation. It was a rare sight, signifying the importance of this occasion as they preferred to blend into the background, unable to alter the events of history.

They nodded solemnly at each other, then veered off in two different directions. The balding man shuffled closer to the sea, his steps heavy with fatigue. His eyebrow twitched when he saw me. I sank lower in the water, uncomfortable at his scrutiny, and hoped that he wouldn't draw any attention to my whereabouts.

Or add me to their tapestries.

When the battle ended and the Chronicle Weavers returned to Cadell, they would weave today's events into detailed tapestries so that future generations would remember.

I blew out a breath, the bubbles drifting to the surface.

I hoped it was Rose's victory they stitched.

Not long after their arrival, the trees shook, the leaves hissing as they twisted, peeling their limbs back to form an opening. Cedrick and Rose strolled out arm in arm, leading their people from the woods.

Matching crowns adorned their heads, their clothes a mix of red and green.

I sputtered in the water, surprised to see that my sister wore men's clothing—pants and a tunic over her large stomach. If only Mother could see her now.

They stopped. Cedrick raised his hand in a gesture of peace.

King Galon crossed his arms, refusing the meeting.

Cedrick tried again, yelling across the beach, "The queen is to remain unharmed as she is carrying a child."

"All is fair in war, little king. Don't bring your treasures if you don't want them stolen."

Cedrick turned to Rose, whispering harshly as she shook her head. Perhaps she was the only person more stubborn than me.

Prince Vian walked out, and the enemy line booed and hissed verbal barbs. His jaw tightened, resolute in his decision to stay and fight on our side.

More Enchanters and guards poured out from Mistbrooke armed with swords, others juggling sparks of fire. Men and women of varying ages stood shoulder to shoulder, waiting for the signal.

What was the signal? How would we know when to start?

A horn blew from the north, and the Windcrest soldiers hooted in excitement.

Not one ship. Or three. But ten ships sailed with a navy banner whipping in the ocean wind. These weren't quaint fishing boats from the docks but a fleet of warships. Large vessels, they easily transported over a hundred men per ship.

Ryken growled at the sight of them approaching. The other Merfolk joined in and snapped their jaws, ready to attack. Some dunked under, swimming with pent-up fury.

"What?" I asked.

"We hate ships," Ryken explained. "They come to attack our people and take our possessions. We will enjoy ripping the wood apart plank by plank." His tail curled protectively around me.

"See the windows?" I pointed. "They have cannons. Stay to the front and underneath."

Ryken nodded, passing on my instructions.

My stomach dropped when fake Zarek stood on shaking legs and sagged to her knees in defeat.

But I knew the truth.

I whistled, hundreds of heads spinning my way. Immediately I wanted to hide from the attention, but this time, I couldn't.

"Marigold," my sister cried, jogging to the tide.

Whispers spread down the lines in both kingdoms. Confusion over our arrival. Yes, the Merfolk were here, but were they friend or foe?

Rose stopped ankle-deep, cautiously waiting. She placed a protective hand over her stomach.

424

I swam closer, keeping my head above the water. "Rosey."

At her name, she ventured deeper into the waves, reaching out a hand until our fingers touched. "Thank goodness you're all right. And Ryken?" She glanced over my shoulder and sighed in relief.

"That's not Zarek," I blurted before we were interrupted.

Rose blinked.

"It looks like him, but it's a woman. She's an Illusionist."

"What?" Rose spun around, doubt in her eyes. "But they don't exist."

"They killed Zarek," I choked out.

Her green eyes flicked to mine. "No. I refuse to believe you."

"They are trying to trick you. Egon saw it too."

He clicked in agreement behind me.

"I . . . have to go tell Cedrick."

"Don't trust them," I said to her retreating back.

Fake Zarek shrugged off her ropes, scowling at me. No longer struggling, she rose to her feet and lifted her hands to the sky. But the air didn't shift. Instead it darkened, like a blanket covering our eyes.

It was pitch black. A void that weighed on me, pressed into my chest like I suddenly couldn't breathe.

Then the screams started.

I Am With You

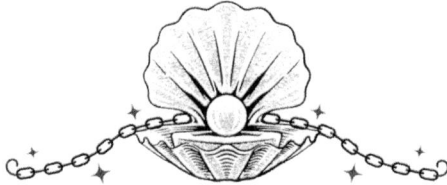

Chaos broke out on land. Voices shouted over top of each other. Metal clanked against metal. Smoke rode on the wind, a fire burning nearby.

I cringed, the screams amplified because of my heightened senses. I wanted to sink below the surface to drown them out.

A voice sounded in the distance. Not words, but a song. The notes trembled with fear before they cut off abruptly.

Rose.

Before I could panic, I felt Ryken's presence behind me, the water rippling. Breathing my scent, he sought me out until he brushed my spine, his hand softening at the contact. He wrapped an arm around my waist, pulling me into his chest.

I'm here, he whispered through our connection.

As much as I wanted to curl into him and hide, courage filled me, jolting me away from him.

"Marigold," Ryken said, startled at my rejection.

"Let me do what I'm supposed to do. What I was designed for," I declared. I swam through the darkness using my other senses. The heat of the sun still burned my face despite the void I swam in. Echoes helped me pinpoint my distance from land, and I followed the cool rush of the current up the shoreline.

My vision was made for the depths, and yet I was blind.

An illusion . . . I reminded myself. That's all the girl, Tifa, could do. *It isn't real.*

My heart thudded in my chest, Tzedek's message flooding my thoughts. *The darkness is coming, and it's time for you to sing.*

Sing. I had to sing.

But what? I had to trust that Ruah knew.

I'm ready.

I am with you. Ruah's voice filled my soul, replacing the darkness with light . . . and song. The notes were suddenly not in me, but were me, my voice ringing through the water like ancient magic. The water swirled—listening, obeying. A large wave lifted me up, the wind rushing across my face the higher we ascended.

The rope of my song fell into my hand, solid and stronger than before. I turned my thoughts on Tifa, remembering the battered girl underneath the façade. I sang to her, calling her with each note.

Listen to me . . . Follow my voice . . .

The darkness cracked, random beams of sunlight filtering through the nothingness. It was enough that I saw her, the real her, even through her disguise. Her hurt, her pain, her loneliness . . . the emptiness where her heart should be.

Come to me . . .

She swayed, her illusion dropping like a cloak onto the ground. In a trance, she turned, stepping behind the archers, her eyes still holding mine.

Other sounds faded until it was just my song. Long, beautiful notes hung in the air. Her head craned back, staring at me on top of the crest of the wave.

Bring back the light . . .

Blinding me, the daylight returned, and I stumbled over my song. The wave crashed down, bringing me with it into a foam of bubbles.

I resurfaced, scanning for my sister. Windcrest soldiers had gained the upper hand, attacking Mistbrooke and Cadell when they were unable to defend themselves.

Cedrick rushed out, his arms covered in scarlet flames, and erected a protective wall around his kingdoms.

Rose rushed to his side, thankfully safe and unharmed.

"Get out of here, Red," Cedrick called out, his face lit by his flames.

"I'm not leaving you. We are stronger together." Rose held up her hand, a small ball of flame dancing on her fingertips, the end tipping toward Cedrick.

Cedrick's eyes flashed molten amber, and the wall of fire rippled then spread, pushing the Windcrest troops into a retreat.

"Keep fighting," King Galon said, rallying. "Archers, in position."

"Ean, take her back to safety," Cedrick ordered. Sweat beaded his brow, his arms trembling to keep up the length of his wall. Arrows flew through the fire, burning to ashes.

Ean dashed from the sidelines, practically dragging my sister toward the woods. She pushed a finger into his chest, screaming at him. The trees barricaded her in, smacking away arrows that flew too close.

A yellow bird flew from a treetop, cawing angrily and attacking an archer who had Rose in his line of sight.

Orion called my name, pointing at the ships setting anchor. I nodded, letting them do what they always do and rip the wood apart plank by plank.

Ryken and the other Collectors stayed behind. A whirlpool formed around each silver-tailed merman, the light of the armor covering them from head to toe.

Blank eyes turned from me and then to the king of Mistbrooke. They marched through the water. White light hummed through their circlets, the scallop shells pulsing.

"Good luck," I whispered as they passed.

Tzedek frowned at me. "No luck needed, siren. Ruah is with us. We will take the marked ones." He pulled his weapon from the water, the clear sword swishing. They stalked across the sandy beach and entered the fray with a deadly purpose.

An arrow ripped through my left side, dangerously close to my heart. Stunned, I realized I was paying attention to everyone else and not protecting myself.

"Marigold," Prince Vian called out.

I slipped down under the surface, the water turning red and metallic. The salt stung the wound. Holding it closed, I swam toward the woods, surfacing to see Prince Vian pivot from where I had been and sprint to where I appeared.

"Marigold," he cried again, kicking up the surf as he ran through the tide.

"Prince Vian?" Why was he over here chatting with me when the battle was underway across the beach?

"Enough with the Prince. I told you—it's just Vian." His eyes dipped to the red trickling down my side. "You're injured."

He turned, standing in front of me, his sword in hand.

"I don't need your protection," I said.

"Where is your merman?" he asked and swung his short sword to knock an arrow away.

"Fighting—as you should be."

"I'm better served here. They don't trust me—despite me fighting next to them."

Shots fired from one of the ships, taking out a handful of Cadell soldiers. The ship sailed closer, the other four behind it. The Merfolk had already sunk half their fleet.

A horn sounded, and over the large sand dune sat Princess Emilia clad in all black, her hair in a high bun encircled in braids. Kohl smudges painted her lids and under her eyes, smoky and dangerous, not the same meek girl I had left. She carried a quiver of arrows and a bow strapped to her saddle.

"Emilia," Prince Vox cried out. He laughed deliriously. "Well done, wife."

A line of warriors flanked her, wearing the same black colors. The last to arrive held up their banner, black and gold, the symbol of the mountain and their homeland.

Glenton had arrived.

Princess Emilia's eyes slid in her husband's direction with disdain. With a sniff, she disregarded him and moved down the dunes, hundreds of giants marching behind her. Their faces were marked in kohl, intimidating by their size alone, not to mention the quantity of them charging over the hill.

"Windcrest has us outnumbered," I said as more Glenton soldiers fell into rank. "My people can't do anything from the sea."

"They aren't here for Windcrest," Prince Vian said. He smirked, cracking his lip. "I asked them to come."

"You?" I turned to face him.

429

His eyes held mine. "I'm smarter than everyone believes." He turned to his sister-in-law. "And she's braver than she lets on. Secrets are the currency, or have you forgotten?"

He whistled, drawing Emilia's attention. She found him in the surf, her brows lifting as her eyes met mine. She angled her head, a picture of grace and power. Her brothers stepped from the line, twice the size of normal men. The royals were known as the giants of Glenton. They said the crown of their kingdom rested on the strongest head.

I absolutely believed it.

They wielded their swords, slicing people as they pushed through the enemy line from the east.

Prince Vox's gloating grin dripped from his face after the first Windcrest soldier was run through. He scowled at his wife, who sent him a dainty wave before she rolled her eyes and unstrapped her bow.

With rapid succession, she shot two arrows one after another, her aim impressive . . . and frighteningly accurate.

The cannons fired again, knocking out a handful of Enchanters. The trees retaliated, lifting rocks and pelting them at incoming attackers who approached Rose.

My sister's song filled the air, different from mine but still coated with magic. A howl sounded from the woods, loud enough to hear over the battle noise. Birds shot from the trees, and even seagulls from the ocean came to her aid.

A white wolf prowled out of the woods with a snarl, snapping at Ean who was too close to my sister.

It seemed like Rose didn't need my help after all.

"I could do more if I was on the ships. Aim the cannon fire on them. We could flank Windcrest from the side," the prince said, flinching at another cannon blast.

"I'll take you," I said. I grabbed his red tunic in my claws, pulling him toward the sea. "You have to trust me."

"I do," he said without hesitation.

Six ships were still left, the others in pieces floating on the water.

"We can't climb the anchors, but you can with your legs. We'll have to swim under the water—*what*?" I scowled at his dreamy expression and swished my tail.

"I thought it would be strange to see you like this. But you're still just as beautiful as before. Being a mermaid suits you."

"Focus." I patted his cheek. "This is important. Hold on to me, and when you need air, squeeze my hand and I'll bring you up."

He took my hand gently as if we were about to dance in the ballroom.

"Vian, hold on tight. I swim fast."

His lips trembled into a smile, his puckered scar stretching across his cheek. "I won't let go."

"Take a deep breath," I commanded.

His chest puffed out, and I yanked him below the surface. Another battle occurred beneath the sea. The Merfolk swam back and forth between the ships, attacking them one at a time.

As fast as I could, I dragged the prince behind me. We only stopped twice for him to breathe, and he nodded when he was ready to set off again. I took him to the closest ship and placed his hand on the iron chain.

"Do you want me to wait?" I asked.

He wiped a hand across his eyes, blinking the seawater away. "No, go fetch more men. Enchanters if you can. We need their magic."

I nodded, diving back in the water to tell the mermen of my task. They followed me back to the shore. A few brave Enchanters volunteered, allowing us to transport them across the sea to the ships.

The three boats that were left had metal casings on the bottoms, impenetrable to the mermen's claws and teeth. They rocked the first ship, pushing it back and forth. Before it tipped over, the metal slide opened, releasing the missing Merfolk into the ocean. Then the rest of the ships opened, and swarms of Merfolk poured into the water around us.

What should have been a happy reunion became a bloodbath.

We Choose Our Own Paths

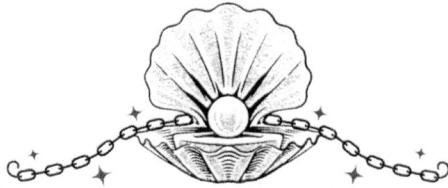

W indcrest had turned the missing Merfolk against us. Confusion broke out, as we were unprepared for an attack from our own kind. Who was on our side, and who was on theirs?

I climbed up the anchor only to slide back into the water. A tail slapped into my chest, slamming me into the side of the hull.

My people, Ruah said. *Remind them who they are.*

Two mermen swam at me, and for a moment I froze in fear, forgetting everything but their angry faces.

Sing, Ruah commanded.

The song filled me again, unable to be ignored. All the Merfolk from both sides turned to me, listening. The heavy rope landed in my hands, and I didn't waste a second before lassoing it around a nearby merman. As I cinched the hold, another rope appeared, and I swam among them, entrancing them as I went.

Stop fighting each other . . . remember who you are.

My chest throbbed from singing and my wound ached, but I didn't give up.

You are made for peace, not war . . . remember.

They blinked, staring at one another as realization washed over them. They were home.

An iron net plunged into the water above me, too fast to avoid. I was tangled inside, unable to chew my way out. Some of the mermen shook at the netting as it lifted me in the air, but it was no use. I was dumped on the deck, still trapped inside.

"Get the shackles and a muzzle for this one," a familiar voice said.

Princess Vella.

"Thought I was dead, didn't you," she spat.

"Please——" I said.

"Quiet!" She screamed the single word, her whole body heaving.

An oily rag was shoved in my mouth and tied behind my head. I squirmed against the net, only tangling my fins more.

"You have taken what I cared about most. My sister. My brother."

"I'm right here, Vella," Prince Vian said. A guard held the prince's weapon at his throat. "Nobody has taken me from you."

"She's turned you against me. Look at you, wearing their colors. You're a disgrace to our family." Her features distorted, her eyes alight with madness. "She is living the life I should have. I should be a mermaid—not her. Why would she be picked over me? She doesn't even know anything about them. Years I've been researching. She didn't even know what Alara was."

The princess signaled to sail closer to land. I fought the netting, ignoring her tirade.

"Honestly, I'll be glad to be rid of you. I'm sick of hearing your name. Since the moment Father ordered your abduction, it's been Marigold this and Marigold that. The lost sister is our key back to the throne. I've had *enough*."

Windcrest had been behind this all along? They had hired Fitz and Desmond to take me?

I gagged on the cloth, trying to argue.

"But I owe you, don't I? A life for a life?" she said, grabbing the bow and arrow from the archer nearest her. She drew her bowstring, aiming at my chest, but swung up to lock on something else in the distance. "Or perhaps a sister for a sister?"

I screamed into the cloth, my throat burning with the pathetic muffled sound.

Her arrow released, whizzing above me.

"Oh drat. I missed," she fumed. More focused this time, she loaded her bow again and took aim.

Prince Vian pushed against the guard and knocked him against his sister as she released the arrow.

"Curse you, Vian. You made me miss again." She signaled to the guards. "Load up the cannons and aim for the queen."

"Vella, stop this madness. We don't need more death."

"Of course we do, dear brother. Has Father taught you nothing? You really are the weakest one of us." She turned away to kick me in my stomach.

Whimpering, I folded inward the best I could, the pain nauseating.

His upper lip curled as he bellowed her name. Shaking off one guard, he jabbed the other in the face to gain his freedom. In a second, he raced across the deck, his face contorted with rage as he shoved his sister overboard.

His face crumbled as soon as he realized what he had done. "*Vella.*" Grip tight on the rail, he leaned over the bar, searching the clear waters.

Guards drew their weapons just in time for three blasts of Glenton's horn, signaling the end of the battle. I fought against the netting, trying to see the outcome.

"We won," the prince said, sounding slightly surprised.

"Your Highness." The guards bowed, dropping their weapons. "We were only following orders."

"Weren't we all," Prince Vian mumbled, glancing one last time into the waves.

He knelt at my side, pulling the cloth from my mouth and untangling the netting, then gathered me in his arms to set me on the railing. "Look."

The Windcrest banner fell, landing in the sand. Their soldiers lifted their hands in defeat. King Galon's charred body rested among the deceased, fire still lapping at the fabric under his armor.

Another loss for the prince. His sister, father, and kingdom were destroyed on the same day.

"I'm sorry," I whispered.

"Don't be. We choose our own paths, whatever the consequences may be." He let out a shuddering breath, reeking of despair.

I placed a comforting hand on his shoulder.

"I surrender," Prince Vox shouted, throwing his weapon down. "I was against this from the beginning."

One of Emilia's brothers stormed up to him, smashing his fist in his royal face, knocking him out cold.

Covered in ash and soot, Cedrick retracted his flames. Rose rushed to his side, throwing an arm around him. They held each other, their mouths moving as they spoke, but I was too far away to hear.

They shoved the Illusionist to her knees, ropes binding her hands.

I jumped from the railing, landing in the water with a hiss, my wound reopening. Merfolk surrounded me, humming and clicking for updates. At the good news, they cheered, roaring louder as they swam off to spread the excitement.

One of the mermen caught me scanning the murky depths.

"She belongs to the sea now," he said, then shot off to join the others in celebration.

The prince jumped in behind me, squinting through the saltwater for his sister one last time. When he accepted the truth, I grabbed his arm, bringing him with me back to shore.

Panting, he trudged through the surf, wobbly on his feet. "I don't know if I'll ever get used to how fast you can swim."

Tzedek stopped me before I submerged, a man over his shoulder. Disappointed, I frowned, wishing it was Ryken greeting me instead. He dropped a man with Windcrest's armor into the crashing waves, and the undertow immediately yanked the stranger into the water, the body disappearing from sight.

Even though I knew it was going to happen, it still startled me.

"Siren, I have a gift for you," Tzedek said, wading closer. "You've more than earned one last venture on land to say your farewells to the king and queen. Then you must return to your new life among the waves."

"Will I forget Rose? And my family?"

"Your memories are gifts from the sea—from Ruah. A love that is self-sacrificing and obedient. You gave everything, and your vow is complete."

I sighed, thankful I had managed not to botch up such an important task.

He scooped me up out of the water as if I weighed nothing. Water

435

dripped from my hair and scales as he carried me through the surf, the waves crashing into his calves. The aftermath of the battle left wounded men and women. Their cries and moans mixed with the crackle of the fire still burning in the timbers and a few bodies in the distance. Innocent people that could have been spared had Windcrest not been so hungry for power.

I pressed my hand against his breastplate, steadying myself. At my touch, it bubbled.

"Sorry." I snatched my hand back.

Tzedek grumbled, shaking his head. "Your mate is one of the most insistent Collectors I've been tethered to. I will allow you this moment with him before we must return to our responsibilities."

In seconds, his turquoise eyes cleared and twinkled as he stared down at me.

"My Marigold," Ryken said, his grip on my body changing from stiff arms to tucking me into his chest, and he kissed my head. With the battle over and my sister safe, my thoughts shifted to the future. Of our new life together.

"I missed you," I said, hugging him.

"I was here even if you couldn't see me. Your song—it controlled the sea."

"Or maybe the sea controlled me." I chuckled, my fingers trailing up the nape of his neck to fiddle with his loose strands of hair. How long ago did I cut these for him?

"You were magnificent——"

I pressed my lips on his mid-sentence, not wanting to hear glorifying words but wanting something real. Him. My mate.

"Marigold," Rose called out.

Ryken pulled back with a groan. "I'm ready for it to be just us."

I laughed at his pouty lip. "I know."

We joined the others just as the shouting began.

"She is of lies and black magic, Your Majesty. Her death will bring peace to the territories."

A guard swung his sword for the Illusionist's head, not waiting for an order.

Prince Vian's blade met his, sparks flying from the impact, stopping the deathly blow. His dark skin covered in sweat and sand, he leaned into the guard with a menacing scowl. "Drop your weapon."

The woman sat emotionless, her eyes inky pools of black swirling like the ocean, uninterested in the scuffle's outcome—even if it meant her death.

Cedrick shook his head. "This is not dark magic. It's the same as mine, though different, but not a reason a person should be killed."

Her eyes lifted to Cedrick, narrowing. "I will not be your prisoner."

"Good, because we don't need any more prisoners. But maybe we can help you? You could meet the Enchanters."

"I'm not an Enchanter, nor do I care to live among them. I just want my freedom."

Cedrick threw his arms into the air.

Prince Vian nervously approached, eyeing Ryken as he sidestepped closer.

"Thank you . . . *Vian*. For fighting beside us, for asking for Glenton's aid, and for saving my sister and me." Grateful, I reached out to squeeze his hand.

Ryken growled for a second, then swallowed it. "Sorry. Habit."

"Marigold," Vian said, his eyes turned to the sea. "I think you may have cursed me. There is a tug in my heart from the sea now. I don't think life on land will ever be the same. The sea is so vast."

"A fisherman?" I asked.

"I don't know. I just want to set sail and see what else is out there. All my life I have lived by the ocean but never stepped foot in it." He sighed. "Besides, there isn't anything here for me. My family disowned me when I left. There is no home to return to."

"What about Windcrest?" Roselyn asked. "You could be king."

"Actually, I think I'll leave that to Vox and Emilia to argue over. I'm tired of fighting."

"Me too," a voice said from the ground. The forgotten girl was kneeling in the dirt, her arm dripping with blood. "If you're going to kill me—do it already."

"Take her with you," I said.

"No," they said at the same time, horrified.

"I want nothing to do with their vicious kingdom. I've been their prisoner long enough. Kill me or release me," she demanded.

"I'm not going to hurt you," Vian said, "but we also aren't stupid enough to just let you go. Your power is too dangerous."

"And hers isn't?" the girl accused. "She controlled me with her voice —how is that different?"

"I do it for Ruah. Who do you do it for?"

"I do it for food. For water. So they don't plunge a knife into my neck," she snapped. "You wouldn't understand."

"You're wrong. I've been where you are: abducted, beaten, starved, and thrown into the sea to die."

"For what? A week? A month? *A year?* Come discuss it with me when you've lived this your entire life." She turned away, her jaw clenched.

"I'll escort her back to Windcrest until we figure something out," Vian said, shaking his head.

"Do you want to take some Enchanters with you?" Cedrick asked.

"Not yet. I have a feeling the castle will be overrun with Glenton's army. Plus, funerals to schedule." He sighed. "It will fall to me to inform my mother she lost her daughter and husband today. If she will even speak to me . . ." Unable to keep it together, he stormed off, his shoulders sagging. A guard picked up the girl, carrying her behind the prince.

"His sister?" Rose asked, her brows raised.

"Princess Vella was on one of the ships. She was aiming the cannons at you. He pushed her into the water to protect you."

"Did she drown?"

"I believe so. The sea took her."

I glanced at Vian's retreating back, my heart aching for his loss. They were still his family.

"*Oh.* I don't think I could be that strong."

"Me either."

"I think you could. I didn't recognize you out there. Look at how much you've changed, Goldie." Rose smiled.

"It's the scales. They make me look older." I flipped my fins, my scales tight and parched for water.

She chuckled. "Maybe, but I think it's more than that. Thank you for bringing the Merfolk with you. I know it wasn't their fight."

"It was Ruah's fight. Windcrest had to be stopped."

"And thanks for Glenton," Cedrick added.

"That was all Vian. He asked Princess Emilia for aid."

Rose bit her lip. "I think I judged him unfairly."

"You can extend him an olive branch."

"I'd prefer him on the throne than his brother. Maybe you can convince him, Cedrick?" Rose suggested.

"Me? I just want to go home, take a bath, and sleep for a week straight. Keeping the wall ablaze was as hard as strengthening the barrier."

"The barrier to what?" I asked.

He opened his mouth, then shut it with a shrug. "It doesn't matter."

I coughed in my hand, my throat dry from speaking.

"We should go soon," Ryken said.

Rose leaned over, hugging me in Ryken's arms. "I love you," she whispered in my hair. "I will see you soon."

"Promise?"

She nodded. "Besides, I haven't given you your wedding present. Cedrick has a wonderful idea for something he's going to build you."

"Build?" I raised a brow at Cedrick.

He shrugged. "I have to test it out first. Maybe Ryken can give me a hand?"

"Maybe in a month or so," Ryken said.

"What do you have planned for the next month?" I asked, irritated he was already leaving. Couldn't we have a day to ourselves? It had been one thing after another.

He pressed his lips to my ear to whisper, "I think you know."

My breath caught.

"It might be two months," Ryken corrected, his eyes scanning mine.

Blood rushed to my face.

Cedrick wrapped an arm around Rose, kissing her temple. "Go on, I know that look. Send word through the trees should you need us. We will check on the injured here. Any Merfolk that needs healing can meet us at the shore."

Ryken nodded.

"Could you start with me?" I asked, tilting my side away from Ryken. Bloody streaks covered his armor where my skin had touched.

"You're hurt," Ryken exclaimed, his hands trembling. "Why didn't you say something? I can get a pearl."

"Or Cedrick can heal her with his magic," Rose suggested.

Cedrick stepped forward at Ryken's nod, moving quickly should the protective merman change his mind. It burned and itched, the same feeling as when the pearl had closed the wound on my shoulder. The gash stitched itself closed, and my skin returned to its pale color.

"There," Cedrick said. He stepped back, wiggling his fingers. "And I managed not to lose any of these in the process."

Ryken pressed a kiss on my head, relieved.

My thank you ended in a coughing fit. The dry air tickled my throat. There must be a limited amount of time I could be on land.

My sister tried to step closer, but Cedrick held her back.

"Let Ryken take care of her," he murmured.

Her green eyes widened at the suggestion. "I guess this is goodbye then."

"Not for forever. I want to meet my niece or nephew." I ended on a cough, my throat itching.

"Water?" Ryken asked.

I grimaced as I swallowed, my tongue sticking to the back of my throat.

"Take her home," Rose said, a melancholy twist to her lips.

I blew her a kiss as we walked toward the sweet crash of the surf. Each wave beckoned me closer, promising relief. I leapt from his arms when he was knee-deep, desperate to be in the ocean again. The cool water refreshed my skin and scales, and I closed my eyes as the current dragged me farther to sea.

No more fear. No more stress. Just peace.

"Marigold," Ryken called out, trying to catch up.

His tail whipped in furious strokes so he could reach me. I dove out of reach, confusing him, and circled him twice, my tail sliding across his chest.

His eyes dilated, focusing on me. He swam closer, but I was already zipping away, swimming circles.

I laughed, spiraling through the water. My golden hair spun with me, shimmering in the last rays of light as I headed for deeper water. "I thought you said you could catch me."

"I'm afraid I won't let you go if I do," he said, his voice like velvet. His gaze followed me, a predatory gleam in his turquoise eyes. "You're playing a dangerous game, Marigold."

I peeked at him over my shoulder. "Am I?"

His nostrils flared, his body rigid. It was a standoff, his tail twitching, the silver scales effervescent and distracting. His heart thudded in excitement, his scent drifting on the current.

"If you swim off, I'm going to catch you," he warned.

"Then catch me," I dared him and darted off with a wink.

And he did.

Perfect

EPILOGUE

S prawled out on the floating dock, my lower half hung off the edge, my fins swaying in the cool water. The autumn nip in the air made the warm rays of the sun more bearable than usual. I rested my eyes, waiting.

I flicked my fins up, splashing droplets over my body so my scales didn't dry out.

So much had changed since summer and my new life had settled into place. The battle might be over, but a revolt was on the rise. The people of Windcrest demanded an end to Prince Vox's reign, the trust severed between them with the lies he had spread. Without Vian to smooth things over, it was only a matter of time before his kingdom crumbled around him.

It was a shame I wouldn't be there when it happened.

Rope creaked from the cliffs above, the knots tightening in a steady rhythm. I counted each one, tracking the sound, so I wasn't surprised by the heavy clump that rocked the wood beneath me.

Footsteps approached, the wood creaking. I forced my muscles to remain relaxed.

"I know you're not sleeping," Ryken said.

I opened my eyes, grinning at his upside-down face as he stood over me, breathtakingly handsome in his human form. He kissed my nose in greeting, and a contented hum vibrated in my throat. Even though it was at my request, I hated when he returned to land.

I missed him.

"How is she?" I asked. Two months ago, Roselyn added a new title to her growing list of aliases—Mother.

"You should ask her yourself," Ryken said. He traced his finger down my cheek and then stood to remove the bulky satchel over his head.

I sat straight, tucking my tail beneath me, the dock swaying from my sudden movement.

"What do you mean?" I asked. "Is Rose coming?"

He was more focused on the items in his bag than me.

"Ryken," I growled when he remained silent.

"You will see. Just be patient. I bought you some things from market day."

Every time he returned to land, either to see my family or check on Mattis, he brought me human knickknacks. At first, they were random, like a fork or a candlestick—the shinier the better. But lately he had been more thoughtful by surprising me with my favorite flowers or chocolates from the castle—though a few pieces were always missing. What I cherished above all were things from my family. Notes from Rose or funny stories from his visit. Those were worth more to me than jewels or gold.

I wasn't jealous but thankful he went in my stead. Most Merfolk still refused to surface, preferring their privacy and safety in the ocean. But Ryken ventured to land at least once a week, transforming into a human to climb up the cliffs on the rope ladder Cedrick had designed. Below the ladder was our meeting point. A floating dock the men had built together.

Where Rose had sit and chatted with me once.

But it had been so long since I had last seen her. Late in her pregnancy she tired easily, the toll of the long journey too strenuous to consider a second trip, even by carriage. Now she was so busy with her sweet baby girl.

I huffed, crossing my arms. I was going to be the last person to see the new princess. All the territories had sent gifts and trekked to see the baby. Even Vian got to hold her.

Ryken was smitten with baby Ivy and chatted about her constantly. How she had little toes and little feet that made his insides all squishy. Hopefully, he didn't sneak her into his satchel one day. Especially since he was very confused about the reasoning behind diapers.

"Don't be upset," Ryken said, digging through his satchel. He noticed my mood swing without even turning around. "Oh, here it is."

He pulled out some ribbons, sparkling gold, deep ocean blue, and bold silks of scarlet. I squealed, the colors alluring. Decorating my hair was to me what fashionable clothes were to the humans on land.

"You don't need accessories to make you more beautiful," he whispered in a sultry tone.

Only my mate could warm my skin with words alone.

I pounced on him, trapping him beneath me to the wooden dock, my hands on either side of his face. It was a little too easy. Almost as if this was part of his plan. My suspicions were confirmed when his hands plunged into my hair to bring my lips to his. Even with the bond between us complete and his mark on me permanent, our attraction to each other only grew stronger.

His hand trailed down my neck, resting on my collar. *I captured a siren.*

I pulled back to smirk, my tail curling around his leg. I purred into his thoughts, *Now what will you do with me?*

A gleam sparked in his eyes of promises of what he would do once we returned to our ship and he transformed. Memories of our time together had me tilting my head away, my scales tingling.

"How are you still shy with me?" he said, kissing my jaw.

"My emotions are tied to my memories. Would you rather I not have them?" I asked.

His lips stilled on my skin. The heat of his breath sent goosebumps down the column of my neck. *"Never.* My favorite part of the day is seeing how many times I can get you to blush."

"I'm realizing that. Should we . . . go home?" I suggested.

"Hello?" a female voice called from the top of the cliff. It bounced between the jagged rocks like a chant until it dissolved into the crashing waves.

Ryken's head flopped back to the dock with a thud of disappointment.

Rosey?

I shrieked in excitement, clawing my way to the ladder. Ryken picked me up, prying my fingers from the rope.

He kissed the inside of my wrist on the pulse of my vein. "You know only one person can climb the rope at a time. Let her come down."

I bounced up and down in his arms, impatient to see her.

"Goldie," Rose called out. She swung her legs over the edge and climbed down. Once again, she wore pants and a tunic as if she'd raided Cedrick's closet. A white cloth was wrapped around her chest. Her long red braid hung down her back, swinging with each rung she descended.

"It's still strange to see you in pants. I don't think I'll ever get used to it," I said. Why was she moving so slowly? *Faster, faster.*

"It's a little more comfortable for traveling and safer for climbing. And honestly, I haven't been interested in squeezing back into a corset. I'm delaying it as long as I can." She laughed, carefully stepping onto the dock.

I leaned in Ryken's arms toward my sister, desperate to hug her after so much time had passed. She held out a hand to stop me. "Wait."

Was she hurt? Injured from the journey? I sniffed at her, my eyebrows shooting up at the unfamiliar scent.

Rose walked closer and peeled back the corner of the white fabric around her chest, revealing a pink-cheeked baby fast asleep.

Words evaporated on my tongue at the adorable bundle.

Black ringlets as dark as a raven's wing curled around her head. Matching black lashes rested on her cheeks, and her rosebud mouth hung open in a perfect little O. Her breath expelled in soft puffs, each one melting my heart.

"Goldie," Rose whispered, taking a step toward me. "I'd like for you to meet Ivy Alysa."

Alysa? I met my sister's gaze, surprised she had given her my middle name.

"Hello, little one," I whispered, already charmed.

Instinct had me inhaling her scent, tasting it so I could remember and find her should ever I need to. It was sweet, like honeysuckle and milk, and something else I couldn't place. Similar to an airy breeze, light on my tongue.

Ryken's hand pressed to my collar. *Don't say anything. You'll scare her.*

Blinking, I inhaled it again, the unknown scent teasing me. She didn't smell of flames or earth or sea. Was she even human? She didn't smell human.

What is she?

I don't know. We'll have to wait until she's older. He sighed wistfully. *But isn't she precious?*

"She is more than precious. She's absolutely lovely."

Rose pressed a gentle kiss on her curls. "I know." She hid Ivy under the fabric cover. "I can't stay long. Cedrick is probably tearing the castle apart looking for us. I, um, snuck out to see you."

"That sounds like you." I held out my hand, and she took it. "I wish I had been there for you."

"Me too. You know I understand. After all the celebration and pampering over Ivy, I appreciate having Ryken help me sneak out for the day. You'd think I didn't know how to function the way people are treating me. Honestly, Mother tried to hand-feed me yesterday. I was desperate to get out. I've missed the open skies, the smell of the forest, and the salty breeze from the sea."

"Everyone loves you. That's all."

"I know . . . and I'm so thankful. I just hate feeling trapped inside. But this wasn't why I came to see you."

"It isn't?" I asked, confused.

"Did you give her my gift yet?" Rose asked Ryken.

"No, she was distracting me." *Not that I minded one bit,* he said through our connection.

I blushed despite myself.

"What is it?" I asked as Ryken placed me on the dock. I rolled over the edge, splashing into the cool water to refresh my scales.

Ryken handed me a wrapped parcel. It was oddly shaped, circular with a pointy top and a soft underside. I sniffed at it, and my sister laughed.

"Just open it."

I tore off the paper and froze at the golden circlet resting on a piece of fabric. Rotating the metal in my hands, I admired the sapphire teardrop that swooped down in the front.

Why had my sister brought me this? I was a siren—not royalty.

"Thank you," I said politely.

"Try it on and then open the fabric," she said, still laughing at me. "Come on, trust me."

I placed it on my head, the teardrop resting between my eyebrows. A perfect fit.

The midnight blue fabric appeared hand stitched, the embroidery work of the corners stunning. Not even Rose or I could sew this well.

"Careful with that piece. I snuck that out too. I have to take it back before anyone realizes it's missing from the Hall of Tapestries."

A Chronicle Weaver created this? I unfolded the last corner, my breath catching at the image of . . . *me*.

Like a queen sitting on her throne, I perched atop the crest of a wave, my tail radiating a soft white glow with shimmering thread. My eyes were closed, my mouth open in song. Resting on my head was a replica of the circlet I was currently wearing. Like light in the darkness, the golden threads of my song stretched into the midnight blue fabric.

"When . . . was this?"

"During the battle. You don't remember?"

"It's hard to see myself without a mirror," I said.

"When the light returned, this is what you looked like. I swear, I didn't even recognize my own sister," Rose said. She tapped the embroidered crown, the sapphire thread glinting in the sunlight. "I wanted to make this for you to remind you of your courage and how your song saved so many people. On behalf of Cadell and the five territories under my domain, thank you." She cradled the white fabric. "You gave us a future."

I ran a hand over the stitching in wonder.

You gave us a future too, Ryken whispered, his thumb grazing the skin above my choker. Shivers raked down my body all the way to my fins.

This wasn't how I had originally envisioned my life. That my pain and trials would lead me here, to this moment—surrounded by love beyond my comprehension.

Perhaps everything didn't go all wrong . . . it actually went perfectly.

And I wouldn't change a thing.

Thanks for Reading

WANT MORE?

Let's stay connected! Want the first scoop on all my writing projects? Or are you interested in when my books go on sale? Then join my newsletter. It includes exclusive author information, giveaways, quotes, excerpts, and my recommended reads.

What are you waiting for? Join today!

- Frozen Hearted: a free chapter from Anjali's POV (Backward Fairy Tales Series)
- Downloadable exclusive bookmarks
- Plus even more freebies on my website

www.authorcalliethomas.com/newsletter-signup-asogc

**Don't forget to turn to the end of the book for bonus chapters from Ryken's POV!

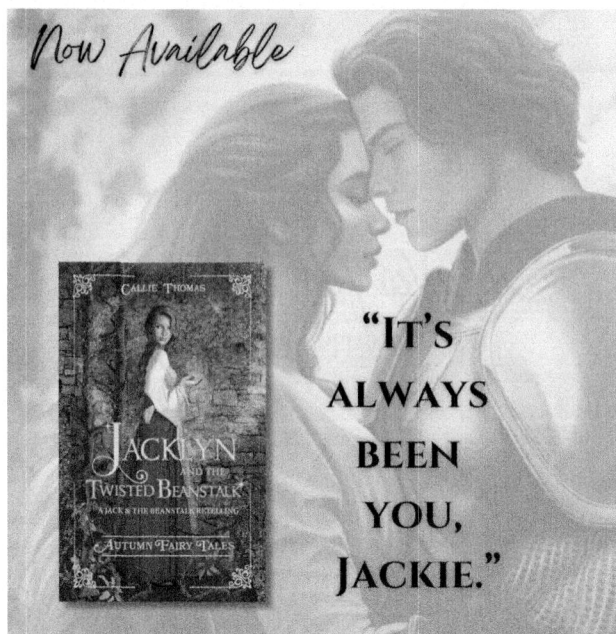

Step back into the past and discover a world long before Rose escaped into an enchanted forest and Marigold fell into the crystal sea. Return to a time when magic was outlawed and Cadell was shrouded in darkness. There you will meet Jacklyn, a fiery peasant who is done with the injustices of the king. To protect her family, she takes matters into her own hands, one magic bean at a time.

Jacklyn and the Twisted Beanstalk is part of the Autumn Fairy Tales series, a collection of eight cozy retellings of your favorite fairy tales. Each book can be enjoyed in any order, so light your harvest candle and get ready to "fall" in love with the romance, pumpkin spice, and everything nice of these sweet and clean novellas!

She has stolen from the king and now must suffer the consequences. He's an honor-bound guard, forced to uphold the law. Can she wish her way out of this disaster, or will their budding romance wilt before it even has a chance to blossom?

Discover Jacklyn's story here: https://a.co/d/4MINJoT

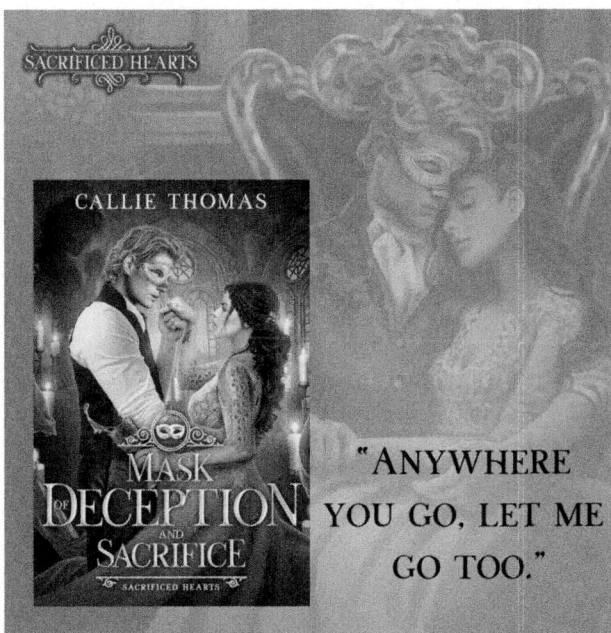

In a castle on a forgotten island in Hanalla, Princess Fiona waits in chains, locked away and only days from execution. The king believes her black hair is the mark of the most vile magic in the land, one that was thought to be extinct. The magic of illusions. Desperate, Fiona must do what she can to survive, including forcing a monster to drink from an enchanted chalice. But she soon discovers there's more to the masked man than what meets the eye...and he's not the only one with secrets.

With a delightful mix of *Jekyll and Hyde* and *Phantom of the Opera* vibes, *Mask of Deception and Sacrifice* is book 3 in the Sacrificed Hearts multi-author series, a collection of stand-alone fantasy romances inspired by monsters of legend and packed with strong heroines, swoony heroes, and sacrificial themes.

If she can remove the monster's mask, she will earn her freedom... but failure will cost her life.

Discover Fiona's story here: https://a.co/d/4iyTPCq

Acknowledgments

Most importantly, thank you to the Lord Almighty for my gifts of creativity and perseverance. Somehow I met my deadlines, and I know it's only by His grace and provision. May the readers hear Your words as they read, and not mine.

A special thanks to my family, especially my husband. This book took over a year to write and edit. He juggled the evening chores with little complaining, sacrificing his free time so I could write. I love you so much. Thank you and the boys for your support and understanding.

To my mom, Diane, who probably loves Ryken as much as Marigold does. Thank you for the laughs with all your messages demanding spoilers and for grabbing the kids so I could sneak in another hour or two of writing.

A big thank you to my editor and sweet friend, Jessica, for all the late-night editing sessions and random texts. I'm so blessed to have you working with me. You are the gentle encourager and most patient editor I've worked with. I know these pages sparkle because of you.

Kindle Vella author friends who were my support system and sounding board, Elizabeth Ash and M.J. Padgett, thank you for all your feedback and kind words. I'm so lucky to have you in my life.

Thank you to all my readers—especially my Kindle Vella readers! I loved reading all your comments and checking in with the poll results. Hanalla has its beautiful name because of you! I appreciate your support by liking and faving my story each week. You're all amazing!

About the Author

Callie Thomas is an indie author who loves all things fairy tales—including twisting tales of her own. Her favorite stories have a mix of sweet romance, laughter, and a pinch of magic. When she's not writing, she enjoys playing board games, reading at the beach, and traveling the world with her husband and two boys. Since she can't live at Disney World, you'll find her near the historical battlefields and lush woodlands where her family lives in Fredericksburg, VA. She recently published her first Vella series, _A Forest of Stolen Memories_ & _A Sea of Golden Chains_, and has more stories on the horizon.

➡️ For more books & updates: https://www.authorcalliethomas.com/

🅰️ amazon.com/author/authorcalliethomas

📷 instagram.com/authorcalliethomas

f facebook.com/AuthorCallieThomas

♪ tiktok.com/@authorcalliethomas

g goodreads.com/authorcalliethomas

BB bookbub.com/authors/callie-thomas

Bonus Chapters

A SEA OF GOLDEN CHAINS

The next two chapters are from Ryken's perspective. The first starts just before he meets Marigold, and the second is after she's been taken to Windcrest without him.

A big thank you to all the readers who unlocked these episodes and made them available for everyone to enjoy!

Happy Reading!

Callie

My Everything

BONUS 1 - RYKEN

T he ship rocked above me, the water angrily pounding on the sides of the vessel. Neither of us wanted them close to the grotto, the area where the Merfolk gathered and hunted. Not that it was my responsibility to guard this area. Llamar was somewhere close, I was sure, but since I was here already, I wouldn't let these trespassers stay any longer.

My people were disappearing.

First Zekel and then Adino four months later, both mermen that were only a few years older than me. Then Gilon, a youngling, vanished in the middle of the night. Never had anyone left Alara, our golden kingdom, by choice, and their disappearances sent a ripple of fear among our people. Who would leave, and why? We were chosen warriors in the name of Ruah. We were more than well provided for, favored by Ruah over all creation based on our obedience and devotion alone. It granted us the freedom of the sea and the gifts of strength, sight, and hearing that carved us into warriors of water, an unmatched design.

Loyalty and honor flowed through our veins. Desertion was so unfathomable among our people that we didn't even consider the possibility. Something had happened to them. But since they were unmated, no one could track their whereabouts.

457

When Liora went missing, a mated mermaid, we finally had the proof we needed. She was taken. Having a mate meant they had an eternal bond that united the two forever. To be apart would be as painful as if their own heart had been ripped from their body. Despair would surround them in a shroud of fog, draining their energy until they were unable to function normally. Days of not eating would eventually lead to their deaths.

Was it even possible to leave your mate . . . and live through the pain?

Rosh, her mate, had smelled her fear in the current and rushed to her rescue, but by the time he had arrived, she was already missing. All that was left were traces of her blood heading to the surface.

Humans, I growled.

With a well-practiced spin, my tail slammed against the hull, rocking the ship back and forth. My first warning.

Attacking outright would violate our peace covenant. Our Merfolk oath kept us to the comforts of the waters and demanded we never use our gifts for destruction but rather for the protection of our people. Compared to the bloodshed on land, we were the peacekeepers. Our purpose was to bring an end to the wars and eventually fulfill our destiny of standing by the Chosen One when the time came for us to defend Ruah's name.

But when the humans sailed into our waters close to our grotto, we were allowed to defend ourselves. And if they were brave enough to enter the sea—a deadly smile pulled at my lips—then I could pull them to the deepest depths and let the ocean decide if they were worth saving.

None ever were.

I slammed my tail into the ship, furious all over again at their presence. Tired of waiting, I clawed at the wood, splintering the wet pieces easily, and what didn't break, I gnawed with my teeth. I didn't stop until I saw bubbles, the water swarming through the opening. The hole was still too small, and just as I opened my mouth to rip it open further, something splashed into the water.

Finally, I thought. They were bringing the battle to us. A direct attack meant I was free to counter with any force necessary. With a snarl, I swam around the ship, ready to tear them into pieces.

I froze at the sight, my heart stopping.

It was . . . a young woman. She flailed about, sinking fast in a foam of bubbles.

Shouts sounded from above, garbled in the water. I frowned. She must have fallen in by accident. Not a battle, then. My adrenaline pulsed beneath my skin, turning into something more, something I couldn't describe.

Her head turned back and forth, panic etched across her beautiful features. Curious, I found myself swimming closer. She was so different from me: soft skin, rosy lips pinched closed, and an upturned nose curved daintily. She sparkled in the sun's rays that streaked through the blue waters. Even her hair shone with color, golden hues that floated like a halo around her. Not dangerous or threatening, but it spun my emotions into a swirling whirlpool so that I couldn't think straight. All I knew was that I needed to get closer to breathe her scent.

The ship forgotten, I stayed behind her just out of sight as her hands fell slack at her sides. Dark fabric floated around her, swallowing her whole like a whale. She was giving up.

For a split second, I thought of saving her. It would take one tail flick to bring her to the surface. And then what would I do with her? Humans and Merfolk were a lethal combination. I had been taught since I was a youngling that humans were the enemy. They were made to destroy and conquer. The opposite of our peaceful nature.

My eyebrows shot up. *Why would I ever want to help a human?* I combed back my hair, my thoughts still scrambled. She was a temptation—a distraction. Besides, I couldn't save her. If the sea wanted to claim her, who was I to alter her course?

My attention returned to the rocking boat above me. It was time for their last warning.

As I flicked my tail to swim upward, a lone musical note gripped my chest like I was caught on the end of a fisherman's hook. I twisted to her and more notes followed, turning into a haunting melody that made my breath quicken. All at once, I was attuned to her and her song. My body shook from the pull of the notes. They beckoned. They teased.

Come to me. Take me. Claim me . . .

This was no human but a siren.

I pressed my hand to my heart, the rhythmic beats matching the tune. I had to see her up close. To touch her. To smell her. For I was sure to perish if I didn't.

Could it be possible that she was for me to claim? I became weak at the thought, my lips parting. I floated closer as the melody weaved its way into my soul.

This was more than unexpected. I was a Collector—an honored gift bestowed to a rare few. My life was dedicated to Ruah, our creator. A mate, though allowed, was never part of my destiny.

Then why? I thought possessively. Why would I feel her call if she wasn't calling out for her mate—for *me*?

Then the song stopped, a gutting silence that made me frantic. I rushed to her side.

Her eyes were squeezed tight in fear. Of me? The thought of anyone hurting her lit a fiery rage in my chest.

I allowed myself one touch and gathered a handful of fabric to bring her closer. Her scent whooshed into me from the movement, a sweetness that shattered my resistance. There was no more time for thoughts. My hand touched the golden band around my bicep. I had to claim her to save her from death.

Her eyes fluttered open, and time stood still. Emerald-green eyes locked on me, capturing me in her net. My breath shuddered out at the realization that I would do anything for her. With a look, she had claimed me. I leaned forward to breathe in her scent, to learn it, to savor it—because from now on, it was mine.

She is mine.

The rightness of the thought sent me into action, and I tore the band from my arm, wincing as it ripped the top layer of my flesh. I clamped it around her throat and watched in fascination as something I had worn my entire life melded into her skin. Bubbles swirled around us, the current pulling us closer.

Her eyes shut as the ancient magic pulsed between us with an explosion of light, blinding as the sun. I closed my eyes, too, trembling as our souls became one. She was my thought, my breath, my heartbeat—my everything.

Did she feel the same way too? She wouldn't look at me, her body limp in my arms. Panicked, I placed my hand over her heart and waited. Silence.

Was I too late?

Picking up her hand, I placed it over my own heart and trembled at the electric power pulsing between us. There was no doubt I made the right choice.

My mate.

She was dying. Her energy slipped from her one drip at a time, and with each drip, she took one from me to replace it.

What I did was reckless. If she died . . . then I did too. Our heart-beats were linked and required the other for survival. My heart would have to beat for both of us. I didn't know how I did it, only that it was instinct. Like exhaling a breath, the electric current raced down my extended arm and tingled against my palm on her chest, my fingers touching my bonded collar around her neck. *Beat,* I commanded. My next heartbeat exploded through our connection, her own a delayed thump after mine.

Don't give up.

Her heart pulsed weakly in response. At least she was fighting.

Again and again.

With each thud beneath my fingers, it grew in strength, matching mine beat for beat.

Don't leave me now that I've found you.

Her lips parted, and a trail of bubbles drifted up. Warmth spread from her hand on my skin as she unconsciously tested our connection. Even asleep, she called to me.

Pulling my hand away, I studied the pulse at her neck and sighed in relief to see her heart working on its own again. I pulled her closer, her head lolling back from the movement, and adjusted my grip. For a human, she was small. I would have to be careful not to bruise or hurt her. She would be fragile until she had fully transformed.

What would she look like afterward? Would she keep her green eyes, or would they turn blue like mine? What color would her fins be? A female's scales changed to a dual color that matched her mate. So she would have my silver and what?

My tail curled around her legs, tangling in the loose fabric.

This was going to be an excruciating few months while I waited to find out. I wanted to know everything about her—the sparkle in her smile, the lilt of her hums, the caress of her fingers, and her graceful movements when she swam.

I touched my forehead to hers, an intimate gesture I had never done with anyone else.

I was in awe. *Thank you, Ruah. I'm grateful you chose her for me.*

The current picked up, swirling around us before it settled again. Ruah didn't always speak aloud. Most times, it was in the quiet moments I felt a powerful presence.

Holding her to my chest, I swam to the Crystal Caves, a place I'd had no interest in entering before. Nor would I have been allowed to. An unattached merman in these caves received a death sentence, not by law but by jealous mates who refused to let anyone near their mermaids until the bond was complete.

I tilted her face back, my thumb brushing over her cheekbone. The unreasonable urge to protect her clouded my brain from anything else. I'd probably attack Orion if he approached me right now.

Cringing, I remembered the training I had missed. Orion, the Grand Counselor of Alara, helped organize the daily operations of Ruah's kingdom. He focused most of his attention on training and defense, as he was once a Collector himself. Because I was born with my silver tail, the mark of a Collector, Orion had been training me into a warrior since I was a youngling. And after all those years, this was the first time I had ever missed a training. The other Collectors, Egon, Jayco, and Pike, would be furious with me. Whenever one of us made a mistake, Orion punished the others instead—a longer, more vigorous session that made our fins ache for days. It taught us a basic fact of our existence: our decisions had repercussions that overflowed to others.

I'd have to drop my mate off and return to Alara. I whimpered, pulling her closer to my chest. The thought of leaving her made me physically ill.

What had I done? I had chained myself to a human, and now I could barely function.

Finally arriving at the caves, I rolled the stone away enough that I could squeeze both of us through. My mate's fabric refused to obey and caught on the stone entrance, a piece ripping off the bottom.

What was this called again? Shirt? Long shirt? With most human items I found, the names and words didn't stick in my mind as they

462

should—much to Orion's disappointment. Our human studies taught us about our enemy's world and how to use that knowledge so we were strategically prepared in battle.

I glanced down at her face. Not that I thought of her as the enemy.

I glided past the cave openings, including the ones that were unoccupied. Some mermen growled as I passed, a warning should I think to bother them. Protectors by nature, we were even more so with our mates. The humans were defenseless in their transformational slumber until the process was complete. While they slept, we stayed close by, tending to their needs and keeping them safe. The instinct to protect was so intense that we were known for attacking our own kind if we felt threatened. So, I swam quickly past and didn't engage in their warnings.

Purple crystals lined the ceiling, sparkling a path that led left. It reminded me to grab a pearl for her to gain strength, especially if I was going to leave for training.

The last cave was smaller than the others but empty and had enough distance from the others, so if she sang again, the other mermen wouldn't hear her. The need to keep her voice a secret surprised me. I wondered if it was for her safety or if my jealous behavior was already kicking in.

Would her voice call any merman to her? My fist curled at the thought. Sirens hadn't been around for the last century, maybe even longer. They were our fiercest warriors. Sleek and fast, they easily outswam a merman. Where they lacked physical strength, their voice was their persuasion, convincing any foe into the waters and into our battleground. Though we preferred peace, sailors and treasure hunters still sought us out.

They had taken enough from us. Where the siren's call was seductive, it was also addicting to the human ear. The humans wouldn't rest until each one was destroyed. And with their deaths started the decline of our people. Our numbers dwindled at an alarming rate due to the lack of female babies. Only sirens could birth their own kind.

The humans that transformed were only shadows of sirens. Mermaids that offered the illusion of what once was. But we were desperate. Even if my mate only carried males, I would be thankful to have any younglings.

Picking the chain off the floor, I gave it a strong tug and nodded when the anchor remained in place. I clipped her to the end, my touch commanding the magic of the mate's band to meld to the golden chain. The chain would keep her from drifting too close to the jagged rocks along the cave ceiling while she slept.

Now she would stay for a few months until her transformation was complete.

But after waiting, and waiting, and *waiting*—a year, to be precise—she had still not changed much in the way of transformation.

Though I was always hopeful. Every night I spent time with her. I spoke of my day and about the ship I had found for us. Deep in the nesting process, I gathered items for our ship so she could feel at home when she arrived. Even after a year of collecting things from shipwrecks and scavenging the ocean for treasure, it still felt like we needed more.

I wanted it to be perfect for her.

I breathed in her scent, human and a sweet floral—a mix that was just her own.

"My heart," I clicked and hummed to her impatiently, "would you please hurry?"

A constant fear that her heart would stop when I wasn't around consumed my thoughts. So I spent every night with her, watching her float in her sleep. My body didn't require human necessities, and I only needed a light rest to relax my fins from swimming. Secretly, I loved this time the most. Sitting in the quiet with her while I dreamed of what our future would look like. I touched a fingertip to the back of her hand, enjoying the jolt of electricity between us. How much more would it be when she was awake? When she would call me with her song because she knew who I was and couldn't bear another second without me?

Sunlight slipped through the porous holes in the cave ceiling. Though this cave had daylight, the others were pitch black since that area was burrowed deep under the connecting continent. Some believed the purple crystals that grew along the ceiling were part of the old magic and connected to the sacred place above it. We were forbidden to touch the crystals but were allowed to collect the clams that accumulated mysteriously among the seaweed where they grew.

Inside each clam was a precious pearl. It could cure anyone—even humans—from any ailment. The pearl of healing.

It was the only thing fueling her strength after months of starvation.

When she didn't take it, she tapped into my energy. Those days, I rested with her in the cave. I was more than willing to share whatever I had to keep her alive.

I wished I could stay with her longer, but my ceremony loomed closer, and with it, the duties and responsibilities I had been ignoring. Soon, I wouldn't be a trainee, and my time as a Collector would begin. According to Orion, it sometimes took days to retrieve a person who had broken a vow.

Days? Without my mate? I sighed. Hours already seemed excruciatingly long.

Each morning, I returned to Alara for training. I swam past the guards on duty, their nods respectful of my position. They allowed me to travel through the quarters and straight into the training hall.

Pike rolled his eyes as I entered, immediately shooting a wave of water in my direction that I barely dodged. He clicked in our language, "You're slow, Ryken."

"You still have never hit me, so I wouldn't be bragging too much if I were you."

Pike smiled, flashing his sharp teeth. "We have target practice today."

I shrugged. The excitement of the challenge was missing.

"You're late. Orion isn't thrilled."

"Egon isn't even here yet," I pointed out.

"He's on an errand for Orion. So you're the only one late."

"It's the girl," Jayco added, joining in the conversation from the weapon's rack in the far corner of the open room. He pulled out a long spear and twirled it as he searched for another. "She's a distraction."

Moaning, Pike jerked his head back dramatically. "Can we go one day without talking about her?"

I growled, "I don't bring her up. You all do." I wished they wouldn't.

"Only because she's always on your mind," Egon said, entering through the floor-to-ceiling windows lining the wall. When he whistled, Pike chucked the spear at him, and he caught it one-handed without breaking my stare. "You're late, by the way."

"How would you know? You weren't even here."

Egon, the oldest of the four of us, swam in front of me, his long

465

brown hair floating around him. He clicked in disappointment, scolding me like he was the next Grand Counselor of Alara. "You smell like guilt."

Pike and Jayco chuckled when I snarled. Egon pounced on me the moment I turned around, trying to pin me to the golden wall with his spear. Though Egon was cunning, Jayco's aim had unfailing accuracy, and Pike was a streak in the sea with his speed—I outmatched them all with my strength. In a matter of minutes, I had Egon's spear in my fist and him pinned against a pillar with my forearm.

"You win," he groaned and let out a wheeze when I released him.

I bobbed my head, a friendly gesture which he returned. Our scuffs were a competitive game we kept tallies on for boasting rights.

I smirked at Pike now that I was in the lead.

These three were the closest I had to family. Years of training, fighting, learning, and embarrassing moments were the glue that held us together. But since I had found my mate, I hadn't been around unless it was required.

"Any change?" Jayco asked. Quietest of us all, he was stealth personified. He'd make a great Collector, probably the best of us. "With your mate?" he added when I didn't respond.

What was I supposed to say? I hated this topic. "No."

The three of them glanced away, avoiding my eyes.

Thinking of her again spiked my anxiety. I glanced longingly at the exit, desperate to be in the caves with her again. Maybe there was some truth in their words. I was distracted.

My spine tingled just before Pike pounced into my back. I flipped him over my shoulder and slammed my tail into his face. *I mean, I'm not that distracted.*

The rest of the day we dedicated to target practice above the water, lobbing spears until my arm went numb. The others grumbled at me. It was my fault we stayed later, and as soon as Orion gave us the nod to leave, I was racing across the sea to the Crystal Caves. Before stopping in to see her, I grabbed a clam from the pile, knowing she'd need her dose for today. Her heartbeat had been weak when I left this morning.

I halted at the entrance, surprised to see a pair of wide green eyes staring at me.

She was awake.

466

Hers to Command

BONUS 2 - RYKEN

T wasn't sure why I had been fighting sleep. Once I was in a dream, I never wanted to wake. This one was no different, lulling me with Marigold's sweet song—a melody I couldn't resist.

My lips parted when I saw her, her golden hair drifting in the ocean's current. It was always the thing I noticed first: the way the light shone through the strands with a sparkle that called to me like treasure. The fierce need to swim to her, to touch her, to *claim* her clawed at me until I couldn't ignore it another second. I glided through the water to get closer. My fingers itched from want, a primal need to complete the process I had started but had yet to finish. She was mine . . . and yet she was not. Her scent still had that lingering aroma of land, things from her past like dirt and fire that I wished would stay there. I snarled in frustration, wanting it to be my scent she carried.

Battling my emotions, I fought for patience, remembering I had promised to wait. My tail swung forward, stopping me a few feet from her. I had to wait until she was ready for me.

Even if it killed me inside.

She didn't notice my distress, her head turning this way and that, searching for something. Her heartbeat quickened, vibrating in the water. It beat strong and steady in a way I hadn't felt before.

I couldn't help but smile at her newfound strength.

Her pale legs kicked out, propelling her forward as her maroon gown floated behind her. I tilted my head at the fabric. Something wasn't right about it. She had been wearing this when I first met her, hadn't she?

Memories threatened to overtake me, and I pushed them away, not wanting to ruin this beautiful moment. Somehow, I knew if I remembered the truth, everything would disappear. And I wanted every second I could have with her.

Click, clickety-click, hummm, click.

She froze, listening to me. My tail twitched as she began to turn, so agonizingly slowly, and I hoped that for once, fear would not cloud her eyes.

Long hair tangled across her face, and she brushed it aside before her emerald-green eyes locked on mine. Then she smiled. Small at first, then it stretched, showcasing her flat teeth.

My chest expanded. It was all I wanted. Her joy was my joy. *Marigold. My mate.*

She held out her hand, so small compared to mine, and I raced through the current to place her palm on my chest. Our connection was instant. Warm tingles heated my skin under her fingertips. Did she feel it too? The way my heart synchronized with hers and a peacefulness settled between us.

"Ryken, look at me," she said in my language, then laughed when my eyebrows jumped to my hairline.

"When did you learn to speak like this?" I asked.

She just smiled and leaned in, the answer less important the closer she got. "Look."

"I am looking. I'm always looking." Didn't she know that?

Inches from me now, those strange human feelings coursed through me. A longing mixed with a desperate want . . . to do something I couldn't explain. The new emotions danced in my chest, my gills malfunctioning. Her intoxicating scent didn't help; her feelings and desires flowed on the current.

"Look down," she stressed, pulling away from me so quickly I almost missed the violet of her tail as it flicked up and sent a wave of water crashing into me.

My heart skipped a beat. *Her tail?*

She twisted, spinning in a circle with her arms stretched outward. Chunks of her dress tore away from her, floating upward until it was only her, fully transformed.

She was so beautiful that I couldn't tear my eyes off her. I refused to blink. Ducking her head, she averted her gaze, a rosy tint to her cheeks, the light silhouetting her profile. The need to protect—to claim her—returned a thousand times stronger. Gritting my teeth, I fought for restraint.

As if she could hear my thoughts, she giggled, a tinkling sound matching the tune of her song.

"Do you like it?" she asked.

Words couldn't form, so I nodded instead. I could see why Collectors shouldn't have mates. Images of her filled my mind and all my responsibilities faded like a misty memory in the background. Nothing mattered but her . . . and that thought alone was terrifying.

I was hers to command. But did she feel the same for me?

My heart knew the truth. Our bond was held together by a frail string, and no matter how hard I tried, the ends kept fraying. What was I to do? How was it even possible that a mate rejected the other? *I didn't agree to this eternal commitment.* Her angry words still haunted my thoughts.

How could I convince her? Did I need to prove it? My strength, my possessions, my heart—it was all hers. Nobody would dare lay a finger on her as long as there was life in my body. It would be my pleasure to tear them limb from limb.

"Ryken," she called out as she swam toward me.

My eyes locked on her movement. How did she learn to swim so fast?

Her tail was blue now, aquamarine from the tip of her fin to the crisscross of her chest. I blinked, watching the color change again to a burnt amber, similar to the sky just before the sun dove into the sea. Twice she circled me, the color of her tail changing with each revolution. Shaking my head, the colors swirled in my mind. Changing colors wasn't normal. The thought distracted me as she curled around me, her arms encircling my waist as she rested her cheek on my shoulder.

Why was her tail changing colors?

I tensed when a crack ripped through my reality, the truth flooding my thoughts. How could I know the color of her tail if her transformation hadn't happened yet? A trick of my mind. This was only a dream—and Marigold was still a human.

An illusion . . .

My heart ached as I cradled her cheek in my hand, her green eyes my new favorite color. *Not real,* I reminded myself as another pang sliced through me. Her smile, the adoration in her eyes, the touch of her hand as it slid across my chest—none of it was real. I couldn't torture myself any longer. Dreams were painful reminders of what would never be. I hung my head, disappointed that I had fallen for the illusion again.

With a gasp, I opened my eyes, panting as if I had been drowning on land.

Now I remembered why I fought sleep. Waking from dreams stung, and the cold slap of reality tingled for the remainder of the day. I pulled at my cloth—*no,* blanket—to reveal the feet that had replaced my magnificent tail. I grimaced as I wiggled them, ugly stubby things. How did they attract females when they were so plain? Where was the shine?

The human world was backward and confusing. Nothing made sense.

Here, I was weak—*sickly* they called me. I couldn't walk, and I did things humans gave me strange looks for. I could handle their fear, but pity?

I just wanted to take Marigold home.

The bedroom door slammed open, hitting the wall hard enough that wood chips crumbled to the floor. I snapped up, muscles tensing.

"Get up, whatever you are. You aren't welcome here any longer," Jacek said, a spear in his hand. He motioned it upward. *"Now."*

A pit dropped in my stomach. "Where's Marigold?"

"Far away by now. She left while you were sleeping."

My fingers curled into the blankets, the protectiveness from my dream still lingering. "Liar," I roared, the sound vibrating in a non-human way. I didn't care. Anyone that came after me with a spear had to know what they were in for—death.

"I don't care if you believe me. She's gone, and I want you gone too."

She would never leave me. I meant more to her than that. Didn't I? My eyes narrowed, furious that Jacek had me questioning my mate at all.

470

A low rumble rattled in my chest, echoing through me until my hands trembled. Rage fueled me across the room in a second, my palms slapping the wall on either side of his head, pinning him in place. My nails dug into the wood as I battled the urge to rip his lying tongue out.

His eyes bulged. "Can you blame her? Look at you—you're a *monster*."

That word. It wasn't the first time I'd heard it. Marigold had called me the same thing when we first met. I knew what it meant—that I was callous and terrifying. When it came to my mate, maybe I was. My lips peeled back, snarling closer to his face. The pulse at his neck beat frantically, the air reeking of fear. It would be as easy as swatting a fingerling. But I didn't, refusing to be what he said I was.

"I don't believe you," I bit out.

"Go look in her chamber and see for yourself."

Snarling, I pushed off the wall and stormed as fast as I could while still keeping my balance. Caitlyn jumped out of the way when I passed, wrapping a protective arm around Mattis. Wide-eyed, the boy stared up at me, mouthing my name.

I turned away, not wanting him to see me like this. My possessive nature would be impossible to control until our bond was complete.

Her door was already open, her scent stale and cold. I sank against the doorframe, the sight of her empty bed twisting my heart.

Please, let this be another dream. *Wake me up, Ruah.*

"See, it was as he told you. There is nothing left for you here," Caitlyn said, sidestepping down the corridor with Mattis in tow.

Marigold promised she would never leave me. Her promise . . . if she broke her promise, then a Collector would come to claim her.

I spun back to the woman. "Tell me the truth; her life is on the line."

"They took her," Mattis blurted out.

Caitlyn gasped, placing a hand over her son's mouth. "He doesn't know what he's talking about. He's just a child."

Her words meant nothing. I focused solely on the boy, inhaling his scent and tilting my head in appreciation of his honesty. Marigold hadn't broken her promise. Caitlyn was right—there was no point in staying here another second.

Scowling, I said, "I'd never hurt him. He is the only one I like. That

471

you're still alive is a gift of my generosity for your provision, as little as it was. Promise me you'll take care of the boy."

"We promise," they said quickly, humoring me.

I punched the side of my fist into the wood, the pressure of it leaving a dent. "A vow to the sea or it means nothing."

"Do it, Jacek," Caitlyn shrieked.

Mattis remained passive despite the turmoil of the conversation. He turned to watch his father.

Jacek crossed his fingers, tapping them on his forehead. "I promise to love and care for him. He will never want as long as we have the means to give it to him. Let the seas take me if I don't."

I tilted my head at the unknown word: *love*.

"Teach him peaceful ways, honest words, and humble actions. Or maybe he should teach those to you."

"I will—we will." As he lowered his hand, the symbol of his promise scrawled across his forehead.

"It is done. I see your mark, the imprinted glow on your flesh. The moment you break it . . . " I dropped my voice to a harsh whisper. "I'll come for you with a smile on my face. Then the sea will deal with you, and I have yet to see anyone survive its judgment."

Jacek swallowed, his color fading to a ghostly shade of cream. Caitlyn sank against the wall, wrapping her arms around her son.

"What are you?" she asked, her voice trembling.

Ignoring her, I nodded farewell to the boy.

"Wait, Ryken," Mattis said. "The castle, you have to go to Windcrest castle."

"Hush now, child," his mother scolded. "Let him leave."

"Ryken, I saw it through my window. A man carried her to the carriage. I think she was sleeping."

"What man?" My blood boiled.

"I don't know. But I saw the seal of Windcrest on the carriage door —it's a royal coach. It was the same one I saw when I visited Windcrest a month ago."

I had no idea what a carriage was, but it didn't sound good. Especially since it took Marigold from me. Whatever beast it was, I would destroy it.

"Mattis," Jacek shouted.

"It's true, Father." The boy turned back to me. "You believe me, right?"

"I do. I'll remember this moment and the kindness you bestowed on me. It is a rare gift, above and below the water. I will return the favor one day."

I left slower than I would have liked, hobbling down the stairs and out the main door. Marigold's scent greeted me outside, but it was as Mattis said. It ended abruptly at the pebbled pathway. To my right, an old scent of hers lingered in the air and headed across the field to a patch of trees.

It was my only lead.

Awkward at first, I was slow, swaying on borrowed legs until I found a steady balance. I crossed the field of wildflowers and entered the shade of the trees, wondering what had lured Marigold from the house. I continued farther into the forest, following the arrows of her scent until it ended at a shallow river. The water smelled strange, not at all like the sea, but fresh like the water Caitlyn poured into our glasses.

Could I still swim in this? There was only one way to find out. I fiddled with the buttons down my chest, struggling to undo them. Human inventions were tedious.

Though I did like their food.

My next breath caught a familiar scent. "I know you're there."

A branch snapped, and I turned toward the noise, not surprised when Mattis slunk out from behind the tree. Back hunched, he tucked his hands behind him, looking sheepish.

I returned to my frustrating buttons. "They will be looking for you. Go back."

"I—I want to go with you."

His topaz eyes stared up at me, large and round, and tugged at my heartstrings. He was so pure that a part of me wanted to keep him. I liked how he saw the world differently, that life was one big adventure. It made me smile. And usually, if I found something I liked, I kept it.

And I liked Mattis.

I could teach him how to use a sword and how to catch fish with his hands. He could tell me stories from his books, and we could watch for shapes in the clouds.

But a new emotion gnawed at me, almost as if I could hear Marigold scolding me from afar.

He's a person, she would say.

But he wants to come with me.

Pretend he was me. How would you feel if someone took me?

My eyes fluttered closed. *Like someone stole my heart from my chest— like how I feel right now.*

Then there's your answer.

Even in my imagination, she bested me in an argument.

A small hand clasped mine, his bones so frail in my palm. "Ryken? Is that a yes? I can come with you?"

I sighed. "No, Mattis. I have to do this on my own."

His eyes filled with liquid. What had Marigold called them? *Tears.* I had made him sad. Why did seeing him in pain make me sad too? My chest ached knowing I had hurt him.

"But why? I want to help her too. Do you think I'm not brave enough? Not strong enough?" he asked, his bottom lip quivering.

I shook my head and kneeled clumsily on the forest floor. "You are brave enough. If I could have anyone at my side to help find Marigold, I'd pick you."

"You mean that?"

I placed a hand on his shoulder. "I do. But the truth is, I don't know where I am going or where she is. It could be days until I find her. That's a long time to be separated from your family." Somehow I kept my lip from curling as I thought of them—*the traitors.*

"I'm grown up now. Almost eight." Mattis stood tall, his chin jutted out. "I can be on my own."

"What about Bungo?"

His chin dipped. "What about him?"

"Who will watch over him?"

The boy glanced away, thinking. "My mother will. Marigold is the one in trouble. I want to help find her."

I smiled. For being so small, this boy was more loyal than any human I had met so far. "I can't take you. I'm not fast enough on my feet, so I have to swim . . . and I swim too fast for you to keep up."

"I know. I overheard what you said."

I held my breath. "What did you hear?"

474

"Everything. That you're from the sea. Talk of Merfolk is common in Amille. But you're not scary to me. Plus, I've read all about your kind in my books. Is that why you can't walk well? You're not used to it?"

For a half-second, I thought of denying it. *But why should I?* "Yes. I miss my tail."

He gave a hoot, jumping in place. "I knew it. Can I see it? Is it like a dragon's tail?"

"A dragon? I don't know what that is. But how about this? Once Marigold is safe, you can meet us by the sea and we will show you. I trust you'll keep this a secret?"

His jaw dropped to his chest. "She is one too? I want to become one."

I chuckled at his enthusiasm. "It doesn't work that way. Besides, we need more humans like you. You restore my faith in humanity."

Mattis pouted. "So, what am I supposed to do? Go back and do nothing? That doesn't sound brave . . . or fun."

"I need you to be my eyes and watch for Marigold. If she returns, tell her where I have gone."

He nodded, his lips pinched in a serious expression. "Will I see you again?"

"Is there salt in the sea?" I asked, raising a brow.

He threw his arms around me, squeezing me tight. "Good."

"Now, go on, my fierce warrior." I patted his head. His thick brown curls were soft to the touch. Unbidden, my thoughts strayed to the future as I wondered what color hair my youngling would have. I hoped it was golden like Marigold's.

My breath hitched. *My youngling?* Where had that thought come from? Though it wasn't as frightening as I thought it would be. The corner of my mouth creased, and I blinked the dream away. First things first—find Marigold.

"Keep on course, Ryken. May the wind be at your back, the waters be clear as glass, and home be on the horizon." Mattis gave me one last squeeze and walked backward before taking off between the trees.

I turned back to the water, watching as it flowed downstream. Marigold was out there somewhere, and I wasn't making any progress by standing in place. The scent of the sea, of home, drifted from my left, and I turned away, walking along the river until the water was waist-deep.

Eager for the cool water on my fins, I jumped in and shifted, my flesh searing from my navel downward. My skin knitted together and hardened into scales in seconds. Cross-eyed from the pain, I forgot how excruciating the transformation was, my tail flicking without a thought to keep me upright. I stared down at my tail, happy to be normal again. Why couldn't my legs be this uncomplicated?

In my excitement, I had forgotten about my clothes. Shredded pieces rested on the rocky riverbed, remnants of the pants I had been wearing. I pressed the pieces together, hoping they would stick. They fell back to the ground, and I grumbled. Without pants, I'd have to stay in this form, limiting where I could go on land. I didn't want to scare the humans more than I already did.

If I didn't have pants, then there was no point in keeping the shirt either. With a flick of my wrist, I sliced through the useless buttons and tore the fabric from my body. It was a relief not to be tangled in human constraints.

I dove under the shallow water. It wasn't as deep as I was used to. I let out a long hum to orient myself on the dimensions of the river and how far it extended. The sound vibrated for miles, twisting and turning until it finally weakened at a fork in the river. It went farther than I expected.

No point in complaining. I shot off, swimming by strange fish that zipped out of the way as I passed. Every few strokes, I surfaced to taste the air before diving back under, hoping to catch her essence to confirm I was going in the right direction. On my last sniff, the smell of blood stopped me cold.

Not mine—but Marigold's.

I surfaced with a growl, my teeth bared at the potential threat. But there was no one here but me and the acidic taste of her blood in the air. Frenzied with worry, I broke one of Marigold's rules and shifted into my human form with a hiss of pain, climbing out of the river. Her scent stopped at a tree at the bottom of the hill. Dried drops of scarlet were splattered on the blades of grass. I fell to my knees, the rocks digging into my weak human skin.

What had I done? It was my fault she was hurt. Why had I let her convince me to leave the ocean?

A roar ripped from me, demanding that I shift back.

Don't panic, I commanded myself. I rested a hand on my heart, wishing I could calm it as easily as I calmed Marigold's. At least she was still alive—that I knew. I had to push away the distraction and worry so I could focus on just her scent.

Then I would bring her home.

I shot up, surprisingly sturdy on my feet. I tracked the scent to the top of the hill, but just as before, her scent vanished. In the distance, a tall structure towered above the tree line, the top almost resting in the clouds. The white circular turrets reminded me of a lesser Alara. Was this the Windcrest Mattis had mentioned?

Blue water glittered like a trail, winding its way from the trees straight through the buildings into the castle. I didn't need legs to enter the kingdom after all.

I dove back into the water, shifting at the same instant. Fire burned down my flesh as it shifted to scales, and I bit my tongue to keep from crying out. It must have been too close to the last time I shifted, my muscles still aching. But I swam through the pain, flicking my tail with powerful strokes to pick up speed and slice through the water.

Fear nipped at my fins, and I tried not to think about the red splatters of blood I had seen. If anything had happened to her . . .

In a swirl of bubbles, I came to a halt at the fork in the river. Panting, I glanced left and right, unsure of which one to take.

Then, as if in answer to my question, I heard her. Marigold's song, a soulful tune, echoed down the current from my right. The low notes hooked me like they had the first time, pulling me through the water with newfound adrenaline.

Was she hurt? Was she scared? I needed to see her *now.*

No matter the distance between us, my body was attuned to her. I would always follow her song when she called for me. Always.

Find me, Ryken.

I will, Marigold. Don't stop singing.

Printed in Great Britain
by Amazon